READING *between the* LINES

READING between the LINES

HOWARD
Fiction

RICK HAMLIN

Published by Howard Books, a division of Simon & Schuster, Inc.
1230 Avenue of the Americas, New York, NY 10020
www.howardpublishing.com

Reading between the Lines © 2006 by Rick Hamlin

Library of Congress Cataloging-in-Publication Data

Hamlin, Rick.
   Reading between the lines / Rick Hamlin.
      p.cm.
   ISBN-13: 978-158229-578-7
   ISBN-10: 1-58229-578-6
   1. Widowers—Fiction. 2. Flute players—Fiction. 3. Man-woman relationships—Fiction. I. Title.

PS3558.A4467R43 2006
813'.54—dc22

2006043699

10 9 8 7 6 5 4 3 2 1

Manufactured in the United States of America

For information regarding special discounts for bulk purchases, please contact Simon & Schuster Special Sales at 1-800-456-6798 or business@simonandschuster.com.

Edited by Ramona Richards
Cover design by Beverly Walbrecht, Resource Agency
Interior design by John Mark Luke Designs

For Sweetie,

who would like Harriet Mueller a lot

ACKNOWLEDGMENTS

HUGE THANKS to Katie Wheelock for her invaluable suggestions. Appreciation to Gretchen Pusch, a fabulous New York flutist who helped me understand the freelance musician's life. Thanks to Arthur Caliandro for the prayer. And, as always, gratitude to Claudia Cross, my tireless agent, for sticking with me.

PROLOGUE

IN LATER years when people asked James B. Lockhart Jr. what got him through that difficult patch, he'd give a quick response about how it wasn't really anything. He got through it as one gets through anything unpleasant, like toughing it out through high-school chemistry or sticking with the wrong job until the right one comes around. Tough times happened to everyone. No one is immune from life's tragedies.

Then he'd look more closely to see who asked the question. Was the person ready to hear the real answer?

Just to test the waters, he'd add something about how if you really look for what you need to survive, the tools are all there. Kind words from family and friends, encouragement, warmth, affection. When he felt brave, he'd admit that he had been fortunate in love and that love could get you through anything.

Most of the time he'd receive a nod and a smile. People would accept that love was an answer.

But then Jim would try to determine how much more of the story to tell. Some things weren't easy to talk about in front of just anyone. They required more explanation than most wanted to hear.

"There was a prayer I learned once," he'd say. "The words are almost as ancient as time. It's hardly original with me. It has been the companion of people all around the world . . . many more worthy than me."

Eyebrows would raise. "A prayer?"

"It's been published in books and described by saints. Most famously it was in a book called *The Way of the Pilgrim*—about a Russian peasant who lived his life by it."

"Is that where you found it?" the listener would ask.

PROLOGUE

"It was a gift really," he'd explain. "We can give so few things that are useful. Most gifts wear out with time. The longer we have them, the more tattered and tired they grow. Not this gift. It becomes only more precious with time and use. It became my lifeline."

At this point he would be afraid he was starting to ramble. If whomever he was explaining this to wandered off to another room or suddenly realized she had to make an urgent call on her cell phone, he would be very forgiving. He knew what she'd be thinking: *You never know if you're going to be stuck talking to a fanatic.*

After all, a prayer, a pilgrim, saints . . . it all sounded a little hysterical.

But the prayer wasn't just meant for church, Jim knew. It was for *every* part of life. In the gym or in a restaurant, beside a hospital bed, or even at the office. It was his lifeline when he felt himself getting lost. He was convinced that no one could be lost with this prayer. It always brought him back to what was important. It supplied thoughts beyond any words. It gave peace to his aching soul.

"Let me tell you a story," he would finally say, because the story itself would explain everything. "It's about love and death and the things that really matter. There's a woman in it—two women, really—a man, a church thrift shop, and a prayer. Although it has a happy ending, it almost didn't turn out that way. It all started in the basement of a church . . ."

What better place to start?

ONE

ELIZABETH ASH tiptoed past the long table of kitchenware—knives, serving spoons, eggbeaters, and Tupperware—as though she might awaken their owners' ghosts. She paused at a set of measuring cups that was missing the one-cup measurement. Picking up a set of copper measuring spoons, she dangled them from one hand like a pair of castanets.

She wasn't in need of any bargains. She hardly had room for anything. She lived on the third floor of a brownstone. One oddly shaped room that had to serve as living room, bedroom, rehearsal space, and studio when she gave flute lessons. Its principal virtues were a high ceiling, two tall windows that faced south, and a deaf neighbor in the apartment next door. She could practice at all hours until the woman across the garden called to complain.

An apartment like that hardly allowed for a rummage sale. What could Elizabeth do with the laminated wood sideboard that stretched against one wall? And where would she put a velvet sofa that could unfold into a queen-sized bed? She might have room for a magazine or two. She remembered making a Christmas tree once out of an old *Reader's Digest* by folding over the edge of every page and spray-painting the whole thing green. But she didn't feel very crafty, and Christmas had come and gone.

Then there were the books.

"Books furnish a room," her mother used to say. An aphorism that never made much sense to Elizabeth until she moved to New York and tried to make do on a freelance musician's spotty earnings. Books would have to furnish her room.

3

And they did . . . double-stacked in one tall bookcase in her living room/bedroom. Stacked horizontally and vertically in a narrow bookcase in her narrower kitchen. Books in the bathroom—those that didn't risk getting damaged by the steam from her shower. Art books and musical scores stacked on the floor so they could form a coffee table.

Now she looked greedily at the table of books at the rummage sale. Maybe there was something here.

"The last thing you need is more books," her friend Dorothy Hughes said.

"There might be something here I'd like to read."

"You can get what you need at the library."

"All the good books are always checked out at the New York Public Library. That's why I buy them."

"And let them fill up your apartment." Dorothy ran her finger through her thick, perfect-for-a-shampoo-commercial hair. She usually wore it in a ponytail, but today she wore it loose—probably to look more alluring.

"I reread them." Elizabeth could reread anything she liked. She could even reread a murder mystery and pretend to forget who had committed the crime.

"A sure sign that you don't get out enough. Remember, we're not just here to buy. We're here to meet people."

It was Dorothy's conceit that two single women together were more likely to "meet people" than one single woman by herself, and therefore in the last few months she was forever dragging Elizabeth to events where they could socialize. Play readings, art openings, book signings.

Elizabeth scanned the crowd. "Who are we going to meet in a church basement?"

"All sorts come to rummage sales. Look at that guy over there. You could meet him."

A tweedy type lingering over a table of garden appliances. Trowels, clippers, hoes, gloves, and pots. Window boxes for fire-escape gardens.

Elizabeth turned to her friend. "Doesn't really look like he's here to 'meet people.'"

"You can't know until you talk to him." Dorothy smiled radiantly so her dimples showed. She crossed the room.

Leave it to Dorothy to do the meeting, Elizabeth thought. She wasn't in the market to meet anyone. She would rather look at the junk.

It was a wonder what people held on to. A cigar box full of bolts, nuts, rubber bands, broken pencils, a shard of pottery, canceled stamps, and paper clips. A card table cluttered with jewelry. A tie pin, a beaded bracelet, a brooch with a huge fake emerald. The prices on these items were overly optimistic. Twenty bucks for the brooch. First-day-of-the-rummage-sale prices. By Sunday anything left on the table would be marked down to ten bucks. Or five. Anything to keep the goods moving.

Elizabeth assumed the money would go to a worthy cause. A soup kitchen or homeless shelter. New pipes for the organ. The church benevolence fund. Elizabeth didn't object to churches at all. She just didn't go in them, unless she was playing at a church concert or hearing one. She was always surprised how chic the ladies in New York churches could be, dressed in their slacks and cashmere sweater sets. Not like the frumpy church ladies of her imagination.

She turned to see if Dorothy was having any luck "meeting" the tweedy man at the gardening table. He looked like a copyeditor or computer programmer. One of those guys who would talk for hours about his job. Deadly dull. He didn't seem the least bit interested in being met. What was Dorothy thinking?

Everyone was completely absorbed in shopping. It was like being in a research library. Or at an Internet café with every person scanning a screen. The people here were in search of bargains. All they saw were objects on tables—knives, spoons, napkin rings, salad bowls. All they could do was calculate prices.

Dorothy was now arguing with a woman over a ratty fox fur. Any moment now they'd pull it back and forth between them. Elizabeth tried to read their lips.

Mine!

No, it's mine!

But I saw it first!

What did Dorothy want with the jacket anyway?

A pillow, the other woman seemed to say.

A pillow out of the fur?

Dorothy had her hand on her hips, and she was explaining, gesturing to the fur. *Trim.*

Possibilities. That's what brought people to a rummage sale. A world of possibilities. Who knew that a ratty old fur could have a second life as a stage prop or a stuffed pillow or trim on an opera cape? People came to try on new possibilities for themselves. They wondered how they would look in that jacket and would they ever find the right place to wear a fake emerald brooch.

Elizabeth sighed. Possibilities are just what she wished she had less of. She preferred certainties. She was certain she was a very good flutist. She was certain she had a job for the next week subbing in the pit of a Broadway show. And she was certain she would never find anybody to share her life with.

Dorothy's hand was off her hip, and now she was rubbing the fur like it belonged to her cat. She was grinning, chatting. She had made a friend. Not a boyfriend, but someone. Dorothy could find a new friend in the Sahara.

Elizabeth cast her eye on a stack of records. Maybe there'd be a recording she'd like. An unusual flute concerto. A piece of chamber music that no one played anymore. Probably not. They looked like old pop recordings, and nothing was more useless than a record anyway. Give her CDs or an iPod.

Books would be better. If she could find one paperback. Something light. Even if it were something she'd read before. Something she'd want to read again.

She ran a finger along the top of the dusty spines, studying titles. Someone's old chemistry textbooks. A collection of Shakespeare. Self-help books. A faded copy of *Love Story*. Volumes of science fiction that didn't interest her in the least.

What she wanted was a late-night comfort book. Something to read when she couldn't sleep or when she felt too alone in her small apartment. Something to give her a sense of certainty. A book with a world that would take her out of her own world. Something that would make her forget.

One cover was too lurid. The writing on the opening page of another was too raw. She needed something with smooth prose. Better yet, a book that didn't make her think of the words at all. A story so big she could lose herself in it.

Then she saw the Harriet Mueller. Historical romance. Now there was something dependable. Every volume was set in Regency England and featured women in high-waist dresses who were swept off their feet by dandified rakes in black riding boots and puffy shirts with collars so starched they scratched the men's cheeks. Women who were sensitive but brave . . . and men who seemed gruff and cool but burned with secret ardor.

Elizabeth had read her first Harriet Mueller when she was a suggestible twelve-year-old with a crush on the boy next door. She had spent the summer reading on her front porch, hoping against hope that he would notice her. He didn't, but she made her way through the local library's entire collection of Harriet Muellers. The librarian couldn't object to a Harriet Mueller. There was nothing too racy in them, and the historical details were all well drawn. Beau Brummel and the Prince Regent. Scenes set at Brighton or in Bath.

Now she was looking at Harriet Mueller's *Secret Vows*. She fingered the corners of the brittle pages. This was a volume that had been passed along and savored, like the score of a great concerto. Somehow that added to the value. *Secret Vows*. She held it in one hand and looked for more.

Yes, there was another Harriet Mueller. *A Lark for Love*. With birds on the cover and a couple embracing in a distant gazebo.

And a third. *What Price Glory*. This one had a military theme. The man on the cover—with dark, fluttering sideburns like a young James Caan—was squeezed into red slacks and a navy blue coat with gold epaulets. Another paperback edition.

Elizabeth couldn't believe her luck. Three Harriet Muellers in one day. She dared not continue looking for more. If she brought any more books into her apartment, even books this thin, she would have to get rid of some she already had. It would be like dumping an old friend.

"So you've found something," Dorothy said.

Elizabeth downplayed the discovery. "A couple books, that's all."

"You'll just stay inside reading instead of getting out and meeting people."

"What about you? You looked like you were having some success."

"With this?" Dorothy held up the old fur.

Elizabeth smiled. "At least you made a friend."

"Next time we'll both come away with boyfriends, I assure you."

TWO

JIM LOCKHART went to the gym every morning. Time on the treadmill was good for his cardiovascular system. Lifting weights decreased his risk of heart failure. It made him feel better and look better. He could comfortably claim that there wasn't much flab on his belly. He could even make a decent muscle in his bicep, like some beach bum.

But the mornings at the gym weren't a source of vanity. He wasn't trying to look good for anybody. Truth was, he went out of habit. Roll out of bed, pull on some clothes, eat a protein bar and drink some coffee, then head to the gym. He showered there, brushed his teeth in the locker room, shaved, got dressed. He even said his morning prayers there, although he wouldn't have wanted anyone to know that.

This morning, as he took the subway downtown, he followed his usual routine. He didn't look at the women in their business suits, their heads in their *Wall Street Journals* or *New York Times,* as they hurried off to work. Out of the corner of his eye he might notice an attractive pair of legs, but he didn't make eye contact with their owner. He sensed beauty all around him—one woman even put on her makeup as she rode the subway—but he always made a point of not looking. He kept his head in the newspaper. Dull habit.

Jim had never considered himself much of a jock. Not since hockey in high school. In college he'd been part of the artsy drama crowd. Didn't even go to the football games. Had very little patience with the rah-rah fraternity bunch. Sometimes he jogged a couple of miles down by the lake back then, but jogging wasn't a jock thing. That was just stress management.

Then in his twenty-ninth year he had developed a bum knee, the result of a hockey accident from high-school days. When he went to see a physical therapist, he was given some exercises, most of which had to be done with weight machines. So he had joined a gym near his office. And after doing the leg lifts for his knees, he figured he might as well do something about the rest of his body. The next thing he knew he was bench-pressing a hundred pounds and running on the treadmill for forty-five minutes. It became habit with alternating routines.

This morning he would be doing an upper-body workout. Bench, curls, overheads for his triceps. Push-ups and pull-ups too.

"One towel," he told the woman at the front desk.

"Hi, Jim," she said.

It always surprised him that she knew his name. "Thanks."

"Have a good one," she added.

He cringed. *Have a good one what?* The phrase was even worse than the unaccountably bland "Have a nice day." Whatever happened to "Good morning" or "Good day"?

"I'll do my best," he said as he swung his gym bag back over his shoulder and carried it into the locker room.

He found an upper locker in the back room where most of the early morning crowd changed clothes. There was the attorney who worked out before being chained to his desk downtown; the architect who ran on the treadmill for miles before designing skyscrapers; and the superbuff I.T. guy who probably never lifted anything heavier than a keyboard at the office but could bench-press twice his weight. Maybe that was the whole point of the gym. You did it because you didn't have to. Stevedores didn't need a gym.

"Hey, Jimbo, you made it."

This amused Jim too. That he had acquired this jockish nickname: Jimbo.

"Hey, Scott."

Scott was a stockbroker. Always trying to interest Jim in some stock or mutual fund. Very friendly, just like a salesman. Not easily dissuaded by Jim's lack of interest in the Dow. "Some morning you'll surprise us and not show up."

"I've missed a few times. You didn't seem to notice then."

"You gave us plenty of warning. Almost took an ad out in the paper warning us of your absence."

Jim shrugged. "It's hard to fit in vacations."

"You work too hard."

"If you worked harder, maybe you wouldn't always be trying to unload those lousy stocks on me."

"Just trying to help you plan for your financial future." Scott put on one of his many T-shirts with a corporate logo on it. Some freebie he'd picked up at a convention. "See you out there."

Jim hung up his long-sleeved shirt and trousers in the locker and changed into his gym shorts. As he pulled on his socks, he muttered the prayer, the same one he said every morning.

"Jesus Christ, have mercy upon me. Make haste to help me. Rescue me and save me. Let thy will be done in my life."

It had become a habit these last fifteen months. The same words repeated again and again. He didn't even have to close his eyes. Even now, tying his shoes, he could say the prayer. *Jesus Christ, have mercy upon me . . .*

Out in the weightroom he took up a position on the bench and started out with forty-pound weights on the bar.

Scott was working on his triceps and getting red in the face. He always turned bright red when he worked out. "Jimbo, what'd you do this weekend?"

"Not much."

"No hot dates?"

"None that I'd tell you about."

Jim had to admit that the gym repartee was something he'd come to enjoy. It wasn't like office talk. People weren't trying to sell things to Jim—except for the occasional penny stock. It was weights and sports and complaints about how eighty pounds felt heavier week after week. Nobody cared that he was a casting director. Nobody tried to slip him a photo and résumé.

"I'm serious now."

"I'm sure you are."

Scott wiped the sweat off his forehead with the back of his hand and gave a toss of his surfer-blond hair. "You got anybody you're seeing regularly?"

"Too many people," Jim joked.

"You object to seeing anybody new?"

"Yes." Jim grabbed the bar. He didn't like the way this conversation was going. Serious questions were not part of the gym routine.

"The reason I'm asking, Jimbo, is my wife keeps bugging me about her cousin."

"It's always a cousin," Jim said, trying to make a joke of it. "They're usually homely with some story about why they aren't married and everybody pretending they're ten years younger than they are." He grabbed the bar and began his reps.

One, two, three. Do it with the prayer. Jesus Christ, have mercy upon me.

"I'm not trying to set you up or anything, but this girl really is nice. Great-looking. Smart."

Four, five, six, seven. Make haste to help me. "The next thing you'll tell me is she has a great body."

"She does."

Eight, nine, ten, eleven, twelve. Rescue me and save me. "I don't know. It's hard for me to find a free night."

"Don't give me that. Everybody has to eat. You can't survive on protein bars alone."

"Try me." *Let thy will be done in my life.*

"You don't buy my stocks, you don't laugh at my jokes, you don't do the exercises I tell you to do, and now you won't even take me up on a free meal."

"That's not exactly what it sounded like."

"You coming off a bum romance or something?"

"I wish." That was the easiest way to settle it. Leave it to Scott's imagination. Jim was sure that Scott's wife's cousin was charming. But he met charming women all the time, and he wasn't interested in getting serious with any of them. Not now. Not so soon. He wasn't ready.

"Well, let me know when you think you want to be social."

"I'll send an announcement." Jim grabbed the bar again.

"One word of advice."

"What?"

"That weight's too light. You're an incredible wimp if you can't do fifteen reps with it." Scott laughed.

Insults were exchanged. Usual gym banter was restored.

Jim returned to his routine. An exercise and the prayer. The clanking of the machines, the strain on his muscles and exhorting the deity. Deep breathing and water breaks in between. It gave him a measure of peace that the world would go on and that he'd get through the long day ahead.

By 8:30 he was ready for the showers. "At least I've done this," he could tell himself. At least he'd been able to do the barbells and dumbbells and chin-ups. Anything to give him some sense of accomplishment.

He weighed himself—178 pounds—and shaved and took a quick shower. He said the prayer while he put on his boxers and laundered shirt. Fresh-pressed cotton and a tie were part of his daily uniform. In this dress-casual era, coats and ties weren't absolutely necessary, but they made a difference to the people he auditioned every day. At least they made a difference to him.

"Good-bye," he said to the woman at the front desk.

"Have a great day."

⸎

"MORNING, JIM."

"Good to see you, Jim."

"How ya doing, Jim?"

He banished all insecurity by the time he hit the halls of Babcock, Crier, and Nelson. Here he was the soul of efficiency, a whiz at decision making, a wit in the washroom, a quick negotiator on the phone. Sometimes he imagined he was a movie and his eyes were the camera taking in the wide smiles, raised eyebrows, and brisk waves as he passed through the lobby with its shiny granite floor and down the gray hall past rows of cubicles.

When he arrived at his office, Jim threw the gym bag under his desk and turned on his computer. He played back the messages on his phone—there were always messages—and sorted through any papers left on his desk. He logged on.

James B. Lockhart Jr., casting director.

His desk calendar alerted him to a couple of staff meetings and a few appointments. He scribbled things down wherever he found a spot. It was going to be a busy morning. Fine by him. He needed to find an actress in her early thirties and a kid who could pass for nine. The photo books were piling up on his desk. The agent calls were already coming in. All of it said to him, "You've got a purpose." Something to keep him busy so he wouldn't have to think too hard. No doubts to consider, no questions to ask. What more could you want from a job?

The certainties of an office were just the thing to keep him focused for the next twelve hours. *Jesus Christ, have mercy upon me. Rescue me and save me . . .*

No more time for that right now.

THREE

"SEE IF you can do that phrase all in one breath," Elizabeth said.

"I don't have the air," exclaimed her student.

"Breathe from your diaphragm. Put the flute down for a minute and take a deep breath."

The student obliged.

"Not with the shoulders up. Keep them relaxed. Take a deep breath. Again. Your diaphragm should expand. Like that. So I can see it."

"I don't feel natural this way."

"It is natural. Practice your breathing at the beginning of each session. Then sing the phrase to yourself before you play. If you think a phrase through beforehand, you won't get into any bad habits."

Elizabeth could tell the girl wouldn't do any of it. She was a bright student, a sophomore at the conservatory, conscientious and musical. But like all of them, she wanted to plunge right into the music instead of working through it slowly. She was bound to make the same mistakes over and over again.

The girl raised her flute to her lips and took a deep breath. The flute gave one long sustained line. A beautiful melodic phrase. Not perfect, but perfectly acceptable.

"That's it! You did it. Didn't you feel it?"

"I guess so." The student lowered her flute. "Is that all?"

"That's good enough for now. I'll listen to the other piece next week." Elizabeth had a show tonight and just enough time to eat dinner and clear her mind before going to the theater.

"Ms. Ash, can I ask you a question?"

Elizabeth felt ancient being addressed as Ms. Ash. "Yes."

"Did you always want to be a flutist?" The girl was taking apart her flute and putting it in its small carrying case.

At your age I wanted to be homecoming queen, a cheerleader, a great novelist, and the finest musician in the world. "It's something I've always enjoyed."

"But did you think you'd end up doing it—I mean—doing it as a profession?"

The way the girl said "end up" made it sound like a penal sentence.

"Not when I was your age. I studied for a long time and worked at it."

"Is it a good life?"

"For me it is. Although not particularly lucrative."

That was one reason Elizabeth thought teaching in her cramped, third-floor, walk-up apartment was good for her students. Give them a realistic idea of a musician's income. Few musicians lived like rock stars.

"I really like playing the flute, but my father says I should be a lawyer so I can pay back my loans after college."

"I think it's important to do what you love," Elizabeth said firmly.

"Do you think I have the talent?"

"You have to make that decision."

Talent wasn't everything. Desire and persistence counted for more. Elizabeth knew many talented musicians who were still working as waitresses and secretaries. And she knew one incredibly talented horn player who was always losing jobs.

The girl put on her coat and pulled her hair back in a clip. "Thanks. I'm just not sure I want to end up like you."

Elizabeth closed the door, not sure if she should laugh or cry. End up like you? As though she were a failure. As though this tiny room at the back of a brownstone was the true measure of her success. Didn't people realize that money wasn't everything? There was another score for success.

It came at the end of a quintet rehearsal when the music echoed in the silence of the room. It was in the phrasing of a solo line that showed all of Elizabeth's mastery of her instrument. It was in the pit of a

Broadway show with a group of musicians who were so good, the music sounded as though there were only one person playing.

That's what was so hard to explain: that she truly loved being a freelance musician. She could put up with the incompetent conductors and the raging egomaniacs. She could tolerate the insecurity of having too few gigs in the middle of August and too many in the month of December. She could adjust to a schedule of teaching because at least it gave her some regular income.

She went into the kitchen—"not even big enough to change your mind in" as Dorothy once claimed—and heated up a can of Campbell's clam chowder. After pouring herself half a glass of cranberry juice, she sat at the small table. She brushed off the single linen place mat and opened up the linen napkin. The rest of the napkins and place mats were in her parents' attic in Connecticut. Part of a hope chest gathering dust.

She picked up one of the three Harriet Mueller books. *Secret Vows.* The paper was almost brown from age, but the binding still held. She could prop open the pages with a knife while she ate. Reading while eating was one of the great privileges of living alone. No need to make conversation. No need to listen to some topic she cared nothing about.

Pretty soon she was lost in a bygone world of waistcoats and servants and gauzy white dresses that showed off a woman's figure. She could hear the horses drawing up on a cobblestone drive and the string quartet that played in the salon. She could smell the lavender water that the heroine had sprinkled on her neck and the bouquet of hydrangeas that filled a Sèvres vase. She felt the formal rhythms of the language, part of the dance of courtship. Just the word *courtship* was so foreign. Who ever courted a woman these days?

Not that Elizabeth wished the world would go back in time. Most women lived in horrible conditions back then—including filth and poverty. There was a high rate of infant mortality. Countless women died in childbirth. But a Harriet Mueller novel was concerned with the life of the aristocracy and landed gentry. There were card parties and horse races and hearts to be won. Elizabeth found it a relief from subways and supermarkets and washing your socks in the sink. A relief from men who "courted" you by bragging about their accomplishments.

Elizabeth read brief passages between changing into her black nylon pants and her black silk top. Her performance attire. The audience couldn't see her in the pit where she sat, but everybody dressed in black. She was a sub for a week in the musical *If You Ask Me*. She'd played the show back in November and a week in December. The money was good and the conductor easy to follow. The musicians were people she'd worked with before. Good colleagues.

The last thing she did was put her flute in her bag and turn out the light. The book she kept in her pocket. She knew the show well enough to read between numbers. That was part of the rhythm of a long-running show. The orchestra read, did crossword puzzles, knitted, crocheted—and all between bars of a song. There was something brazen about picking up a trumpet between a crossword clue for a bird in Patagonia and the name of a director of film noir.

She continued her reading on the subway. As the crowded train clattered on its way, she was lost in another world. In the life of another heroine in another era. If a man had stepped forward and knelt before her to court her at that very moment, she wouldn't have noticed.

JIM WAS looking at photos of actresses. Stacks of them were piled on his desk. Beautiful women and plain women. Interesting-looking ones and drab ones. Women with red hair, brown hair, blond hair, short hair, long hair, white hair, tinted hair. He'd already scrolled through his computer for images, and now he was going through what he'd already printed out. There was something important about holding a photo, as well as seeing it on the screen. Somehow it created a tactile impression of the women he'd interviewed. Impossible to believe how many women had passed through this office in the last six years, ever since Jim had come on staff at Babcock, Crier, and Nelson.

Jim had an almost flawless memory of faces. "I never forget a face," others might say. With James B. Lockhart Jr., it was not only a memory of faces but an uncanny, internal mechanism for filing them away. A producer or director could scratch his head and throw out a few adjectives for a character he wanted on screen, and Jim could come up with a dozen suggestions. He'd know the names, a few vital statistics—like the quirky laugh they might have or the way one eyebrow rose higher than the other—and their agents.

It wasn't something he'd ever known about himself—or anything he'd acknowledged as being different from anybody else—until he began working at the agency. He'd started out as an assistant, but soon found people calling on him with what seemed like basic questions: "Do you remember the name of that woman who interviewed with us last spring for the antihistamine commercial?"

He remembered. He could see her sitting on the tan sofa in her purple top and suede skirt. He could picture her brown hair, hazel eyes, and the small mole near her nose.

"Everybody can do that," he would say.

"No, they can't," his boss told him. It was like having perfect pitch or a perfect golf swing. You were born with it.

Right now he was looking for a woman for a car commercial. She had to be both clean-cut and provocative. Pretty, of course, but if she were too pretty, she'd be intimidating and women wouldn't want to buy the car because they couldn't imagine living up to that intimidating standard.

Not only did Jim have to find someone for the part, he had to guess what the client wanted. Clients were notorious for not knowing their own minds. They could say "sexy" when they really meant "wholesome." They could describe a person as "otherworldly" when they really wanted "down-to-earth." They could baffle you with requests for girl-next-door, athletic, and Midwestern, then leap at exotic, feral, and Southwestern. Go figure.

He looked up and spotted his reflection in the window. Once there was a time when his image had been on an eight-by-ten glossy—when he was on the other end of the business. Actor instead of casting director. If he'd known then what he knew now, would it have made any difference?

A dead-end thought. His face had changed a lot since that long-ago head shot. The same strong chin and aquiline nose and brown eyes, but there was a darker hollow beneath his cheeks, and his smile wasn't as quick or natural. It was his eyes, though, that had changed the most. They used to look out at the world in wonder. Now they had a guarded gaze.

"What are you finding?" a voice behind him asked.

He turned from the window. It was Nan, his best friend in the office. The person he depended on most.

"A few possibilities."

"Show them to me," she said.

"Try this: Sultry but Friendly."

"Not bad."

"Innocent yet Knowing."

Her comeback was quick. "Too obvious."

"Then there's I Told You So."

"What's her voice like?"

"Sultry but friendly."

"You're kidding."

"She can change it to 'innocent yet knowing' if that's what we need. She's a good actress. I saw her in a showcase a couple of years ago."

"Innocent or knowing?"

"Off the wall. A real flaky play. There are a few more on the computer. Check these out." He pulled up a checkerboard of choices. "I can even do sound for these."

"Don't prejudice me. I don't want to get too attached to any one of them yet."

"Spoken like a true professional."

Nan made an attempt at stifling a yawn. "You're quite a case, of course. You have your choice of the most interesting, beautiful women in New York, and you look at them with clinical detachment."

"I'm waiting for the right one."

"And who would she be?"

"I'll know when I find her."

She looked at him with her dark eyes, and her voice softened. "You should get out more."

"I go out all the time."

"Where? The gym?"

"The theater. I probably take in two dozen shows a month."

"That's work. You should do something that's just for fun. Something that's just for you."

"What did you have in mind?"

"Let's get something to eat." She was making light of it too. They were not a couple. They were friends.

"I need to finish up here."

"No you don't," Nan said. "I'm the account exec, and I officially say that you've done enough. Meet me at the elevator in five minutes."

"I'll ruin my record for being the last one out."

"I wish you were kidding," she said dryly.

FOUR

"DOROTHY . . ."

"I can't believe you're calling me this late."

"You're always up late," Elizabeth said.

"Maybe I have to be up early tomorrow for an important audition."

"You don't. You would have told me about it. Dorothy, I need to talk to you about that book I bought at the rummage sale."

"What about it?"

"There's writing in it."

"Of course there's writing in it. It's a book. Books have writing in them."

"Turn down that TV," Elizabeth ordered. "You can't hear me with it going full blast."

Dorothy's neighbors must have been deaf too.

"I keep it on for research," Dorothy explained. "I need to see if they're running any commercials that I'm in."

"Are there any running right now?"

"There just might be." The sound of the TV disappeared. She must have pushed the mute button. "Tell me about the book."

"I took it with me to my job tonight. I'm playing in the pit of *If You Ask Me*."

"Oh, yeah."

Dorothy was still sensitive about *If You Ask Me*. She'd been up for one of the parts and felt she should have been cast. The role had gone to a competitor.

"Anyway, there are a couple of long scenes where the orchestra doesn't play—"

"I don't know how you can stand that show. The acting is terrible. The singing is worse."

"I was using the time to read *Secret Vows*, one of the books I bought at the rummage sale," Elizabeth said, ignoring her, "when I came to this writing at the top of chapter three."

"What do you mean?"

"There was some scribbling along the top."

"Notes for an English class?"

"Sort of like that but more personal. I skimmed through the rest of the book and found more. Some sentences at the top of the chapters or in the margins. You know how you write notes in a book when you're studying it for school? Well, it's like that, except the lines all form a message."

"I get it!" Dorothy exclaimed. "Some man has been kidnapped, and he's locked in the church basement. He's trying to communicate with the outside world." She had a laugh that sounded like a bark, which she'd used to great effect when she'd had to play a dog in a play once.

"I don't appreciate your humor," Elizabeth said, appreciating it anyway. "It wasn't a man. The writing is in a woman's hand—in purple ink. A fountain pen."

"What's it say?"

"Let me read you some of it."

"Darling, I don't know when you'll read this. It might be years from now. Long after I'm gone. I wanted to find some way to reach you, but only when you were ready. I know I could have put this in a letter and left it for you, but there's no telling if you would be ready."

Elizabeth paused to turn a few pages.

"I thought of other places to put the message. In a desk drawer. In my bureau. I could imagine you coming upon it when you had to clean out my socks and underwear. But that seemed wrong. And I couldn't be sure that you'd be the one to

clean my drawers. One of my sisters could find it, and that would be all wrong."

Elizabeth scrambled through some more pages.

"But every couple has a few places known only to them. With you, darling, it could be your grandfather's college mug. The place we kept our extra set of keys. If I left you a quick note there, you'd get it. Like a mom putting messages in her kid's lunchbox."

"Can you believe this?"

"Keep reading," Dorothy said impatiently.

"My private spot had to be my jewelry box. You didn't quite understand what my jewelry meant to me. That a string of pearls my mother wore as a debutante was worth more than any appraiser could say. Or that topaz ring from my grandmother. That's all right. I didn't need diamond bracelets from you or diamond earrings. You gave me many other things."

"How long does this go on?"

"All that's in the first book. *Secret Vows*."

"Lizzie, let me get this right. You're telling me it's all written by hand in the book?"

"Along the margins and at the chapter headings. With a fountain pen. She's trying to communicate with this guy. It's a message."

"It doesn't say much."

"It goes on. She wrote stuff in the second Harriet Mueller I picked up at that rummage sale. *A Lark for Love*. Listen."

"Darling, I'm trusting that you'll come to this book when you think of me. You knew how much I loved these books. Almost as much as I loved you. You used to tease me about them all the time. My comfort literature. Well, I'm using them to speak to you. For the first message, go back to Secret Vows, then read on."

"The point is, she wrote in all the books."

"Same purple pen?" Dorothy asked in the probing tone of a TV detective.

"Same handwriting. She wanted to reach someone. She was trying to give him a message."

"I'd say it was a husband or ex-husband or boyfriend."

"Husband, I think. At least they lived together and knew each other's habits very well."

"But if you were a guy, would you actually look for a message from your wife in a copy of Harriet Mueller?" Dorothy sounded incredulous.

"If I knew the books meant something to her."

"Sounds like she was a fan . . . just like you, Lizzie."

"I can't believe he gave away these books to the church. The messages are too personal. It would be like putting a stack of love letters up for sale."

"Nobody would want to buy any of my love letters," Dorothy said. "Not that I ever received any."

"It seems so callous."

"Maybe he was angry at her. Or maybe he didn't even know the messages were there."

"You think he gave the books away to the church without knowing what was in them?"

"Somebody did."

"That's terrible!" Elizabeth was surprised by the passion and urgency in her voice. She put the books down on the floor.

"There's not much you can do about it," Dorothy fired back.

"I found these books at that rummage sale you dragged me to. Now I feel responsible for them."

"I wanted you to meet a *guy*, not a book."

"The book is all about a guy. At least the handwriting is."

Dorothy yawned loudly. "We can talk about it tomorrow."

"He probably didn't even know what he was giving away." Elizabeth wanted to justify it somehow.

"Don't get too wrapped up in it. It's just writing," Dorothy said. "Get some sleep, OK? Good night."

"OK. Good night."

A cold gust blew in through a crack at the bottom of Elizabeth's window. It skated around her bed and darted out beneath her front door. She put on her warm, long-sleeved flannel nightgown and slid under the duvet. Flicking on her reading lamp, she looked at the three books on the floor next to her. She picked up the second volume and thumbed through the pages.

I hope you realize this is a love letter. There's so much we've said to each other and so much that has been unsaid, I had to write things down. I wanted to go through every moment in our past and remind myself what was special about what we had. I've been reliving it in my mind, remembering everything. Let me give you my conclusion first of all. No suspense. No surprises. Here it is:

I love you.

Elizabeth turned out her light, but couldn't fall asleep. She kept thinking of a woman writing something so urgent, yet so private, that she put it on the pages of a well-worn book. Not a place that someone would naturally look for it, but a place she was sure he'd find, as long as he could read between the lines.

But maybe he didn't find it. Maybe he'd given the books away before he knew they were there. Or he'd been so angry or hurt that he didn't ever want to see them again. Was that why these books had ended up in Elizabeth's hands?

FIVE

"JIM, YOU'RE working too hard."

"There's a lot to get done."

"It gets done when it gets done. It's not like staying at the office till nine or ten at night makes it go any faster. There comes a point of diminishing returns."

Jim dunked two chips in a dish of salsa. The salsa got hotter the more he ate it, but he couldn't stop. What was it about salsa that made it so irresistible?

"I like work."

"A slave to Babcock, Crier, and Nelson," Nan said. "What a cause."

"Maybe advertising isn't a worthy cause, but I've learned to like it."

"You deserve a little happiness."

"I *am* happy."

"I don't believe you."

Nan hadn't smoked in years, but she still held two fingers close together, as though she had a cigarette in them when she gestured. She had beautiful, well-manicured hands.

"I hate people who always talk about being happy. That's so boring," Jim complained. "Life has more to offer than idle, aimless happiness."

"Who was talking about anything aimless and idle?"

The restaurant was a cheery Mexican place with piñatas dangling from the beams. It held no memories for Jim, which is just what he wanted.

"I have an aim," he said. "To please the clients."

"You know they don't give a hoot about what you think. We're just fodder for internal politics. You've seen enough fabulous proposals that get dumped right out of the gate because some pompous supervisor is trying to prove how ignorant he is."

He grinned. "You do have a way with words."

"It's not worth taking your job too seriously. You're not going to impress management on the twenty-second floor."

"I want to be proud of what I do," Jim said.

"I'm proud of what I do. Your secretary is proud of what she does. Mr. Babcock, Mr. Crier, and Mr. Nelson were all proud of what they did a thousand years ago when they founded this noble company. But I'd venture to say they all had a life outside of the office."

"I go to the gym."

"You know what I mean." She dipped her hand in the plastic basket of corn chips. They'd already gone through one order of quesadillas and one of guacamole.

"Work relaxes me. It gives me something to do."

"It's no substitute for an emotional life," she countered. "What you have at work isn't an emotional life. It's a power trip. You're the person everyone wants to meet, but it has nothing to do with you. It's your position. All those phone calls and free tickets. Nobody would invite you to anything if you weren't Mr. Casting Director."

"Give me a break."

"It's not a substitute for the real thing."

The real thing. Had he even experienced the real thing? Was that what he was mourning? "Why do I put up with you?"

"I'm charming, witty, and right," Nan said in a husky voice. "We're friends."

They were friends—just friends. Maybe there was a time when they could have become something else, but that moment had long since passed.

"Nan, I'm doing my best. I'm getting through the days."

"That's not living."

"What do you think I should do?"

"Fall in love with somebody," she suggested. "Fall in love with one of those actresses who come into your office to try out for a commercial.

Fall in love with someone whose work you really liked. Pick out some-one who sings in a cabaret act."

"It's not that easy."

"Pick the wrong person. Just pick someone. You won't know until you try." Nan raised a hand to flag down their waiter. Jim was ready to ask for the bill, but she said, "We need some more guacamole and chips."

"I'm too old."

"How old are you?"

She knew exactly how old he was. Their birthdays were only two days apart. Every year, as long as they'd worked at Babcock, Crier, and Nelson together, they'd gone out for lunch to celebrate.

"The same age as you."

"I will always claim to be younger than you. I say I'm thirty-one."

"I'm thirty-two."

"Just the age for the Picky Bachelor Syndrome."

"What's that?"

"It happens to guys who wait too long for the perfect woman. They manage to find something wrong with every girl they meet. Her bangs are too short; her ankles are too thick; her mother makes bad lasagna. You're headed that way."

"I'm a widower, not a bachelor."

Nan looked away. She had one of the best figures in the office. Her dark eyes and dark hair would have made her a gypsy temptress in some bad movie. But when you talked to her, she was all good sense and warmth.

"How long has it been?" she asked.

"I don't know."

"You could probably tell me down to the exact hour." Her voice turned soft and kind. For all her hard, businesswoman attitude, she could switch over to quiet and pensive in a second.

"Fifteen months, seven days, and four hours."

"Not really that long."

"It seems a lifetime," he exclaimed. "I can't believe I was once married. I can't believe there was a time when I wasn't alone."

"Being alone gets to be a bad habit."

"I hated it for a long time. The apartment was so quiet I heard her wherever I went. I started up conversations. I'd stand at the refrigerator and call into the bedroom, 'Can I throw out this leftover macaroni and cheese?' Then I'd remember she wasn't there. The mac and cheese, the milk, the carrots, and the salad rotting in the vegetable crisper were all for me."

"You'll get over that."

"That's what everyone says. But I haven't. For the longest time I bought her flavor of yogurt at the supermarket. Cherry. I bought rocky road ice cream because I knew she liked it. I bought six-packs of diet Pepsi for her. And they sat in the refrigerator reminding me that there was no one to drink them."

"That must have been hard."

"I thought it would be better when her clothes were gone. Her sisters swooped down one weekend and went through all her drawers. They asked me to stay out of the apartment while they got rid of stuff. I couldn't have stood being there anyway."

"You must have been grateful."

"Even when it was gone, I could still picture what used to hang in the closets. Her overcoat, her green parka, the blue-striped dress, the cream-colored blouse. I never paid attention to those things when they were there, and all of a sudden I missed them."

"You never talked about it."

"You know what I was like back then. I was a mess. You were incredibly kind. I couldn't have made it through those days without you." He couldn't bear to look at her for fear his voice would break or tears would come into his eyes.

"What about now?" Nan dipped a chip in the guacamole. Piped-in mariachi trumpet music drifted down from the ceiling.

"I don't know how to do 'now.'"

"What a line."

"It *is* a line," he agreed.

This was how they talked in the office. Looking at things dispassionately. Keeping their distance.

"Just go out. You're getting too used to being by yourself. You'll start acting like an old man."

"Nan, I *can't* go out. I keep thinking of her. I go someplace—on some errand or something—and I see something that makes me think of her. The tofu she bought at the Korean deli, the red geraniums she could never grow, the shampoo she always used. On the subway in the morning I'll spot someone reading the newspaper the way she did, folded over in one long column, and I'll wonder what she would have thought. Or I'll pass a restaurant where we ate and remember how she dipped her bread in the sauce of the coq au vin."

"Forgive me. I've never lost someone that close to me . . . but don't you get to a stage where all those reminders are comforting?"

He sighed. "They're not. They only remind me that she's so far away."

"Can't I help by distracting you?" She took one of the largest tortilla chips and broke it in half, just to break the mood.

"You do. Work does. It's the only thing that helps. That and the gym. They take my mind off the places it wanders."

She raised one eyebrow. "Babcock, Crier, and Nelson. The perfect cure."

JIM TOOK a detour on his way to the subway. He strolled over to Times Square to get a glimpse of the billboards. The lights had always seemed reassuring, even when they were selling products he didn't care about. Coke, Levi's, Hanes underwear.

He thought of all those flashing lights broadcasting their messages into the sky. Imagined them traveling light-years away to different solar systems, different galaxies, different worlds. Someday, years from now, Times Square would go dark, but the messages would still be traveling in outer space. It was a sort of eternal life—old messages still floating beyond the sun, waiting to be heard. Waiting the way he was waiting to hear from her.

It was now 10:30 at night. Theatergoers were just getting out, the fast ones dashing for cabs. Suburbanites rushed to make their trains at Grand Central. A few stretch limos crawled through the traffic. People on the sidewalk wrapped their wool scarves tighter around their necks to keep out the chill.

Almost every day Jim interviewed actors and actresses who dreamed of having their name up in lights on a movie theater or on Broadway. But did any of them wonder what they'd lose by achieving their goals? He recognized one of the models on an underwear billboard. The fellow had auditioned for a part in a detergent commercial, and now he was stripped to his drawers in Times Square. Some achievement.

Jim turned his back on the Great White Way and walked along a quiet side street with a mixture of anticipation and dread. The restaurant wouldn't be there anymore—he knew that. It had been replaced by something chic with recessed lighting, black walls, and orchids on white tablecloths. No doubt the waiters and waitresses were all beautiful and efficient. None of them would have tolerated a young couple lingering at a table for two hours with only a crème brûlée.

The old place had been run by an aged pair of Breton women who served vichyssoise, celeri rémoulade, and a boeuf bourguignon that would have pleased Julia Child. The floor was green linoleum, and the walls had faded pictures of Montmartre and Mont-Saint-Michel. The dinner specials, which never changed, were scrawled in chalk on a blackboard.

Not so long ago he and Lois had gone there to figure out their future. A golden future full of promise. Newlyweds, they started the discussion in their cramped one-bedroom apartment, but why stay there? The whole thing would go down better with Breton cider and onion soup.

They had talked for over two hours that night, laughing, arguing, changing their tack with each course. In the end they flipped a coin. It was the easiest way. One had to win. One had to lose. But in a marriage, was it ever possible for one to win while the other lost? They were young. They had to take a risk. They had to gamble. They laughed as they left. The adventure had begun.

Jim hoped for some garlicky smell of the old place, something that would take him back. He'd hear an old Edith Piaf song or the greeting from one of the owners: *"Bonjour, monsieur. Bonjour, madame."* He'd see the flashing neon sign.

But the music was gone. No savory scent of onion soup. All he could catch was a whiff of diesel exhaust from a tourist bus and the stench of a hot-dog vendor's charcoal fire. Nothing to set his imagination humming. Only his fading memories, and a sorrow that he couldn't bear. Why did he think it'd be any different? You couldn't redo the past. You had to live with the choices made. Isn't that what she had been trying to show him? Wasn't that what she'd wished for him? But it was hard, so hard.

Jesus Christ, have mercy upon me, he prayed. *Make haste to help me. Rescue me and save me. Let thy will be done in my life.* Then he walked to the subway and took it home.

SIX

WHEN ELIZABETH awoke the next morning, a bright winter sun streamed through her window. She'd dreamed that she was at one of the long tables in the large vaulted reading room of the New York Public Library, sitting across from a homeless woman.

Suddenly the old woman in the dream took to scrawling across her pile of books with a purple fountain pen. Elizabeth tried to stop her. The librarian brought more books, and the homeless woman wrote more with the purple pen.

"Don't," Elizabeth said. "Don't!"

Now she looked down to her bedroom floor. Her three latest copies of Harriet Mueller were still there, the purple scrawl waiting to be deciphered.

Wednesdays were matinee days. She didn't have to leave her apartment until 1:15. She had one lesson in the morning. Then nothing until the matinee. The rest of the time she could read. She boiled some water, added some oatmeal flakes, and sat down with *A Lark for Love*.

This novel opened up at a gaming house, with the hero and other rakes playing for high stakes at whist and faro—games Harriet Mueller was always writing about. The hero, a tall, light-haired man who refused to powder his hair, was in competition with a rich, well-fed fop over the love of a woman. After drinking too much port, he challenged the fop to a high-speed carriage race.

Elizabeth cared little about the race. She wanted to find out what the purple pen said. She skimmed through the pages to read the scrawl at the top of chapter headings.

Darling, when we met, I thought you were the handsomest man I'd ever seen. Arrogant too. You hardly noticed me in our English class. You kept flirting with that obnoxious Helen LeGrand with the pretentious accent. No one was supposed to know that she came from Texas, I suppose. The one time in our freshman year you walked me to class, you seemed very sweet. We talked as we strolled under the elms. Then suddenly you looked at your watch and darted ahead. "I don't want to be late," you said, running to class. I'd never known anyone so rude.

But at least you'd noticed me. Of course I noticed you. I remember watching you on stage in Tartuffe. It wasn't a big part. You were a servant or valet. None of the freshmen got big parts. But none of us could take our eyes off you. I couldn't. It wasn't just because you were handsome. It's because you were good. You were always involved in what you did. Totally committed on stage. "Real actors prove themselves when they don't have any lines to say," our teacher said. That was you.

Now Elizabeth had to read between the lines. The woman had met her husband—if he was her husband—at college. "Darling," as she called him. They were both in the same class and had both studied English and acting.

Sophomore year I was surprised that you remembered my name. You came up to me at that dance in the fall and started dancing with me. It was like you to assume that I hadn't come with anybody else. And just like you to disappear into the night.

I saw you in all the plays you did that year. A piece of fluff by Noel Coward—can't remember what—but you were dashing in a white smoking jacket and black tie. You also did a very convincing English accent. After that there was a Sam Shepard play. Completely off-the-wall. As though you were trying to prove your range. Then you had a big part in Henry V. Another accent. Welsh, this time.

Some of those plays I saw twice. I didn't tell my roommates because I was afraid they'd think I'd flipped over you. I had, but they didn't have to know. I signed up to usher at the last two plays. That way I could see you every night.

It was you, the actor, that I loved first. I appreciated your work. You were unlike any man I had ever seen or known. The guys I dated in high school were into football and baseball. You were part of a different world.

Elizabeth copied a few phrases down. Going from chapter to chapter, the thoughts seemed disjointed, but they made sense when put together. The woman who'd written them had taken her time. There wasn't any crossing out of the purple pen, only breaks where the writer had stopped to think. At the same time, there was something urgent about the prose.

You broke my heart junior year. Helen didn't seem right for you at all. Too glamorous and fake. I used to ask myself why boys couldn't see through her charade. She was such an act. The soft, quiet voice. The feigned helplessness. That inane laughter. I wanted to shake you out of it. You didn't have to fall in love with me, but you could have chosen someone more worthwhile. I seriously questioned my own taste to have fallen for the man who fell for Helen LeGrand. That name!

I was thrilled that she didn't get cast in The Seagull. She would have ruined it. You were much better without her on stage. She had to make a return in Godspell, but that's because it was a musical and they were desperate. At least with you as a director, you tried to keep her from overacting. Finally you also saw how rotten she was. The scales fell from your eyes.

Have I ever told you how much I loved being your stage manager for Godspell? I'd never been a stage manager before and didn't really think I could do it. But sitting backstage and calling all the lighting cues, I discovered it was a place of power.

And sitting next to you in rehearsals, writing down all the blocking, I got to see what your vision was. Darling, don't ever lose that. You have a vision for everything you do. You have very specific standards and taste. It's what makes you precious to me. Don't ever sell yourself short when I'm gone. Keep your vision.

The buzzer on Elizabeth's apartment rang. Her morning lesson! Where had the time gone?

"Just a minute," she called down the stairs. She hadn't even changed out of her bathrobe or made her bed or washed the empty pot of oatmeal or put on some makeup. She didn't like to teach without mascara, even if her students were all women. (Men never seemed to study the flute.)

She dumped the dishes in the sink. She threw her bathrobe into the closet and quickly pulled on some jeans and a shirt. As she buttoned the top of her jeans, she kicked the sofa bed closed and picked up the pillows to cover it. It would take the student a minute to hike up the three flights of stairs to reach Elizabeth's apartment. Great for breath control.

The doorbell rang.

"Just a sec," Elizabeth called through the closed door. The girl could catch her breath on the landing. Elizabeth pulled the music stand from the corner, put some music on it, and unlatched the door.

"I hope I'm not early," the Korean student said. She was very earnest. Tireless in her practicing.

"Not at all. I had a slow start this morning. Let's do some scales." Elizabeth was the one out of breath.

The student took her flute out of its case. At least no one had to lug a forty-pound instrument up the brownstone's narrow stairs.

"What first?"

"Let me hear your scales."

The student began with a two-octave C major scale, then played C-sharp major, D, D-sharp, E, etc.

"Keep it smooth," Elizabeth said. "Don't think of a scale as separate notes but as one long phrase. The way a string of pearls makes up a whole necklace."

Where had she come up with that analogy? Harriet Mueller, no doubt. The romance of words. It was part of what she liked about being a flutist. She tried to make her music like poetry, and images from books often floated through her head.

"Now the arpeggios."

Elizabeth sat on the sofa and watched her student. The girl had the unfortunate habit of raising her eyebrows on the high notes and lowering them on the low notes.

"Be careful of the intonation on the way up."

"Intonation?"

"You were a little sharp. Try it again."

Elizabeth thought of the books by her sofa bed and who had owned them. If she had stumbled on a package that was addressed to someone else, she would have taken it to the post office and mailed it. If she'd found someone's dog wandering down West Ninety-third, she would have done all she could to return it. What about a message scrawled on the pages of an old book?

The arpeggio came to an end. "Nice," she said. "Have you practiced the Prokofiev?"

"Yes, ma'am."

"Let's hear it."

What if the loving messages had been rejected? What if he'd wanted nothing to do with them? What a terrible thought! Like any lover, the woman had expected him to treasure her words. Surely if he'd read all that purple ink, he wouldn't have given away the books to a church rummage sale.

The books were meant to be kept. He must not have known what was in them.

Flute music floated through the apartment. The old plaster walls and wooden floors served as a sounding board, amplifying the music. Elizabeth wondered if her student heard it. The girl's eyebrows shot up. A wrong note. She played it twice. Was she hoping that Elizabeth wouldn't notice? Elizabeth would wait until the piece was over. Her mind went back to the books.

How would she find the man who was supposed to read those messages? How would she know he was the right person? She couldn't go up to someone at that church and say, "Are these books yours?" She couldn't ask around, "Do you know anyone who likes Harriet Mueller?"

The only answer was to read more. Find out as much as she could. Get to know him as she would any Harriet Mueller hero.

"OK," she said to her student. "There were a couple of wrong notes. Let's go back and see if we can correct those passages."

The Harriet Muellers were still on the floor. Elizabeth slid them under the sofa with her foot. Somehow the books seemed sacred, and Elizabeth didn't want to share even their presence with anyone else. She couldn't explain it to herself—that a voice was speaking to her from the pages of a book.

That she was a part of someone's quest to be heard.

That she was getting to know a woman who wanted to say "I love you" to one extraordinary love.

SEVEN

"I HAD no idea that's the kind of girl they were looking for," Nan said.

"You'd think after all the time we've been doing this, we'd be better at guessing."

"We were way off this time."

"They said they wanted Sultry Girl-Next-Door. And that's what I gave them."

"What they really wanted was Girl-Next-Door . . . with some un-stated Sultry."

Jim sat on the top of his desk next to a stack of photos and résumés. "I knew it was going wrong as soon as the girl came into the room, wobbling on her high heels."

"My fault. She was my choice."

"I hadn't realized that."

"She didn't sound like Marilyn Monroe singing 'Happy Birthday, Mr. President' when we first interviewed her."

"She was a flake. I should have known. Toss me a stack of those." Nan sank down in the chair opposite his desk.

"I don't know if these are going to be right. This pile comes from when I was looking for something else."

"It'll give us a start."

"How much time do we have?"

"We should have had somebody last week. They keep changing their minds."

"Does that ever bother you about this business?" Jim was looking through his own stack of photos and résumés. Faces. More and more faces.

"It comes with the territory. Everybody is allowed to change their mind."

"Every once in a while I'd like to be the one to shake things up. I'd like to be the one who tosses a stack of photos and résumés on someone else's desk and says, 'These are all wrong.' Think about how much power I'd have."

"If we really wanted power, we'd go into another business. We'd be up on the twenty-second floor."

Nan and Jim were silent as they looked through photos. It was the shared silence of colleagues focused on the same goal with a huge deadline looming. They sorted the possibles into a small pile. The impossibles went back on Jim's desk.

"Why did you go into advertising in the first place?" Jim asked.

"I expected to stay in academia."

"What did you study?"

"Sanskrit."

Jim looked up in disbelief. "You're joking."

Nan didn't even give him a glance. "I was very good at it. I've got a good ear for languages. If I'd gone into the military, they probably would have sent me to one of those full-immersion language schools. To make me fluent in Urdu."

"It's amazing how many smart people end up in advertising."

"Include yourself."

"I never studied Sanskrit," Jim said, returning to his pile. "Finding anything?"

"A couple of possibilities. She's got the right look." Nan held out a photo of a woman with a clean-scrubbed face, freckles, transparent eyes, dimples that went with a lopsided smile, and thick brown hair in a ponytail. She looked a little rounder than the usual underfed, made-for-TV model, but she certainly wouldn't be intimidating—if that's what was bothering the client.

"She's been here before. Cute, energetic. Good laugh. Nice eyes.

Dimples. I think she was up for a cologne commercial. She didn't get the part."

"Dorothy Jane Hughes," Nan said slowly. "I don't know her."

"She pops up off Broadway from time to time. She's usually the lead's best friend. Smart, funny. Never gets the guy. Once she played a German shepherd."

"You're kidding."

"No animal costume—just a gold leotard, a leash, and a very good bark."

"You see too many plays."

He grinned. "Hazard of my profession. I'll call her in."

"The sooner the better." Nan paused at the door. She was wearing a short skirt and high heels that really showed off her legs. If Jim didn't know her better, he'd think she was being flirtatious.

"I'm sorry I unloaded all that stuff on you last night," Jim said.

"Hey, I'm a friend. If you can't talk to me, who can you talk to?"

"You're a good listener."

"I try." Nan winked and made a quick turn on her stilettos.

Jim watched her go with some relief. She would never push a point too hard. She knew how to keep to the boundaries of personal and business. That's what was good about the office.

He picked up the phone and dialed the agent for Dorothy Jane Hughes. "Hi, this is Jim Lockhart at Babcock, Crier, and Nelson . . ." One advantage to being a casting director: your calls were put through right away. "Can you get Dorothy Jane Hughes over here first thing tomorrow morning?"

❧

DOROTHY ALWAYS felt that being an actress was an exercise in patience. You just had to wait, hoping that the right parts would come your way. Knowing that if you just stayed at it for a few more weeks, the right casting director would call . . . and he'd have a part suited perfectly to you. But sometimes believing you'd eventually get a part wasn't so easy.

Truth to tell, Dorothy was coming through a dry patch, working part-time as a receptionist to cover the rent and sending out her photo and résumé to every ad she found in the trades. As she answered phones, made the coffee, and opened envelopes in her temp job, she was keeping her options open. *I don't have to keep doing this. I don't have to be an actress. I can do other things. I could start another job.* But she couldn't get over the feeling that she was meant to be doing what she did.

Between business calls at her receptionist's desk, she checked for messages on her cell phone. Who knew when her agent would call? Who knew when a friend would give her a good tip on a possible job? Who knew what director was planning a show that required talents exactly like hers?

Dorothy had learned to live in the light of hope. She practiced it, studied it, lived it. She'd tried to explain to Lizzie that hope was something you could acquire. There was a recipe for it: "Think three hopeful thoughts before you get out of bed in the morning. Stare at yourself in the mirror when you're brushing your teeth and believe in yourself. Believe in the things you were meant to do." You could practice hope, like practicing the piano or the flute.

No calls yet. But still there was hope. Soon there would be a call. She was sure of it.

⌖

ELIZABETH'S STUDENT was interminably slow at taking apart her flute, wiping it free of saliva, putting it in its green-velvet-lined case, putting the case in her bag, and wrapping herself up in a sweater, scarf, mittens, coat, and hat before heading out the door. The last thing she did was hand Elizabeth a check.

"Thank you so much for your teaching. I'll practice very hard on the concerto," she said.

"I'm sure you will. I'll see you next week."

Elizabeth pushed the door closed. She went into the kitchen and washed the dirty dishes, then put some water on for tea. While waiting for it to boil, she finished her makeup. The teakettle whistled. B-flat.

Not quite in tune. Every time it whistled she always wanted to tune it. The curse of perfect pitch.

She changed her clothes for the matinee. The black pants. The black top. Flute in her bag. She let the tea bag steep. The phone rang, but the answering machine could pick it up. If someone was canceling a lesson or changing a rehearsal time, it could wait. The rest of her day was planned. Reading, lunch, matinee, and evening performances.

She sat on the sofa bed and read the purple lines from *What Price Glory.*

> *Were you relieved when Helen LeGrand decided to study abroad senior year? Were you glad that she wouldn't be around? I have never noticed in your chest of drawers a stash of love letters from her. Did you burn them? Did you throw them away? Or have you saved them in some secret place—as dear to you as these volumes of Harriet Mueller are to me?*

"These volumes of Harriet Mueller." There must have been more than three. What happened to the other ones? Were they at another table at the rummage sale? What was written in them?

> *Maybe you were disappointed to be cast against me. You, the big glamorous star on campus, and I who had only made my mark as a stage manager. I would like to say that I was completely surprised they gave me the part. I should pretend to be modest. Sorry. I knew I deserved it. All right, it was just a comedy by Neil Simon. I would make it great.*
>
> *This is what I want to tell you: I couldn't have been great without you. Every time I looked at you on stage, things were happening. You were always in the moment. You were right where I needed you in a scene. It was like playing tennis with someone better. You made my game look good. Naturally I would get a better review than you. (Does that still sting, darling? Don't let it.) I was the newcomer. You were the old hand. They had to make something of me. They'd made enough of you already.*

suddenly we were a couple. On stage and off. Farewell Helen LeGrand. I don't feel sorry for her at all. She got Paris. I got you.

Spring is supposed to be the season for love. The flowers blooming, students playing their stereos out the windows, Frisbee games under the magnolias.

Forget it. Our season was winter. Remember sledding when it was zero degrees? Remember ice-skating on the lake? I was sure we were going to fall into a hole in the ice. You reassured me that the ice wouldn't melt until March. Maybe you had some Hans Brinker ideas about the two of us skating around the lake. We looked more like I Love Lucy.

What I remember most are the walks we took. From the library, to the dorm, to the theater. Our breath cast a shadow. I put my hand in your pocket to keep it warm. You didn't run off ahead to beat me to class. Sometimes you were late. We sang Christmas carols outside in December. A two-person caroling team, singing outside dorm windows at two o'clock in the morning. You were pretty good on "Deck the Halls." I thought my "O Holy Night" was inimitable. (You fell to your knees at just the right moment of the song, dear.)

I have every note you sent me that Christmas. I've saved them. Too bad I couldn't make transcripts of your phone calls too.

She had saved his love letters. Had he kept hers too?

My sisters thought I'd gone around the bend. I guess they were right. I'd had crushes before. But you were my first and my only love. Don't forget that.

My One and Only.

How could this guy give away these books? How could he be so callous? Clearly he didn't give a hoot about what she thought. He was cold and unfeeling. Maybe he'd wanted to clear out these memories. Start over from scratch. Elizabeth tried to imagine him cleaning out an apartment or house after a breakup or divorce. But giving away these books with their heartrending messages?

Unless he wasn't the one who gave them away. Maybe she did it. Perhaps she wrote all these messages, then changed her mind. The Harriet Muellers sat on a shelf for a couple of years until she couldn't take it anymore. Fed up with the outpourings, she'd tossed the books in the garbage, thinking, *Good riddance to emotional overkill.*

But maybe someone had found them and donated them to the church rummage sale.

Elizabeth winced. She'd had moments when she'd said something heartbreakingly honest—and regretted it. It wasn't fun to be that vulnerable.

Elizabeth imagined living with those Harriet Muellers on a shelf. Feeling the weight of their convictions and passion. If she were living alone and had to see reminders of a love that had been "My One and Only," she would have wanted to get rid of the evidence. Even if they were vintage Harriet Muellers.

Then another scenario dawned on her. What if "darling" had died? What if the man who was supposed to read this history of a love story was no longer alive? She imagined his heirs going through his things and boxing up the old books.

Why bother to look inside? Nothing but a bunch of ancient paperbacks. Throw 'em out. Give them to the church. At least somebody could make a few cents on them. Better than leaving them in storage for generations.

Elizabeth had to find out who had given the books away. For the past few months she hadn't wanted to see anyone or "meet people," as Dorothy put it. Now she'd been pulled in by an incomplete story. Not the one Harriet Mueller wrote, but something written in the marginalia. She hadn't been able to make things right in her own life. But for this couple—and this woman writing to her "One and Only"—Elizabeth had to do something.

EIGHT

"LIZZIE, WHERE have you been? I've been calling you all afternoon and evening."

"Just got in."

"Glad to hear it. I hate to think you've been sitting there all day, screening your calls on the answering machine."

"I'd never do that to you, Dorothy."

"I hope not. But you never know. You get into these moods where you don't want to talk to anyone. You just want to stay holed up there with your flute and romance novels and hot tea."

"Don't you ever feel like closing out the world?"

"I like reading and I like watching movies and I even like drinking tea, but I'd rather do all of them with someone else."

"I'm just quieter than you. *Phlegmatic* is the term they use in Harriet Mueller novels."

"You're not really phlegmatic," Dorothy said. "You're actually quite passionate. Even if you don't talk about it. You OK?"

"I'm fine. Really."

"OK." Dorothy pressed on. "The reason I called is that I have this audition tomorrow."

"Great."

"My agent says they're really excited about me. The casting director remembered me from *The Dog Show*."

Elizabeth stifled a laugh. "All you did was bark."

"I must have barked well. He wants me to come in."

"Is it a dog-food commercial?"

"Very funny," Dorothy said sarcastically. "It's a car commercial, and

I'm supposed to ride in this car in the desert with a guy who races a camel. I'm supposed to be good-looking but not so good-looking that people don't look at the car instead."

"Some compliment."

"I get to leave the guy in the desert and drive off with the car."

"What are you going to have to do for the audition?"

"Be smart and pretty and clever and perfectly charming while showing that I have a natural appeal for any car owner." Elizabeth could hear the anxiety in her friend's voice.

"How old are you supposed to be?"

"Thirty-one."

"That's how old you are."

"But I have been going on these young-mother auditions and overworked-secretary auditions where I'm supposed to be somebody with a terrible cold. I haven't ever been considered car bait. What do car girls wear?"

Elizabeth thought a minute. "What kind of car is it?"

"I don't know . . . a Dodge or a Chrysler or maybe a Ford. It wasn't one of those foreign cars. Definitely not Japanese. Maybe a VW."

"What do you have in your closet?" Elizabeth took off her coat, switching hands with the phone, still listening. Then she got some yogurt out of the fridge.

"The young-mother pants and sweater won't do."

"Do you have anything short?"

"In this weather? It's thirty degrees outside."

"You've got great legs. Car girls should show off their legs." Elizabeth took a bite of yogurt.

"Even if they're never seen on TV?"

"Ever been to the car show? The girls are always draped over the hoods."

"My legs aren't long enough. I'm too short."

"Second option: Overdress. Wear a formal. Act as if you're on your way to a debutante ball."

"At ten o'clock in the morning?"

"Think *Breakfast at Tiffany's*. Think Audrey Hepburn." Elizabeth savored the yogurt. Cherry. Her favorite.

"That's still pushing it. I don't begin to have Audrey Hepburn's figure or neck or her cheekbones. Let's go back to your short dress idea. I've got that gray dress I always wear to parties. If I wear high heels, they make me look taller than I am, and the casting director should be able to remember me."

"That sounds good. What about the weather?"

"I'll wear an overcoat." Dorothy had it figured out, thanks to Elizabeth. "Now, tell me what's on your mind."

"Nothing's on my mind. I didn't call you," Elizabeth said. "You called me. You were having the crisis this time."

"Something's on your mind though. I can tell. You're sounding too subdued."

"I've just come back from playing two shows."

"Is it Alberto? Are you still thinking about Alberto?"

"I haven't thought of him in weeks." Elizabeth didn't want to talk about Alberto.

"I'll take you at your word. It must be those books. All that purple ink."

"Yes. I've been reading them." It was so much a part of what she'd been thinking about, she wasn't even sure she should tell Dorothy.

"What's so interesting?"

"I'm getting to know more about the guy and the girl." Elizabeth dropped the empty yogurt carton in the trash and washed the spoon. "In the second volume the woman tells how they met. She talks about falling in love. Evidently they went to college together and finally dated senior year. They were in a show together and got cast opposite each other."

"It'll never last," Dorothy said.

"What do you mean?"

"You can never stay in love with someone who plays opposite you in a play. At first, you become completely obsessed with the guy. You think of him all the time. You have dreams about him. But the infatuation can't last beyond the closing night."

Elizabeth felt defensive. "This couple stayed together. She writes like they did. She calls him her One and Only."

"Were they married?"

"I can't tell. But she loved him. She still loves him when she's writing. It's a series of love letters."

"Written on the corners of old romance novels? That seems so unlikely."

"She chose the books because they were something she treasured. Something that she kept. I keep all my old Harriet Muellers. I wouldn't give any of them away. I reread them too."

There was a pause at Dorothy's end of the line. "But in the end, he did give them away. What kind of jerk would give away all these sentiments from his wife or girlfriend?"

"He didn't know she'd written in the books. Maybe he didn't even open up the books before they ended up in the rummage sale."

"What do you think happened to her?" Dorothy sounded pensive.

"I don't know. But I feel obligated to make sure he reads what she wrote."

"Why?"

"If you found someone else's love letter lying in the gutter with no postmark on it, wouldn't you mail it?" Elizabeth asked.

"Yes. But you're talking about doing something more complicated. You want to find out who was supposed to receive these messages and get them to the guy. We could be looking forever. We could search the whole city. There are eight million people in New York, and most of the guys would rather be watching football than reading what some ex-girlfriend wrote them."

"I have to try."

Dorothy exhaled in exasperation. "I suppose I have to help you?"

"That would be nice. After all, you were the one who dragged me off to that rummage sale to 'meet people.'"

"I didn't think you'd be meeting a dead person."

Elizabeth took a quick breath. "What made you say that?" She could hear Dorothy turn on the TV in the background.

"An instinct," Dorothy said. "The books, the rummage sale, the purple pen."

"Do you think it's the guy?"

"No, the girl. She's gone, and that's why the books were given away."

"That's exactly what I feared. It's so sad."

"Tomorrow we can go to the church and see if we can find out who donated the books to the rummage sale."

"What about your audition?" Elizabeth asked.

"We'll go after it's over. I'll be in an adrenaline meltdown. I'll be desperate for some company."

"I've got a flute student at eleven. Can we meet at the church at twelve-thirty?"

"OK."

"Break a leg on the audition."

"The short dress?"

"Absolutely. You're a knockout in it."

NINE

JIM HAD a good night. It was the first time since Lois's death that he'd been able to sleep all night. No staring at the ceiling. No looking over to the other side of the bed. No reaching across for an embrace. No waiting for the good-night kiss in the dark. Just sleep. It made him feel slightly guilty that he was able to forget her enough to rest. But he told himself that she would understand. He needed his rest.

Today he walked from the subway to the gym with a real lilt in his step.

"Morning, Jim," the woman at the front desk said. "One or two towels?"

"One. Thanks."

"Have a great workout."

This used to be his time away from Lois. His private time. Sitting on the subway. Lifting weights in the weightroom. Running on the treadmill. Saying his prayer. She had rarely been awake when he'd left the apartment. He used to kiss her before he left, but had stopped that because he didn't want to wake her. He'd call her once he got to the office and check in. Mornings were his.

"Morning, Jimbo," said Scott.

"You're here bright and early."

"I've got a meeting first thing." Scott was sitting in front of his usual locker, his shoelaces untied. His T-shirt said Smith Barney on it.

"Finishing up?"

"Just starting. I'm going to do a quick round of the machines, then I'm out of here. Wish I had hours like you and could go in late."

"And stay late."

"No matter what, you come in here at seven o'clock sharp. Even in the winter when nobody can see if you're in good shape. No bathing suits. No Caribbean trips for you."

Jim shrugged. "It makes a difference to me."

"You must be working out to look good for some girl. You must be doing all those crunches and squats for a reason. Ah, the life of a single guy."

"Tell me about it." It was easier to let others have their fantasies about his life. Too hard to dissuade them.

"Anytime you want to meet my wife's cousin . . ."

"Not until I can bench-press ten more pounds."

"Fat chance." Scott pulled up his T-shirt and glanced in the mirror for a second to see if his crunches were making any difference on his gut.

No abs yet, Jim noted. But he didn't say that aloud.

Scott headed to the weightroom.

"See you there," Jim called.

What made him so hesitant about Scott's wife's cousin or going out with anybody? Time was supposed to heal all wounds. It had been fifteen months, nine days, and thirteen hours. The clock kept ticking. No end in sight. For months Jim had thought that the first year was his goal. If he could only make it to twelve months, things would go back to normal. He'd stop feeling the ache inside.

Maybe the ache had dulled, but the emptiness hadn't disappeared. It had grown worse. The hours, days, and weeks just added up. He went through his life by habit. Even the thought of going out with a woman didn't appeal. The ability to woo, to talk, to court, to charm, to intrigue, to tantalize, to entice—it was gone. He used to think of himself as a fairly sophisticated guy. But he was afraid he'd act like a twelve-year-old.

Listen to his gym talk. All macho bravado. He shook his head, disgusted with himself.

He preferred to forget. Forget everything. That's all he wanted to do. Yet the clock kept moving on. By six o'clock tonight it would be fifteen months and ten days. Any milestone in that? Any freedom?

As he lay down on the bench and did three reps of bench presses, he said the prayer. It was part of his habit.

Jesus Christ, have mercy upon me. Make haste to help me. Rescue me and save me. Let thy will be done in my life.

He could see Scott across the room doing dumbbell curls, getting red in the face. Why didn't he walk over there and say to Scott, "Hey, I'd love to meet your wife's first cousin"? What harm was there in that? The four of them would go out to dinner. No big deal.

At some point he would have to go back and rethink everything that happened with Lois. He would have to unearth the arguments he'd made years ago and justify himself. If she were alive, he could talk to her. She'd tell him where he was wrong. She'd reassure him that things were going to be all right. But that was the whole problem, wasn't it? Lois was gone. There was no second chance. Nothing could be said that hadn't been said. Hurtful conversations couldn't be redone. She was gone.

He grunted through his last set. *Jesus Christ, have mercy upon me . . .*

He put down the weights with a clank. "Ugh."

You could get angry in the weightroom, and people would think you were just yelling at the weights. You didn't have to let on that you were angry at yourself. And right now Jim knew he needed to get out of himself. Show a little courage. Take a risk. Change something.

Scott sat down on the weight bench. "I don't see those ten extra pounds you're lifting."

Jim took the weights off the floor. "Hey, about your wife's cousin. I wouldn't mind meeting her."

"Really?"

"If she can deal with somebody as out of shape as me."

ELIZABETH CHECKED her watch in front of Christ Church. She couldn't do this errand without Dorothy's help. It sounded too bald: *"My friend and I were at the rummage sale last week, and we wanted to know where you got some books that we bought here?"* How inane.

She stood by the sign that advertised the sermon for next week, "Seek and Ye Shall Find." Not all things could be found so quickly. Happiness, peace of mind, friendship. Love. The seeking didn't necessarily guarantee the finding. She knew too many people who had sought fruit-lessly. Sometimes she felt like one of them.

Then she saw Dorothy, hurrying down the sidewalk. Her audition makeup was on. Lots of eye shadow and mascara, two shades of lipstick, and enough blush to be seen from ten feet away. She'd probably been up since six, working on her hair. It boasted enough product to survive a hurricane.

"I was great!" she said, grabbing her friend's hand.

"I'm glad."

"They loved me. I almost didn't make it here. They kept me there for an hour and a half. They had me read five times and walk back and forth in the hall. I'm supposed to walk a lot. They asked me what I knew about cars."

"What'd you tell them?"

Dorothy wrinkled her nose. "That I got in a car accident on my first day of driver's ed. Ran into a turquoise sports car."

"Is that true?"

"Sort of. I wasn't driving, but I was in the backseat. It felt like it happened to me. I've thought about it so much it seems like my story."

"Are they calling you back?"

"That's the best part. They want me to come in tomorrow to meet the client."

"Congrats."

"This could be great, Lizzie. A car commercial for a national audience. It could run for years. Think of the mailbox money."

"The what?"

"Residuals."

Elizabeth hated to tell her that a car commercial would have a very limited run. There were new models every year. New commercials. "I hope it runs forever."

"So what are you doing waiting out here? Let's go in. A church is the perfect place for a day like today. We can thank God for callbacks."

They walked through a wrought-iron gate, past a tiny garden, and opened a heavy oak door.

The receptionist sat behind a grille like a teller in a bank. She had a round, moonlike face and bright red lipstick that only served to make her skin look whiter. She was folding sheets of eight-by-ten paper. "May I help you?" she asked. The expression on her face discouraged idle chatter.

Dorothy did the talking. "We were at the rummage sale last weekend, and my friend here picked up a set of wonderful books—Harriet Muellers—that turned out to have something written in them. She wanted to see if she could find out who donated them, in case the donor didn't know they had messages inside."

"The rummage sale?"

"Yes."

"You'll have to speak to Mrs. Halladay. She's always in charge of the rummage sale."

"Can you tell me where I might reach her?"

The woman looked at Dorothy with some surprise. Evidently everybody knew who Mrs. Halladay was and where she was to be found.

"Mrs. Halladay volunteers in the Thrift Shop on Tuesdays and Thursdays."

"I love thrift shops," Dorothy exclaimed with a theatrical outburst of enthusiasm. "I have bought some of my favorite things at thrift shops. Such good deals."

"Today is Thursday," the woman said.

"What time is the Thrift Shop open?"

The moon-faced woman pointed to a sign. It gave the hours for worship services, Bible study, AA meetings, NA meetings, Al-Anon meetings, choir rehearsals, and the Thrift Shop: Open between 1:00 and 5:00.

"It's almost 1:00," said Dorothy. "If we could just wait here for a few minutes."

"Suit yourself." The woman gestured to a bench against the wall. "The entrance to the Thrift Shop is outside and around the corner. Near the front of the church. You'll see the sign." Her job completed, she went back to folding sheets of eight-by-ten paper.

TEN

"COME IN," the silver-haired woman said. "You're my first customers of the day." She was unlocking the door of the Christ Church Thrift Shop.

"We had to wait upstairs," Elizabeth said.

"It gave us some time to meditate on bargains," Dorothy said.

"That's what we're here for." The woman had a strong Southern accent and a hairdo that was demonstrably south of the Mason-Dixon line. Large and wavy with lots of hairspray—straight from the salon. "Bargains that raise money for good causes."

"Sounds like a good deal."

"I think of it as stewardship," Mrs. Halladay said. "People donate used things they want to get rid of. Others get a real deal buying what's been donated. And all the money goes to a worthy cause."

The Southern accent was infectious. "We were here last weekend for the rummage sale," Dorothy drawled, matching Mrs. Halladay's enthusiasm.

"Wasn't it wonderful? Our biggest fund-raising event of the year."

"Very impressive."

Mrs. Halladay unwrapped a cashmere scarf from around her neck and hung up her coat. "We get a lot of donations at the rummage sale. It's a huge draw."

"I look at a rummage sale as a great excuse to clean out my closets," Dorothy said. She sounded like some heroine from a Tennessee Williams play. Full of phony charm. "Land sakes, I do love a good rummage sale."

"You're just like everyone else. They hear about the sale and bring things in. Lovely things. Silverware, costume jewelry. We even had a nineteenth-century sideboard."

"When do you start accepting donations?"

"In the fall. In time for tax deductions."

"Where does the money go?" Dorothy asked.

"Different church funds. Benevolence, outreach, missions. Depends on the need. Once we used the money to restore a stained-glass window."

"My friend and I"—Dorothy gestured with her eyes to Elizabeth—"were thinking of the stuff you had at the rummage sale. Did you sell all of it?"

"Of course not. We had plenty of leftovers. We bring a lot of it here. It gives us a second and third chance." Mrs. Halladay laughed, showing off a pair of teeth that looked like a china doll's. Small and neat.

"Sounds like a good system, ma'am."

"We can sell things all year long at the Thrift Shop. If the ideal buyer doesn't come to the rummage sale, he'll show up here. There are things that require time to sell. It took me three years to sell a silent butler. One day the right person finally walked in. Can you imagine that? He was the one person in this big city looking for a silent butler." Mrs. Halladay eyed her potential customers, lingering over Dorothy's audition makeup and short skirt. "Anything in particular you're looking for?"

"I like antique clothing."

"You must be an actress."

Dorothy gave her best theatrical smile, good to the back of the house.

"Many actresses come to us for costumes. We're known for our vintage clothing."

"My name's Dorothy Hughes."

"I'm Veronica Halladay."

Feeling completely out of her league, Elizabeth spoke hesitantly. "I'm Elizabeth Ash."

"Nice to meet you."

Dorothy headed to a rack of vintage clothing, leaving Elizabeth to address their real concern. "Have you ever heard of Harriet Mueller?"

"Was she an actress too?" Mrs. Halladay asked.

"She wrote romance novels. Most of them are set in the Regency period."

Mrs. Halladay furrowed her brow and adjusted a single strand of silver hair. "Books are hard. It's a certain kind of person who likes books. I have customers who'll come in and spend an hour looking. They don't have anything particular in mind. They just like going through our shelves."

"I found a couple of old Harriet Muellers at the rummage sale. I was hoping to find more."

"Check on the back shelf."

"Are the books arranged alphabetically?" Elizabeth asked.

"I'm afraid not. That's too complicated. Anyway, I get a lot of decorators who buy books by the yard. They don't care about the contents. All they're interested in are the covers. They want different colors. Cordovan, malachite, burnt sienna, taupe." She made the latter a two-syllable word.

Elizabeth wished Dorothy could help, but her friend was completely absorbed by a white linen dress at the end of the shop. Elizabeth was on her own. "Thanks, I'll look."

She turned to the shelves, running her fingers along the books' dusty spines. A Latin primer, self-help books, weight-loss books, cookbooks, a history text, historical novels, old bestsellers, an atlas, coffee-table tomes, half a set of the Encyclopedia Brittanica, *Reader's Digest Condensed*, and books whose only value seemed to be their bindings. The perfect thing for those decorators.

Why had she come here? She'd never find another Harriet Mueller and hadn't come close to explaining why she wanted one. The only thing her fingers had collected was dust.

Dorothy approached.

"Since when did you speak with a Southern accent?" Elizabeth whispered.

"If it helps . . ."

"Doesn't make any difference. I don't think Mrs. Halladay pays any attention to books. She won't know anything about who donated them."

"Bet she'll go for a love story though."

"You're shameless," Elizabeth hissed.

She continued her search and listened with one ear while Dorothy spun her tale to Mrs. Halladay. The messages in purple ink on the romance novels. The heartbreaking words addressed to "Darling." The text meant to reassure the loved one of the lover's undying devotion. The whole thing was like a packet of love letters left for someone very special. "My One and Only," as the purple pen put it.

"Can you imagine anything more romantic?" Dorothy gushed.

"Why would anyone give those books away?" Mrs. Halladay looked puzzled.

"That's what we were wondering."

"He couldn't have known what was written in there."

"Do you think so?" Dorothy acted shocked.

"Men can be insensitive like that. They overlook things. I'll bet the man who owned those books donated them to the rummage sale without ever once looking inside."

"How callous." Dorothy clucked her tongue.

"He just didn't know, dear. Men aren't always aware of what they're doing. Sins of omission."

"What do you suppose happened to the lady who wrote the messages?"

Kneeling on the floor, looking through books, Elizabeth peered toward Dorothy. Her friend had allowed herself to get a little teary-eyed with these last words. She was playing to the back row. A real theatrical performance.

"Maybe she's not around anymore," Dorothy continued. "Maybe she died. Maybe his estate sold the books."

Mrs. Halladay took this with equanimity. "We get many donations from estates. Relatives of the deceased will ask us to clean out whole apartments, little aware of what they have. If there's something valuable, we'll call their attention to it. We're not here to take advantage of people."

"Would you have any idea where the books came from?"

"We give receipts to people, but we don't keep copies for our records. Was there a name inside?"

"No."

"Any inscription?"

"No."

Down on her knees, her fingers running along the books' spines, Elizabeth burst out, "Here! I've found another."

Another Harriet Mueller. A vintage copy. *The Changeling Prince.* Pulling it out of the stack, she opened it up, thumbing through for a sign of the purple pen.

As Dorothy and Mrs. Halladay rushed over, Elizabeth kept scanning the pages.

"There's nothing inside," she said. "No writing." The depth of her disappointment startled her.

"No purple ink?" Dorothy asked.

"Not in this one." Elizabeth rose from the floor and held it up for their viewing.

Mrs. Halladay thumbed through it herself. "I'll try to think of who might have donated the other ones to our sale."

"Do you keep lists?" Dorothy said suddenly.

"I'm afraid not."

"Just let us know if you have any ideas."

Elizabeth scanned a low bookrack near the front of the shop and spotted something familiar. She thought she knew almost every Harriet Mueller by sight. This one was set in Bath, as she remembered. She walked slowly to it, as though she were stalking it, and pulled it from the rack.

Dorothy and Mrs. Halladay were talking—paying no attention to Elizabeth as she opened the book and scanned the pages. A flood of purple ink was splashed across them. The same handwriting. More messages addressed to "Darling."

"It's her," Elizabeth said to herself. "It's them."

JIM THUMBED through a pile of photos and résumés, at first looking at them with only a professional eye. But then he found himself thinking, *I wonder what it would be like to go out with her.* The potential dates were all over the place. There were too many attractive women to consider.

He paused at a photo of a brunette with the longest eyelashes and the most alluring smile. *No*, he told himself, *I can't go out with her. Professional conflict. She'll be looking at me as a business contact.* It was like going into a candy store after just being told that you're diabetic. Was this the result of his daily prayer? God rescuing him?

When he was married, it didn't seem to matter. He could appreciate a woman's beauty and know she was off-limits. And for over fifteen months as a widower he'd had no emotional interest at all. The women he interviewed and auditioned were assignments for work. That was all.

But now, because of a casual invitation from a buddy at the gym, he started to think that maybe there was something he did want.

He was sitting at his desk, finalizing his choices for the car commercial and thinking about dating, when Nan came in.

"I've got my list," she said. "Do you have yours?"

"I've narrowed it down to three women."

"I wonder if they're the same as mine."

"You go first."

Confident of her judgment, she read them off: "Eleanor Kaisson, Leigh Butler, Dorothy Jane Hughes."

Jim gave a slight whistle. "My three choices exactly."

"Your front runner?"

"Dorothy. Hands down. I think she'd be great. She's just what they want, even if they don't know it yet, and she'll be able to communicate all the allure they need."

"Let's not even give them a choice this time," she said. "We'll tell them that we're sure Dorothy is it."

"I'll call her agent."

"She should come back tomorrow. Have her wear that same gray skirt. It's not perfect, but it'll work. Don't get her nervous, but let her know she's a finalist. She's almost there."

Nan, ever efficient. A real take-charge personality. If she weren't such a good friend in the office, would he want to take her out on a date? Could he risk thinking of her that way? She was beautiful in a faintly exotic way, but she never traded on her dark good looks.

"You know, if I were to begin dating again, this job might prove a real hazard."

"What on earth are you talking about?" She walked closer to his desk and sat on the armrest of the chair opposite him. It was safer than actually sitting in the chair. A gesture that meant she didn't intend to stay for long.

"All these pictures. All these women I meet on the job."

"If they weren't a problem before, why should they be a problem now?"

"Before . . . I was attached. Now I'm not."

She made a dismissive gesture with one manicured hand. The nails were Chinese red this morning. "As though your opinions of them have changed?"

"They're starting to look more dangerous."

"What do you want me to do about that?"

Jim grinned. "You could make sure I don't make a fool of myself."

"That's always a possibility. You can't avoid it." She narrowed her eyes, as though she were reading a client's mind. This time, though, the mind was her friend and colleague's. "Are you going out with someone?"

Jim hung his head in a boyish way. "Not exactly. I did, though, agree to meet the cousin of a friend's wife."

"Pretty threatening," she said wryly.

He looked up. She was teasing. "It was OK to make a fool of myself when I was twenty-two. It's a lot less OK when I'm thirty-two."

"Nobody's sending you to the wolves."

"I don't think I even know how to ask a woman on a date."

"We could do some role-playing to give you practice."

"What if I actually like the cousin of the friend's wife?" he worried aloud. "What am I supposed to do?"

"Go out with her. Get to know her. No one's asking you to propose marriage right away."

"I don't know."

How could he explain that every morning for months he had said this prayer at the gym, *Jesus Christ, have mercy upon me . . . rescue me and save me*, and not for a moment was he interested in any other woman? Then one morning after saying it, he agreed to meet a woman, and his world was turning upside down. What had come to replace the pain was just too confusing. He could fall in love with anybody. Even Nan. It was like one of those myths, where people drink love potions and flip over the wrong person.

"Good luck." Nan rose from the armrest. "I'm not very good at being Lucy the counselor."

"Thanks for your help. Dorothy Jane Hughes will be great in the ad."

"I hope so."

ELEVEN

"THEY MOVED to New York."

"Of course, they did," said Dorothy.

Listening on the phone, Elizabeth could hear her friend filing her nails in the background. The TV was on as usual. It was interminable, like an ancient aunt who couldn't be shut up. Did Dorothy pay any attention to it? Was she listening to Elizabeth or trying to catch Conan O'Brien's last joke?

"That's why the books turned up at a New York rummage sale." Dorothy's tone was matter-of-fact.

"Coming to New York together sounds so romantic. They had each other. They didn't do it alone. They had each other for support."

"Where are you getting all this?"

"Listen." Elizabeth read the purple ink:

> *"New York was everything I wanted it to be. Loud, noisy, crowded, pushy, competitive, raucous, and exciting every minute. The hope in the air was unbearable. It's what got us up every morning to pound the pavement looking for our big break. We both had such hopes. I wanted you to succeed. You wanted me to succeed. We could feel it."*

"They were actoring," Dorothy said.

"Actoring?"

"Doing all those things you're supposed to do when you move to New York to be an actor. Auditioning, interviewing, waiting tables, taking a bus-and-truck tour out of town."

"Why do you say that?" Elizabeth asked.

"'Pounding pavement looking for our big break.' It's such an actorish phrase."

"Well, they both were involved in theater in college. So it makes sense that they were budding actors in New York."

"That's right."

"You said it would never work because they played opposite each other."

"So I was wrong. Go figure."

"Here's what happened." Elizabeth continued reading.

"When we came back home for the wedding, I think my parents just assumed we'd stay in St. Louis. Why pay all that money for a crummy, lightless, cold apartment on the Lower East Side when we could live in splendor near my childhood home? Why did we have to stick it out in New York? We'd tried and nothing big had happened. We'd proven ourselves. Now it was time to come home.

"I didn't ever tell you about the conversation I had with Mama before the wedding. She took me to the beauty salon—her regular place—and I had the works. Nails, facial, mud treatment, waxing. I was waiting at one point, wrapped in towels, when Mama sat down and said, 'Honey, you don't have to go through with it.' For a minute I had no idea what she was talking about. 'He's a nice boy,' she said, 'but there are tons of nice boys around here who are making lots more money.'

"Don't get mad about that. She always liked you. Dad did too, but their ideas of what was marriageable material were pretty conventional. Still are. It took them years to figure out that you were actually making money. Sure, we got the new apartment and I was starting to get work, but they had no idea how things balanced out. I'm afraid they thought I was footing all the bills. My fault. I should have tried to convince them otherwise. Showed Daddy your checks. But you can't change your parents. It's too much work.

"It doesn't sound like it was easy sledding," Elizabeth said.

"Never is."

"Somebody was earning some money."

"Hard to believe it came from acting." Dorothy spoke from experience.

"There was some tension with the family."

"There is with any family."

"But she loves him—"

Dorothy broke in. "At least that's what she says."

Elizabeth could hear water running. What was Dorothy doing now? The dishes?

"She's speaking up," Elizabeth defended. "She's saying things. Isn't that a good sign?"

"She's probably making up for all that she didn't say but should have said when they were together."

"What do you mean by that 'when they were together?'"

"They might be together physically but they're apart emotionally. You can tell."

Elizabeth found that jarring. She felt such a bond with the writer and had grown so fond of the voice. She could picture the woman writing these things in the pages of Harriet Mueller. It was an admission of true love. Never a crossed-out word. Everything came straight from the heart unedited. Would that she could love like that!

"I guess," she said very carefully, "what I like about her—the writer—is that she reminds me of me. She's trying to set things right. She wants to make sure everything's OK. She wants him to know what she really thinks."

"Is that what you wish you could do with Alberto?"

A pause. It was a topic they hadn't addressed in a long time. "Not fair," said Elizabeth.

"He's still on your mind."

"How could he be? He never writes."

"You never set things right with Alberto."

Elizabeth frowned. "There was never the chance."

"Just as well."

No, what she had known with Alberto was nothing like this. She could never have written something like this about him. "Let's change the subject. Any more word on the commercial?"

"Not yet."

"Keep me posted."

"Don't worry. The world will hear."

The last thing Elizabeth did before falling asleep was to turn to the last passage in the book and reread it.

> No, darling, we didn't let my parents get between us. We made the right choice of staying in New York. Moving back home would have killed us both. Dad would have set you up in some good-ol'-boy job, I would have joined the Junior League, we would have had three perfect children, and we would have been miserable. None of it would be ours. You would take to drink, I suppose, and maybe I would have been one of those awful suburban wives who needs a tranquilizer to get through the PTA meeting and the country club dinner dance.
>
> Still, I suspect it cost us something that neither of us knew. We were on our own. We were too proud to ask for help. Pride goeth before a fall, you know.
>
> You would have been furious if I had called Daddy and asked for a loan. You remember the times when we needed it. Sometimes I think you blamed yourself. You thought that I didn't like living in the Lower East Side apartment. You thought I wanted to be rescued.
>
> Listen closely. You didn't have to do anything on my account. I would have been happy for fifty years living in a cold-water flat if it would have made you happy. All I wanted was your happiness. I prayed for it all the time. Still do.
>
> You are still my One and Only.

Elizabeth turned out her light and tried to sleep.

LYING IN bed, Jim wondered what had gotten into him. Why had he said he'd be glad to meet Scott's wife's cousin? What Pandora's box had he opened? As long as there were no girls he would consider dating, he didn't have to make any decisions. He could be like a monk with sworn vows. If all women were off the radar, he didn't have to confront any notions about what he liked and what he didn't like and what he possibly wanted. He could turn down Miss America as fast as he turned away from a harridan.

But by one rash act he'd opened the door on thousands of possibilities. There was no reversing it now. *Jesus Christ, have mercy upon me.* If he could only close the door. It wasn't only the women he interviewed who would be temptations. He'd been shocked at the office to feel that flirtatious urge with Nan.

He wanted to woo her, wow her. Those great long legs . . . why had he never noticed them before? That husky voice, the intense eyes, that sensuous mouth, and the smooth white skin of her neck. An image passed through his head of wrapping his arms around her and kissing her. Right there in his office at Babcock, Crier, and Nelson. Why not just close the door and go at it?

He shook his head. Not only would it be scandalous, it would go against every company policy-and-procedure book, not to mention his own ethical standards.

Fantasies like that had been gone from his life for so long that he was shocked when they crept back in. Prompted, it seemed, by a simple invitation from a guy he knew from the gym. Preceded by a prayer. He wanted to be rescued and saved, but he didn't want all this tumult.

So he'd say no. He'd simply tell Scott that he couldn't go out to dinner with the wife's cousin. He wasn't ready yet. It was completely possible that he'd act like an adolescent. Awkward and shy one moment and flirtatious the next.

He flicked on his bedside lamp and looked at his alarm clock: 2:13. That meant fifteen months, ten days, eight hours. and thirteen minutes. He'd had the whole bed to himself all that time, and still he slept on one side of it. His side. The other half was still her side with her bedside table, her books, and her clock that now said 1:13. He never adjusted it, didn't even change the time after daylight savings. He was waiting for the batteries to go out—as though that would be some sign. Some release.

Jim shuffled into the bathroom and glanced at himself in the mirror. His body was in pretty good shape. Nothing to complain about.

"Must be getting into shape for some babe," as Scott had put it.

No, Jim hadn't been. He'd been getting into shape for himself. Going to the gym out of habit, good or bad. Holding on to some schedule to stay sane. To keep the grief at bay.

There was a time when getting in shape had not mattered. When Lois was there on her half of the bed, he never worried about how he looked. He just looked at her. He loved staring at her when she was asleep, her breathing as regular as the bedside clock. His eye followed the line of her body, each curve familiar but somehow new. He was like a boy discovering it for the first time. Sometimes he thought she could feel his eyes on her and only pretended to be asleep. She would wake up and smile, then fall back to sleep. Such an actressy thing to do. How she loved an audience even in sleep.

But what about those times when she couldn't sleep? After her treatments, she'd toss and turn in such discomfort that he couldn't begin to fathom it. When she'd finally fall asleep, she'd cry out from some bad dream. He'd hold her, then she'd slip back to sleep or take a sleeping pill. For months on her bedside table there had been a full array of pills—brown bottles with labels on them.

Take two, twice a day.

Take three, three times a day after mealtime.

Take as directed.

Take when needed.

Take as necessary.

He'd thrown them all out. No hesitation about that. He opened the medicine cabinet now, relieved to see no pills anymore.

But none of her makeup was there either. No skin creams, no lotion, no eyebrow pencils, mascara, or lipstick. No comb, no toothbrush, no tweezers, or nail files. All of it gone and gone so long that it was hard to re-create in his imagination. *Rescue me and save me.* This is what he really wanted to be rescued from: the loss of her memory. Seeing her slip into nothing more than a phantom, a fading image in a photo.

He closed the medicine cabinet. He turned on the water, splashed his face, and went back to bed.

When she was well, she read in bed late at night. "Does the light bother you?" she would ask.

"Not at all," he would say.

She would read for an hour, then turn off the light and fall back asleep.

He moved over to her side of the bed and laid his head down on her pillow. It was the closest he could come to her now.

As he stared up at the ceiling, he remembered how much she loved old paperbacks. She could read the same book over and over again. Sometimes she wrote in them. Comments to herself. Something she discovered on the tenth or twelfth reading. She said they were like old friends—her favorite books. There was always a short stack on her bed-side table. He hadn't removed the ones that had been there at the last. The cleaning lady came in every other week and dusted around them. When her sisters helped him empty her closets and her drawers and her desk and her bookshelves, he'd asked them not to touch the small stack on the bedside table.

He rolled on one side and reached for a tattered volume. *Quite the Thing* by Harriet Mueller. A couple embraced on the cover—the man in a brilliant yellow jacket and the woman in a pale blue dress. Her hair was upswept in a bouffant reminiscent of the early sixties. A man on horseback could be seen in the distance.

Harriet Mueller had been one of Lois's favorites. There'd been a row of them on the old bookshelf her sisters had sent back to Missouri. "I read them to relax," she said. If she was worried about something or under a lot of stress, she took out a Harriet Mueller. She said it was her reassurance that the world was all right after all.

That was the reassurance Jim needed now. He had never opened a Harriet Mueller before. Never even cracked a page. They were her books. Girl books. Not his type of thing. But on a sleepless night when she'd been gone so long that he couldn't remember the color of her toothbrush or her brand of lipstick, at least there was this link.

He turned back the cover and flipped to chapter 1 and stopped.

All he saw was his wife's handwriting. Her pen with the purple ink all over the pages. The same ink she used for Valentine's cards and thank-you notes and anniversary cards. Her messages to him. She wrote at the top and down the sides and on the next page and the next. She was writing him.

Darling, today is not a good day, but I need to keep up with this project. If you're only just discovering it now, I will repeat what I've written elsewhere. Look back in the other books. It's something I knew you would discover. Not immediately. Only when you were ready.

This is not how it was supposed to end. The two of us were supposed to live forever. For our sixtieth wedding anniversary we'd invite everybody to our country place—I always pictured a cottage on Cape Cod—serve them an elegant meal, and thank them for all the happy memories we've had. Here we've barely made it to our sixth, and our seventh seems unlikely. Celebrate on your own though. Don't forget. You've never forgotten that date ever.

The problem with not having sixty years is that we have to fix things and make everything right right now. No waiting. We have to cram too much of life into too little time. If we'd known we'd only have this much, we would have done things differently, I'm sure. We would have paced ourselves. We would have given ourselves a better last act. You always used to say, "Save the best for last." The audience always remembers what you do last.

Everything's been happening so fast that I haven't been able to keep track of half of it. I can't process it, and I fear you can't either. I say a prayer for you every night. I pray for you to be safe. I pray for your happiness. Be happy without me.

Just remember that I love you. I always have. You're my One and Only.

Jim could hear her voice, the inflection she put into the words. He could see her in the bedroom taking off one of her audition dresses and putting on her pajamas. He imagined her saying all this as effortlessly as she took off her necklace and put it in the jewelry box on top of the bureau. The jewelry box that used to be there.

It was too painful to recall. She was as alive as the writing on the page. Unable to bear it, he put down the book, got up to turn off the light, and lay down on her side of the bed again. He put his hand to his face and hid it, even with no one in the apartment to see him.

Then he let the tears come.

TWELVE

"JIMBO, WHERE were you this morning?" It was Scott on the phone.

"You won't believe this. I overslept. I didn't even hear my alarm." How could he explain that he had not needed his alarm to wake up— not for fifteen months and ten days.

"We missed you. I thought the world had ended. The place wasn't the same without you. The receptionist didn't know what to say to any-one this morning. She forgot to give me my towel because she was so distracted waiting for you to walk in that door."

"Give me a break." Jim was at his desk, ready to return all phone messages and attack his e-mail. He hadn't even had his second cup of coffee. It was bad enough to sleep through his workout, but to arrive at the office twenty minutes late was unconscionable.

"I wanted to set things up for tonight."

"Tonight?" Jim paused.

"Yeah. We've got a baby-sitter for the kids and everything. We're all ready. Karen's cousin is great. You'll really like her. But don't get all uptight. It's just for fun. No pressure."

No pressure? Jim felt himself panicking. His blind date tonight. What had he gotten himself into? He was famously cool under pressure. Everybody knew that. He wasn't supposed to panic. His reputation depended on it.

"Let me see." He checked his calendar. A useless exercise. Big com-mitments like a dinner on a Friday night were not things he usually forgot. He wished he had. He wanted to go home. Go to bed. Read over Lois's message. He did not want to go on a date.

"You're not busy all of the sudden, are you?"

"I'll have to see." He wished the calendar would lie.

"There's a Viennese place we could go to. Strudel, weisswurst, Linzer torte, that sort of thing. Karen's been bugging me to try it."

Could he say there was an off-Broadway show he couldn't miss? That he'd promised some budding star he'd come and see it that night? Other people came up with social lies. Why couldn't he? "I don't see anything on my schedule, but there's something in the back of my mind . . ." *Yes—fear, terror, boredom!*

"Then you're on. You're a prince. I don't have the address. I'll get my assistant to e-mail you the details." There was a muffled sound in the background.

"I'm not sure about this."

"If you'd been doing your usual bench presses, you'd be better prepared. Too bad. You'll have to show off your muscles a different time. Hey, I've got to run. A customer calls."

The phone clicked before Jim could say any more. Scott had never called him at the office before. It had been strictly a gym relationship. Until now.

Lisa, his assistant, stepped in. "I've got a Dorothy Jane Hughes on line one."

"Who?"

"Dorothy Jane Hughes. For the commercial. Do you want me to have her call you back?"

"No. I'll speak to her . . . Dorothy?"

"I can't tell you how pleased I am," the voice on the other end of the line said. "I swear I'm floating on air. I've called everybody I know. Even people I don't know. This is the best choice you've ever made. You will not be disappointed."

Jim could hold the phone six feet away from his head and hear every word. The enthusiasm of actresses was not foreign to him, but he'd rarely met one so exuberant.

"My agent said I shouldn't call you," she went on, "but I had to thank you personally. You came to that show I did, *The Dog Show*, and obviously my German shepherd—I'm sorry, it was really over the top—

made some impression. Thanks for choosing me. I was afraid I was out of the running, but then you called. You made my month. My year!"

Nan appeared in the doorway with a questioning look on her face. Jim rolled his eyes. "Thanks, Dorothy. Thanks for calling."

"The clients will love me."

"Just wear the gray skirt," he urged her. "We'll see you this afternoon. I'm sure everything will go fine. Keep your schedule clear next week. We'll talk to your agent about when we film."

"I love cars. I love all kinds of cars. It doesn't matter. I'll snuggle up to a VW or Rolls or a Kia—"

"Got to go now. We appreciate your enthusiasm." He hung up before she could say more.

"A live one?" Nan said.

"Everybody is at me today. I haven't even checked my e-mail, and I've got a half-dozen voice-mail messages to return."

"That's what happens when you come in late."

Jim reddened. "I overslept. I was up late, thinking about things." *I heard from Lois. She got in touch with me in a weird sort of way. She's been trying to speak to me all this time.*

"No need to apologize. No one works harder than you."

"I didn't even make it to the gym."

"The place will never recover."

"I don't need your sarcasm."

She raised one eyebrow and put a hand on her hip. "You appreciate it. You just don't realize it."

"And that guy I told you about who was trying to set me up with his wife's cousin? He's trapped me into going out with them tonight. I don't even know if I'm wearing the right thing for meeting a blind date." He had on a button-down shirt, a black cashmere sweater, and brown slacks. His jacket was hanging on the back of the door.

"You look fine."

"Remind me again at the end of the day." *Be like Lois. Make sure my collar isn't up in back. See that my tie matches my suit and that my socks don't have holes in them.* Who could ever replace Lois?

"I'll put it on my agenda." Nan turned to go.

"One more thing." Had he gone soft in the head?

Nan looked at him expectantly.

"Thanks," he said. "I do appreciate you, even if I don't always say it or show it."

IF HE were an actor, Elizabeth might have known him. She could have played for him in the pit of some show or watched him perform. Or maybe they'd been at the same party sometime. But that seemed unlikely because Elizabeth avoided the company of actors and actresses. Most of them were so self-involved. All they ever talked about was their careers and what part they almost got or were sure to get. What really irritated her was the way they dominated a conversation. At a party with actors and actresses, everybody had to perform. Everybody preened and showed off, and a flutist was expected to listen. To be the perfect audience.

Some actors I like, Elizabeth thought.

Take Dorothy. She talked a lot, and Elizabeth listened, but when Elizabeth wanted to talk, Dorothy listened. It went both ways. It was a dialogue.

Not with a lot of other actors. They talked. You listened. They performed. You were the audience.

Well, she was a performer too. She had an ego, too, thank you very much. When she had to be the center of attention, she could rise to the occasion. That's what bothered her about actors. They took her at face value. The shy redhead in the orchestra pit. The flutist who stared at her music and followed the conductor's downbeat.

"I'm more than that," she said to no one in particular on the subway train. "Much more." She did chamber music and gigs with her quintet. She enjoyed playing with pickup orchestras around town. She taught with colleagues who were some of the best in the country. She had her own solo career. And when she did a Broadway show, she put her whole heart into it.

She looked at the other riders on the subway. Actors and dancers in their theater jackets with logos advertising their shows. Other instrumentalists, like her, dressed in black and carrying their horns or violins or cellos. Techies in their grungy backstage clothes. Everybody headed to work on a show.

Maybe "Darling" was among them. He could be in a musical. Maybe she had played a flute line for him once. She could be playing for him tonight.

A self-absorbed, domineering actor. An egoist. That was the last thing she needed in her life. Then why did she feel protective of him? She worried about his happiness. All those prayers his wife had been saying for him. Were they answered? Had he found his bearings again? Was he striding out on the stage, as sure of life as he was of his lines?

She had a vivid picture of him. Tall, long-faced, strong nose, slightly tortured expression, sensitive gray eyes, brown hair. But when he smiled, he lit up the stage. She could imagine walking up to him at a rehearsal with the Harriet Muellers under her arm. "I have something that belongs to you," she'd say. She'd want to talk to him about his wife and their relationship. A partnership of equals. Real love.

RED VELVET curtains hung inside the door to The Vienna Woods so that you had to push them back to make it into the restaurant. Jim supposed it was atmospheric, but all that plush red reminded him of a saloon in a Hollywood Western, not old Vienna.

Inside it was more convincing. Crystal chandeliers hung from the ceiling with gold tassels dangling from them. Gold braid ornamented the red-upholstered benches and chairs, like military trapping from a Viennese operetta. The walls were hung with huge gold-framed mirrors, and more plush red fabric framed the windows. A waltz was coming from a speaker in the ceiling, and at any moment the Merry Widow herself would swoop out from behind a bronze candelabra.

Jim passed his overcoat and hat to the coat-check girl and glanced at himself in a smoky mirror. How staid he looked. Boring, stiff, not much fun. More like he was a CPA than a casting director. If he'd remembered he was going out tonight, he would have worn something different. His one Helmut Lang suit or maybe a suede jacket. Lois would have had the right idea.

It irritated him that he was doing all this fussing when he was certain that he wasn't that interested in Scott's wife's cousin. He was here as a favor to a friend. And because of Lois. *I pray for your happiness. Be happy without me.* That was her command. Lois wanted him to get out and enjoy life. He'd try it for an evening. All he had to do was make polite conversation for a couple of hours, then he was off the hook. From the look of it, Scott would be shelling out a lot of dough for dinner.

"I'm meeting Scott O'Donnell tonight," he told the hostess.

"Jah," she said with an Austrian accent straight from the ski slopes. "Vil you come this vay?" She took tiny steps in her tight black leather skirt. He expected her to start yodeling any moment.

"Jimbo," Scott called, "you made it."

Seated on one side of him was a pageboy blonde with a Florida tennis tan. On the other, a rosy-cheeked brunette with earnest brown eyes.

The blonde stood up and gave Jim a kiss. The perfect stockbroker's wife. "I've heard so much about you."

Probably said it to every friend and client of Scott's.

"I don't know what he's told you," Jim said.

"I don't ever look at any of the women at the gym, right, Jimbo?"

"He only has eyes for the mirror," Jim said. "Checking out his form."

"I said you were the best-looking, hardest-working, iron-pumping casting director who came to the gym."

Jim smiled. "As far as I know I'm the only one who comes to the gym."

"This is my wife, Karen."

"I figured as much."

"You are so nice to come out like this on short notice," Karen said. "Not at all."

The rosy-cheeked brunette stared at them hopefully, waiting to be introduced.

"I want you to meet my cousin, Adele," Karen said.

Adele? "Very nice to meet you."

She extended her hand and Jim took it. It was damp and cold, as though she'd been clutching her glass of Perrier for dear life.

"Karen said I'd enjoy meeting someone closer to my own age after a day at work."

What was she? A nursery-school teacher? One of those nice women who spend all day speaking on a four-year-old level?

"Adele is a gerontologist," Karen said helpfully.

"How interesting." So she spent her time forcing crafts on octogenarians.

"I wanted to do something that would really make a difference for people," Adele offered.

"You should have seen her with our grandparents when they had to move out of their house," said Karen.

"I've always liked old people."

Jim sat down with a sinking sensation. The chair, decorated with gold leaf, creaked beneath him. Maybe it would collapse.

Adele was the sort of girl women would say had really nice hair or a nice complexion. Men wouldn't notice either.

"Scott tells me you're in advertising. That must be so interesting."

"Not nearly as worthwhile as gerontology."

"It is a growing field," Adele said. "People over eighty are the fastest growing demographic in America today. Now that some baby boomers are hitting their sixties, the needs in our country for trained gerontologists will only increase. We need to be prepared for the demographic shift."

"How interesting." Jim wanted to disappear into the walls, get swallowed up by the red velvet drapery.

"But that's not the only reason I went into gerontology. I found that I was involved in a field of study that crossed all cultures and races. The aged and highly aged are treated so differently. If you look at the figures, you would be surprised how badly off our seniors are compared with those in Japan or Western Europe, where the state takes such good care of them."

"I hadn't realized that."

THIRTEEN

ALL NIGHT Jim listened to Adele, prodding her with more questions. Finally he couldn't take any more details about the astonishingly high rate of Alzheimer's or what high-protein beverages were good for adults who couldn't masticate. Desperate to change the subject, he asked, "Have you seen any great movies?"

"Yes," she replied. A slight overbite made the *S* whistle as she spoke.

"Tell me." He was practically pleading with her.

"There was an excellent documentary on TV about why the Finns and the Swedes live so much longer than the Americans with a diet that's very heavy in cholesterol and fat."

Wait until I tell Lois about this, he thought. He could imagine describing every moment to her, from the first meeting to the farewell in front of The Vienna Woods. Only she would see the humor of it.

"Thank you so much for a nice time," he said to Scott and Karen. "I enjoyed meeting you," he told Adele.

"Likewise," she said.

Likewise? He could hear Lois imitating that response, hissing on the sibilance.

What surprised Jim was how disappointed he was. He thought he'd be relieved if they didn't get along and he'd never have to think of her again. Adele would just be an unspoken joke he and Scott shared at the gym. A bond beyond barbells. But sitting beside her, hearing her explain how she got into gerontology, he discovered that despite his protestations, he'd come to The Vienna Woods hoping for the most.

Back at his apartment he found himself looking for Lois. She'd be in the bathroom washing her face or reading in bed, waiting for him to come home. "You won't believe this," he heard himself say. He wanted her reaction, her laugh, the shared viewpoint. *All I wanted to do was tell her about you*, he thought. Introduced to a new woman, and all he wanted to do was talk about his dead wife.

That night Jim left the lights on, as though Lois were the one who had gone out, and he would doze off, ready to wake up when she came in.

He'd once heard that mental patients were in the most danger when the antidepressants had kicked in enough to give them energy but not enough to relieve the depression. That's what he felt like now. Over the worst of grief but without a sense of where he was supposed to go or what he was supposed to do next. He was aimless, rudderless.

Where, Lois, where?

HE AWOKE at three. Looking over to Lois's side of the bed, he saw her small stack of books on the bedside table. The one on top, *Quite the Thing*, was right where he left it, full of her last messages to him. He'd already checked the other books for messages. Nothing.

Suddenly he remembered. There were other Harriet Muellers! Where had they gone? Jim sat bolt upright. He thought of Lois's bookcase with her favorite books. The ones she reread and reread. A sort of meat loaf and mashed potatoes of literature. Comfort food. For weeks they'd stayed there. He hadn't had the heart to get rid of anything. Her dresses in the closet, her makeup in the bathroom cabinet, her pantyhose in her top bureau drawer.

Then her sisters had helped him. They had come and taken out armloads of clothes. What they did with them he never knew. He didn't want to know. The apartment needed to lose some of her things. A box or a bundle at a time. It would help him let go.

So the sisters came back again and took more. A clean, brutal sweep. He'd already saved what he wanted—things that would mean little to them. A silver-backed hairbrush, the fountain pen she used, her collection of theater playbills. A couple of photo albums. The rest could go. His memories would be the things that he'd hold closest.

His sister took the bookshelf because it had belonged to a grand-mother or great-aunt or somebody. But what had happened to the books? There were other Harriet Muellers there.

He bounded out of bed and into the extra room. It had been their guest room and study. Someday they'd hoped it would be the baby's room. He turned on the overhead light to get a full view of the book-case on one wall. There was his collection of Patrick O'Brian and Dick Francis. An old set of Dickens he'd inherited from his grandmother.

But where were *her* books? Now that he wanted something of hers, where were they?

Sprinkled on the shelves were a couple of volumes. Two Jane Austens, a *Book of Common Prayer*, a history of eighteenth-century France (he'd never had much patience for the French), some bound play collections. William Saroyan, Noel Coward, Anton Chekhov, and Neil Simon. He didn't remember ever buying them, especially not the Neil Simon. They were probably for some class in college. He opened a volume and saw her underlining and notes. The same purple ink even back then. But no messages. And no Harriet Muellers.

Where had they been sent? Thrown away? He wasn't home when her sisters boxed things up. He couldn't bear to watch them. Jim would have hated to see any of her stuff go. He was afraid he'd change his mind about getting rid of it. The bookshelf was there one morning and gone in the evening. The Harriet Muellers that had been lined up like schoolgirls on the shelves had disappeared.

Three o'clock. Too late to call her sisters, Emily and Melinda. They'd think he'd gone off his rocker. What would he say? "Hey, it's Jim. I was just wondering what you did with all your sister's books on that bookshelf?" At three in the morning?

Those books were a secret language between husband and wife, a secret that would lose all its power if it had to be explained. When Lois took out a Harriet Mueller, he knew she was considering something that was beyond thought. She needed time. She didn't want to be bothered. They could talk and joke and laugh on a Harriet Mueller day, but the book was a sign that she was vulnerable. She needed to be someplace else for a few days. Someplace between the covers of a romance novel.

Jim cursed himself for not thinking of them. Of course that's how she would communicate with him. A note in her jewelry box would have been too obvious. He would have read it days after her death when he was completely numb and not known what to do with it. He wouldn't have been able to process it.

But anything between the pages of a Harriet Mueller required his close attention.

"Lois," he said to the empty apartment, "where? Where are they? What more did you want to say to me? Where are the books? Tell me."

He returned to his bedroom and picked up the one volume that he had and reread the note:

> *Darling, today is not a good day, but I need to keep up with this project. If you're only just discovering it now, I will repeat what I've written elsewhere. Look back on the other books. It's something I knew you would discover. Not immediately. Only when you were ready.*

He was ready.

❧

"I GOT the part!"

"So I've heard. You've already left a dozen messages." Elizabeth rubbed her eyes. What time was it? Eight o'clock on a Saturday morning. Why did Dorothy have to call so early?

"You should have called back. I wanted to share the good news with somebody."

"It was late when I got home. I was tired." Elizabeth sat up in bed. "How did the interview go? From the sound of your voice, evidently they liked you?"

"Loved me. Lizzie, this is really my moment. A commercial for national TV. I always knew I'd grow into my looks. 'Give 'em time,' Mom always said. Well, the time is now. And you'd better believe I'm going to take every advantage of it."

"When do you film?"

"Wednesday and possibly Thursday. I've taken both days off from the temp agency. No receptionist gigs for me."

"I'm really pleased for you."

"Glad you're in a good mood. Because I have another favor to ask of you."

"Another rummage sale?" Elizabeth could imagine looking for more Harriet Muellers. Maybe this time she'd find the guy.

"A show. I'm supposed to see a staged reading of a new play on Sunday, and I don't want to go alone."

"I have a matinee on Sunday."

"This is in the evening."

"Why can't you go to the reading by yourself?"

"Antoine is going to be there, and I can't bear seeing him." Antoine was a persistent but unwanted suitor.

"Why are you going?" Elizabeth asked.

"The director is a friend. He says there's a part in this show that would be perfect for me."

"You should be in the reading, shouldn't you?"

Dorothy sighed. "The playwright wanted someone else. The director had to go with his choice. If it goes into production, they'll audition me."

"By that time you'll be too busy selling cars on TV."

"Just come with me," Dorothy pleaded.

"What time?"

"Six o'clock. We can have dinner afterward. I'll pay."

"You haven't earned any money yet."

"It's as good as in the bank."

Elizabeth opened the refrigerator for some yogurt. "The things I do for you."

"You're a doll."

"We can meet on Forty-sixth Street after the matinee."

"Have you found anything else in those Harriet Muellers?"

"I've read everything I've got."

"Do you see anything in it?"

"I see somebody I want to help." She opened the top of the yogurt. "I wish you'd look for the real thing."

⤸⥁

THE REAL thing. That was the problem.

Would Elizabeth ever find the real thing? Would she ever meet the real person in the messages? The person she'd come to imagine was more interesting than anything remotely real. She figured he had a good career as an actor. Did a couple of musicals, made some money, went on a national tour. Picked up a pilot for a TV show in California and filmed a horror-movie spoof.

The surprising thing was, he was modest about it all. Probably because of the tempering love of his darling. His wife. She was his anchor. They'd moved to New York together and had made it. Now he was bereft without her, and Elizabeth had to find a way to bring him her words.

There was always the chance that he'd wander into the Christ Church Thrift Shop and look for the books, realizing his terrible mistake. A slim chance. But still. Mrs. Halladay would alert her that he'd come. They'd get together. Elizabeth would console him over his loss. She'd know the secrets of his heart. They'd talk about the woman who wrote in the Harriet Muellers. And then what?

Did she actually believe he would sweep her off her feet? All because of a few messages scrawled in some old books? Her imagination had leaped far ahead of reality. What she needed was more evidence. Some ballast for her dreams. More books. More stories.

That morning Elizabeth had to give a few lessons at the conservatory. Walking downtown she stopped at a small hole-in-the-wall bookstore on Columbus Avenue.

The owner was a scruffy, bearded fellow who always wore a tweed jacket, no matter the season. The same brown tweed that was steeped in the city's smells. Cigarettes, exhaust, pizza, coffee, greasy fries.

"Morning," she said.

"Morning."

"I was looking for some old romance novels."

"Anything particular? I get a lot of stuff." He had a voice that sounded like he gargled with glass.

"Harriet Mueller. Have you seen any of her books lately?"

The interior of his shop was no bigger than a walk-in closet and every square inch was filled with used books. Elizabeth couldn't begin to fathom how he filed them. Fiction, nonfiction, romance, mystery, history. Wilkie Collins was next to a manual on shipbuilding, and Jackie Collins was on top of an econ textbook.

He closed his rheumy eyes to scan his inner card catalog. "No. You don't see them much—Harriet Muellers. They're good ones. Well written. Well researched."

"I know."

"You might check some of the thrift shops around here. There's one at Christ Church. They have a great rummage sale every year. I've found some real bargains there. Things you don't find anywhere else."

"I'll keep my eyes open," Elizabeth said and resumed her walking.

The man she was looking for had to be here somewhere. He could be just around the corner. At the Korean deli, at Barnes & Noble, at the fish market, waiting in line to mail a package at the post office, waiting to buy tickets for a movie. Shopping at Tower Records. At the pharmacy, the bagel shop, the dry cleaners. He couldn't be far away.

❧

JIM CALLED Melinda and Emily in the morning and left identical messages on their answering machines: "It's Jim. I know it's been a while since we've talked. I'm doing all right. Sorry I'm so bad at keeping in touch. I guess it's because I have nothing new to say. I was wondering, though, if you know what happened to all the books in Lois's bookshelf. There are a couple missing that I was looking for. Do you remember what you did with them?"

He sounded full of self-pity. As though there really was nothing new to say. On the contrary, he had a lot to say. More than he'd tell them. He missed Lois desperately, but in the past few days he had felt a change.

Like when spring was near. That budding-crocus, thaw-in-the-air sensation. He wanted to talk to Lois and listen to her. Her words would be in the books. More books. If only he could find them.

He picked up a pile of shirts for the laundry and grabbed the list of groceries to buy. He kept a running tab on a pad of paper by the refrigerator. *TP, mustard, parm cheese, dental floss, frozen peas, spaghetti . . .*

He and Lois used to do the shopping together. Even when they were at their busiest, they could join forces with separate lists and a grocery cart. He did dairy, she did cereal; he did frozen foods, she did fresh fruit and vegetables. He would still forget things that would have been on her list. Where were the apples? Where were the carrots? *Lois should have picked them up.* Then he'd remember.

Outside the air was cool and damp, just above freezing. Diesel exhaust from the crosstown buses hung in the air. Garbage in black plastic bags sat on the sidewalk waiting for collection. Dirty old snow lay in a few patches. Soot was sprinkled on the white like black pepper.

Jim dropped off his shirts, picked up some mouthwash at the pharmacy, and was about to go to the supermarket, when he remembered the used-book shop down the block on Columbus. Just a hole in the wall. He'd never bought anything there and often wondered how the man managed to earn a living. Who would want some old paperbacks that had been read a hundred times?

Lois! he thought. She recycled there all the time. Giving up a handful of rejects and coming away with another handful. The small shop was her lending library.

A scruffy man in a tweed jacket was arranging books on a cart outside his shop.

"Good morning," Jim said.

"Can I help you?"

The Used Books—Bought and Sold sign needed repainting. The Sold part of the equation was growing dim.

"My wife, Lois, used to bring her things here."

"I don't know most people's names." The man spoke English as though it were a foreign language.

"This place was important to her. She was able to sell the books that she didn't want anymore and buy new ones to replace the old. Perhaps you remember her."

"Lots of people come here."

"She hasn't been here in a while."

"I don't keep close track of my customers."

"She's away," Jim said. He couldn't bring himself to say, "She's dead." He shifted his weight. "What I'm wondering is if her sisters brought some of her books here to sell. She had lots of favorite paperbacks that she never would have sold off herself, but someone else might have."

"People have different tastes."

"Did anyone sell you some old Harriet Muellers recently?"

"No."

"Have you seen any Harriet Muellers lately?"

The man scratched his beard and narrowed his eyes. Jim felt an enormous hope in the long pause. If only he were patient enough. If he listened closely enough. If he remembered her and what she loved. Visiting a hole-in-the-wall bookstore where she shopped from time to time. She probably knew the tweed jacket's pattern by heart.

Jim waited expectantly. Hope had swooped down and caught him.

"No," the man said curtly. "I haven't."

FOURTEEN

SATURDAY AFTERNOON he saw a third-rate production of a David Mamet play. He didn't even stay for the second act. That night he took in an experimental production of a Brothers Grimm fairy tale. Second row center was a bad place to sit—right next to the sandpit on stage. He got quite sandy, but he was entranced by one beautiful woman in the cast who had eyes the color of blueberries and blond hair worthy of Rapunzel.

Sunday he skipped a matinee in favor of a movie set in Ethiopia. No possible actors in the film, but the man who did the voice-over was said to be perfect for any travel ads. A comforting travelogue voice. Sunday night there was a reading of a play set in a prison. A play within a play. The main character was a novelist who rediscovers her calling volunteering in the prison. A do-gooder play.

As usual Jim was in the second row. The performers sat on stage in a semicircle. The set from the afternoon show still filled the space. A huge tree dominated stage left, the roots stretching down into the orchestra pit. It might have looked impressive during the performance, but under the glare of houselights, it reminded him of a bad Disney prop. Why was he here? Which performer had he come to see?

A woman on stage caught his eye and winked theatrically. She must have been the one. Her picture and résumé floated through his mind. He smiled without giving too much encouragement and raised one finger.

If he'd been the director or producer, he wouldn't have known where to begin to improve the play. It was so half-baked. It needed more than a staged reading. He never understood why playwrights had to inflict their early drafts on an audience. A novelist or poet would never conceive of such a thing. Lois would have said, "The process is everything. Not the goal, the process." The process, bah!

He couldn't wait for the intermission.

"THAT'S HIM!" Dorothy said from their seats in the back of the house. Polite applause at intermission. The actors were bowing.

"What?" asked Elizabeth. She was actually enjoying the play. She had feared it would be mournful, set in a women's prison with a bunch of ex-druggies and prostitutes. B-movie-ish. But the script was remarkably intelligent, and the play within the play wasn't bad. "Antoine?"

"No. The guy from Babcock, Crier, and Nelson. I think he's cute. Even cuter without the coat and tie."

"Which guy?"

"The casting director. Jim Lockhart. My fan. I'm sure I got the part because of him. He saw me as a German shepherd."

The actors were walking off the stage. Jim stood up.

"Jim!" Dorothy cried out, waving her hand.

Elizabeth scanned the faces in front of her. Several people turned to see who was calling. Only one of them could be Jim. Brown tousled hair, brown eyes, tall and lean but not too thin. A theatrical type but not the kind you saw on stage. Not a narcissist waiting to be recognized. A little more self-effacing than that. He flashed a quick smile, as if embarrassed by the attention.

"We've got to go talk to him," Dorothy said.

"You go."

"You're coming with me."

"Dorothy!" A short, beady-eyed man intercepted her at the aisle. "I'm so glad you came."

"Antoine, I'm not speaking to you."

"That was last week."

"This week is even worse," she retorted.

Jim walked up to the three of them . . . most likely out of politeness. Dorothy turned her body so it was practically a barrier in front of Antoine. Elizabeth was closest.

"Hi," Jim said.

"Hi," Elizabeth returned. "I'm a friend of Dorothy's. At least she's the one who dragged me here."

"I work for an ad agency that just cast Dorothy in a commercial."

"So she told me."

"I expect she's told lots of people."

Dorothy smiled at Jim. "I didn't expect to see you here. I didn't expect anyone here. This is my friend Elizabeth. A musician. She plays the flute."

"Where?"

"This week I played in the pit for *If You Ask Me*. Next week I'll go back to teaching and doing some chamber work. After that I've got to go out West for a solo tour." Why was she saying all this? She wished Dorothy would take up the conversation.

"You must be good."

"There are a lot of good musicians in this city," she said modestly.

Antoine pushed himself between Dorothy and Elizabeth and thrust out his hand to Jim. "I'm Antoine Moreau. I do stand-up comedy. I'll give you my card. You work for an ad agency? I'm really funny. Ask Dorothy."

"Nice to meet you."

Antoine pulled out his card.

"Are you ready for the shoot next week?" Jim asked Dorothy.

"I spent all morning at the gym and I'll go all day tomorrow."

"Don't worry. You look great," he assured her.

"I would be really good for a TV commercial," Antoine went on. "You probably need someone like me. Short, dark, really funny. Anyone who can sell himself in stand-up can sell a product."

"Antoine," Dorothy said, "can't you tell he doesn't want to talk business?"

"Send me a tape," Jim offered graciously. "We'd be glad to look at it." He turned to Elizabeth.

Antoine moved closer. "Call me in. People don't really know what I can do until they see me in action. When I go into an office, I leave everybody laughing. The secretaries, the execs, the janitors. Everybody gets a taste of my humor. Just let me drop by."

"We prefer to work through agents." Jim was being incredibly gracious.

"I'm not one of those airbrushed, cookie-cutter types."

"He's already promised to see your video," said Dorothy in exasperation.

"We can go out after tonight's show," suggested Antoine.

A shadow fell across Jim's face.

"He's got work to do," Dorothy said.

"Yes," Jim replied, "I'm supposed to meet with both of these ladies after the show. Dorothy's friend—"

"Elizabeth," Dorothy prompted.

"Elizabeth is coaching her in the part. We needed a musician to help Dorothy's breath control. The shoot will demand a lot of breath control."

"She's a flutist," Dorothy added, improvising. "They're famous for their breath control. Her apartment's on the top floor of a brownstone. She gets a lot of exercise going up and down."

"You're getting together to discuss breath control?" Antoine looked bewildered.

"And other things," Jim said.

Elizabeth glanced at Jim to see how serious he was. He seemed to be completely in earnest. Not a hint of duplicity.

The lights in the theater began flashing. Time for the audience to take their seats.

"I'll send you that video." Antoine pointed his fingers like a gun at the casting director.

Bang, bang. You'll die over my talent, Elizabeth couldn't help but think.

"I'll look forward to seeing it," Jim said kindly.

"It'll knock you dead." Antoine followed this up with a punch in the air. Overkill.

"IS IT always like that?" Elizabeth asked at the restaurant.

"Some actors are even more aggressive," Jim said.

"You aren't actually going to watch his video?"

Jim shrugged. "He might be good. He's a type. Commercials need all types."

"He's a complete jerk," said Dorothy, mincing no words as always.

"Is he any good?"

"In that obnoxious, audience-as-hostage, stand-up comic way."

"Perfect for hocking antianxiety drugs," Jim said wryly. He was sitting in between them in a booth, turning back and forth like a spectator at a tennis match. "But thanks for rescuing me."

"How did you get into the business in the first place?" Dorothy asked.

"It's just one of those things you fall into," he said.

"Not like being an actress."

"Or a flutist." He turned to Elizabeth.

"You'd be surprised by how many people stumble into that," she said.

He had a startling gaze, as if he could read right through her. Right between the lines of her character. She didn't want to think of what he saw. His was a face that asked for emotional honesty. As though he'd been through some sadness and wasn't going to tolerate anything short of the truth. No one would fake anything for those eyes.

"How did you get to be a flutist?"

She didn't hesitate. "I've always loved music. My mom says I loved it even as a baby. She could get me to stop crying if she sang for me. I could carry a tune when I was pretty young. Mom taught piano at home, and she found me picking out 'Happy Birthday' when I was only two."

"A veritable Mozart," Dorothy volunteered.

"Evidently you stuck with it," he said.

"Music was big in my house. Playing an instrument. Singing. Everybody did something. My dad worked as a lawyer, but he could play violin. After dinner he would play duets with Mom at the piano."

"A lot of people grow up around music but don't go into it professionally."

He seemed to be talking to both of them, but his head kept turning to Elizabeth. It was as though she couldn't escape, caught by those probing eyes.

"My dad could have been a professional violinist. Mom said he didn't try because he hated to be at the mercy of a conductor."

"Yet you made that decision."

"Sometimes I think the decision was made for me. There was nothing else I wanted to do. I studied the flute in fifth grade. I was glad I could do something other than piano but was also glad that it was in the key of C."

His eyes urged her on. "Do you have perfect pitch?"

"Yes," Dorothy said. "She does."

"It's not such an advantage for a musician," Elizabeth explained. "Perfect pitch is more of a hazard. It'll drive you nuts if a conductor wants to take the pitch down slightly or you work with a singer who wants to do something in a different key. Once I accompanied a tenor who had everything transposed down because he was losing his top notes. We had to pretend that his high B-flat was a C."

"Where'd you study?"

"At Eastman in Rochester."

"And then you just moved to the city and got jobs?"

"Pretty much."

"She's the envy of every actor," Dorothy said. "A performer who has never had to wait tables. A rare breed."

"How did the two of you meet?"

"In a show," Dorothy said. "A terrible play."

"I played the flute."

"And I was supposed to be some nineteen-thirties Hollywood goddess who could whistle anything. Hence the flutist. Whenever I whistled, Lizzie played. We got so good at it I could just pucker up my lips and she'd start playing, stopping just when I'd run out of breath."

Elizabeth laughed. "The whistling was the only good thing about the show."

"It was a real technical feat. The playwright was some heiress from the Upper East Side. Coffee or tea or pharmaceuticals. Lizzie, what was it that family owned?"

"Pharmaceuticals."

"That's right. This was her big piece. She'd been working on it ever since her graduation from Sarah Lawrence. I whistled, Lizzie played. Until one afternoon—I don't know what came over me."

"Good sense," Elizabeth said.

Jim kept staring at her. Not Dorothy.

"One afternoon there were only seven people in the theater," Dorothy began.

"Two of them must have been relatives and the other five were from an old folks' home." Elizabeth turned to Dorothy to continue.

"That matinee I was doing my whistling trick, and Lizzie was playing when one of the old folks said to the other in a voice so loud you could hear it down the block, 'Why does she keep making that kissing face?' and her companion whispered back, 'She's supposed to be whistling.' Of course the deaf old lady didn't hear it, and they went back and forth a few times until I started giggling. I was supposed to be whistling a Cole Porter tune, but all I could do was laugh. Trying not to laugh made it even worse."

"I started laughing too," Elizabeth said. "I couldn't help it. And when you laugh, you can't play."

"I was gagging from laughter. My stomach hurt, but no sound was coming out. And I heard this giggling offstage. No flute music. And that made me laugh harder. It was like she was my voice. Even my laughter."

Elizabeth rolled her eyes. "We had to be friends after that."

Jim's brown eyes looked amused but distant somehow. "I can see why you laughed. Things like that are especially funny in the theater."

"Did you ever do theater?" Elizabeth asked politely.

"A while ago," he said evasively. "Most people in New York have done some theater somewhere. Scratch any banker or lawyer in town, and you're sure to come up with a frustrated actor."

"And you?"

"I came to New York to help put people like Dorothy in commercials."

Easy self-deprecation, Elizabeth thought.

"I'm glad you did," Dorothy said.

The waiter was about to circulate, asking if anyone wanted anything more.

"We've managed to avoid Antoine," Jim said.

Dorothy looked at him gratefully. "Thanks so much for helping us."

"I should get going," Elizabeth said. "I've got a student coming first thing tomorrow."

Jim raised his hand and mouthed "check please" to the waiter.

"I look forward to the shoot," Dorothy said.

"I'm sorry I won't be on location to see it. My job is over. They'll fly you out to Arizona, do thousands of takes, and fly you back."

"I won't disappoint you."

"I'm sure you won't."

When the waiter came, Jim said, "Here, let me."

The two women objected, but in the end Jim won, putting it on his credit card. Then all three of them stood up.

"Which way are you going?" Dorothy asked.

"Eighth Avenue. I take the B or the C uptown."

"We need to walk over to Seventh to take the one or the nine," said Elizabeth.

They shook hands as they parted.

⤬

JIM WALKED to his subway, smiling like a tourist. It was as though he were seeing the city for the first time: The garish billboards, flashing neon signs, carriage drivers taking their horses back to the stables, a mounted policeman, sidewalk vendors selling pretzels and hot dogs, a homeless guy with a sign advertising that he was a poet: *Let me write a poem for you. Two bucks a stanza.* Two street evangelists were handing out pamphlets that said, "Jesus Christ is Lord."

Jim took a pamphlet and muttered his prayer. *Jesus Christ, have mercy upon me. Make haste to help me. Rescue me and save me. Let thy will be done in my life.*

"She was beautiful," he said to himself. "Red hair like a Pre-Raphaelite painting and those green eyes. Sweet too—and modest." Like no one he had ever seen before.

Fifteen

"WHY DID you say we take the one or nine train?" Dorothy asked, a safe distance away.

"We usually do," Elizabeth said.

"But we could have taken the B or the C and walked the extra blocks. We could have talked with him some more."

"He wanted to get away from us. Couldn't you see that? He was being nice by saving us from that stand-up comic. I didn't want to take advantage of that."

"He was interested in *you*."

Elizabeth stopped dead in her tracks. "What are you talking about?"

"He kept staring at you. I watched him. He hardly looked at me."

"He's a casting director. He's used to studying people. That's his job."

"Lizzie, get it into your head. There are looks, and there are looks. He was looking."

As they headed down the stairs to the subway turnstile, Elizabeth felt in her coat pocket for her Metro card.

"He wasn't wearing a wedding ring. I saw no photos of children in his office. He doesn't look gay," Dorothy continued. "So what could he like better than taking a subway uptown with two gorgeous females like us?"

"He's a little sad."

"What do you mean?"

"We told one of our best stories and he was nice about it, but there was some other vibe coming from him," Elizabeth said.

"You've been reading too many of your books."

"When he smiles, the smile doesn't go all the way across his face. It stops halfway."

"Don't you think he's nice?"

"Yes." Elizabeth thought he was a lot more than that. "But he wasn't really interested."

"Listen, girl, it does you no good to read too much into every situation. You're always looking for the story under the story and people's private motivation as though you were going to write them up in a novel. Well, I can tell you that sometimes it's a waste of time. If you think things out too hard, you won't feel anything at all."

Elizabeth had to shout over the noise of an approaching subway train. "More advice for the lovelorn?"

"He's yours to lose, I tell you. He wasn't flashing those eyes at me. I will do one last favor for you."

"Don't." Her words were lost in the screech of brakes.

"Well, if he happens to ask, I know your phone number by heart."

AT TWO thirty Jim woke up ready to talk. He had to tell Lois how he felt. He rolled over to her side of the bed, where he could see her copy of *Quite the Thing* on her bedside table. He could read her words and hear her voice. But he'd already read the message a dozen times. He was tired of talking back to the same sentiments. He wanted to hear other words. What would she think, for instance, if he fell in love with another woman?

Maybe she'd written in other books. Something other than a Harriet Mueller. A romance by another writer perhaps?

He turned on the light, got out of bed, and headed to the living-room shelves.

Would the romances be among the mysteries? Would he find a few of them shelved by author in the hardcover section? Lois wasn't ashamed to have her Mary Stewarts or her Victoria Holts in the ranks with more solemn writers.

Under *H* on the big shelf he found a few Donna Howells. He took them down and thumbed through their brittle pages carefully. Cheap old paper that crushed like leaves in the forest. The pages were brown, but none of them had purple markings.

Genevieve West was represented under *W*. These paperbacks were a little newer and in better shape. The women on the covers were still dressed in Regency garb, but their hair owed more to Farrah Fawcett than the Empress Josephine. Jim thumbed through the books but found no messages from Lois. He moved to the front of the collection in the other bookcase and found two volumes by Cynthia Gooden Brown, a writer he'd never noticed before. No messages in them, though, just Lois's name. A loopy script scrawled, from the appearance of it, when she was a teenager.

Had she taken them to school? Did she hide them in her book bag and sneak a glance at a few pages during algebra or physics? He'd seen photos of his wife taken back then. Tall and gawky but with the same dark eyebrows and fair skin that made her so striking. That she didn't know she was beautiful was one of her charms.

These books were a lifeline back to her, something precious— volumes that had followed her from high school to college to New York and this place. They were all he had to go on.

He held them up to his face, hoping for a trace of her perfume. All he could catch was the damp of New York and the dry chemical tang of ink. Surprising that it would still be there.

Taking two of the Cynthia Goodens back to the bedroom, he sat on the side of the bed. Then he grabbed a pen that lay on his bedside table. A ballpoint, not a fountain pen. Maybe the world's great literature came from a quill dipped in ink, but for Jim a twenty-five-cent Bic was good enough for his deepest thoughts. He found an empty space above a chapter heading and wrote:

> *Dearest, they were telling our story. The two women I met tonight after the play. One is an actress soon to appear in one of our commercials, the other a flutist I've never seen before. Enchanting. Beautiful thick red hair and a complexion so fair that it seemed translucent. The best thing about her were her*

eyes. *If women only knew how much men look to the eyes. For reassurance. For warmth. For something shared. She had eyes of dark summer green.*

I wanted you to know about her because for the first time since you left I met someone who makes me feel like you did. Someone who delights me and makes me smile again. I didn't think it was possible. At first I didn't even trust my reaction to her. I thought it was just a fluke.

Then I went out after the play with her and her friend. They'd been trapped by some creep, and I was supposed to rescue them. A noble deed. We were chatting at our table when she and the actress started telling a funny story about cracking up during a performance, getting a serious case of the giggles.

I tried not to be rude, but I stopped hearing her. I heard you. I thought of that time in summer stock when I was running my fourth show at night and rehearsing the fifth show during the day. I was goofy from exhaustion. You came on stage for just a minute. I looked at your wig and saw a wisp of hair coming out of it. I started laughing and couldn't stop. You joined me. We both managed to say our lines and make a graceful exit. Just barely.

But I still can't let you go. I measure everything I hear against you. Everything I see in a woman makes me think of you. That's why I'm writing this down. I need to look forward, not backward. Help me. Let me move on.

Your One and Only

Jim turned off the light and fell fast asleep. Lois's bedside clock said 4:12.

"OK, JIM, what'd you think of her?" Nan asked, sitting on the armrest of his extra chair.

"She was beautiful. Hair, eyes, complexion, and a voice that was otherworldly. I was almost relieved to hear her laugh. When she laughed, I knew she was real."

"That must have been a surprise."

"The laugh made her seem human. Until then she was like a goddess."

"Come down from the heavens to rescue you?" Nan looked askance at him, clicking her red nails against each other.

"It was almost like that."

"I guess you never know what a guy from the gym can fix you up with."

Jim caught himself. There was no way Nan would know about the redhead. She must be talking about his Friday night date. "Oh, that. It was a riot. A hoot. I was laughing about it with Scott this morning at the gym. I don't know how they could think I would be interested in their gerontologist cousin."

"A gerontologist?"

"Got her degree in studying old people. She works at an old folks' home and couldn't stop talking about their diet, their chances of getting Alzheimer's, their symptoms. I couldn't bring up anything without her talking about gerontology."

"She was beautiful?" Nan said.

Jim improvised. He wanted to hide his confusion. What he'd felt for Elizabeth was too new. What was he thinking? He couldn't explain it to Nan. "She wasn't bad looking, but her conversation was so limited."

"Who?"

"The cousin."

Nan shook her head. "It's hard to keep up with your love life."

"The funny thing is, Scott said this one wasn't even the cousin he had in mind. He thought his wife was bringing someone else."

The phone in Jim's office was ringing for the third time. When it bounced out to his assistant's office, he heard her pick it up.

"Jim," she called from her cubicle, "it's Melinda. She says she's returning your call."

"I'll let you go," Nan said.

Melinda was Lois's older sister. The one who had made all the conventional life choices. Married the guy from back home, bought a house close to the parents. She had two perfect sons and a pretty daughter, and she worked part-time at the school library so she could be home with them.

"Jim, how are you? I'm so sorry I didn't call you back earlier. Your message got lost on the answering machine, and I didn't get it until now. Kids, you know."

No, Jim didn't really know kids. But it was Melinda's perennial refrain. The kids. They prevented her from sending her Christmas cards out in time and buying birthday presents until months after a birthday and going to New York to see her sister and brother-in-law for a weekend.

"I guess it's risky to leave a message."

"This time it was."

"I was wondering about Lois's stuff. When you and Emily were here last year, do you remember what you did with all her books?"

"We left most of them there. It was too hard to figure out which were yours and which were hers."

"I don't mean the ones in the living room or the guest room. I was thinking of the ones on the small bookshelf. The one you took back to Missouri."

"Those?" She said it with some disdain. "They were just some old paperbacks. I wondered why Lois kept them for so long."

"She would reread them."

"The only person I've ever known who could read so many romance novels. And reread them."

"What did you do with them?" He tried to keep the eagerness out of his voice.

"You'll have to ask Emily. I think we donated them somewhere. We might have sold them to a used bookstore."

"The one around the corner?"

"I can't tell. I never know where I am in New York. I get completely turned around. Anyway, there were so many books, it was hard to figure out what to do with them. I would have just thrown them away, but you know Emily. She hates to waste anything."

"I've got a call in to Emily too."

"She'll get back to you . . . eventually." Another refrain of Melinda's. That Emily was bad about doing the conventional things like writing thank-you notes and returning calls.

"Thanks. Give my best to the kids." He could hear them in the background arguing about a Monopoly game.

"Jim, how are you?"

He winced. In college Melinda had majored in psychology. She took it as her license to ask probing questions.

"How is the grieving process going?"

"I'm OK." He could feel his lip contract to one thin line.

"You should come out and visit us." Melinda's voice turned whispery and earnest, the echo of a radio psychologist urging the buttoned-up male to open up. Her kids were still arguing in the background.

"Someday I will."

"You've been through so much in the last year and a half."

"Things are getting better."

"Let me tell you something. I've studied the grieving process—in college I wrote a long paper on it—and according to the experts this should be the time that your numbness wears off. Don't be surprised if you have thoughts about other women. That's only natural. You're right on schedule."

"OK." It appalled him that his emotions could be on any schedule. As though he were some lab rat going through a maze.

"I'm sure Lois wouldn't take it as an act of disloyalty if you started dating again." A child called in the background. "Just call us if we can ever help. You're still family."

"Thanks, Melinda. Gotta go." He hung up.

Just to be contrary he would have chosen never to go out on another date ever again. The *grieving* process! What was happening to him wasn't part of the grieving process. It was the *living* process. The purple pen, the romance novel, the green-eyed redhead were all urging him to do something with his life. He had to take a risk and get unstuck. Wasn't that what Lois would have wanted? If he could only find the rest of the books.

In the middle of the day he tried calling Emily again and sent her an e-mail. She was in graduate school at the University of Missouri and sometimes got lost in research. Nobody would hear from her for days, then she'd eventually resurface. "Resurface now," he said to himself.

At 4:55 he checked an urge to call Dorothy Jane Hughes on some pretext about the commercial just so he could ask for the redhead's phone number. *Stop calling her the redhead,* he told himself. *She has a name. Use it. Elizabeth.* If he'd remembered the last name, he would have looked it up. But it wasn't fair to telephone Dorothy. Communication with actors was best done through agents.

All he wanted was a phone number.

SIXTEEN

DOROTHY FLEW to Arizona on Wednesday. She'd gone to the gym every day before then, trying to make up for months of no exercise. As she said herself, she didn't do anything by halves. She got her hair trimmed slightly, made sure the roots were dyed, and drank gallons of water all week so her skin would be smooth and moist. She would have taken a suitcase full of bottled water with her, but Elizabeth reassured her that there was plenty of bottled water in Arizona. Elizabeth was thrilled for Dorothy. A two-day shoot, rooms at a deluxe hotel, all expenses paid, a fat fee, not to mention the possible residuals. It was the boost Dorothy had been waiting for. Just what she needed. She had hoped for a big break . . . and finally had received it.

But Elizabeth was also relieved to have her gone. The ringing phone made her jumpy. Every time she picked it up, she found herself thinking, *What now, Dorothy?*

It wasn't the talk about Dorothy's career that wearied her. It was Dorothy's plans for Elizabeth. What kind of guy would be right for her? Where would she meet him? Was now the right time? No matter how hard Elizabeth tried to divert the conversation, the questions would boomerang right back.

Elizabeth was glad to have the time to herself—like a wife whose husband was on a business trip. She did her laundry. She memorized a short fantasia for her upcoming concert tour. She reread a Harriet Mueller, one that hadn't been marked up with a purple pen. (There was a relief in that too.) In the middle of it she wondered if Dorothy had ever given her phone number to the casting director at Babcock, Crier, and Nelson.

And if she had, why hadn't he called?

JIM DID some extra workouts all week. Monday, Wednesday, and Friday for weightlifting, Tuesday and Thursday for cardiovascular work—running on the treadmill or doing the Stairmaster. Doing intensive reps made a difference. Shook his system up a bit. The muscles could get used to the usual routine. They needed a surprise. His whole psyche needed a surprise.

Friday morning he could feel the result of the extra reps. Fatigue had set in. The final set of every weightlifting set was a struggle. But he pushed through it. Pushed through the pain. Pushed through the aching muscles. No pain, no gain.

Jesus Christ, have mercy upon me. Make haste to help me. Rescue me and save me. Let thy will be done in my life.

Unfortunately the prayer didn't seem to have its usual effect. It didn't bring him the peace he was accustomed to. It only made him think of what he should be doing with his life. What would Lois want for him? And instead of finding forgetfulness in exhausting exercise, he found that he was thinking of a girl whose phone number he didn't even have.

He focused on the exercise. Bicep curls. Three sets of fifteen. He didn't grunt and groan. The guys who sounded like they were lifting four hundred pounds were showboaters. Noise was a wasted effort. He stared in the mirror to make sure his form was correct. He looked up from the straining muscles to his face. Was he still attractive to women? Did the redhead have any interest in him? Couldn't somebody help him find her? God or Google or Dorothy Jane Hughes?

"No wild TGIF parties tonight," Scott said with a toss of his blond hair.

"You wore me out last Friday."

"Just in case you're tempted, I can set you up with that other cousin." Scott was wearing his Merrill Lynch shirt.

"I'll take a rain check."

Anything but another blind date. He'd rather come back to the gym in the evenings. As it was, Jim went to the theater every night just to be exhausted enough to fall asleep. He hadn't gone out with Nan. He didn't want to hear any more advice from her. Didn't want to be tempted by her charm and looks.

He preferred the busyness of work. The constant pressure. He could let it take over, and he wouldn't have to think of whom he wanted to meet and what he would say if he saw her again.

He woke up early on Saturday. If he ran, it would be his third cardiovascular day in the week. The sidewalks and streets weren't icy. No need to go to the gym. He could do a long run in the park. He read the newspaper, then put on his sweats, a wool cap, and some gloves. They would keep him warm enough.

The serious runners were already making their way up and down the rolling hills of the park. The sun was blinding, brighter than it ever was on a warm summer day. No haze to filter it. Pure sunlight pierced through the bare branches and bounced off the snow left on the ground. Patches of snow lingered under the trees like dusty shade. It was exhilarating running outside. Much better than the treadmill.

As people passed him, he felt himself looking. Searching. He could never forget a face. That's what made him good at his job. *Make haste to help me.* He would see hers again.

He did the long loop. When he came out on Central Park West, he felt like he could run another five miles. Instead of going into his apartment building, he slowed his pace and kept jogging along the streets in his neighborhood. He admired the curving limestone fronts and the dour brownstones. He imagined people waking up inside, having their first cup of coffee dressed in their bathrobes and pajamas. He felt the companionable silence. Admired couples being together without having to say a word. The way he and Lois had been.

For a minute he was sheltered from the wind between buildings. He could feel the sweat drip down the sides of his face and roll from the pores beneath his arms. His T-shirt was damp, and his hands were wet inside the gloves. He took them off and held them in his fists.

His route took him over to Broadway and back across to Columbus. Just as he turned the corner he knew where he was headed. Just to see. Just to check it out one more time. Even on a frigid morning like this the scruffy man with the tweed jacket would put out his used books in carts along the street in front of his tiny store. Maybe the passersby hadn't read the latest Tom Clancy. Maybe they'd enjoy owning a faded copy of *Wildflowers of America*.

Jim stopped at the corner to lean against a building and stretch the backs of his legs, then turned and jogged slowly to the shop. That's when he saw her strolling toward him.

She wore a maroon overcoat and a large gray scarf. The tips of her red hair flew out from under her hat like tassels on a cord. She had a large bag over her shoulder, but she didn't seem to be in any hurry. She stopped at the used bookstore and ran her gloved hands across the spines of the books outside as though she were in a library. Another book lover.

Jim pulled his gloves back on. "Hi," he said.

She looked at him as though she wasn't sure who he was. A friendly "Hi" on a Saturday morning on Columbus Avenue didn't rate much as a pickup line. Then her green eyes smiled in recognition. "Hello."

"Dorothy's done a great job. That's what all my reports say. The client is pleased, the director is pleased, and we're pleased." He sounded like a politician on the stump. Couldn't he come up with something more interesting?

"She was so excited to get the work. It was a big boost to her. The kind of thing she's been waiting for."

"If this one goes well, I'm sure they'll want to use her again. It could be a real sinecure for her."

"Mailbox money," Elizabeth said.

"What?"

"That's what Dorothy calls it. Checks that just arrive in the mail. Residuals."

Jim laughed. "Maybe she'll earn enough to allow her to do an avant-garde play in the East Village with a flutist in the pit."

"Don't make me laugh."

"That was a very funny story. Nothing is funnier than laughing when you shouldn't be laughing."

"We thought we were funny."

"You were." He paused. "Where are you headed this morning?"

"The conservatory. I give lessons to high-school kids on Saturday mornings. Some of them are quite talented. Some are just pushed into it by their parents."

"Sounds like harder work than getting mailbox money."

"It is." Elizabeth nodded and the red hair worked out from beneath her hat. "I could never do what Dorothy does. It would drive me nuts waiting so long between jobs. I like having work every day."

She was forthright, not shy.

"I know what you mean. But if it's something you really love, then it's worth waiting for. That's probably what motivates Dorothy."

"That and sheer nerves." She looked down at her gloves.

Now for his big moment. He could even hear a drumroll in his head, his own personal soundtrack. He didn't know what made him so nervous. This is what he'd wanted, what he'd hoped for. Normally he didn't hesitate doing something that he'd put his mind to. But this moment wasn't just in his mind—he had to act, and acting had the gravest consequences.

"You're probably busy tonight," he began.

"No," she said.

"Aren't you playing in that show?"

"Not this week. I was only a sub."

"That's right. That's what you said. You don't do it all the time."

"Just once in a while for the money."

"Could I take you out for dinner?"

There. He'd said it. Now he wished that he could disappear. That a trapdoor could open in the sidewalk and he'd vanish. He couldn't bear standing face to face with her. Seeing her expression. Figuring out if she were making an excuse or not.

"That would be nice," she said. "What time? I've got a private student making up a lesson at six o'clock so it would have to be after seven."

"You don't have to."

"I'd like to."

"Really?"

"Absolutely."

"We can eat late. European style. 8:30. Do you like Thai food?"

"Sure."

"There's a good place on Sixty-eighth Street. We can go after the Lincoln Center crowd has cleared out. Have the place to ourselves."

"Great."

"The Purple Lantern." He gave her the address. "Meet me there," he said and didn't know what to say after that. "I know you're in a hurry to get to your students." He shook her gloved hand with his. Then he jogged off, resisting the temptation to look behind to see if she were looking back at him.

Only when he'd gone a couple of blocks and was nearly at his building did he bewail his lack of gallantry. *Meet me there!?* He should have said, "I'll come by and pick you up." Isn't that what you were supposed to do on a date? Pick a girl up. He hadn't been on a date since college. He didn't have the faintest idea of what a guy was supposed to do.

When he got home, he showered, had a huge breakfast, did his laundry, paid his bills, and cleaned his refrigerator. There was still a box of baking soda on the bottom shelf. Lois had put it there almost two years ago to swallow food odors. It had long passed its usefulness, but he didn't have the heart to throw it out. It was the same with the half jar of capers she'd bought—how many years ago?—for a chicken recipe. And the orange marmalade an aunt had sent from Florida. They stayed on the shelf. All he had managed to throw out was an old jar of pickles. She never ate pickles.

In the late afternoon he remembered to check his answering machine. One hang up and one long message from his sister-in-law Emily:

"Hey, Jim. Melinda said you called. Sorry. I've been really busy working on my dissertation. I won't bore you with the details. Anyway, you were wondering what we did with all of Lois's old books. Most of them went to a church thrift shop. I can't remember the address, but it wasn't far from your apartment. They were collecting stuff for a rummage sale.

Most places don't take books, but they did. It's sort of a gray stone build-ing. Gothic architecture. I can't remember what street. The thrift shop is in the basement. Miss you. Hope you're doing well. You need to start having fun again. Lois would understand. See ya."

Foolishly he stood by the phone with a pen and a pad of paper, ready to write down a location. Emily never said where. No address was given. And if the church had a rummage sale, who knew if the books were still there?

But that voice. The cadences were so much like Lois's. Sweet and unusual and smooth. You could take the girl out of Missouri, but you couldn't take Missouri out of the girl.

"Thanks, Emily," he said aloud. "And yes, I am having fun." All this concern over his "fun." He was doing fine, OK? He had a date to prove it.

⌘

ELIZABETH COULDN'T find a single purple lantern at The Purple Lantern. The lanterns were brass with fake candles in them. Grass mats covered the walls, wooden shutters shielded the windows, ceiling fans sputtered overhead, and plastic orchids rose from Chinese pots. The whole thing was more *Road to Mandalay* than *The King and I*. A Hollywood hodgepodge of Eastern Asia rather than a pure homage to old Siam. The one thing that was demonstrably Thai was the silk pillows and curtains. Bright orange, fuchsia, lime green, popsicle yellow—like parrots in the jungle.

Standing there, Elizabeth wished she had spoken to Dorothy before coming here. Except Dorothy would have probably said not to go out on such short notice, or at least pretend she had to cancel five other things. She was supposed to dissemble. Look hard to get and delighted to be found. But what about clothes? Dorothy would have known what she should wear.

First there were all the concert dresses in her closet. Not the dignified black she wore in an orchestra but bright silk dresses she sometimes used when she was soloing.

113

"Soprano dresses," Dorothy called them.

"It's what I wear," Elizabeth argued back. When people went to a concert, they wanted to feel they were going to a real event. A woman in a pretty dress was part of the package.

But a date dress? It couldn't be too dressy, and it shouldn't be too casual. She wanted to look like she had made an effort, but she didn't want it to appear that her expectations were too high. He'd set the time for 8:30, which gave her over an hour to get ready. Too much time to fret.

She had put two dresses on her bed, a silk print that looked too summery and a black shift that looked funereal. She settled on the latter and found a scarf to brighten it up so it wouldn't look like she'd just come from a funeral home. She added pearls, something she'd never wear on stage, and a gold bracelet, which she couldn't wear if she were playing the flute. It would slide right off.

Of course, now that she was at The Purple Lantern, she felt overdressed. Why not jeans and a sweater? What kind of statement was she making? She was foolish to accept the invitation anyway. He was a nice guy, and she felt like damaged goods. Why raise anyone's expectations? She was no more ready to go on a date than fly to the moon. If he hadn't asked her so boldly and looked so hesitant himself . . . if she hadn't seen that sadness in his eyes. That's what had made her say yes almost in spite of herself. She wished she had her flute with her. Some prop.

"Would you like to check your coat?" the hostess said.

"Sure." She took off the reliable maroon overcoat and felt even more at sea. "I'm here to meet Jim Lockhart."

The woman checked the list of reservations. "He's here already. Come this way."

She led Elizabeth through the restaurant to a table in the back. Jim stood up. His eyes were on her all the way. That was even worse than not having anything to carry, Elizabeth thought. Worse than walking from the wings to center stage for a solo recital, with everyone looking at her and no music to hide behind. She depended on music to lift her out of herself. She'd concentrate on it. She'd hum the first few measures so she wouldn't die of self-consciousness. She hummed now.

"You look great," Jim said. He was in a jacket, no tie.

Should she tell him the truth? "I couldn't figure out what to wear."

"You came up with just the right thing."

An awkward pause. Should they kiss or shake hands? The table was in the way. She extended her hand. He took it and leaned across the table to kiss her on the cheek.

"You're nice to say so."

"You're nice enough to come out on such short notice."

"Dorothy will die when she hears. She would hate to know that I didn't pretend to be booked on a Saturday night." She sat.

"Let's not talk about Dorothy now."

"She's my alter ego."

"We can talk about you."

Elizabeth could feel herself swallowing the flattery—hook, line, and sinker. She would be more guarded next time. She was going out with him only just this once.

"Not fair," she said. "As I remember, I talked a lot about myself the last time we went out. Your turn."

"Menu first."

SEVENTEEN

THE MENU had so many pages it was like reading a novel.

"What's lemon grass?" Elizabeth asked.

"I don't know. Lemony grass?"

"Whoever wrote this got so creative it's hard to know what anything is. Listen to this." Elizabeth read: "'Tastes like an open field between two forests after the gentle fall of a spring shower.'"

Jim started laughing. "Tastes like dirt, I guess."

"Or how about this? 'Imagine swimming up a river on the first day of summer and finding yourself on a plate of fresh noodles covered with a flavorful sesame sauce.'"

"I think I'd rather not."

"'These birds will create songs in your heart upon eating that will make your insides sing.'"

"Sounds like indigestion."

"I'm probably better off not reading the descriptions."

"Just settle on the names. What do you want? Fish, chicken, shrimp, vegetables?"

"Shrimp."

"And how are you on sweet or spicy?"

A waitress in turquoise silk and with a master's degree in engineering— as she explained—helped them order. She recommended the shrimp and broccoli and described the sauces. They made their choices and she left. Then there was a pause. It reminded Elizabeth of the silence at a concert just before she played her first note. Expectant.

"Are you from New York?" she asked.

"Wisconsin. Where are you from?"

"Connecticut. Close enough to come to the city for concerts and shows, but not close enough to go to Juilliard for high school."

"Would that have made a difference?"

"I used to think so. All those connections I would have made. On the other hand, it doesn't matter that much. You make contacts when you come here, and talent is the first prerequisite."

"You must like it," Jim said.

Elizabeth was about to tell him about how much she loved the music, and how she was glad of every moment she played even if the stress of the business sometimes drove her nuts. But she stopped herself. Not so soon. Not yet. "I thought we were going to talk about you."

"I work in advertising. Not nearly as glamorous as being a professional musician."

"Is that what brought you to New York?"

"I was going to be an actor." He took a sip of his green tea. "Sounds like a real cliché. Coming to New York to be an actor, but I didn't want to go to California, and I figured I'd just be postponing the inevitable if I went anywhere else."

"Did you come to the city right after college?"

"Pretty much. But it wasn't just my idea." He took another sip of tea.

Was he stalling, looking for a pause that would keep him from having to tell more about himself? Elizabeth wondered. Why was he so hesitant?

"I came here with a friend," he said finally. "It was her idea to live here as much as mine."

"Was she an actress?"

"She was. She was very good."

"I don't usually like actresses or actors," Elizabeth confessed.

"I know what you mean. I work with them all day long. They can be so self-involved."

"Not all of them." Elizabeth didn't want to be disloyal. "Dorothy's not so self-involved when you get to know her."

Jim reached his hand across the tablecloth as though he was going to stop her. "I thought we weren't going to talk about her."

"We were talking about actors. And actresses."

"My friend wasn't self-involved either. And she was very talented. We figured we'd both find jobs and that would be that. Even when you hear that the odds are really tough, you don't believe it. I don't think either of us expected it would be as hard as it was." He had a beautiful speaking voice, soothing and strong.

"Auditioning, you mean."

"Just getting the chance to audition while trying to make enough money to eat and sleep."

"Where'd you live?"

"We both lived in about ten different places that first year. Sleeping in some friends' living room, housesitting for this crazy decorator in SoHo, subletting when people went on tour. I moved, she moved, we both moved all the time. It drove her crazy, but it was the only way to survive."

"What'd you do for money?"

"The usual things. Catering. Waiting tables. Proofreading for a law firm at night. My first big break was being a spear-carrier in the Shakespeare festival that summer. I finally got my Equity card."

"I know how hard it is to get cast."

"I fit the costume. That's probably the only reason I got cast. The money wasn't much, but it made me feel legitimate. We got married that September, and at least I could say I was a working actor."

Married? Elizabeth was surprised at how disappointed she felt. "You were married?" she said, trying to sound disinterested. Their first and last date. She'd tell him she was too busy.

"I was." Jim kept talking as though the words would obliterate the awkwardness that came over her. "I felt proud of myself at the wedding. To be a working actor. I even felt like I deserved the honeymoon. We came back and got our own apartment on the Lower East Side—a place friends had moved out of. Then for the next year I didn't get any work."

"Equity card or not."

"I did one showcase and it was terrible. I couldn't get any agents to come to it, and I was working so hard to pay our rent and expenses I wasn't really focused on what I was doing."

"Is that why you gave it up?"

"Not exactly." Their first course had arrived, and Elizabeth was glad of the distraction of dipping meat into sauce and cutting up the noodles.

"Lois was looking for work too," he said.

"Lois?"

"That was my wife's name. She got a couple of modeling jobs. She found out she had a perfect size to be a shoe model." He was staring at his food.

"Did she get any acting jobs?"

"A few. A showcase here and there. At least she managed to get an agent. He only returned about one in ten phone calls, but she could get him to send her on some auditions."

"Did she have other jobs too?"

"She'd do temp work on Wall Street and waitress at night and take her acting classes and dance classes. Some weeks we'd hardly see each other. We both got fed up with it. One night we both skipped our classes and went out to this little French restaurant. We needed to talk." He plunged his chopsticks into the noodles and took a big bite.

"You don't have to tell me this," Elizabeth said.

He chewed for a moment, then went on. He wasn't looking at her. He gazed far back into the room, as though he was trying to see through to the past. "We sat at that restaurant and talked about why we'd come to New York in the first place. To act. And neither of us was doing it. I mean, maybe if somebody was giving us money, we could have managed, but we were both working so hard that we weren't giving it anything."

"It can be hard to make a living." She wanted to make it easy for him to tell this story, whatever it was.

"That's when I had my brilliant idea. I said, 'Let's take turns.' We couldn't make enough money doing all the odd jobs that we were doing, but if one of us got a real job, then the other could be the actor. Pursue the career full-time. And then we'd switch off."

"How'd you decide?"

"We talked a lot about who should go first. Women often need to be younger to get their start in acting. And an argument could be made that a guy could have a great career in his late thirties and early forties."

"So you bowed out?"

"It wasn't so easy as that. I volunteered, but she said no. She launched into a whole argument about why I should go first and she would have the money job. She said she'd be a paralegal. She'd gotten some jobs at a downtown law firm and thought she could be hired full-time. Get trained on the job. But I said I didn't want her to resent my career."

"How'd you settle it?"

"The most democratic way." He grinned, looking back at her. "We flipped a coin."

"Who won?"

"She did."

So Jim was damaged goods too . . . just like her. He'd sacrificed the start of a good acting career, devoted himself to another job, then got cheated when his wife divorced him. Was that it? Elizabeth wished she could find some comfort in that.

"I'm sorry," was all she could say.

"You shouldn't be. Fair was fair. That's what I agreed to do. I convinced myself that I wanted to do it. I'd been temping at an ad agency, and I told them I wanted to go full-time. I got into casting there—my background was helpful—and I've done pretty well in it. I was good at it. I have no complaints. You can't look back."

"WHAT A lie," Jim thought. That's all he was doing. Constantly looking back.

"I guess not," Elizabeth said softly.

"We went ahead. She did pretty well in her career. Got a part on a soap opera that lasted two years. Did some good roles off Broadway. Went out to LA for the pilot season. Got cast in a pilot that looked like it'd be picked up. She got to a point in her career where I could stop mine in advertising and we'd do OK for a while."

"What happened?"

"The deal was for five years. Her turn for five. Then the time was up. My turn. We went back to the French restaurant. We had something to celebrate. It had all worked out. Now I could give up advertising, and we'd both be actors. It should have been the happiest day of our lives. It wasn't."

This was the part that he knew he couldn't tell. The cruel turn of events. The reason he'd started praying the prayer: *Jesus Christ, have mercy upon me. Make haste to help me. Rescue me and save me. Let thy will be done in my life.*

"Some things," he went on, "don't turn out exactly like you think they will or even how they should. I went to that restaurant with a small bouquet of roses. My congrats. She came with big circles around her eyes. I knew she'd been crying. She wasn't a weepy person. Something was up."

"You don't have to tell me this," Elizabeth said. She looked uncomfortable. Like she was sitting next to some stranger on an airplane and suddenly having to listen to his life story from LaGuardia to Dallas–Ft. Worth. Being a captive audience in a Thai restaurant.

Except Jim wasn't eager to tell this narrative. He just couldn't stop himself. It was as though he wanted her to know the worst about him.

"I've been thinking of it too long not to tell you." He would control his emotions. Like an actor in the middle of a difficult monologue.

"What did she tell you?"

"It didn't seem too serious. We tried not to be scared. When you hear the word *cancer*, you don't want to think the worst. It's not an automatic death sentence. You talk to doctors and sign up for treatments, and everybody keeps up a brave face. You hear the statistics, but you meet people who have beaten cancer. You think, *More and more people survive. Things can't be so bad. She is going to get well.* We just had to change our plan for a while. Her job was to beat cancer. Mine was to support her."

"You didn't get your five years?"

"All I wanted was five more years with her. That would have been heaven."

"No resentment?"

"You always resent something with cancer. And you have to bury that too. You just want the person to get well. I wanted her to get well. That's all I wanted. But she didn't . . ." He stopped himself. "Anyway, I told you it'd be an interesting story."

"You never went back to acting?"

"It was too late."

"That sounds absurd. You don't seem too old to go back to it if you wanted to."

He could hear the annoyance in her voice . . . as if she didn't want to spend any time with a guy who was smarting over thwarted gifts. He shouldn't have told her about Lois.

"You're right," he said. "I could throw myself into it now if I wanted to. I certainly have a lot more contacts than I ever had. That was one of the initial thrills of being a casting director. Being on the buyer's side. Suddenly I was putting people on hold who would never return my phone calls when I was an actor shoving my résumé under their doors." He smiled wryly. "Power is never as tantalizing when you're on the inside."

"Why haven't you gone back to it?"

"I've gotten too good at what I do to stop."

"As long as you're not just doing it to bide your time."

"It's a paycheck. My insurance is covered. And I meet people like your friend Dorothy."

"I thought you said we weren't allowed to talk about her tonight." She looked amused.

"You've already heard my life story. We broke all the rules with that."

"We did break the rules," Elizabeth said.

They should have started out with small talk. Movies, books, music, the weather. Instead they'd leaped into the heavy stuff all at once. She'd asked the questions and he'd talked.

"I didn't want to get heavy like that," he said. "I'm sorry."

"You've been through something. Something big. I'm flattered you wanted to share it with me."

That was the point. For fifteen months, nineteen days, and three hours, he hadn't told anybody at all, and suddenly he was talking about Lois to a woman he barely knew.

"You should be flattered," he said. "I don't ever talk about it."

"Maybe you should."

"People will just feel sorry for me. That's not what I'm looking for." *What are you looking for?* he asked himself. What did he want? "I figured I could be honest."

"So what do we do now?"

"Talk about the things people normally do on first dates. Have you read anything good lately?"

"That's too private," Elizabeth said, laughing.

EIGHTEEN

THE REST of the evening Elizabeth kept waiting for the other shoe to drop. He would tell her something else about himself, another secret that he had told no one else. Was it really flattering to be a man's confessor? Was he engaging in emotional blackmail? It was bad enough to get involved with a guy who was on the rebound from some girl. But what if the girl happened to be his dead wife?

After the story was over, he moved on. He didn't insist on showing her photos of his wife. He didn't give her any more anecdotes about their perfect life together. He wasn't maudlin at all. He allowed the story to end where he had begun.

"It's an interesting story," he'd said. That was all.

They ate dinner, and dessert was coming. They were talking about music. She told him about the concert tour she had coming up. Places like Davenport, Cheyenne, Boise, and Ogden.

"What do you think about when you're performing?" he asked.

"All sorts of things. It can be very surprising. Different images come to me that are connected to the music. Landscapes sometimes. A tree I've seen. A lake. Mountains. But other things go on in my mind that have nothing to do with the music. I'll be thinking about the hotel where I'm staying. I start wondering about checkout time. I'll notice someone in the front row who is falling asleep with his mouth open. I'll be reminded of a good friend back home."

"That must be distracting."

"Only if I let it be. Mostly I'm focused on my music, and this other part of me is balancing my checkbook. It's like doing two things at once."

"When I do two things at once, I do at least one of them badly."

She was sure he was being too self-effacing.

"Do you ever get a song stuck in your mind?" she asked.

"Everyone does."

"You know how you can write a letter and read a newspaper article or watch TV and still have the same song in your mind?"

"Yes."

"That's what it's like."

"It's like having a person stuck in your mind while you're doing lots of other things."

A person? Who? Was he thinking of someone in particular?

"Maybe," she said cautiously.

"Do you like performing?" he asked.

"Only when I'm playing. I dread everything else about it. I hate the traveling. I don't like being by myself in an unfamiliar city. I'm not good at meeting people afterward and accepting their congratulations. I get very self-conscious about the clothes I wear." *Like what I'm wearing now.* "But when I perform, I forget it all."

"You must be very good."

Elizabeth felt herself blush and felt Jim watching her blush. "Not fair."

"Only because it's true."

"This is just the kind of thing that happens to me after I perform. I get flustered and don't take compliments graciously."

He turned his head to one side. "You remind me of someone . . ."

I remind you of the dead wife? Is that what you mean? she wondered. "I'll take that as another compliment."

"It was meant as one."

When the check came, he wouldn't hear of her paying half the bill. A real date. He took her coat-check number and got her coat while she went downstairs to the restroom. When she came back up, he helped her put it on.

"Where do you live?" he asked.

"West Ninety-fourth."

"Let me take you there."

"That's not necessary."

"I'd like to." He stepped out to the curb to flag down a taxi. Half the yellow cabs of the city were converging on Lincoln Center. The opera and the symphony had both let out. Music lovers were chasing after cabs. Jim would have to be quick to beat them.

"No," Elizabeth said boldly. "Let's walk." It would give them a chance to talk more. "I mean, if you don't mind the cold."

"This is nothing. I grew up in Wisconsin."

He took her elbow gently and steered her through the crowd. They started up Columbus Avenue.

"You probably played hockey on frozen lakes in zero degrees," she said.

"I hated hockey. What I really loved was speed skating. I was fast."

"Hans Brinker," she said.

"It was fun. I did a couple of races in junior high and won."

"So you were a regular jock?"

"Not at all. I played hockey because I had to."

"And hated it?"

They were walking side by side, separating when someone came toward them or walking single file if necessary. It made for a disjointed conversation.

"I did it for my father."

"He must have been a big hockey fan."

He steered her away from a plastic garbage bag blowing in the wind. "Worse. He was the announcer for our school games. He really got into it. He did this whole Howard Cosell spiel. Actually changed his voice. It was one of those father-son things. I realized how much it meant to him. If I quit, he would feel like he couldn't do it. So I kept playing hockey for him, even when I didn't enjoy it. I would have been happier speed skating."

"Do you skate anymore?"

"Not much. I've never wanted to skate on that tiny rink at Rockefeller Center. It's always crowded, and there's nowhere to go. It'd be like skating on a postage stamp."

"You should go up to Lasker Rink. Up at the top of the park. There's more room there."

"Would you come with me?" he asked.

Was this going to be another date?

"I don't really know how to skate."

"You can learn." He stopped at a signal and turned toward her, like they were skating already.

It gave her a vision of slipping and sliding on the ice, and Jim coming to the rescue. She didn't want to be rescued. It was fine when it happened in books, but it was too messy in real life. Someone was always left wishing for more. "I don't know . . ."

"I wouldn't make you do it if you didn't like it. We could just try."

They crossed the street and walked past a boutique window that featured a mannequin with a ravishing pink silk dress and . . . army boots. "Those are so ugly," he said.

"Can you imagine me walking out on stage in a pair of shoes like that?" she asked.

"No, but I could see you in a dress like that. In green. That's your color."

The remark caught her off balance. She'd been so careful all evening, but that comment nearly knocked her over. That he thought of her in a ravishing green dress.

He surprised her again by taking her hand. She didn't resist. They continued walking north.

This part of Columbus Avenue was less crowded. Fewer people to pass. In the warm spring days, the restaurants would be open, their tables spilling out onto the sidewalk. Now there was only the sound of a jukebox inside.

"Do you ever go to any of these places?" he asked.

She shook her head. "Too yuppie."

"Too many people who look like they're in advertising?"

"You're teasing me." She didn't want to blush again.

"I was thinking when I asked you out," Jim said, "that I didn't really know how to go on a date anymore. I mean, the last time I ever did it was in college. I'm not sure what the rules are now."

"You've done all right."

"I'm improvising." He gave her hand a squeeze.

They were passing the supermarket and the school, coming to her block. A kid delivering a pizza on a bicycle zipped past them.

"I'm on the block between Columbus and Central Park West."

"The one with all the trees on it."

"They're bare now." To her irritation a phrase from the opera *La Boheme* came to her. Not even a flute part. The soprano singing to the tenor. That she'd see him again in springtime when the leaves returned to the trees and the flowers bloomed. Shamelessly romantic.

"They'll bloom in the spring." He stopped and bent down to kiss her. It was short and sweet. He stood back and looked at her.

"I don't know," she said. The words just came out.

"You don't know what?"

"You're a nice guy and I like you, but I still don't know."

"What's not to know?"

"I'm not sure I'm ready for this."

He frowned. She knew what he was thinking. She could put the words right into his mouth. He was the one who'd lost his wife to cancer and had spent months grieving her. He should have been the one to decide if he was ready or not. That was just the trouble. He had all the emotional cards to play.

"It'd be fun to go out again," he said.

"Yes, if it were only fun." She couldn't get into an argument with him on the corner of Columbus and Ninety-fourth Street.

"I'm not asking for more than that."

"I know you're not," she said. "I just want to know what I'm getting into before I get into it. I can't tell right now."

Was he hurt? Hadn't he been the one who opened up?

"Fair enough."

No way could she say what she really had to say: *I don't want to be the one to get hurt. I don't want to be the one left to pick up the pieces. I'm not strong enough anymore.* "Skating would be fine."

"You SAID what?" Dorothy asked on the phone.

"That I wasn't sure."

"You're not sure of what?"

"If I really want to get involved. He understood."

"What are you, out of your mind? You haven't gone on a date since that obnoxious, self-absorbed joker got a job in Germany and left town, leaving you high and dry, and you say no to the nicest, best-looking, most decent guy who comes along?"

"I didn't want to rush into anything."

"Who's rushing? It doesn't sound like he was proposing marriage in one date. He wants to go out with a beautiful woman. Isn't that what he said?"

"Not in so many words."

"He wants your friendship."

"I'm not sure I can deal with even that," Elizabeth said. "Maybe I'm not ready."

"I'll brainwash you into readiness. What is it? He's a good guy. He reeks good guy. He's successful, good-looking, and kind. All those other casting directors are jerks compared to him. He remembers names. He goes to people's shows. He seems to even like theater."

Dorothy had been back in town for less than forty-eight hours, and she was already giving Elizabeth a piece of her mind.

"Maybe you should go back to Arizona," Elizabeth said.

"It's looks like I got back in just the nick of time. Who knows what you would have done if I'd been gone any longer?"

"So what am I supposed to do?"

"Let him know that you had a great time. Men are insecure. They need constant reaffirmation. They need to know they're appreciated." Why was Dorothy always the expert?

"There is no way I'm going to call just to say that I had a good time. He'll think I'm chasing after him. Guys hate that too, as I remember." Elizabeth hoped her friend would hear the cynical tone in her voice.

"What do you find wrong with him?"

"He's high maintenance. Too high for me."

"How do you know? You've only had one date."

"The first thing he talked about was the death of his wife."

There was a pause on Dorothy's end of the line. "I didn't know he had a wife."

"She got cancer and died."

"That's really sad. How long ago?"

"He didn't say."

"He must be over it by now."

Elizabeth shook her head, confirming her own worst thoughts. "How could you ever get over something like that?"

"By falling in love with another woman. You're helping him get over his grief."

Elizabeth was getting exasperated, and she found her exasperation exasperating. "I don't want to be anybody's therapy."

"Does it bother you that you're not the first?"

"Not at all."

"So it's just like falling in love with a guy who's broken up with another girl."

"There's more than that going on. He needs someone. I'm not sure I want to be needed that badly."

"Lizzie, you're chicken. You're afraid you'll fall in love."

Elizabeth lowered her voice because it was almost painful to admit the truth. "Maybe I am."

"Indulge me for a moment. Let me give you one of my theories. When two people are meant for each other, nothing can stop them. It's fate—just meant to be."

Fate. Elizabeth wasn't sure she believed in that kind of thing. "So why are you working so hard at getting us together?"

"Sometimes fate needs help." Dorothy laughed.

Elizabeth didn't want to talk about Jim anymore. "How was Arizona?"

Dorothy went on to give minute details about the shoot, the film crew, the director, the makeup artist, the weather, the hotel, the restaurants where they ate, and the flight back. Elizabeth listened willingly. It was a relief to have someone else's story to fill up the phone wires.

Almost like having a good TV show on for an hour. As reassuring as reading Harriet Mueller.

JIM WAS exhilarated. He opened a soda and flipped on the TV, but he didn't want to watch anything. He wanted to close his eyes and see Elizabeth. The redhead. The flutist.

He knew he'd done a stupid thing by talking about Lois's death, but Elizabeth had looked so earnest and interested that he couldn't help himself. What had encouraged him was her reaction. She didn't exclaim over the whole thing. She didn't take out a handkerchief and get all teary-eyed. She seemed to understand that this was part of his history, like where he went to school and what ad firm he worked for. He closed his eyes and pictured the pearls against her fair skin. He loved seeing them next to the freckles at the back of her neck when he helped her with her coat. It was all he could do to resist kissing her there.

She was a relief from most of the girls he saw in the business. The actresses who were so polished and practiced. When they were casual, it was always a studied casual. They could come to an interview in jeans and a T-shirt, and he could tell they'd spent hours picking out just the right pair of jeans and ironing the T-shirt. When they laughed, it was to show they could laugh on camera. When they listened, he could always tell they were seeing the camera watching them listen.

Elizabeth Ash wasn't like that. She didn't beg for his approval. She didn't trip over herself to be flirtatious. She had a great sense of humor, and a clear sense of herself. He bet she was a fabulous performer. Unflappable. She could probably play through a hurricane.

He could see her standing in front of a crowd—breathing deeply, closing her eyes on the slow passages, swaying slightly with the music. He could see her in the silk dress, a green version of it, with her hair up so that the freckles were showing. A class act.

How was he going to convince her that he was truly interested? She wouldn't be overwhelmed by the big gesture, the floral bouquets, or the boxes of candy. Dinner at a ridiculously expensive restaurant. Long ago he could never afford those things. But now that he could, he'd found a girl who wouldn't flip over them. She wanted something more. But what?

He looked at the two Cynthia Gooden Brown books by his bed. He picked up the one he'd already written in. His scrawl filled the top of several pages. It was an impractical way to send a message. Why had Lois chosen to write in a book by Harriet Mueller? It would have been so much easier to just write a letter and put it in some secret place. But he would have found it in the days after her death, and the words would have meant nothing.

Or everything.

She had chosen the Harriet Muellers for a reason. She wanted to speak to him when he was ready. He looked at the one volume he had. Tomorrow he'd go to the church and find out if the other ones were still there. A rummage sale? They'd be gone by now. He could imagine trying to explain that they had "great sentimental value." Old paperback books with purple writing on them. What could anyone do with them?

He sat on his bed and opened the Cynthia Gooden Brown book. Another message to his wife. He took out the pen and did the writing.

Dearest, don't be upset with me. I told someone your story. Our story. Letting it out was such a relief. I've kept it inside too long. I shouldn't have dumped it on Elizabeth tonight, but as I was staring at her, I realized I couldn't go much further with her without telling her about us. It was what I needed to do.

Now I need to move on. I've needed to move on for months. This looks like my chance. We walked uptown afterward. It was easy to talk to each other. Then we came by that shop where you bought your one fancy dress. There was a beautiful long silk gown in the window. I was reminded of you, but this one was for her. Wrong color. She needs green, not pink, but it was rich and beautiful. I wanted to buy one just like it for her.

I'm sorry I never bought you fancy presents. For years I could never afford them. When I could, you were too sick to be able to wear them. Or more likely it was a failure of imagination on my part. I want to be different with her. Extravagant and generous. This is my chance.

He put the book down and looked across the room at Lois's clock. 9:13. What was that? It was much later than that. Past midnight. Then he noticed that the second hand wasn't moving. The clock had stopped—right in the middle of his dinner with Elizabeth. Just at the moment when he was moving on.

"'Night, Lois," he whispered before he turned out the light.

NINETEEN

THE CLOSER she came to a recital tour, the more focused Elizabeth became about her playing. She would start wondering why she had picked such a difficult repertoire. Why hadn't she chosen more pieces that she had performed before? She would begin to count how many weeks or months it had been since she had soloed last. Maybe she had lost her nerve. Maybe this time when she was on the road she would go blank in the middle of the Bach or the Scarlatti and have to start over from scratch.

She started to talk to herself. "Elizabeth, don't be ridiculous," she chided. "You've played half this repertoire before an audience several times. Some of those pieces you could do in your sleep. Especially the Bach and Scarlatti. Once you get up on stage and start playing, all your nerves will go away. The music will carry you. It has in the past. It will now."

With each day before her departure she became more single-minded on what she had to do. She closed everything else out, anything that was unnecessary. She still had teaching and a couple of studio jobs to do, but part of her brain was always practicing.

Over the years she'd learned that it was important to rethink each piece musically. At night after her students had left, she opened her scores and played things over in her mind. She thought through the phrasing. She reconsidered every breath mark. She practiced tempos. Nothing was worse than starting a piece and discovering by the fifth bar that you were going too fast. There would be no conductor to blame. She was on her own.

Dorothy called, as usual, but promised, "I'll be quick. I know you're practicing."

And Dorothy was quick.

Despite her nerves, the concentration of giving a recital was exactly what Elizabeth loved about being a musician. This is what it was all about. Bringing beautiful music to an appreciative crowd. Audiences in New York could be horribly jaded. They'd heard it all and seen it all. Not so in Ogden, Boise, and Cheyenne.

Now was not the time to worry about her social life. She had a higher calling. The work was so absorbing she didn't have to wonder why she thought so much of Jim Lockhart or how interested he really was in her. She didn't have to worry that she'd scared him off. So be it. She was meant to be an artist. Why concern herself with such mundane matters?

But then, late at night, when she finally had to take a break from the musical scores and phrasing and breathing, she picked up a copy of Harriet Mueller as an escape. Escape it wasn't. It reminded her of what was lacking in her life. There was no one she could begin to call "My One and Only."

They had gone ice skating as promised. It was fun. Elizabeth had skidded and slipped on the ice, but in the end she got the hang of it. It was a little like a scene from Hans Brinker. His confident hands guiding her around the ice. They ate dinner in a small restaurant in Harlem, then he took a cab ride home with her. He was careful. He didn't even get out of the cab.

After that they'd gone to the Metropolitan Museum. She'd been there dozens of times, of course. She was used to taking friends from out of town through the galleries. Now, though, there wasn't a rush to see all the big hitters—the Rembrandts, Van Goghs, Monets, and Picassos. Jim moved through the museum in a languid way, stopping at a small ivory cross that he said he'd always loved and a Dutch landscape that showed a sky with perfect clouds. They had dinner in the cafeteria and talked about painting. Not a conversation where anyone was competing to show off, but a probing talk on what made one picture better than another. Again he rode with her in a cab back to her apartment but didn't get out.

"I know you're working hard to prepare for your recital," he said.

The trip to the museum had been the perfect break. She could enjoy him, but they didn't have to get serious. She could go back to her practicing.

Thursday night, as she was cleaning the flute and putting it in its case, the phone rang. She picked it up, expecting Dorothy. It did no good to hide. Dorothy would keep calling back until Elizabeth picked up the phone.

"I'm just about to close up shop," she said.

A pause on the phone. "Elizabeth?" a man's voice asked. She recognized it immediately.

"Hi," she said. She couldn't pretend to be disappointed.

"Sorry to call so late."

"Are you still at the office?"

"No, I'm at home, wondering what you're doing." His voice was warmer and kinder than she could even remember.

"Getting ready for my recital."

"Practicing this late?"

"I've been going through the music in my head. I like to rethink everything I'm doing so I don't do it by rote."

"That takes a lot of concentration."

"There's always the fear factor to keep me going. I know if I don't do this, I won't be any good and I'll make a fool of myself on stage."

"I don't believe it. You're an artist. You want to do your best."

"That's a nice thing to say." She half wished he wasn't so kind. It would be so much easier to put him out of her mind.

"Are you going to give a practice recital before you go on tour? I'd like to hear you play."

"Not this time. This gig sneaked up on me. Playing in *If You Ask Me* really slowed me down. I haven't had time to schedule a dry run."

"Would it help?"

"There are several pieces I'm doing for the first time. It might help to have a friendly audience to hear them first. Just to see how they work." Was she really inviting him?

There was a pause, then, "I'm the friendliest of audiences."

"You don't want to sit and hear me play the flute, do you?" Now she was asking—trying to gauge his interest.

"Sure I do. Think of me as your slightly above average audience member. I can appreciate all music, but I'm not a professional musician."

"I'll have to check with my accompanist. We only have two more rehearsals ourselves." Her heart was beating so loud she was afraid he'd hear it over the phone.

"What about without your accompanist? I want to hear all your solo lines. You can tell me what the accompanist does."

She stiffened. "That's not really the same." Her professionalism was being challenged. She'd once heard that Frank Sinatra never sang outside a studio or off a stage. Never improvised at a party with a stranger at the piano. "If you hear me, I want it to be the real thing."

"Is there anything you do without an accompanist?"

"Three pieces. Two modern ones and a baroque fantasia."

"Great. I'll come and hear you play them."

"There's hardly any time left. I have to make sure they're ready." *No no no!*

"Let's do it tomorrow night."

She'd run out of excuses. "You sure you like flute music?"

"I will tomorrow night."

She hung up the phone in horror. What was she thinking? She was supposed to be preparing for a recital, not entertaining. Just look at her apartment. It was always neat, of course, because of her students, but having a nerdy seventeen-year-old girl visit the place and having a charmingly persuasive single man come by were two different things.

She noticed the smudge marks on the back of the door and the dust balls under her table. Her mirror could use some Windex. Her rug should be vacuumed, and her curtains cleaned. And her books. What could she do with all her books? What would he think of a woman who had romantic novels stacked two rows deep in her bookcase or on her floor? Two Harriet Muellers peeked out from under the bed, where she had another stack of paperbacks.

The phone rang again.

"I forgot to ask what time."

She drew in a breath. Too late to say no now. "Seven thirty would be fine."

"Which apartment?"

"Three B."

"NAN," JIM asked, "if a man's just gone out on a date with a woman, what are appropriate presents for him to send?"

Nan stood in front of his desk in one of her dark, pressed suits. She looked at him quizzically. "Hypothetically?"

"Yes, hypothetically."

"Candy or flowers."

"Nothing more original than that?"

"A book or CD maybe."

"I thought you women were all liberated."

"We are. But we want to know that a man knows the rules before he breaks them."

"Wouldn't you rather see how imaginative a man can be?"

"He can send freesias instead of roses. Anything but long-stemmed red roses. They're such a cliché."

"CDs?"

"Something to prove that he has good taste. Country's OK, rock's OK, pop would be all wrong. Classical if he's willing to take a risk and knows his stuff."

"Books?"

"If he's read the book. Something he's capable of talking about. He shouldn't show off by sending something to prove how smart he is. And nothing too specific. Nothing like *How to Find the Right Man*."

"How about clothes?"

Nan frowned. It was the expression she made at a meeting when a client proposed something that wouldn't be right for the campaign or the agency. The space between her eyebrows creased. "Are we still speaking hypothetically?"

"Say that I'm the one. Picture me doing the giving."

"You don't know her size. You are taking a big risk on her taste. You are only guessing in the most conventional way on her colors."

"What if it's something that she's said she liked?"

Nan bit the top of her lip. "Is this the blind date?"

"The flutist. She's going away on tour. I want to send her something very special while she's gone. What's wrong with that?"

"Clothes are too bossy. It's like you're trying to prove that you're in charge. You're trying to make a woman look a certain way to please you."

"I'm not."

"It'll look that way."

"This woman is different, Nan. She's an artist. She has a very strong sense of herself. She knows who she is on stage. I want to share that."

Nan shifted her weight. She didn't sit down. "Don't go too fast, Jim. You're out of practice."

"I haven't gone too fast. I've been very careful. I don't call her nearly as often as I think about her. She's busy getting ready for her tour. I've respected that. I'm going to hear her play some of the music tonight."

"Bring her some chocolates."

"Not flowers?"

"She can take the chocolates with her. The flowers she'd have to leave behind."

❦

"PRETTY BRILLIANT," Dorothy said.

"It wasn't exactly my idea."

"I figured you'd have the accompanist there, and instead of the two of you there'd be three. What a mess. But just the two of you. That's excellent."

"I shouldn't have told you," Elizabeth said, the phone in one hand and a dust rag in the other.

"Of course you should. You tell me everything. I tell you everything. That's why we're friends."

"I don't think this is going to be good for the recital tour. I keep stopping my practicing today to clean the apartment. You should have seen the mess under the kitchen sink." She shook out the rag in the sink.

Dorothy laughed. "He's not going to look under the kitchen sink."

"But I'll know what it's like under there, and that's enough."

"What are you going to greet him with when you open the door? An apron? Sign of the domestic goddess?"

"Very funny."

"Just don't wear one of your dowdy performance dresses."

"They're not dowdy."

"They're OK on stage. But they'd be too much for your little apartment. Want me to come over and pick out something?"

"No. I need to practice. I don't have time for this."

"Then I'll get off the phone."

VERONICA HALLADAY sometimes thought it was a mistake to even have books at the Christ Church Thrift Shop. They took up an enormous amount of room. They could stay on the shelves for months before anybody bought them. You couldn't make much money from them, and they didn't attract deep-pocket buyers. The only way the Thrift Shop had ever made big money on them was when a decorator would come by and say, "I need five yards of books." They'd even specify the volumes by color. A yard of cordovan, two yards of pool-table green, one of navy blue. As though books were like wallpaper or upholstery.

Truth to tell, she wasn't a big reader. Although she always took a book with her on their annual summer vacation, she was lucky if she finished it by Christmas. She preferred historical fiction because she felt it improved her mind. She usually had a volume of historical fiction on her bedside table. But after reading a page or two, she always fell asleep.

Nevertheless she knew what books other people liked. She was good at arranging them on shelves at the Thrift Shop. It was a little like arranging cereal at the supermarket. The things that had the most demand she put high or low—they would disappear anyway. The slow movers she put on eye-level shelves so they'd be seen.

She was taking books out of a box left over from the rummage sale. She dusted them with an old handkerchief. Too bad there were so many paperbacks. The interior designers didn't go for paperbacks. The cover illustrations could be picturesque, but most of the spines were brown and frayed. Not much to look at. They would need real readers.

If Mrs. Halladay had to find a way to make a living, she would run a shop. She liked matching products to customers, old merchandise with new owners. It was like arranging guests at a dinner party. Triumphs came when an unlikely buyer found a previously unnoticed castoff. Like the wallflower finally getting a dance.

"Somebody will want these books," she told herself as she unpacked them and studied their titles. *Gardening on a Budget, Know Your Word Processor, Accounting for Dummies, The Balkans—Toward an Unlikely Peace.* What an odd assortment to end up in one box. Even arranged alphabetically, books could find the most unlikely partners.

At the bottom she found two slim paperbacks with florid covers: *The Captain's Dream* and *Stalwart of the Ionic Club.* A man in a red uniform embraced a golden-haired woman on one, and on the other a well-dressed card player looked up from a winning hand to gaze at a raven-haired beauty with diamonds and décolletage. Both books were by the writer Harriet Mueller.

Harriet Mueller. Why was that name so familiar? She'd heard it before—not too long ago. She searched her memory and recalled the two young women who had been looking for Harriet Mueller paperbacks. She had written their names and numbers down on a yellow Post-it note. Yes, it was still there, right by the cash register. She called and left a message: "This is Veronica Halladay at the Thrift Shop, and I've found two more books by Harriet Mueller. I'll save them at the desk for you."

Two Harriet Muellers with purple ink all over them. Wasn't that what the young woman was looking for?

TWENTY

JIM ARRIVED empty-handed. He'd left his briefcase at home and had taken off his tie. He didn't want to look too formal. He didn't bring flowers or chocolates. No CD or a book. He wanted to present himself as a music lover. In the entryway of the brownstone he hesitated before buzzing 3B. The nameplate said A. Wong, not E. Ash. He looked up at the number 16 carved over the doorway. He had the address right, and he was sure she had said 3B. He pushed the buzzer.

"Hello?" came a voice.

"It's Jim."

"Come right up."

He took the steps two by two. Someone on the first floor was cooking Indian food, and the smell of curry went with him. The staircase narrowed as he climbed. Two apartments per floor. Newspapers were piled outside the doors, and a pair of old boots and kitty litter were in front of one. On the top facing the back was 3B. He rang the bell.

Elizabeth opened the door. This is when he wished he had flowers. Something to offer that was more than himself.

"Who's A. Wong?" he asked.

"She lived here before me. They never got around to changing the name on the buzzer."

She was wearing slacks and a light green sweater.

"You get your exercise going up and down those stairs."

"I figure it's good practice for my breath control." She stepped back to let him in. "Going up every day."

Her apartment was incredibly neat. It reminded Jim of a boat. A place for every item and an item for every nook and cranny. Books lined a narrow bookcase and were stacked up along the floor in neat piles with the spines all facing the same direction and the stacks going from big to small. Music scores lined the top of the bureau and huddled under it like puppies. A music stand was in the center of the room, and the flute lay across the sofa bed. A magic wand at rest.

There were only two chairs at the small table next to the kitchen and only one place mat. Room for one only. Next to it was a door that Jim assumed led to a bathroom and beside it a door for the closet. If he opened the closet door there were two possibilities: that everything was as neat as in the room, or that in a mad rush to clean she had stashed all her extraneous things—old newspapers, dirty clothes, unanswered mail—and if he opened the door, it would all come tumbling out.

"Great place," he said.

"It's small but right for me. The location is easy for my students, and in between lessons I can practice all I want."

"No one complains?"

"One neighbor is deaf and another never comes home."

"Too bad. I bet they miss out on some good music."

"And a lot that isn't so great. When I practice, I can make some pretty ugly sounds."

"I can't believe it." He couldn't believe that she'd ever done anything ugly. Even the tiny apartment had a certain Bohemian beauty. The small framed pictures on the wall. Rose prints. The silk pillows on the sofa bed. The little Oriental rug on the hardwood floor. The linen place mat on the table. The curtains. The worst thing about the apartment was that it didn't seem to allow for another person in Elizabeth's life. Just the flute.

"At least I need to feel that I can make ugly sounds in here," she said. "When I'm practicing, I'm practicing. It's not a performance."

Jim gestured at the window. No curtain. "People can stare in from across the way."

Elizabeth laughed. "I never think of that. I like the light."

"Have you been here for long?"

"A couple of years."

"When A. Wong moved out?"

"I don't know who she was—or he was. I got the apartment from a friend. Could I get you a Coke or something?"

"A Coke would be fine."

Jim took his coat off and tossed it on the sofa bed while Elizabeth got the Coke. She came out of the kitchen carrying it in a glass, with a small napkin. *Even that is classy*, he thought. She wasn't going to let him drink it from the can.

He took the glass with a thanks and sat on the sofa bed. "Do you ever think of doing something else?"

"All the time. I'd be great at real estate. Or as a legal secretary. Sometimes I think it'd be fun to organize someone else's life. For about a day. Then I'd miss it."

"The music?"

"Everything." She gestured to the book-lined walls of her room. "The freedom. The friends. The tours. Especially the music."

"You're nice to give me a preview of the concert."

"As long as you don't fall asleep. Then I'll know I've failed."

How could he fall asleep? Just the two of them in the one room with Elizabeth looking ravishing. This was her world, and he felt flattered to be included. He was in awe, as though he'd been invited into a writer's study and was going to be shown the secrets of her craft.

"Can you tell me anything about what you're going to play?"

"The first two pieces are modern. The last is a baroque fantasia. It goes all over the place. The real challenge is to get the runs down right. They need to be smooth. All in one breath and motion. There should be something sweeping about them, but they need to have shape. They can't be notey."

"Like a sentence instead of words on the page?" He was struggling to find an appropriate comparison.

"Or like the voice. Musicians are always talking about imitating the sung voice, but when it comes down to it we're all snobs about singers."

"You, a snob?"

She was the most real, unsnobbish, generous, openhearted person he'd ever met.

"Musicians can be terrible snobs."

She sounded nervous about playing for him. Performance anxiety. It was almost as nerve-wracking as that first kiss.

"Where do you want me?" he asked. But he wondered, *Should I leave right away?*

"You're fine there." She picked up the flute and stood no more than five feet away from him. She held it up to her lips and played a quick arpeggio—a warmup. She was stalling for time . . . Jim could tell. "This first piece opens the recital. No accompaniment. Just me."

He nodded. She raised the flute and began playing. The music transformed her. The awkwardness was gone; her body was relaxed. She seemed enormously tall, like a basketball player. And although the sound was coming out of the flute, it seemed to rise out of the top of her head. It floated into the room and filled it. Her own little Carnegie Hall.

Jim hadn't even asked her the name of the piece. If he had to give it a title, he would have called it "Shepherd's Song." For a moment they weren't in New York but in an open field, and a lonely melody was floating across the moors. The lines of the tune were long and sinuous. Between each phrase, Elizabeth took massive breaths, like an Olympic swimmer coming up for air, but the breathing didn't interrupt the song. It was part of it.

He closed his eyes and felt himself in the music, riding it up and down. She had him in the palm of her hand. Then the song made an abrupt shift from minor to major, and with it, he felt a flood of happiness.

But when he opened his eyes, he saw that Elizabeth wasn't smiling. Her concentration was so intense she made no acknowledgment that Jim was even in the room. At the same time he felt the song was for him . . . and him alone. It couldn't have happened without him there.

The tune kept getting softer and higher. It climbed and climbed. Then, on a note that was so soft Jim could barely tell it was there, the music stopped. Elizabeth put down her flute and smiled. The mood was broken.

What words could he use? "That is really beautiful."

"Isn't it? I'd never heard it before a friend played it in a recital here. The composer is only twenty-four years old. English. Terrifically talented."

"You're the one who's terrifically talented."

"Thank you."

But she looked uncomfortable with the compliment, he noticed.

"It must be hard to open a concert with a piece like that. You're so exposed."

"The first piece is always the hardest. It's like any first impression. With some listeners you only get that first chance. I used to start out with things less challenging, but now I go all out."

"Will you have any breath left?"

"I hope so," she said modestly. She lifted the flute to her lips and played the second piece. This one was lighter, less intense. It reminded Jim of two birds chasing each other and then flying apart. He thought he saw a smile on Elizabeth's face as she played. He couldn't take his eyes away from her. He started to feel inadequate. Why had he suggested this? What could he say to her? All words were so insubstantial.

When Lois performed, he was the dependable, trustworthy audience. But that was so different. He knew what she was doing. He knew the words and was familiar with her every expression, her every gesture. He spoke to her with authority.

With Elizabeth he had no authority at all. He looked around at the apartment. The books, the pictures, the tiny galley kitchen. This was her world. She was entirely self-sufficient. She didn't need a man in her life at all.

The chirping flute brought a spring day into the room. Birds darting through trees and singing. The light airiness of it. This piece finished with a soaring flight.

"That's my comedy routine," she said, laughing.

"It works. The audience will love it."

"This third piece is my chance to show off. My teacher said there should always be one piece in a recital that makes an audience say, 'Wow.'"

"I figured they've already said it."

"If I'm lucky," she said.

The flute was raised for the third time. Again Elizabeth transformed herself. Or was it that the music transformed her? This time she was earthy and wild. Jim watched her fingers. The piece that was supposed to "wow" did so with runs and roulades that traveled faster than the speed of light.

Why did he think she would go for him? His self-confidence was exaggerated. Her control was amazing. She seemed to be burning with passion as she played, but everything else about her was icy cool. As if nothing would shake her.

He wasn't even sure he liked this piece, but it was having its desired effect. *Wow, that must be hard*, he thought. *Amazing. How can you play that fast?*

When she was finished, she gave a short bow and he burst into applause. He looked at her to see if she was the same person. That happened with Lois too, when she was good at her role. He would forget she was even his wife.

"That was great!" he said. "Use that as your encore. They'll give you another ovation."

"It's not really as hard as it looks."

"Who cares? No one will know."

"You liked it?"

"I liked the whole thing. I had no idea how good you were. You become someone completely different when you play."

"That's what Dorothy says. 'The terror of Ninety-fourth Street.'" Elizabeth took apart the flute and swabbed it with what looked like an old patch of pajamas.

"How often do you go on tour?"

"Twice a year at the most. It takes a lot of preparation. I have to psych myself up to do it. But when I do it, I fall in love with performing again. I'm a two-week-a-year soloist. I've got the ego for that. Not much more."

"Wouldn't you like to go more often?" He heard himself adopt a tone he'd forgotten he had. The artist's advisor, dispassionately telling a performer what she should really be doing.

"There's not a huge demand for what I do. The audiences who want to hear a flute are not filling auditoriums and football arenas. Twice a year is about all my agent can muster. I figure I'm lucky at that." She put the flute away in its velvet-lined case.

"If you could get the money to record a few CDs, that would put you on the map."

"Next you'll be telling me that I need a gold-plated flute."

He looked at the flute in its velvet-lined case and then back at her. "Too dazzling. You're pretty enough to look at."

She closed the case with a snap. "It helps to have an audience. I'll be able to tell myself, 'I got through this once. I'll be able to get through it again.' More Coke?"

"Thanks."

She took his glass and went into the kitchen. She came out with two filled glasses.

"Tell me again what cities you're going to."

She picked up a typed sheet of paper that was on the table and read from it. "Des Moines, Davenport, Cheyenne, Boise, and Ogden."

"That's a lot of traveling."

"I'll be exhausted when I come back." She sat next to him on the sofa bed.

"I'll miss you."

"You don't know me well enough to miss me." She said it as a simple fact, but he couldn't help thinking she meant more.

"Now that I've heard you play, I don't know you at all."

She was indeed a mystery. Shy and self-effacing one minute, all confident the next. Light and flirtatious, then guarded and distant.

He put his arm around her waist. "You're about a dozen different women with that flute. I couldn't keep up with them all."

"It's what I do." Her green eyes searched his.

She leaned toward him and he kissed her. A short kiss. Just the smallest intimation of what he felt.

"There's a lot for me to get to know," he said.

She backed away suddenly. "Can we wait until I come back? My mind is full up with the tour and my recital and what I need to take and all the phone calls I have to make before I go."

He looked again into the green eyes. "It seems to me like you're organized already."

"Only externally. I'm a mess inside."

"So am I." He was thinking of his wife and the extraordinary sensation of having a woman so close to him again. Smelling her hair, his hand at her back. Seeing the freckles on her neck. He could almost hear her heart beat.

"You know what I mean. I'm thinking of too many things at once."

"When you're gone, I'll be thinking only of you."

She looked puzzled. "What about your work?"

"Thinking of you will make it go better." Was he being too bold? Had he said too much?

"I look forward to seeing you when I come back. But right now I have to get ready to go." She stood up.

"Then let me take this with me." He held up the piece of paper that showed her itinerary. "I want to think of you each day in each city you visit."

THAT NIGHT, before falling asleep, Jim picked up the book next to his bed and began writing.

Darling,

Something odd happened tonight while I was listening to Elizabeth. For the past few weeks I've been thinking that falling in love was the way I could forget you. It would be an escape from the pain. It would be my chance to move beyond the past. My recovery from grief.

But tonight, in her apartment, I felt especially close to you. I could remember sitting and watching you perform. I loved being your best critic, your most trusted ally. I loved being at opening nights and hearing all the people applaud you and comment on you during the intermission. Then coming home and rehashing everything off stage and on. Going through all the performances of your fellow actors and actresses. Critiquing every moment.

Tonight, there was a moment when I leaned to one side as though I'd whisper in your ear about how wonderful she was. I wanted to tell you about her. How odd to share this happiness with you. Oddly enough, I think that you would be the happiest for me. You would understand it. True love is wanting more than anything else the happiness of the beloved.

Forgive me for all the mistakes I ever made with you. Save me from making them again.

That was as far as Jim got . . .

TWENTY-ONE

JIM DID research on churches in his immediate neighborhood. He phoned the big red brick one on the corner with its Byzantine architecture and banners out front that advertised dances, plays, and concerts. No rummage sale or thrift shop there. He dialed the Catholic church down the block with the large Virgin Mary under a protective disk. *Our Lady of the Satellite Dish*, he thought of it. The recording made no mention of a rummage sale or a thrift shop. He tried a storefront Pentecostal church that played loud music on Friday and Saturday nights. The woman spoke Spanish and Korean before using English—as though single-handedly she could reverse the curse of Babel. She would be glad to receive any donations of clothes, she said, but no books.

That left Christ Church. It mentioned the Thrift Shop in its newspaper ad. Was there a rummage sale too?

He was told to call back when Mrs. Halladay was present. She knew all about the rummage sale. When could he reach her? Tuesday and Thursday afternoons, at the Thrift Shop, the voice on the phone said.

So he phoned the Thrift Shop on a Thursday afternoon and got a recording telling when the shop was open. "And remember," a woman's voice added, "all items donated to the Thrift Shop are tax-deductible. Receipts provided upon request."

On Tuesday he explained to Lisa, his assistant, that he had a lunch meeting that would keep him out of the office until after two, then grabbed a slice of pizza and took the subway uptown, eating en route. He walked the three blocks from the station to the church.

"Mrs. Halladay is in the Thrift Shop," the moon-faced receptionist told him. "Today is Tuesday. Mrs. Halladay always comes in on Tuesdays." As though Mrs. Halladay's name was synonymous with certain days of the week.

"Thanks. I'll look for her there."

At the Thrift Shop he had to assume that the silver-haired woman with pearl earrings and a large diamond on one manicured hand, a sapphire on the other, was Mrs. Halladay. Her navy blue suit didn't seem to collect any dust from the objects surrounding her.

"A customer!" she exclaimed. Clearly she was not a let-them-roam-around-on-their-own saleswoman. Rather, she was of the dripping-with-charm, help-them-until-they-buy school. She was folding a large quilt. Its pattern of spades, clubs, and diamonds was so ugly that giving it away would hardly count as charity.

"How do you do," he said. All thought of just asking about the books disappeared. He'd be a customer.

"You're the first here today. Tuesdays can be slow until the nursery school around the corner lets out. All those mothers and baby-sitters come by to see if we have anything for their children. I can usually sell them something."

He barely suppressed a grin. "I'll bet you can."

"My husband says I'm a natural. Tells me that I could sell the Brooklyn Bridge if I set my mind to it."

"You have some very nice things." Jim gestured to the objects on tables, bookshelves, racks, and chairs. Someone had put fresh carnations in one of the Vaseline glass vases.

"We're very fortunate," she said. "People give to us because it all goes to a worthy cause. And every donation is tax-deductible."

"That's what the phone message said."

"'Wise as serpents, gentle as doves,'" Mrs. Halladay quoted.

Fitting, Jim thought. *Words from the Bible in a church basement from a thrift-store lady.*

"We try to accommodate everybody," she said. "Is there anything in particular you're looking for?"

"Maybe a present for a friend." He didn't want to declare himself just yet. "Something for a thirtieth birthday."

"What did you have in mind?"

"Something to tease him about how old he is. Something that would give him a big laugh."

"We have some nice men's hats," she said. "Homburgs and Borsalinos. People find those amusing." Mrs. Halladay spoke as though she didn't entirely approve of people using the Thrift Shop just for comedy. It had a higher purpose. "We've had some nice canes in the past. Don't have any right now."

"How about an old pocket watch?"

"No pocket watches. But we have some pipes up here." Mrs. Halladay took an old humidor down from a top shelf. "You could give him a pipe."

For several moments they stood over the box, admiring the pipes. Wood, ivory, and ebony, scented with tobacco. Then Jim glanced to the back of the shop, looking at the books. Two large bookcases full.

"The big pipe would be best. It's the most outrageous."

"Beautiful workmanship. It's all ivory. And the carving is very nice." She smiled proudly, as if the pipe were her find.

"Must be from the Orient."

"A real bargain."

"Can you wrap it up?"

"I have some tissue paper at the front." Her high heels clicked on the linoleum floor as she turned with a purposeful stride.

He followed her, trying to make his tone casual. "You had a rummage sale earlier, didn't you?"

"Our biggest fund-raiser of the year."

"My sister-in-law brought a big box of books to the sale, and now she's having second thoughts. You know how book lovers can be."

"Sometimes I wonder why we even keep all the books we do. The money isn't great. I've come to think of them as a loss leader. They manage to attract a certain clientele. People come for a book or two and end up buying a tweed jacket or a brass desk lamp."

"What about the books my sister-in-law brought to the rummage sale?"

"We get all the overflow. Anything we don't sell at the rummage sale comes here. We rarely throw anything away. Do you know the titles or the authors?"

Jim ran a hand through his hair. "They were romances. Certain writers in particular. Cynthia Gooden Brown, Genevieve West, and Harriet Mueller. Harriet Mueller especially. Vintage paperbacks. I think she liked them for their covers as much as their content."

Veronica Halladay's ears perked up at the mention of Harriet Mueller. And then she paused. The most natural thing to say would have been, "Someone else around here was looking for Harriet Mueller," but her years as a volunteer at the Thrift Shop had trained her in discretion. Sometimes one branch of a family wanted to get rid of an antique fire screen or a tea service and another branch of the family wouldn't sell it for pure gold. Who was this young man anyway?

"You can check the shelf back there," she said.

"Are the books arranged alphabetically?"

"I'm afraid not. More by size and shape." No need to justify her idiosyncratic system.

Jim walked over to the shelf and glanced across the spines. "Would you know if you have any Harriet Muellers?"

"I don't believe we have any for sale," Mrs. Halladay said. The two she had were spoken for. That was the best way to put things. Not a lie, a clarification. Mrs. Halladay never lied.

"My wife used to read them. She loved them."

Jim ran his fingers across the paperbacks on one shelf.

"Are you looking for them for your wife too?" She followed him to the back.

"She's not alive anymore."

"I'm very sorry."

"It happened a while ago."

"I'd love to help you." Mrs. Halladay was softening on the young man. "Just leave me your name and phone number, and I'll call you if I find anything."

"Thank you." He gave her one of his cards.

"It's ten dollars for the pipe," she concluded. She would save the card.

Connecting people with donated goods. Bringing new life to something used. That's what she did at Christ Church Thrift Shop. It was the very reason she volunteered on Tuesdays and Thursdays. To provide second chances for things . . . and people. It was her calling in life, her God-given gift.

HIS CHASE after the Harriet Muellers was foolish. Why did he think he'd find them? And what did he suppose he'd find in them? Some last connection with Lois? To hear her last words to him? What was he chasing after? It was impossible to communicate with the dead. And why should he bother? What she'd wanted to say she should have said directly to him when she was alive. Now it was too late.

He walked down Columbus Avenue, irritated with himself. He'd wasted his time in a fruitless pursuit. His future was with Elizabeth the flutist, not with some scribbling from his dead wife. That was over. Finished—like her alarm clock.

Snow was coming down gently, landing in his hair as he walked. Hollywood snow. Charles Dickens's snow. It would look beautiful in New York for a day or two, and then it would be a muddy, dirty mess. That was the problem. If you put anything white down in New York, soon it showed the dirt.

He thought of Elizabeth on her concert tour in some Western city, where the snow stayed white. The air would be clear and dry and cold. The sky so dark at night that thousands of stars could be seen. The men would wear string ties, and the women long dresses. Hearing live classical music was a noteworthy event, not something to yawn over. Some geezer in cowboy boots and his only suit would be sitting in the front row admiring her. His wife had forced him to come to the concert, but when he saw the pretty redhead swaying as she played, he was delighted.

Jim said the prayer. He needed to focus his thoughts.

Jesus Christ, have mercy upon me. Make haste to help me. Rescue me and save me. Let thy will be done in my life.

But the rote prayer did nothing to lift his mood. It didn't help him, rescue him, save him. He found himself saying the words, but he couldn't concentrate on them.

He'd found the Thrift Shop vaguely depressing. All those old used goods looking for new owners. Abandoned, gone on the block. It reminded him of the loss in his life. But he no longer wanted to linger in the past. He was looking for something old so he could get on with something new.

"I'm listening for you, Lois," he said. "Still looking to you."

He treasured the last night he'd had with Elizabeth in her apartment. Her music had left him emotionally spent. She had given his longing a tune. It seemed impossible that she could know what a man felt for a woman and put it to music.

The night in Elizabeth's apartment should have ended with magic. Instead it concluded with an awkward promise. Then she was gone, and he was left searching for some Harriet Muellers with Lois's writing in them.

He came to the boutique that he'd passed with Elizabeth on their first date. One of their few dates. The pink dress was still in the window. The wrong color but the right dress. At once he was struck with the urge to see if they had it in the right color. Elizabeth had to know what he really thought of her, how important she was to him. He had to take a risk—let her know. He darted into the store.

"Can you help me?" he asked the saleswoman.

"Yeah?" Barely looking up from her magazine, she chewed her gum loudly. Not helpful like Mrs. Halladay.

"Do you happen to have that dress in the window in green?"

"What size?" she said, popping the gum.

"I don't know for sure, but I've got a pretty good idea."

Ten minutes later, he walked out of the store and headed back to his office. There he found a FedEx box, consulted Elizabeth's itinerary, and found out where she'd be the next day. He was never much for buying

Hallmark cards with printed sentiments. Instead he took a sheet of office letterhead and scribbled on it:

> *To the most brilliant of flutists,*
> *You take my breath away.*

He paused. Should he say what was really in his heart and on his mind? Or was it too soon? Dare he take such a risk?

But then there were all those times when he should have taken a risk with Lois—and he didn't. He didn't want to make the same mistakes again.

So, before he could second-guess himself, he added two more lines and sealed the envelope.

He took the box to the FedEx office himself. He didn't want it to go on the company account. He even paid extra for early delivery to Cheyenne, Wyoming. It had to get there as soon as possible.

MRS. HALLADAY had attached a leather belt of sleigh bells to the door of the Thrift Shop so that it sounded like Santa Claus whenever anyone entered. That way, if she was in the back of the shop sorting through boxes and bags of donations, she could know that she wasn't alone.

Not that she worried about personal harm. Nothing bad could happen in the basement of a church. She just wanted to know when people came in.

The sleigh bells rang.

A young woman called, "Hello!"

Mrs. Halladay scurried from the back.

"I don't know if you remember me . . . ," the young woman said.

Mrs. Halladay smiled. "Of course I do. Hello, Dorothy."

"You called my friend Elizabeth Ash to tell her that you'd received a recent shipment of Harriet Muellers."

"I'm afraid they're not recent at all. They've sat in this box for who knows how long. I don't even think they were put out for the sale."

She took a small Bergdorf Goodman bag out from under the counter. "There are only two in there."

"Elizabeth will be pleased."

"You're not the one interested in them?"

"They're really for Lizzie."

"As I remember, she was looking for ones with writing in them," said Mrs. Halladay.

"Exactly."

"These have writing in them."

"A whole series of messages?"

"With a purple pen."

Dorothy took one out of the bag and thumbed through its pages. "Just like the other ones."

Mrs. Halladay was a discreet woman. That was another reason she was such a good saleswoman. She was not one to pass on gossip. But there was the man who had come in looking for books by Harriet Mueller. He said they were given by his sister-in-law. Then he had mentioned his dead wife.

"I didn't really read what was written," Mrs. Halladay said.

"The words all form a story. They're messages from a woman to a man."

Veronica Halladay wavered. She had arrived at a crucial moment. The decision felt monumental, as though she could be violating some secret pact of client confidentiality. But if she didn't speak up, she may regret it forever. Who could know but that the good Lord had put these pieces of a puzzle in front of her, so that she could put them together?

"Does your friend Elizabeth know any of these people?" Mrs. Halladay asked.

"No. She's trying to put their story together, but she can't because she doesn't have all the books. She wants to get them back to their rightful owner."

"I know who he is," Mrs. Halladay burst out.

Dorothy's eyes widened. "Who?"

"He was in here about an hour ago. He was looking for Harriet

Muellers. He said his sister-in-law had brought some books in. His wife loved reading Harriet Muellers and he wanted to find them."

"He has a wife?"

"Not anymore."

"What do you mean?"

"She died. He said it happened a while ago."

"What did he look like?" Dorothy's expression turned eager.

"Tall, about thirty years old, I'd say. Handsome with brown hair and kind brown eyes. A baritone voice. He spoke with great self-assurance."

"What's his name?"

"I asked for his card. I told him I would call him if I had any information. I wasn't sure what to do." Mrs. Halladay tucked a loose strand of silver hair behind one ear and said in her most Southern accent, "I finally explained that we didn't have any Harriet Muellers for sale." She spread her arms wide. "After all, these were already spoken for."

"Who is he?"

"Let me get you his card." She took it from the top of her desk, where she'd only just left it.

Dorothy read the name on the card and read it again. "Oh no," she said under her breath.

"Yes?" Mrs. Halladay said. For her good detective work she felt she was at least entitled to a little explanation.

"Let's just say this is someone we know."

TWENTY-TWO

HOW MANY times could Dorothy say, "You'll never believe this! You'll be so amazed"? How many times could she exclaim into the phone, "It's so amazing! It's not at all what you'd expect!"?

And then she'd gone on about how many calls she'd made to track Elizabeth down. First to Elizabeth's agent, then a concert-hall adminis-trator in Boise, who said she was still in Cheyenne, and in Cheyenne they said she hadn't left Davenport yet. And the person in Davenport said to try Miss Ash at her motel.

"But how did you find out?" Elizabeth said, trying to understand what Dorothy was talking about. "How do you know?"

"The lady at the Thrift Shop found him. Mrs. Halladay. She knew. I went there today to check up on those books she called us about."

"But how?"

"She said a man came to the shop looking for the Harriet Muellers. He said some books had been donated to the church by his sister-in-law."

"Her books?"

"No, they belonged to his wife."

Elizabeth took a deep breath. "He's still married?"

Of course, he was married. All the best men were married. There was nothing out there for a single woman of her age.

"Not anymore."

"Divorced?"

"A widower. His wife died."

"So all the purple notes . . ." Elizabeth's thoughts whirled. A heavy sadness settled on her. So she had loved him, then lost him, because she had died. It was all too sad. Too unlike the Harriet Muellers, where the hero and heroine always ended up together, forever. "Did Mrs. Halladay know who the man is?"

"Yes," Dorothy said slowly. She sounded hesitant—not like Dorothy.

"Then who?"

"Elizabeth, it was . . ." Another pause. "It was Jim Lockhart."

"Jim?" Elizabeth felt the wind go out of her, as though she'd just played an impossibly long phrase on her flute. "Are you *sure*?"

"He left his card at the shop."

"That doesn't make any sense. Why would he give the books away?"

"He didn't. I guess his sister-in-law was cleaning out his wife's stuff and just boxed up the books and took them to the church. That's how we found the ones at the rummage sale."

"But Jim . . ." Elizabeth thought of what she knew about the couple in the books. What she'd read. They'd met in college, they were both involved in the theater, they came to the city for their big break. But she'd assumed that the man was still an actor. "Jim's a casting director."

"Yes, and his wife was an actress," Dorothy said. "And she died of cancer. While she was ill, she wrote to him in the books."

"Why is he looking for them now?"

"He didn't know what had happened to them. He never knew she'd written in them."

"But I still have them. I didn't know they were his."

The whole thing was so wrong. "Darling" in the books was warm, passionate, dashing, sincere. He'd worked his way into her heart as any character of fiction had. She saw him, pictured him, imagined where he lived. He was as vivid to her as any Harriet Mueller hero. How could he be Jim Lockhart?

"Will you tell him, Lizzie?"

"Of course I'll tell him. I have some things that belong to him. He'll want them back."

"I wouldn't tell him."

Her chin stiffened in determination. "I have to."

"It's weird knowing stuff about him that he doesn't know we know."

"It's awful," said Elizabeth. "If I'd known the messages were meant for him, I wouldn't have read them in the first place."

"That's ridiculous. They were in the open. On sale at a church rummage sale, for goodness' sake. It's like reading a postcard. Nobody could have stopped you. Don't blame yourself."

"I should have returned the books as soon as I saw the writing inside." It was one thing to picture some character in her imagination. It was dreadful to know who it really was. Worse to have dated him. Elizabeth could never measure up to the devoted woman who wrote in the Harriet Muellers. She couldn't compete.

"Think of it as a coincidence. You bought some books that were meant for him, and then you met him. New York's a small place."

"It is not, Dorothy. Des Moines is a small place. Davenport is even smaller."

"Well, the universe of Harriet Mueller readers is small."

"Just because you've never read her books."

"Tell him that it's a coincidence that both you and his dead wife had the same tastes in literature."

"I know more about him than I should. Than anyone should. And we've only just met." She couldn't merge the two: Jim and the man in the book.

"Can't you see it was meant to happen?" Dorothy asked. "It's fate. I know you don't believe in that kind of thing . . . but I do. And you have so much in common with his wife. She was an incurable romantic, and so are you."

"It doesn't feel like that at all. She had a history with him. They knew each other for several years in college before they ever started dating . . . I hate knowing that."

"I'm sure he would tell you all that if you asked. What's so private about that?"

"It was written in a private place. It was intended for an audience of one."

An audience of one. Like Jim listening to her play in her apartment.

"He'll be grateful to you when you give him the books back."

Elizabeth exhaled. "Just because I've restored his wife to him? I don't think so. I'll only be reminding him of what he lost."

"I shouldn't have called. You have enough on your mind already."

"It's Jim . . ."

"Don't think about any of this stuff until you come back to New York."

If that were only possible. If she could put Jim out of her mind. It was worse now that she had to connect him with a figment of her imagination.

"One more thing. Do you want me to tell you what it says in the two Harriet Muellers I just picked up?"

"Absolutely not!" Elizabeth practically shouted. "Now that I know who they're meant for, I'd rather not know."

"I'll get my whiteout."

"They don't belong to you. They don't belong to me. They're his."

"JIMBO, ISN'T that weight a little too heavy for an old guy like you?"

"Give up. You're just jealous." Jim was doing bicep curls. Fifteen reps for his third set, but he felt like he could go on for another three or four sets and at twice the weight.

"You're really pushing yourself, old man."

"I've been feeling good."

"It's amazing how this place heats up right after Christmas and then slows down in February."

Jim did a few more curls just for the fun of it.

Jesus Christ, have mercy upon me. Make haste to help me.

"All those guys who want to lose weight after Christmas give up after two or three weeks."

"New Year's resolutions," said Scott. "They never last."

"Things will start picking up once everybody starts thinking about wearing a bathing suit again."

"The battle against love handles." Scott was positioning himself to do overhead lifts.

"How's your wife's cousin?"

"Devastated that you haven't called."

"Give me a break."

"The people at the old folks' home keep her busy, so I guess she's happy. We don't really see her much."

"Your wife's not mad at me, is she?"

"She saves all her anger for me. Take my word for it: don't ever get married."

"I have been married."

"Oh yeah. I forgot." Scott grunted under the weights. He was always lifting more than he could handle and then having to drop the dumbbells onto the floor.

"Funny thing is, when you are married, you don't realize how wonderful it is to have someone there every morning when you wake up or someone to call in the middle of the day to talk about mundane things like what you should eat for dinner that night."

Scott groaned. "Somebody there to complain about what a slob you are and why you don't make more money and to ask why you have to spend so much on that car."

"You'll probably think I'm crazy, but I miss talks like that."

Rescue me and save me. Let thy will be done in my life.

"You are crazy." Predictably enough, Scott dropped the weight to the floor.

"Tell your wife that I appreciated her setting me up."

"She's got a thousand other single friends and cousins she'd love you to meet."

"Tell her that I already have somebody in the picture."

Scott sat up on the bench. "Serious?"

"I am."

JIM TRIED to gauge just when the FedEx package would arrive and when Elizabeth would actually receive it. According to her itinerary she would arrive in Cheyenne on Wednesday afternoon. Would she go straight to the concert hall or would she stop at the motel first? He'd sent it to the motel because that seemed safest. No telling who might get it at the concert hall.

He could picture the place. One of those old converted movie theaters that booked acts from out of town. Lois once went on a bus-and-truck tour to dozens of places like that. They always had a group of civic boosters and arts committee representatives, modern-day versions of the mayor's wife from *The Music Man.*

Would Elizabeth wear the dress that night or save it for later in the tour? Jim didn't doubt that it would fit. He had an unerring eye for sizes, something that came from his job. Once he had to arrange a photo shoot with different fashion models, and to the designers' surprise he could accurately name the dress size for every woman. A hazard of the profession. Maybe Elizabeth's new dress might need some minor adjustments, but seen from a distance at a concert, a safety pin would do the trick.

He was trying to anticipate her reaction. Imagining it. Picturing it. She'd see the FedEx package, look at the return address, and wonder. She'd go up to her room and open the box. *He shouldn't have,* she'd think. The color, the cut, the fabric—it was perfect.

Of course, the present assumed a lot. It presumed that their relationship was far more serious than Elizabeth might have been prepared to believe. But that was a risk worth taking. Maybe things would have been better with Lois if he'd allowed himself to be more extravagant. To give in to the craziest impulses. Nan had told him to stick to chocolates and flowers. Well, with Elizabeth he had to do more.

Her music still reverberated in his head. He wanted to share it, celebrate it. That was the message of the dress: *I think you're fabulous. And here's a dress to prove it.*

Think how she'd look in it!

Twenty-Three

ELIZABETH SHOULD have guessed. It all fit. All those things he had told her over dinner at The Purple Lantern. Coming to New York with his wife. Living in a dozen different apartments. Throwing themselves into their careers. It completely matched what she'd read in the books. It was such a familiar scenario. Everybody came to the city to make it big. A lot of people came as couples. Most of the time they didn't make it big. His story wasn't much different from thousands of others.

Except the death of his wife. He had insisted on telling her, as if it were something essential about himself. She couldn't dismiss it as a bid for sympathy. He wasn't the least bit morbid about it.

But when she thought about the man in the books—"My One and Only . . . my darling"—

Jim Lockhart had known a love that was outrageously romantic. There would never be room in his life for something more. She, Elizabeth Ash, could only be a poor second. If you'd had that kind of marriage, what would be left?

She imagined the conversation she'd have with him back in New York. They'd meet someplace for dinner. She'd bring the books with her. They'd start with a first course. Before they'd even finish their salads, she'd take out the Harriet Muellers. "These belong to you, Jim," she'd say. "It's a complete accident that they ended up with me."

A terrible mix-up.

Elizabeth would pass the books across the table. He'd look inside. He'd recognize the handwriting immediately. She'd see the expression on his face. Remembering the great love of his life. "I didn't know it was you when we first met," she'd go on. "Otherwise I would have returned these books immediately."

She'd admit that she read them. She'd tell him that, yes, she was moved by them. He'd known a love unlike anything she'd ever experienced. Years of devotion and self-sacrifice that made a ridicule of the one relationship she'd ever had. An artistic partnership and passion. And then she'd say . . .

What would she say? That she didn't think it would work out for them at all? That she didn't want to follow in the footsteps of such a predecessor? That he was very charming and handsome, but she didn't want to be a poor replacement for "my One and Only"?

All those phrases that had seemed so romantic when she was first reading them now left her cold: *I hope you realize this is a love letter. . . . I wanted to go through every moment in our past and remind myself what was special about what we had. I've been reliving it in my mind, remembering everything. Let me give you my conclusion first of all. No suspense. No surprises. Here it is: I love you.*

She'd been interested in Jim. Something good was going on between them, but better to call it quits now before she got too involved.

THE THEATER in Cheyenne was an old wooden turn-of-the-century opera house, a little jewel box. She could imagine girls in bloomers dancing on stage and miners throwing gold nuggets at them. The crowd at the concert was more sedate. They seemed to like the two unaccompanied pieces and the baroque fantasia. Toward the end of the fantasia, when she was in the middle of an impressive series of arpeggios, she looked out and saw an older man in a string tie beaming at her.

She did one encore, as usual, then was called back on stage for another encore. This time, instead of doing something new, she repeated the piece that she used to open the recital, the one she had played in her apartment for Jim. The haunting flute tune had always delighted her, but this time as she played it, thinking of Jim despite herself, she felt a horrible sense of loss. What was beautiful was gone. What might have been would never be. The piece sounded to her ears like a funeral song, a shepherd on a moor mourning his lost love. To her surprise it brought tears to her eyes.

She made a quick bow and listened to the applause in the wings. Still strong, but not strong enough for another encore. She was relieved. She didn't have it in her to play another encore even if she were asked. Someone threw a bouquet of flowers onto the stage, which she picked up. One last bow and she was gone.

Her motel was on a lonely strip outside of town. The chairwoman of the Cheyenne Friends of Music had volunteered to put Elizabeth up, but Elizabeth had declined. She preferred a drab motel room to all the homemade charms of an extra room in a lady's house. Performing on stage was demanding enough. She didn't need the added anxiety of being the perfect guest.

She and Eric Weissinger, her accompanist, checked in at the motel after the concert. She desperately needed to unwind.

"We have a package for you, Ms. Ash," the woman at the front desk said, handing Elizabeth a large FedEx box.

"Thank you." Elizabeth looked at the return address with a sinking sensation.

"Who's it from?" Eric asked.

Eric was a brilliant pianist, but he was perfectly oblivious offstage. All of his sensitivity was reserved for his instrument.

"I don't know," she said. *Babcock, Crier, and Nelson.* It could only be from one person.

"Good concert," Eric said, standing in the hall outside their rooms. "You were right to repeat the opener for your encore. It was especially good tonight."

"Thank you."

"We've got all day to drive tomorrow, so don't get up too early."

"I won't," said Elizabeth crisply.

"Good night."

Sometimes, away from New York, people liked to imagine that there was something romantic going on between the red-haired flutist and her brooding, dark-eyed accompanist. Not a chance.

Elizabeth dreaded opening the box. Anything to delay it. Maybe she could send it back without even looking in it.

She changed out of her performance dress, a presentable gray silk number that communicated seriousness of purpose. She opened her suitcase and got into a long-sleeved flannel nightgown. The FedEx package was on the bed. She stared at it as though it were a time bomb.

What if Jim Lockhart had sent her something that would make it even harder to return the books? Something that would make it impossible to keep him out of her life? She shook the box. Not books or CDs. The shape and weight were wrong. Certainly not flowers or candy.

Marshalling her courage, she pulled the tab, but it came off in her hand. Why were FedEx boxes so hard to open? She took a pair of fingernail scissors out of her bag and cut along the top. All she could see inside was a brilliant malachite color shimmering through a white gauze of tissue paper. She picked up the envelope, then put the note aside without reading it. She pulled off the tissue paper. A dress so well packed that there wasn't a wrinkle in it. A lady's maid in a Harriet Mueller couldn't have done better. She laid it out on the bed.

The fabric was ravishing. A green Venetian silk, thick enough to hang gracefully but light and smooth to the touch. The neck had a modest curve, and the top was sleeveless, perfect for playing in concert. Not too tight around the middle. She'd have plenty of room to breathe, but the skirt wasn't so big that it would make a swishing sound. The color was just right. People would say she'd picked it out to match her eyes. He knew the exact color. How could he?

Elizabeth opened the envelope and read:

> *To the most brilliant of flutists,*
> *You take my breath away.*
> *You are the one and only.*
>
> *Love, Jim*

No! she wanted to shriek in the room. How could he have used that phrase? What was he thinking? *I'm not your One and Only. That's someone else.*

He was imagining a relationship beyond anything she could give. Impossible. She wanted to pick up the dress and throw it across the room in fury. She tried to convince herself that it was the wrong size. Surely he had made some mistake.

She slipped out of her nightgown and put on the beautiful silk dress, willing it to be wrong. Completely wrong. Give her a mirror. That was one thing that motel rooms always seemed to have too many of. Mirrors. She hoped she looked foolish in it. Laughable. She turned to the mirror, challenging it to make the dress ugly.

It was perfect. She held her arms up as if to play the flute. Perfect. More extravagant than anything she would ever buy or that anyone had ever bought for her.

Why? she asked herself. Why did he feel the need to do it? Why couldn't it have been a box of chocolates? Why not a bouquet of flowers from FTD? What was he trying to say?

She picked up the flowers that had been given to her at the theater and put them in the ice bucket on top of the bureau. Walking around in the green dress, she felt like a movie star from the thirties. Greta Garbo or Jean Harlow. The way they wore long dresses as though they had a whole wardrobe of them. Elizabeth couldn't get the zipper all the way up the back, but she could still walk around in the motel room like a princess.

She put the fingernail scissors back in the cosmetic bag. She sat in front of one of the mirrors and took off her makeup. She brushed her teeth. She should call him and say no. She should send the whole thing back. But when she looked in the mirror, she wanted to keep the dress. She wanted to say yes. She knew what Dorothy would say. That it was a sign. That she and Jim were meant to be.

Well, Dorothy was wrong. Because Jim wasn't really interested in her. He was just replaying the love of his life and recasting the leading part. Using the same lines too. A lot of originality in that!

She heard Eric in the next room watching a talk show. The voices reverberated through the walls. Tomorrow they would drive all day. They would discuss Bach, Scarlatti, Vivaldi, and Gluck. No one but Eric ever discussed Gluck. He would never once ask about the FedEx box.

He wouldn't even feel compelled to discuss her performance the night before. They would navigate across a cold, dry stretch of America, and she would be grateful to be completely out of touch, far from a man who thought she was the world.

WEDNESDAY NIGHT Jim didn't hear from her. And Thursday he knew she'd be on the road. He checked the itinerary on his desk. There was no phone number for Thursday. She and her accompanist would stop at some motel on the way. Maybe she'd call from there.

"Any calls for me?" he asked Lisa.

"Only the ones you took," his assistant said.

"Any others?"

"No."

"Thanks."

Nan came in. Time to reconnoiter at the end of the day. She sat, as usual, on the armrest of the chair opposite his desk. "You keep checking for calls. Anyone in particular?"

"An agent."

"I have never known an agent not to return your calls," she replied. She looked at him out of the top of her eyes, as though she were peering over a pair of reading glasses.

"Maybe it's someone we want to come back for another interview. I want to make sure she got the message."

"Actors and actresses and models call you back, Jim Lockhart. Everybody returns your phone calls."

"There might be someone who didn't get my message. Sometimes answering machines don't always work. You can't always trust the phone company."

"Where's the flutist?"

"Who?" asked Jim, innocently enough.

"Is she in New York?"

"Did I tell you about her?"

"Yes. And your manner tells me even more about her."

"She's on a recital tour. Somewhere out in the Midwest or West. I'm not sure."

"Then why do you have her itinerary sitting right there on your desk?"

Jim blushed. "So I do."

"You didn't do what I said."

"Nan, I do everything you say. That's how our working relationship thrives. I follow your every order. And you follow mine."

"You didn't buy her chocolates or flowers."

"Flowers wouldn't last, and she wouldn't take chocolates on a concert tour."

"What did you buy her?"

Jim looked sheepish. "A dress."

Nan clicked her tongue. "A dress? What kind of dress?"

"Green. Silk. Something for her to perform in. It'll be perfect."

"How do you even know it'll fit?"

"I know sizes. I'm good at figuring out women's sizes. Hazard of the profession. Don't tell anyone."

"How many times have you gone out with this woman?"

"Once and once we had dinner with her best friend." It wasn't worth explaining that the best friend was Dorothy Jane Hughes, who'd just acted in a commercial produced by Babcock, Crier, and Nelson. "We went to the museum too, and we went skating once."

"If a man I'd gone out with only a couple of times sent me a dress, I'd seriously think he'd gone mad."

"I have. I'm crazy about her. Why can't I show it?"

"A card. A telegram. A phone call. Flowers, remember. But a dress makes you look like Svengali. You're trying to control her, shape her. You're being her manager and agent, and it's not your role. She's not someone you've just cast for a commercial. You're not her boss."

"It's a present."

"How much did you spend?"

"The money is immaterial."

"Probably more than you've ever spent on a girl before."

"It's what I wanted to do."

172

"Have you heard from her?"

"Not yet."

"Then call her. You can apologize. Say it was some foolish whim."

"She's on the road. I don't know where she is going to be tonight. It's not on the itinerary. I have to wait for her to call."

DOROTHY JANE Hughes did not have any of Elizabeth's compunctions about reading something that was not meant for her. She'd spent a dreary afternoon and evening temping at a law firm. Five hours at a reception desk, saying so many names into a phone that she wondered why law firms didn't just give their companies acronyms. In between she read boring back issues of *People* magazine. Nothing dated faster than gossip.

At home she switched on the TV, took a hot bath, heated up some Chinese takeout from her refrigerator, and sat down with the two volumes of Harriet Mueller she'd picked up from Mrs. Halladay.

It surprised her how hard it was to make sense of the purple handwriting. The paragraphs didn't fit neatly on the page. She'd get a couple of sentences at a chapter heading, then skip to the next for more, and then to the next for more. It was almost as though the woman had wanted to put her messages into some code. Who else but a devoted husband would go through the trouble of deciphering them?

Dorothy had to transcribe what she read just to get the sense of it. She worked through one volume, then the next to see which one went first. She started to understand why Elizabeth had found it so compelling. These were heartfelt words. Everything about them was unveiled. If she'd been acting them, she'd say half of the lines with tears in her eyes. The woman was speaking from the heart.

> *Darling,*
>
> *I can't put my finger on just where things went wrong. Maybe it was after we made that agreement at the restaurant. Who could know that I would be so successful? Suddenly everything I touched was gold. Fool's gold.*

I couldn't refuse. Don't you understand that? I had to do that movie. I had to go out to Hollywood to do that pilot. I had to be on the soap. You'll think I'm lying when I say I did it for you. The clock was ticking. It was my turn. I wanted you to be so proud of every achievement. I wanted you to be smiling in the audience. When I was on tour and you couldn't be there, I imagined you. I pictured you in the face of every man in the audience. It's what saved me from being unfaithful. I was being a radiant star for you.

I should have known that it ate you up. I should have seen that. The job wore you out. You were miserable at the beginning. I saw that but couldn't admit it. I had only my five years. I had to make the most of them. For us. That was the agreement. Don't you understand? It was for us.

Agreement? What agreement? And why five years? It seemed to prove what she always said. Actors and actresses who played opposite each other on stage shouldn't try to marry. Nothing could live up to their idealized onstage passion. Dorothy opened two packs of soy sauce and dumped it on her rice.

It was the dress that made me realize how bad things were for you. I'd been so wrapped up in being a success, making the career work, I hadn't been paying attention. Then came the dress. Something so stupid and small. I needed a dress to go to the Tony Awards ceremony. We both knew I wasn't going to get any award, but it was so important for me to make a great impression. I wanted something lavish. Something completely over the top.

When you said we couldn't afford it, I should have listened. I could afford it. I could have paid for it ten times, and we wouldn't have noticed. The money was flowing. Finally. But that's not what you meant. I realize that now. I'm sorry. I can't tell you how sorry I am. You were thinking about freedom. Your freedom. The future. I had no idea how much you wanted it to be your turn.

Sacrifice. You sacrificed for me. You put your life on hold for me. You've had to do it again since I've been sick. And as much as I hope to get well, I fear that it will only be more months of sickness. More chemo. More radiation. More misery.

Darling, I'm so sorry. The dress didn't mean anything to me. I shouldn't have insisted. I should have gone to the Tonys in jeans. I told myself I was doing it for you. For us. I owe you a thousand Italian suits and ties and perfect cotton shirts. All for a stupid dress. I'm sorry.

Dorothy went back and forth between the pages to find out if there was more to it than the dress. She decided that the woman bought the dress and wore it and "darling" was peeved.

The writing in the second book was about some sort of performance.

You came to everything I ever did. You saw the worst and the best. I hate to think of some of the awful things you sat through. Loyalty. Your great virtue. You are so loyal. The worst of it was, though, I took you entirely for granted. I couldn't do an opening night without you in the audience. I never looked for you until the final curtain, but I could tell you were there. You have no idea how identifiable the rustle of a program is. I heard your cough, your laugh, your chortle, your sighs. Remember Phantom? Five thousand people—and I could hear you cough.

I couldn't always see you when the curtain went up. But I always knew where your seat was. I looked in that direction. Do you realize that? Didn't you know that I was bowing to you? Flirting with you? I loved flirting on stage, knowing you were in the house. What a dreadful flirt I was. But it was only because I knew that you took me seriously. On stage I could pretend to be in love when the one who really loved me was watching all along. (Please say you were jealous!)

"A real coquette," Dorothy said out loud.

Then one night you weren't there. It shouldn't have mattered. It wasn't a great play. I was only doing it as a favor to the director.

some nice people in the show. We had a good time afterward, hanging out. You didn't seem to mind how late I came home. You were good enough to wait up for me.

Opening night. I listened for your cough, your laugh, your sigh. It was a small theater. I could have heard it all—seen it all. A minute into my first scene I realized you weren't there. OK, so later I got the message. Much later. What was it? A dinner with clients? A presentation for the boss?

The problem was, we never had a scene. We behaved perfectly. Dignified, in fact. Wasn't I understanding? Didn't you think me the model of the tolerant wife? Weren't we the modern couple? You explained and I understood. You saw the play the next night; I asked you about business. We were fine.

What a joke! We weren't fine at all. I was miserable. Couldn't you tell? For the first time I thought I'd lost you. I wanted to reverse the clock. I wanted to stop all this acting nonsense. I just wanted to go back to us being us, but I couldn't. It was too late. Too many people were dependent on me, and I wasn't strong enough. I couldn't say no. I didn't have the courage.

I kept on telling myself that I was doing what I was doing for us. That every success was ours. That you should have been as proud as I was over every accomplishment. What a laugh! We forgot how to care for each other. We should have fought. I could have cried. But I didn't. It was wrong.

That's what I'm most sorry for. Not telling you how hurt I was. Never letting on about all the hurt after that. Something died, and I couldn't bring it back to life.

I'm trying now. I hope by the time you read this I will have succeeded. I hope you remember how much I loved you and will always love you. I have to believe that we can make our love come back.

Dorothy closed this volume, not sure if she would share its contents with Elizabeth at all.

TWENTY-FOUR

ELIZABETH FOUND the landscape incredibly bleak. Everything was brown. The grass was brown, trees were brown, the pickups they passed were brown. Houses were brown, and the ghost towns were light brown, bleached by wind and snow. The only color was in the sky. A bottomless blue, but otherwise the feeble winter sun was incapable of adding color to anything it touched.

Eric drove first, which was a mistake. Elizabeth thought he would have less time to talk. On the contrary. He insisted on talking music, and it only made his driving worse. At a speed of eighty miles an hour, he'd go on about the court of Louis XIV. Suddenly he'd slow down to forty-five to demonstrate the proper ornamentations for a Rameau piece. And this in the fast lane! What if he should do a dramatic demonstration of a Gluck aria with an eighteen-wheeler behind him? Elizabeth promised herself she would never let him do any highway driving again.

"We'd better get some gas at the next exit," she suggested.

"We've got half a tank."

"You never know where the next station will be."

"I love driving here. So much better than the Jersey Turnpike. There's nobody on the road."

"Maybe you can let me try."

"I was thinking about the composer Lully . . ."

Her dress was in the trunk. She'd wrapped it up so that it could be shipped. All she needed to find was a FedEx drop-off location. She imagined a dusty Western town like the ones in cowboy movies with a dirt road and an orange and gray FedEx shop on the main drag, right next to the general store. What she hadn't anticipated was how few towns there were, let alone FedEx shops.

"Lully wasn't really all French, and that's something you can hear in his music," Eric said. "It's an Italian name, and the baroque derives from the Italian. Even Bach got stuff from the Italians. What's amazing is how Lully managed to make something French out of his music composed at Versailles . . ."

Elizabeth put her foot to the floor, braking unconsciously. "You're getting too close to that truck."

Eric didn't even appear to hear her. "His music isn't performed all that often anymore, but he's one of the truly great ones. You'll see his name inscribed at the top of the Garnier Opera in Paris. Part of their pantheon, lowercase *p*—"

She interrupted. "Can we get off at the next exit?"

Maybe they'd come to a town with a post office. She'd mail the dress back express delivery. It'd get there just as fast. There had to be a post office somewhere.

Eric went on. "You should look into the French flute repertoire. There's a lot more there than most people realize. Rampal played some of it—some of it dreadfully—but he didn't dig deep enough. A flutist like you could do more with it."

Jim knew her taste. He had chosen a dress more sophisticated, more glamorous, and more expensive than any she would buy, but it was exactly what she would have wanted if she had the nerve. Somehow he'd seen into her soul. Her deepest *Vogue* magazine moment.

"I was thinking that you looked very good last night," Eric said.

"What?" The non sequitur took her by surprise.

"You're really very pretty. With your red hair and fair skin, standing in front of an audience, you make a very good impression." He said it as though it were a historical fact, like the operas of Gluck. "It adds to your charm when you perform. The audience sees this striking Pre-Raphaelite beauty, and then they hear music that is otherworldly."

Elizabeth stared straight ahead. He was tailgating an eighteen-wheeler. "Thank you."

"Three hundred years ago they cared about how music looked too,

178

not just how it sounded. Writers spoke of what singers looked like. In our age we think the more serious a musician is, the more solemn the clothes. That's why I think you need a different dress."

"What?" She raised her voice.

"Green, I'd say. It would match your eyes and go with the red hair. Give your audiences more to look at. It will affect your playing in small ways. You'll look out at a concert and see more of them looking back at you. Green silk, I'd say."

She was dumbfounded. "Have you been talking to anyone about this?"

"It's just my professional opinion. I don't consult with any other experts, unless they're musicologists in fields I'm less familiar with. The best ones have a way of amplifying what knowledge you have . . ." Eric was back on his arcane musical topics.

And Elizabeth was more certain than ever that she had to send back the dress. "Green's wrong for me. Too obvious."

"Maybe at a dinner party, but not on stage," Eric threw in. "The bold gesture always works, as long as it's tasteful. Men know these things better than women. It takes a man to dress a woman."

"An arrogant man," she muttered.

⌘

"CAN WE talk?" Nan asked.

"Anytime you want," Jim said.

They weren't in the office but at a boring, slick, orchids-on-the-table restaurant Jim had chosen. The walls were shiny and black, the pictures were bland and tropical, and the waiters were impersonal. Dinner was Nan's idea. They'd finished their main course but were only getting to the main subject.

"I've been worried about you."

"So you've said."

She rushed on. "This is different than before. I used to be worried that you were closing yourself off from the world. Now I think you're going after it all wrong. You're like a teenager with your first crush."

179

"Sometimes I feel like a teenager." He gave her his best boyish grin. "Nan, I used to think life was forever. That there was loads of time. That I could do everything I wanted if I did it all slowly. I don't think that anymore."

"But if you rush into everything, you'll never be able to do half of what you want. You'll spoil it."

"How will I know until I try?"

Their waiter, dressed all in black, came to their table and recited the dessert menu like a Disney robot. Perfectly polished and with no charm. He looked at them both hopefully, as though he were waiting to be told that he'd earned the part. "I'll come back," he concluded.

"Why did we choose this place?" Nan asked.

"There was another restaurant here when I came with Lois."

"Better than this, I hope."

"I wanted to be reminded of it," he said. "I didn't want to forget it."

"You're going to make a big mistake," she warned.

He leaned back in his chair. "I'd rather act boldly and make a big mistake than be too careful and never know."

"Flowers would have been fine," Nan insisted.

❧

IT WAS Friday morning, and Jim still hadn't heard. He didn't know where Elizabeth had spent the night. He had no phone number. He'd made one call to FedEx to see if anyone had signed for the package. He was reassured that it had been delivered to Elizabeth's motel and signed by the desk clerk. He tried to convince himself that he didn't expect to hear from her. When she returned to New York, they'd go to a ball at the Waldorf or the Plaza and she'd show off the dress.

But what if his estimates of her size had been wrong? Perhaps she'd been insulted. He'd misjudged the height, say, or the waist. It was never good to guess that a woman was larger than she truly was.

At the gym he did an extra set of crunches and an extra set of pull-ups. He did fifty push-ups like a marine at boot camp. He'd already worked up a healthy sweat by the time he got to the weight machines.

Jesus Christ, have mercy upon me. Make haste to help me. Rescue me and save me. Let thy will be done in my life.

He was out of touch. What did he know about dating anymore? It had been too many years. He thought of his first dinner with Elizabeth. He'd talked too much about himself. Why had he wanted to give her his whole life story?

Bicep curls would make him feel better. They always made him feel better. Bicep curls were like cleaning the dishes or scrubbing the bathroom sink. Instant gratification. You could see the difference. It didn't last much longer than clean dishes or a clean sink, but you could feel it in your arms. "Beach muscles," his high-school PE teacher called them. They did no good for you on the ball field or in the gym, but they'd make you look good on the beach.

What nonsense! What kind of girl just went for a guy's biceps?

"Jimbo," Scott said, "got a hot date this weekend? Crunching iron to show off?" This time his T-shirt said eBay.

"A quiet weekend at home with the TV."

"You think I'll really believe that?"

"A new reality show."

"You're living it. The bachelor life."

Was he living it? For the first time in over fifteen months he was truly interested in going out with a woman, and he had nothing to distract him from it. He hadn't scheduled himself to see any theater or cabaret acts or independent films with up-and-coming actors showing off.

He put down the barbell. "Scott," he asked, "if there was a girl you were really interested in and she was halfway across the country, would you go there to see her?"

"If I had enough frequent-flyer miles." Scott put another forty-five-pound weight on the bench press.

"I'm serious, now. Would you travel there to see her? Would you surprise her if you hadn't heard from her in a few days?"

"Girls love surprises."

"What if she's working? Wouldn't that be an unpleasant surprise?"

"Your call, buddy. If she's not glad to see you, she's not worth crossing the street for."

Scott slid onto the bench. "Spot me on this."

"Sure."

He grunted as he lifted. "Just go."

"What?"

"We're tired of seeing you mope around here." *Pant, pant.* "You've got it pretty bad, and nothing's going to make things better until you see her. Go."

Jim waited while Scott struggled with the weight at the end of the set, then asked, "You've noticed?"

Rescue me and save me. Let thy will be done in my life. Was this the answer? Was *she* the answer to what he'd been looking for ever since Lois had died? The meaning behind his existence that seemed so elusive? The *something* that would make him want to get out of bed every day?

"The whole gym has been talking about it. We'll take up a collection for you. Go."

The girl at the reception desk who handed out towels gave her own benediction. "Enjoy," she said as he left.

HE WANTED to see her in the dress. That was the extent of it. He wanted to see her on stage with the lights on her, a pianist behind her, the flute held up to her lips, and the dress falling in luxurious waves around her. He wanted to feel the audience falling in love with her as he had fallen in love with her when she was playing.

The itinerary sat on his desk, the names of cities and theaters calling to him like sirens on a South Sea isle. He clicked on the Internet and checked Boise. There was no direct route from New York City. He'd have to go to Denver and fly from there. He checked the departure times and his schedule for the day. Even if he canceled his afternoon appointments, he would barely make Boise for the opening notes of the "Shepherd's Song."

Nan came by to give him a rundown of some new commercials on a mouthwash. All the people the director would want to see.

"Should I go to Boise?" he asked in the middle of their discussion.

"No," she said. "You don't know her that well."

"But how will I ever get to know her if I stay here?"

"She'll be back in New York soon enough. You can pick up where you left off."

"I'd like to see her perform."

"You can see her perform in New York."

"It wouldn't be the same," he said. "She rarely does solo work here."

"OK, then go," she said, giving up. "You need to figure out who she is to you. But don't surprise her. A woman doesn't want a surprise unless it involves jewelry."

"All I've got is an itinerary. She doesn't have a cell phone with her."

"Leave a message at the hotel."

"That I'm coming? She won't know what to think."

Nan put down the folder she was carrying and looked Jim in the eye. "She won't know what to think when she sees you."

"Nan, I want her to know that I really care. I don't want to hold back. I have to say everything. There's not a moment to waste." He thought of Lois and how fast it had gone. There were too many wasted moments. He wanted things to be different this time. He wanted to *be* different.

"I hope you're not disappointed."

"How can I be?"

Jim felt a burst of energy. A new hope for the future. If he stepped out and took a risk, could wonderful things happen? For him? For Elizabeth? Was there such a thing as a second chance? A way not to go back, but to go forward—and do things right? Could this be what the prayer was really all about? What Lois had known he would need to do, when he was ready?

"Cancel all my afternoon meetings," he told Lisa.

His words sounded right out of show biz. Yes, cancel the auditions and interviews and meetings. None of it was really that important. He could pick it all up on Monday. Cancel the advertising business for an afternoon. It changed completely every forty-eight hours anyway. There'd be new disasters on Monday.

"Everything?" Lisa asked.

"Yes," he said. "I have to make a quick trip out of town. Nan, you can handle things on your own."

"I'll do my best," she said.

By noon he was taking a taxi to LaGuardia.

THE VENUE in Boise was a school auditorium, as different from the charming old opera house in Cheyenne as it could be. Signs painted on butcher paper hung from the ceiling saying, Go, Tigers! Beat the Bucks! Plaques on one wall honored the top scholars since 1967, the year the place had been built. The walls themselves were hospital green, and the seats were upholstered in what must have been jade green but was now a dirty yellow. The trophies in the trophy case were a tarnished lot.

By some perverse accident the acoustics of the place were superb. Precise for instruments, lush for the voice. You could hear a pin drop on stage from the last seat in the house. Connoisseurs in town called it the Carnegie Hall of the West. Musicians from around the world asked their agents to book them into Boise just so they could try it out.

Elizabeth played a few notes from the stage. The acoustics *were* superb. Nothing sounded muddy. The runs and trills were crisp and lyrical. Not dull and clinical. As she rehearsed that afternoon, the sound reminded her of singing in the shower. The music went out to the house, then came back, improved.

Good thing, she thought, because she was still in turmoil about the dress. She and Eric had spent the night on the road in a motel outside Soda Springs, Idaho. They had seen a store with a FedEx sign in the window—and half a dozen other signs. By then Elizabeth couldn't bring herself to send it back. It was a gift. Returning it by mail would be unforgivably rude. She'd take it back with her on the plane and deliver it to Jim by hand, thanking him, but saying . . . what?

Saying it wasn't appropriate? Even that sounded lame.

She was glad of the night off from performing. She had stepped back from the vulnerability of the limelight. How nice it was to be anonymous in front of a blaring TV with a slice or two of pizza for dinner. No makeup on, her hair a mess. She hung the dress up on the back of the door of the motel room. It was like a second person in the room, asking her who she really was. The glamorous flutist or the frump in her long-sleeved nightie? She put it back in the box so she wouldn't have to listen to it or look at it.

Now that she was in Boise she was glad to see that the color of the dress was wrong for the hall. "It'll clash with the green walls," she told herself. "It'll be completely wrong."

She played a few more notes, then put her flute away.

The girl at the front desk of the Boise motel gave her a cryptic message, saying that a friend had called.

"Dorothy," Elizabeth assumed. Dorothy could wait. Elizabeth needed a long bath, an hour in front of the mirror to do her face and hair, and another hour to go over the program in her head. One night off and she had an irrational fear that she had forgotten the whole thing.

She had to become bigger than the Elizabeth who worried about other people's opinions and her reputation and what was the right thing to do. She had to become the vessel for the music. She would be putting an audience in touch with the immortals. Bach, Scarlatti, Mozart.

If I wear the green dress, she told herself, *it will have nothing to do with James B. Lockhart Jr. or how he thinks I should look on stage. It will be the right thing for the music.*

She stepped out on stage that night, looking ravishing. After a cordial round of applause, without a piece of music in front of her, she lifted up her flute and began her solo concert.

Twenty-Five

JIM'S PLANE was late landing in Denver. He missed his connection to Boise and barely made the second flight. He had to run all the way down one long hall to a pair of flight attendants who were about to close the door. Good thing he had no checked luggage. All he had was a bag with his sweaty gym clothes, a change of underwear, his toothpaste, and shaving stuff.

The only car he could find to rent was a huge Lincoln Continental. He felt like a chauffeur, ready to take a pair of local teens to the prom. He drove to her motel, a low-slung building with a Western motif. His room was decorated with cedar shingles, Lincoln Log furniture, and a moose head. The glass eyes stared at him suspiciously. At the front desk he got directions on how to get to the concert, but on the road he got hopelessly lost. Twice he was headed out of town before he found the high school.

The concert was well underway when he entered the lobby of the auditorium. Two ladies were counting ticket stubs, and two younger men in tuxedo shirts were pouring apple cider into plastic cups. He wished they had been serving baked potatoes at intermission. Isn't that what Idaho was famous for?

"I'd like one ticket," he said.

"The concert's almost half over," said the woman behind the cashbox.

"I'd still like to hear it."

The woman bit her bottom lip, as if trying to decide if she should charge him half price for only half the music.

"Gloria," her companion said, "give him a ticket at the full rate."

"That'll be forty dollars," said Gloria.

"Worth every cent," her companion insisted.

186

His heart pounding, his breath slowing, he stepped into the back of the house. With eyes barely adjusted to the dark, he couldn't see anything but the stage. If he moved, he'd trip over a seat or an usher.

All he saw was the beautiful red-haired flutist, her head cocked to one side, the silver sheath of her instrument catching the light, her music coming in a flurry of notes. It was the last movement of a concerto, with the pianist playing the orchestral part. The flute was spinning a dizzying melody above the accompaniment. The audience seemed to be on the edge of their seats, whipped along the music's jagged path—except for one dozing art patron in an aisle seat.

At last Jim's eyes traveled from her red hair and fair skin to . . . a plain gray dress. The outfit of a frumpy musician. Not a star.

Jim felt sick. He would head home on the next flight. The trip had been a fool's errand. Some romantic fantasy of his overheated imagination. Nan had said no about the dress. His heart had said yes. He should have listened to Nan. Paralyzed with remorse, he stood rooted in the lobby at intermission and listened to the audience. Not the people talking about real estate or fishing. The people talking about Elizabeth.

"Sure can play," said one fellow in cowboy boots. "Pretty too."

"Makes you want to take her home and give her a good meal."

Boise was small enough that everybody seemed to know each other. Piano teachers and band directors. Prosperous-looking boosters and small-town grandees. Parading the civic pride that said, "Someone would come all the way out from New York to play for us."

The conversations made Jim feel incredibly lonely. Why didn't he have any buddies to discuss fishing trips with or golf games? He didn't even have a wife. All he had was a job and an empty apartment.

A wallflower, he stood with his back to the trophy case and watched. One elderly lady smiled at him, and he smiled back but not long enough to encourage conversation. Feeling self-conscious, he thrust his hands in his pockets. The only person he knew was on stage, and by the looks of it she wouldn't be glad to see him.

One fellow in a tuxedo shirt walked through the lobby ringing a cowbell. Intermission was over. People threw back their heads to finish their cider. Those who had gone outside for a frigid smoke crushed their cigarette butts against the wall and flicked them into the snow. They hurried into the auditorium to hear more beautiful music. Jim stayed back in the lobby.

A lady who was collecting empty cups walked by and said amiably, "Aren't you going to hear the rest of the concert?"

"I'll wait here," he said.

The woman who had taken his forty dollars looked up bewildered from her cashbox, as if to ask: "All that money for only one piece of music?"

The doors separating the auditorium from the lobby were now closed. Applause filtered through, sounding like distant rain on a tin roof. Her crowd was greeting her warmly. That's who she was meant for. Not an audience of one. Even if he drove his rented Lincoln back to the airport, he wouldn't be able to catch a plane to Denver and New York until morning. He was rooted to the linoleum tiles under his feet.

How he'd hoped to write a new script this time, create a new beginning. He turned to face the trophy case. All those names of students long forgotten who'd been best at tennis, best in French, tops in math, recognized by the DAR for their outstanding citizenship. One tarnished plaque honored the best actresses and best actors in each graduating class. That's the award he would have won in college. One for Lois too.

"Lois, I wanted to do it right this time," he whispered. Just like any widower still talking to his wife. Except instead of reminding her to take out the trash or balance the checkbook, he was promising to be better than the husband he'd been. He'd read somewhere that grief went on longer when the relationship wasn't resolved at death. Was any relationship ever resolved by death?

Why, he wondered, was it so hard to show love? Why, when that's all that anybody wanted to receive in this world?

He could imagine all too easily what had happened with the green dress. He was being too controlling. He was trying to play all his cards at once. He was showing off. He was moving in on turf that wasn't his own. He'd heard all the arguments before. He and Lois had had them all. Couldn't he see that there was a difference between being supportive and being intrusive? How long had he known Elizabeth?

But couldn't she see that he needed to be extravagant? He needed to go all out. He didn't want to hold back this time.

To add to his turmoil, he could hear her music through the closed doors. The low quiet parts were barely audible, like a slow wind on a summer's day, but the thrilling runs and arpeggios came stumbling through the walls and bounced around in the lobby, echoing in his heart. She was magnificent, and the applause that greeted each piece only confirmed that.

He wanted to share her triumph. He'd stand at the back of the auditorium and bask in the praise like a proud father. Why, though? He had earned none of it. The praise was hers. There was no glory in reflected glory. Only more loneliness.

He tried the old prayer: *Jesus Christ, have mercy upon me. Make haste to help me. Rescue me and save me . . .*

Then he added an addendum. *Don't let me blow it.*

The sound of a final ovation reached him. He heard her speak. The words of the spoken voice always seemed paltry after the music that had soared. She was announcing an encore. There was a bit of polite laughter from the audience at some self-deprecating remark she must have made. Then silence.

The haunting shepherd's tune came out through the doors, the song that she had played for him. The sound became louder as an usher opened a door.

Suddenly Jim wanted to look at her and see. He stepped quietly across the lobby to the doorway so he could get a good view of her on stage. The red hair, the face focused on the music, the willowy white arms holding the flute. He looked in bewildered fascination and stepped into the house. He couldn't believe it. She was just as beautiful as he expected, and then some.

And she was wearing the green silk dress.

⬿⬲⬲

ODD WHAT you could hear from the stage even in the middle of an all-absorbing piece. Elizabeth remembered a recital her mother had come to at Eastman. In the dead of a Rochester winter, with snow piled up halfway to the windows and more forecast for the next week, she had no expectation that her mother would be there. She'd actually discouraged her from coming, downplaying the whole thing. In the darkened auditorium she'd fretted over the classmates and professors who would complain about tempos and grace notes and intonation. She had a mental map of where they were sitting.

Then during the adagio of a concerto, when she was sustaining a line through a perilous three-measure passage, she heard the snapping of a purse. It came to her in a flash. She knew which purse, which dress went with it, which handkerchief her mom would be taking out of it, which pair of reading glasses went back in. She could hear her mother's quiet sniffle, and knew her mother was there. Over on the left side.

Now in the Boise auditorium, in the middle of her encore, she heard a man at the back of the house clear his throat. Although she had only known him for a short while, she was as sure of whom it was as she had been when her mother snapped the purse. She looked at the silhouette in the doorway, and her heart skipped a beat.

Her mind flew faster than her fingers. This was not the sort of interruption she needed in the middle of a concert tour. Think of all that she would have to explain.

Why she was in the green dress, which she meant to give back to him.

Why she had some books, which belonged to him.

Why she wasn't right for him.

If only she hadn't seen him in her imagination first. If only he could have retreated back to the pages of a book. Instead, Jim was as real as the man in the front row in the string tie. The one who had let out a wolf whistle when she entered on stage in the green dress.

Idaho, she thought. *Farm boys and cowboys.* She was glad they liked the way she looked. What surprised her was how the dress affected the way she played. She was just a little more willing to take risks, a little more eager to stretch a phrase or a note, willing to gamble on her breath control. Isn't that what they'd expect of a soloist in a luxurious dress?

She should have been grateful, overjoyed at seeing Jim Lockhart. But she wasn't. She dreaded talking to him, dreaded having to explain herself. She dreaded making a scene.

THE AUDITORIUM emptied out quickly, and Jim followed the line of people going backstage. He could have been back in school, with his parents waiting to see a favorite teacher.

She was radiant—like a teacher on Back-to-School night. Her arms laden with a bouquet of roses, she smiled at him where he stood at the end of the line. Then she paid all of her attention to each fan, acting as if there were no one else in the world she wanted to talk to more. Jim listened to snippets of conversation:

"That's my favorite piece. The way you played it brought tears to my eyes."

"What you did on that fast part reminded me of the recording I have, except you did it better."

"Tell me where you got this beautiful dress. It goes so well with your eyes."

"Our daughter lives in New York. Can we give you her telephone number? It would be good for her to meet a nice girl like you."

These were the music teachers and PDQ Bach listeners and fans of the Saturday afternoon Metropolitan Opera broadcasts. Jim wanted to tell everyone that he knew the flutist and that the green dress had been his brilliant idea. The Boise Friends of Music were pouring more cider in plastic cups.

Even before Jim got to the front of the line, one woman was raising her glass. "I would like to thank Ms. Elizabeth Ash for a brilliant evening of music." The voice rose in crescendos of self-satisfaction. "She has transported us to another world with her playing. Elizabeth, we thank you so much for coming all the way to Boise with your music, and giving us this delightful, memorable, spectacular concert."

A round of applause.

Elizabeth said a few words, and there was more applause.

When it was over, Jim found himself face to face with her. He kissed her cheek. "You were wonderful."

"Thanks."

"The dress looks even better than I expected."

"I'll explain." She looked down.

"You don't need to."

"When'd you get here?"

"I just flew in."

"Business?"

"I wanted to hear the concert."

An older woman whispered to another woman behind him, "He must be her boyfriend."

Elizabeth turned away from the comment and greeted another fan. As soon as the fans left, she said quickly, "I'll go change."

Jim was left with Eric.

"All I play are orchestral transcriptions," Eric was explaining. "They're not meant for piano. Sometimes I don't have enough fingers to play all the notes, and I have to minimize the accompaniment. Other times I get frustrated because I can't make a nice lyrical orchestral sound."

"I see," Jim managed to comment, but he was distracted, waiting for Elizabeth.

Elizabeth finally came out wearing jeans and a T-shirt. She was carrying her gray dress on a hanger and the green dress was in the FedEx box he'd sent it in.

Eric burst out of his usual oblivion. "The green dress was great."

"Thank you," Elizabeth said.

"You should wear it all the time when you perform. That was your best performance yet," Eric insisted.

"I'm glad you feel that way." She turned to Jim. "Where are you staying?"

"A motel outside of town. There's a big moose head in the lobby and in my room."

"It sounds like the same place we're staying."

"It is."

If she took in this fact, she didn't linger over it, Jim thought.

"Do you have a car?" she asked.

"A rental."

"Follow us."

Jim almost wished that Elizabeth and Eric were an item so he could understand why she was being so cool. She had smiled at him in the line, so she must have been glad to see him. And she had worn the dress for the second half of the concert, so his gift must have pleased her. But there was something else going on.

He followed them in his wide Lincoln to the outskirts of town. The motel sign rotated above the highway like a high-flying carousel without its horses. They parked and went into the lobby. The stuffed moose greeted them with his glazed eyes.

Eric stood between Jim and Elizabeth, like a younger brother who hasn't gotten the hint to ditch.

"Do you want anything to eat?" Jim asked Elizabeth.

"I'm really tired," she said.

"I've got some protein bars in my room," Eric offered. "If anybody wants them."

"I was thinking we could go to a restaurant," said Jim.

Elizabeth held the FedEx box in front of her like a shield. "We've got to get up early tomorrow to go to Ogden."

Jim studied her. "I'd like to talk."

"Protein bars are an excellent way to snack without adding excess fat or carbohydrates. You know, carbohydrates can be as bad as sugar and fat."

"I'm exhausted," Elizabeth said. And she did look tired.

"Maybe there's a place we could sit for a little bit," Jim suggested.

"I always take protein bars with me on tour," Eric rambled. "Otherwise it's tempting to eat a lot of junk food on the road and that just makes me more tired."

Elizabeth looked into Jim's eyes. "You've come all this way."

"I loved your concert. You were fabulous."

"It was one of our best performances."

"Especially the second half," Eric said. "When you came out in that great dress, it was like you were another person. Everything popped in the second half. Everything connected. It was completely over the top."

The expression on her face changed, as if she knew a conversation was inevitable. "Can you wait here for me? I want to leave some things in my room."

"I'll bet we can sit in the breakfast room," Jim said.

"I'm going to bed," Eric announced.

Twenty-Six

JIM HAD no reason to go up to his room. He had no luggage. Nothing but his gym bag. In the half light of the empty breakfast room he waited. He heard the elevator doors open and listened for her step. She walked into the room as though she were meeting the school principal.

"I've been terribly rude," she said. "Thank you for the dress. It's stunning. It's prettier than anything I've ever owned, but I can't keep it."

"Why not?"

"We really don't know each other well enough."

"I like you."

"I like you," she said, a note of equivocation in her voice, "but that doesn't mean you should buy really expensive dresses for me."

"Why not? You're a performer. Performers should get used to accepting all sorts of gifts from their admirers."

She compressed her lips. The light came from behind her so Jim couldn't see her face clearly. "I fear there are strings attached."

"Of course there are," he said lightly. "You should feel absolutely devoted to me because of it."

"How did you even know my size?"

"I'm good at guessing. It comes from the work I do. All the actors and models I meet in casting."

"I'm sure they're all smaller than I am."

"They come in all sizes."

"I think," she said hesitantly, "you think I'm somebody I'm not." She knew who he'd really loved. She'd read the woman's very words. She knew all about their life together and its perfection.

"When I saw you standing up there on stage I saw the most incredibly

195

beautiful woman in a stunning dress playing some beautiful music. You took my breath away," he said softly.

"In your note you called me your 'One and Only.'"

"It's a phrase."

"How can I be your One and Only? You've already told me about being married."

"My wife died nearly sixteen months ago." He could have given her the exact number of days and hours. "And you're the first woman I've met since then who seems worth going out with. You're the first I've ever wanted to spend time with or see."

"I'm flattered."

"I apologize if I've done it wrong. I'm out of practice. I haven't dated since . . . well, since I was in college. All I can remember from then is being too careful, and I don't want to be too careful this time. I thought Lois and I would have a lifetime together. We'd have fifty more years to do all the things we promised to do. It didn't turn out that way. Everything went too quickly. It makes me feel that if I don't take my chances, I'll lose out on the best thing that's come around."

"I fear I've been dishonest with you."

"How?" Had he been wrong about Elizabeth and her accompanist? Was there something alluring about Eric's long stringy hair and rambling speeches? "Is there someone else? Are you and Eric . . . an item?"

Elizabeth laughed. "No. Even if he were interested, he would drive me nuts. That's not it."

"What is?"

She took a deep breath, almost as though she were going to start a long phrase of music. "This dress, for instance. I didn't really plan on wearing it. I didn't for the first half of the concert."

"I know." Jim nodded.

"But when I came backstage at intermission and saw it in the box, well, I just knew it would be right for the music I was playing. And it was. It felt great."

"I'm glad. You looked beautiful."

"But I can't keep it. I would owe you too much because of it."

"It's just a dress."

"It cost so much."

"I thought it would make a difference. An audience sees a performer before they ever hear a note played. It would prepare them for how good you were. They'd see you at your best."

Elizabeth's eyes narrowed.

Was she upset with him? Did she think that he was trying to remake her? Tell her she needed more makeup or a different hairstyle? Had he made another error in judgment?

"I like my other dress very much," she said in a stiff tone.

"I do too. But I figured . . . well, I figured that if you could afford it, you'd go for something even nicer. I'm not trying to run your life. You should make all your own decisions about performing and what to wear on stage and what's right. But when you and I walked by that store and saw that pink dress, I knew what I wanted to get you. I didn't want to waste a moment. The chance might not come again."

"You flew out here to hear me." She appeared puzzled.

"Frequent-flyer miles. I had to cash them in. They've been piling up. Use 'em or lose 'em."

"I like to be warned before I'm surprised."

Was that fear he saw in her eyes? Or nervousness?

"But then . . . it wouldn't be a surprise." He flashed her a grin.

"I guess not."

"I wanted to hear you perform. After hearing just those three pieces in New York, I wanted to hear them in a concert. And I wanted to see how an audience responded to you." He could hear the recklessness in his voice, but he couldn't stop. He had to tell her—continue taking the risk.

"Why couldn't you have waited until I performed closer to home?"

"I didn't want to wait so long. I don't know how I can say it any clearer," he went on. "You are spectacular. You amaze me. You delight me. I think about you all the time. You're smart. You're talented. You're beautiful. I think we'd be great together. We'd have fun. We like a lot of the same things . . . and I like you. I'm falling in love with you. It's not the dress. Forget the dress. Don't get hung up on it. It's you."

He'd said it now. What more could he add?

Elizabeth was looking down at the floor. "You don't know me. I think you expect far more of me than I can ever deliver. All those nice compliments . . . I can't live up to them. I'm not all those things."

"You are to me."

She ran the back of her hand across her face. Jim could tell in the darkness that she was crying.

"I don't want to hurt you, but no."

"What can I do to convince you otherwise?" he pleaded.

He dreaded hearing that horrid phrase—the cliché that had to be avoided at all costs: *"Can't we just be friends?"* Better that she remained silent.

"Do you even want to see me again?" he asked.

"Sure," she said, sounding straightforward and honest. "Maybe we could go out with Dorothy sometime. She likes you too. I mean, not like this, but as a friend."

"Could we go out for dinner again?"

"Maybe."

"I hope there's some favor I can do for you." He didn't want to cry. He couldn't let her off the hook. He loved her. She was the best thing that had happened to him. It couldn't be over like this. She had worn the dress, after all.

"I don't know."

"Because you have done a huge favor for me."

"Oh." It seemed like she could barely speak.

He held her gaze with his warm brown eyes. "You have made me feel alive again, Elizabeth. After fifteen months—more than fifteen months—of feeling that my life would never happen again, that I'd be forever in this dull place where everything was gray, I met you. And I could see for the first time that there would be something new for me. I wouldn't be repeating the same old scripts and patterns. I would be creating something new."

"I'm glad I could be helpful," she said in a measured tone.

"These past few weeks have been wonderful. Just thinking about you has been wonderful."

"Good."

Any moment she'd get up, and it would be all over. All the dreaming and hoping—and praying. Yes, praying.

"Thanks for that." He stood up, as if he knew she couldn't take talking much longer.

She rose too. Jim kissed her on the cheek.

"Good night," she said.

⸎

ELIZABETH'S ROOM in the motel was done up in an Indian motif. There were paintings of wide-eyed Indian children in teepees framed on the walls, the bedspread was printed like an Indian blanket, and the chair was painted with Indian symbols. They could have been hiero-glyphics or ancient Sumerian script for all Elizabeth cared.

The evening had turned into a disaster in a few short minutes. She couldn't get over the feeling that she'd done something terribly wrong, but she couldn't imagine having done things differently. If she had writ-ten down a list of all the qualities she wanted in a man, surely James B. Lockhart Jr. would have met every qualification. He was generous, kind, romantic, funny, earnest, sensitive, confident, warm, cultured, good-looking, and successful.

It wasn't him. It was her. The wife. The woman who wrote in the purple ink. Elizabeth couldn't be a paragon like that. She could never give so devotedly. She'd tried before and it hadn't worked.

His One and Only.

She put on her nightgown and picked up the book she'd brought for the trip. A novel to pass the time when trying to sleep in a dreary motel room like this one. It was meant to take her back to an era when men courted their women with fine words and extravagant gestures.

Like a green silk dress.

She'd come to the moment in the plot where the hero and heroine had a misunderstanding because of two letters that got lost in the post and then were found too late. Page 234 with another 83 to go. Elizabeth didn't even need to look ahead to know that things would work out all right. The hero would demonstrate that he was a changed man, not the rake he appeared, by doing some kind, generous thing, and the heroine would realize that the gallant man in black was really a smarmy thug only interested in her money. At the last moment, the hero and heroine would get together. It was guaranteed.

Why couldn't life be like that? She'd always thought that if two people were meant for each other, as Dorothy believed, then no matter what happened, some force would make sure they got together. Now just the opposite seemed to be happening. Reason would argue for James B. Lockhart. But reason didn't convince her heart.

Elizabeth slammed the paperback shut and hurled it across the room. It hit the wall with a *thud* and knocked down the painting of a wide-eyed Indian maiden. They both crashed to the floor. She should have been shocked and horrified, but she wasn't. She was tired of every romantic notion she had ever read. They were a sham. Life was so much more difficult. People were so much more complicated.

Pulling the pillow over her head, she cried. There was nothing else to do. She wept into the rough motel sheets, muffling the sound. She didn't want anyone to hear her.

VERONICA HALLADAY woke up at midnight in her large apartment overlooking the Hudson River. She thought perhaps it had been Mr. Halladay's snoring that had awakened her. But no. He was sleeping silently in his striped Brooks Brothers pajamas, one hand over his chest. She listened in the dark for any sounds down on Riverside Drive. A car alarm or maybe the rumble of the garbage truck making a late pickup. All was quiet.

Then she became aware of what had awakened her. The Thrift Shop. Where others worried late at night about bonds falling or the rise of the dollar, Veronica Halladay worried about secondhand things. She had once had a conversation with her pastor, fearing that her obsession for used knickknacks was unhealthy. She had explained how she sometimes prayed that a pair of brass andirons or a set of fine tea towels or even a slim volume of poetry found the right owner. She said she was convinced it was a matter of God giving new life to old things. Her pastor, bless him, had told her there was nothing wrong with that. It was just another way of praying for people—for good to come into their lives. And God knew we all needed more of that kind of prayer. Mrs. Halladay had rested easier after that.

Well, it was a set of paperback books that woke up Mrs. Halladay this time. Harriet Mueller paperbacks. Mrs. Halladay could see the striking beauty with red hair and fair skin who had held the books so lovingly. She remembered Dorothy, the shorter friend who had come to pick up the books. She could also picture the handsome, tall young man who had asked for the books himself. She saw again the sorrow in his brown eyes—like the sorrow found in a chipped mug or a tarnished silver tray. Something that was missing a bit of itself. Something that had some of its beauty rubbed off its soul.

There was sadness in the redhead too. Was it the books that had made her sad, or did they relieve the sadness? She couldn't tell.

Mrs. Halladay thought of the two young people who had shown up, like used goods, at the Thrift Shop door. Most of the things donated just needed a bit of love and affection. With a dust rag, glue, polish, and elbow grease they could shine. All they needed was a new home. Plenty of people had found precious keepsakes at Christ Church.

But what could the Thrift Shop do when the people themselves seemed like castoffs? When she could feel the sadness seeping from their souls? Was there some way she could help?

Mrs. Halladay turned to her side. "Lord, about the redhead and the handsome young man—two people with sad eyes—would you help them find what they are searching for? Please?"

And as she attempted to go back to sleep, her thoughts mulled over the reason God had awakened her in the middle of the night. Was there some additional role she was supposed to play? Something to bring those two secondhand people together?

TWENTY-SEVEN

DOROTHY DIDN'T expect to hear from Elizabeth on tour. Elizabeth would be busy enough performing. In the meanwhile Dorothy saved up things to talk about. The purple ink messages she'd read, the auditions she was going on, the boring temp job, the phone call she wanted to make to James B. Lockhart but didn't out of extreme discretion. Dorothy had so many speeches saved up that, at one o'clock, when the phone finally rang, she assumed it had to be Elizabeth.

"Coming, Lizzie," she yelled to the phone.

One o'clock. That would mean eleven o'clock mountain time. Lizzie's concert and the reception afterward would be finished by now. The accolades would have been received. She'd be back at her motel and ready to dish.

"'Bout time you called," Dorothy said into the phone, so certain was she of the caller.

"Didn't know you had been waiting that long," said a male voice.

"Excuse me?"

"However accustomed I am to women waiting for my calls all across the globe, I'm rarely greeted with such exuberance."

She exhaled with exasperation. "Alberto."

"Good guess."

"Where are you?"

"Germany. Earning a decent wage and trying to handle the language. Too many declensions as well as the subjunctive. Who even knew there was a subjunctive?"

"How is it? Do you like the job?"

Typical Alberto Battista. To be working in Germany for months without a word and then to call out of the blue. There could be only one reason.

"Same old, same old. I don't know how many more times I can hear *Il Trovatore* sung in German. I don't know how many times I can play *Il Trovatore* for that matter. Plus *West Side Story*, in badly accented English and *My Fair Lady* in German. Can you imagine *My Fair Lady* in German?"

"Ever the musical snob."

"Don't deny me my prejudices," he tossed back. "They're all I've got."

"Do you like it there?"

"What can I say? The food's good, and the girls are beautiful. But not as beautiful as one American girl I remember."

"Elizabeth's not here," Dorothy said defensively. "She's on tour. She's in Idaho or Utah right now."

"Good for her." There was something patronizing about the way he said it, as though soloing in Boise was several notches below playing in the opera house of Dusseldorf.

"She works hard on tour."

"I know she does. Playing Bach and Scarlatti for the hoi polloi. Bringing culture to the heartland."

Dorothy grew more irritated. "Why are you calling me?"

"I had the urge to check in."

"We haven't spoken in months."

"I'm bad at sending postcards. I figured if there was anything really wrong you'd let me know."

"She's not ready to start over again." Dorothy wanted to make things clear. Cut to the chase.

"How do you know?"

"She's still feeling burned."

"It was over when I left. I wouldn't have gone if it weren't. See, that's the subjunctive. If it *weren't*."

"She's happy now," Dorothy countered.

"I'm glad she is. So am I. Deliriously happy. I told you the food was good and the girls are gorgeous. Everything's nice here in Germany. It's not a constant hustle like it is in New York. People even say please and thank you."

"You've never been one to say please and thank you. In any language."

"I've gotten manners. You wouldn't believe the difference."

The audacity of the man. The cheek—the pretensions! "I'll have to see it to believe it."

"That's why I'm coming to New York. To give you a chance. The end of next week. Look how polite I am. I'm calling to warn you."

"You should warn Lizzie too."

There was a pause, then, "This seemed safer."

Just when Dorothy wanted to think the worst of Alberto, he would say something like that. Reveal his softer side. Remind her that he had some good qualities.

"We can be friends," Alberto said. "We promised each other that. I sent her a Christmas card just to prove it. I miss Elizabeth."

"Now isn't the best time," Dorothy insisted.

"There is no best time. I have to see her. But don't tell her. Let it be a surprise."

"I don't think she's really in for surprises—," Dorothy began. But it was too late. Alberto had already hung up.

Alberto coming. Dorothy couldn't think of anything worse. Things were complicated enough already. Elizabeth looked like she was doing all right. She'd actually gone on a date with another man. She even seemed interested in him, for all Dorothy could tell.

There was no telling where things could go with Jim Lockhart. But with Alberto around . . . well, he could botch up everything. Make a complete mess of it. Swooping in from Germany, expecting to be the center of attention. Dorothy had to warn Elizabeth. Call some motel in Idaho or Utah. Get her on the phone right away.

On the other hand, what if Dorothy didn't call? What if she left things as they were? What if Alberto just turned up?

Elizabeth would have a good object lesson at hand. Alberto moping around. Alberto thinking he could just start things up again. Alberto playing for the prize. Talking, talking, endlessly talking. Wouldn't Jim Lockhart look pretty good by comparison?

Sometimes—most of the time—Dorothy liked to make things

happen. But this could be one of those times when it would be best to step back. At least for now.

No, she decided. She wouldn't call Elizabeth. Maybe, perhaps if the subject came up, she'd say something, but not yet. Not just yet.

She practiced the conversation she wished she could have with her best friend. *Lizzie, trust your feelings. Trust in a new love. Things will turn out OK if you just trust and wait.*

SATURDAY MORNING Jim was still wearing the same clothes from the night before. Elizabeth saw him at the front desk checking out. He'd called about flights, he said, and there wasn't anything out until late afternoon so he'd be stuck in Boise for several hours. She imagined him in the lobby all day, sitting beneath the stuffed moose with his gym bag in his lap. Pathetic. It surprised her how much she cared.

"We're headed to Ogden," she said. "We have a concert there tonight. Do you want to drive down with us? You could probably pick up a bus to Salt Lake City from there."

"That would be great," he said with relief. "I wasn't really looking forward to hanging out here all day."

"We've got a rental car."

"So do I."

"Come with us. You can turn yours in here."

It was easy enough to be friends.

Then she remembered the green dress. It had made such a big impact on the audience and her playing that even Eric, who was obtuse about all things other than music, had noticed. She really needed it. Would it be so bad to keep it, as a gift from a friend?

"Thanks," he said.

Elizabeth drove this time. Anything to avoid Eric driving. Jim sat in front next to her and Eric sat in back.

Eric talked for a good hour about French musical traditions in the baroque era, and neither of them had to contribute more than an "Oh, really?" or "That's amazing!" for the lecture to continue. She could feel Jim gazing at her as she stared at the road. She was glad to have Eric dominate the conversation because she didn't know what to say. Anything that came to her was far more serious than she wanted it to be. The weather was bitter cold, and the few lakes and rivers they passed were frozen solid with little houses on the ice for fishing.

"The sky is so blue you forget it's brutally cold," Jim finally said.

"Until I see a frozen lake." Then, all of a sudden, other words came to her mind:

Our season was winter. Remember sledding that night when it must have been zero degrees? Or you trying to teach me to ice skate? I was sure we were going to fall into a hole in the ice. You reassured me that the ice wouldn't melt until March. Maybe you had some sort of Hans Brinker ideas about the two of us skating around the lake. We looked more like I Love Lucy.

Elizabeth was surprised by how much she remembered. Whole passages about him. The story in purple ink had made such an impression on her.

"I like the cold," he said.

"The Hudson doesn't freeze over like this."

"It hasn't in a long time."

"You think this is cold?" Eric exclaimed. "In the late seventeenth century the weather was so cold that wine froze at the palace in Versailles. And all the canals in Holland were frozen for skating."

"Like Hans Brinker?" Elizabeth said. *Hans Brinker.*

"Exactly," Jim said, looking out the window.

"Composers modified their operas to suit the audiences," Eric continued. "Fascinating when you think about it. Even the theater took on different subjects. A playwright like Molière adapted his ideas to the cold. We don't think about it now, but imagine how you'd structure a play differently if most of the audience was freezing."

More of the purple words flooded back to her: *I remember watching you in Tartuffe. He had been in Molière back in college. It wasn't a big part. You were a servant or valet. None of the freshmen got big parts. But none of us could take our eyes off you. I couldn't. It wasn't just because you were handsome. It's because you were good.*

"Molière is hard to act," said Jim.

"You were in *Tartuffe* once."

"Did I tell you that?"

"Yes," she said, catching herself.

She was afraid to open her mouth, not sure what would come out. She could imagine him on that frozen lake playing Hans Brinker and she could see him in *Tartuffe*, an impossibly good-looking valet. How much easier it would have been to fall in love with him back then. Both of them would have their lives stretching out ahead of them, ready to be molded by their experiences. They would form natural parts of each other instead of having to remake what was already there. Their history would be shared. Now it would have to be wiped out and written over, like old script on a blackboard. Or like purple ink in the margins of a book.

"You don't see Molière plays very often," Eric said.

"I guess not."

"They're particularly hard to translate. Especially the ones in verse. Contemporary audiences don't know how to handle poetry . . ." Eric went on until he dozed off in midsentence, seemingly exhausted by his own talk.

Elizabeth and Jim were on their own. What to say? She gripped the wheel and stared at the road. "Do you like living in New York?"

"As long as you don't take it too seriously, it's a good place."

"I'm afraid I couldn't do my career in any other American city."

"You could play the flute anywhere. You attracted a good crowd here."

"But to have the variety of work I have as a freelancer. I could only do that in the New York area. And all those other things, like auditioning and getting a manager and finding different chamber groups to play with. Being in New York makes it easier."

Jim was looking at her. She could feel his eyes on her as she drove. "Tell me, if you could do all that and live elsewhere, would you?"

"Maybe. I always tell myself that I don't have to be a flutist. I could do something else."

"Like what?"

"Be a potato farmer in Idaho."

He laughed. "Onions in Colorado?"

"Or be a rancher in Utah."

"That would be a tragedy for the rest of the world."

"Why?"

"You're a really good flutist."

How much easier it would be if he weren't kind and thoughtful. If only he hadn't praised her and sounded as though he meant it. If only she hadn't known so much about him.

"Do you want to drive?"

"What about Eric?"

"No!" she whispered. "He's terrible on the highways."

"OK."

They reached Ogden in plenty of time for the concert, and Jim picked up a rental car to take to Salt Lake City. Elizabeth kissed him good-bye on the cheek with a heavy heart. She was afraid she'd never see him again.

Good friends. Could they really be friends? It seemed like she'd said good-bye to that already.

"Someday I hope I can do a favor for you," he said.

"You don't have to," she replied.

"I wish I could."

NEW YORK sucked him back into its whirlwind. Jim went to the gym first thing in the mornings and stayed late at work in the evenings. He checked out movies and shows at night that had performers he needed to get to know. Cataloguing talent—that's what he did. Nan asked how things went in Montana or Idaho or wherever it was he went. Fine, he said. They'd gone fine. But he said it in such a way that even a friend like Nan didn't ask more questions.

ONCE SHE was back, Elizabeth got a call from a flutist friend who had to go out of town because of an illness in the family. Could

Elizabeth sub for her in the pit of *Out of Mind*? It'd only be for a week. Elizabeth said sure. She could use the money. A freelance musician always needed the money. Some months, like December, there'd be too much work. Too many *Nutcracker*s and *Messiah*s. But other months, such as August and January, nothing might be going on. Better say yes to every offer.

Much harder to say yes to a man.

She was glad of the tight, claustrophobic spaces of the city. No bleak winter landscapes with clear blue sky and wide-open fields for brooding. Manhattan had only short vistas down narrow concrete canyons. Even if she'd climbed to the top of the Empire State Building, the view was obstructed by low clouds. She wouldn't have to look too far into the future. She could bury herself in work. Lessons during the day, rehearsals with the quintet, the Broadway show at night. No time to think of Jim at all.

Dorothy called late one night, but Elizabeth said she was just too tired to talk. Too tired to listen.

Then, on Thursday night, when Elizabeth was coming home from the theater, the finale of the show was stuck in her head. It was one of those facile tunes that can't be erased from the brain. The only cure was Bach. Ten minutes of Bach was the cure for everything. Humming Bach to herself, she took the two flights up and came round to the last flight. A body was slumped in her doorway.

A burglar! She'd scamper down and dial 911. Suddenly she realized she knew that figure as well as she knew her own name. The two-day growth of beard, the dark hair spilling over a broad forehead, the thick lips and thin argumentative nose, the same dark green corduroys he always used to wear when he lived in New York. Hadn't he managed to find any new clothes in Germany?

"Alberto," she whispered. She could have stepped over him without waking him.

"Hmmm."

"Alberto," she said, "wake up. It's me."

He rolled his eyes half-mast, and closed them again, smiling. "I thought you'd never come."

Twenty-Eight

"I DIDN'T have the key to your front door."

"Good thing, I really would have mistaken you for a burglar and called the police. How'd you get in?"

"Easy. Somebody propped open the front door."

She didn't want Alberto inside, but she couldn't bear to think of him sitting outside on her step. He was capable of that. Waiting all night. "Would you like some tea?"

"Thought you'd never ask." He picked up his knapsack, made of some handwoven Peruvian fabric, no doubt his link with the proletariat. Next to it was his horn case. The black leather was battered and worn, but the instrument within would be immaculate. That much could be said for Alberto. However much he neglected his hair and his clothes, his horn was always beautiful. He treated music seriously no matter what was going on around him.

He put down the horn and knapsack and sat in one of Elizabeth's folding chairs.

"Make yourself at home." Why even bother saying it? Of course he would.

"I will." He took out a pack of cigarettes.

"No smoking please."

"I forgot how puritanical Americans are about cigarettes."

"Puritanical nothing. They stink up everything." She took off her coat and put her bag down. At least the place was clean. That was something she gave herself credit for. Her place was always clean. "You could have called."

"I did."

"I never heard anything."

"I spoke to Dorothy. Figured she'd warn you. She tells you everything."

"You can't stay here," she said. *Let's get that settled early.*

"I wasn't intending to."

"What brings you back to the States?" She stepped into the kitchen to boil some water for tea.

"I was getting bored with Germany."

"What about your job?"

"Don't worry. I'm still gainfully employed. One advantage to those European countries. Once you're hired, you're on for life. You have to skip rehearsals for a week before you even get disciplined. It's not like the crazed military life of an American orchestra."

"You skipped rehearsals to come here?"

"We get this week off. The opera house is closed for renovations. I figured it was an opportunity to get in touch with my roots."

"Earl Grey or Sleepytime?" She held up the two boxes of tea.

"Earl Grey. If I can't smoke, the least I can do is get some caffeine into my system."

"Did you just land?"

"Just got into JFK."

Warning bells should have gone off with Elizabeth. Warning bells always went off when she was within twenty feet of Alberto. She'd already been successful at rooting him out of her life. She didn't want him to worm in on her territory again. She couldn't afford it emotionally.

"What do you intend to do for a week?" she asked.

"Hang out. See friends. Listen to some music. See you."

"I'm really busy this week. I've got rehearsals and teaching, and I'm playing in a Broadway show."

"Broadway?" He frowned in exquisite musical snobbery. "Why do you do it?"

"The money and the people. I enjoy the work too."

"You know you're better than that."

An old argument she'd rather skirt.

She lifted her chin. "I don't consider myself above anything. If I'm being paid for the work, I do my best to make sure I'm giving it my best."

"All to pay the bills."

"It's part of being a musician in New York," she said. "Doing a little of everything. It helps me fund the other things."

"Like what?"

"Like going on tour. I just came back from a week of concerts in the West and Midwest."

"Tell me what you played."

"Not now. It's too late."

She knew he'd want to talk about every note. He would take apart each piece musically and put it back together again. Remade and reconfigured by Alberto Battista. The sheer brilliance of his musical mind was dazzling and devastating. But tonight she was not in the mood.

"I've never met anyone who plays the flute like you. You could have a brilliant career in Europe."

"I have a very nice one here in America."

Alberto took a big gulp of tea from his cup and wiped his mouth with the back of his hand. "Lizzie, I've changed."

"Your table manners haven't."

"Lizzie, I want to get back together."

"What do you mean?" The very tone in her voice should have stopped him. But then, Alberto was always oblivious to such things.

"We were meant for each other. That's always been clear."

"Meant for each other?" She crossed her arms and dared him to challenge her.

"We balance each other out. You are lyrical. An adagio movement. Tuneful. I'm quick, biting, anything in a minor key. A major chord means nothing without a minor one. It's the contrast that makes beautiful music."

She couldn't believe what he was saying. Not only was it corny, but he spoke as though there had been nothing wrong between them. As though every moment between them, every date and dinner, had been perfect harmony. Had he forgotten so soon? Had he reimagined their whole relationship?

She winced. "The contrast can also be cacophony."

"I've been thinking of you a lot in Germany."

"How would I know? I've barely heard from you in eight months, and now you want to start something?"

Alberto shrugged. "We needed the time apart. Things needed to cool off a bit."

"That's not how I recall it." When it was over, she knew it was done.

"You thought we could still be friends."

That phrase. Being friends with Alberto was different from just being friends with Jim.

"Friends stay in touch," she said. Friends were polite, courteous, considerate. They didn't appear at your doorstep out of the blue.

"I was too hurt to say anything else." Alberto wiped his mouth with the back of his hand again. All the years she'd known Alberto, Elizabeth could count the few times he'd used a napkin. She used to spend entire meals waiting for him to wipe his mouth with a napkin. She'd break down and just hand it to him, then feel guilty about it. She thought she could be bigger than that. More forgiving. If she really loved him, why was using a napkin so important?

"I've thought of all the places I'd like to show you. Incredible palaces. Beautiful churches. Concert halls with amazing acoustics. I've been thinking of the way you play Bach. All the notes are accurate, but you always keep a sense of the musical line. It never sounds like a computer."

"Thanks," she said, trying to hear it as a compliment.

"Here in America we think we should hear every sixteenth note, but I've been to places where Bach first played. The acoustics are wet and muddy. All the music gets slurred. It would take a player like you to keep it musical. You were meant to play there."

She looked at him, wishing he would finish drinking his tea and be gone. "I enjoy playing Bach here."

"You could have an amazing career in Europe. They'd understand you and appreciate your playing. Here in America a musician has to have a gimmick. A solid gold flute with diamonds on it. Glamorous photos. Fancy ball gowns to play in."

She thought of the green dress. "There's nothing wrong with looking good."

"I could introduce you to agents. They'd send you on tour. Eastern Europe is desperate to hear new things."

"And where would I stay all this time?"

"I've got friends in Dusseldorf. They'd put you up."

"When am I supposed to leave?"

"Come with me next week. This time of year it's easy to get a cheap flight."

"Doesn't it occur to you that I might be busy? That I might have a full musical life here?" She was getting angrier by the minute. "Have you stopped to consider that I'm happy where I am? That I don't want to play in the capitals of Europe? Quite frankly, I'm thrilled to go to places like Boise and Ogden and Davenport and bring them stuff they've never heard. That might be something you wouldn't know."

Alberto refused to be baited. He ran his fingers through his hair—admittedly, it was thick, luxurious hair—and looked around the apartment. "At least you could find a bigger place than this."

"I used to admire your arrogance," she said. "I told myself that if I had your confidence I might have more success. But I was wrong."

"Lizzie, you're making too much of this."

"Too much? You arrive at my door unannounced—"

"I called Dorothy," he broke in quickly.

"You could have called me. After being away for eight months, and you come back and immediately assume that I'm ready to follow you anywhere in the world?"

"Is there someone else?" His lips curled into a smile, daring her to have a boyfriend.

"No," she said emphatically. "There's no one." *But not for want of one man's trying.*

"You and I have a history."

"You have so much gall."

"Lizzie, you're the only woman I've met who I respect musically."

"I suppose I should be flattered."

"At least you could admit that we were friends."

"I invited you in for tea. I didn't invite you in to take control of my life."

Alberto yawned. Clearly, this was not going the way he'd planned it. "It's late. I shouldn't have come straight here from the airport. I should have waited until morning."

"I have a busy day tomorrow."

"I'll play my horn outside your door."

"You would." She picked up the empty tea mug. "Do you have a place to stay?"

"I sort of figured I'd stay with Melvin and Dave," he said sheepishly.

It figured. A trombonist and trumpet player. Brass players stuck together.

"Did you call Melvin and Dave? Did you tell them you were coming?"

"Nobody answered."

"So you dropped by my apartment because you needed a place to stay, and you assumed I'd let you." She dropped the dishes in the sink and turned on the water. "You're not."

"Any suggestions on where I should go?"

"Try the Y."

"It's late."

"Or the youth hostel."

"They have a curfew."

By sheer force of will Alberto got people to do the things that he wanted them to do. Like a spoiled three-year-old, he was so insistent that people just caved in. Well, this time she was not going to cave. She would not let him sleep on her floor. She did not want to trip over him in the morning. She didn't want to be kept awake by his snoring. Most of all, she didn't want to be the person that for six years she had tried to be for him.

"I'll find a place for you," she said.

She'd find some other friend he could stay with. Not Dorothy. Dorothy always got along with Alberto because she was completely wise to him, but she'd go bonkers with Alberto on her floor. Elizabeth wouldn't do that to Dorothy. There had to be someone else. Someone who wouldn't be too put out.

"I hate to call anyone this late," he wheedled.

"So do I." She thought of someone but thrust the possibility out of her mind. It wouldn't be fair. It would be taking him at his word, and she didn't want to take him at his word.

"Lizzie, I really missed you. That's why I'm here."

"It's too late." She turned to the kitchen to avoid his eyes. She didn't want to see the warm, tender pleading that would be there.

"Forever?"

"It's too late to be talking about this right now."

Jim had asked if there was anything he could do for her. He had repeatedly said he wanted to do her a favor someday. There could be no greater favor.

"I'll sleep in the hall," Alberto announced.

"You can't do that." Elizabeth turned back around and spotted the FedEx box with the address label still on it. Jim's phone number would be there. It was as though the piece of paper was begging her to call.

"I've slept in German railway stations at night."

"Well, this isn't a railway station." She went to pick up the box and practically tripped over Alberto's knapsack.

"Can I use your bathroom?"

"Sure."

Dorothy was always saying that sometimes things appeared in front of you and gave you choices that you had to take . . . even if they weren't easy. Maybe this was one of those times.

Elizabeth picked up the receipt. Jim's home address and number. She went to the phone and dialed.

IT WAS a terrible show. All about this guy and girl who lived together in a one-bedroom apartment while they were dating other people. It was supposed to be some tour de force because the couple also played the other people in the show. So when the guy was going out with someone else, the girl played the girlfriend. And the guy had to play the boyfriend when the girl roommate was going out with someone else, except you couldn't really tell which part they were playing. The first act had ended with a screaming match between roomies, which took Jim five minutes to realize was between the roommates and not between respective love interests.

He had slunk to the lobby, wishing he could go home right away. If only home wasn't so empty and silent. Then Nan had come through the front door.

"Nan."

"I've come to take you away from all this."

"Just in the nick of time. I can't even remember which actor I was supposed to be checking out." He was so ready to leave, any second, that he carried his raincoat under his arm.

"It's the playwright you're here for," Nan reminded him. "He's a part-time copywriter for us."

"He should stick to copywriting."

"Let's go get something to eat."

He couldn't object. She led him down the street to a restaurant that featured a small jazz combo. As long as there was no flutist playing. He couldn't bear hearing any flute music just now. He had even walked right out of a drugstore the past week, putting down a basket full of things, when he identified a solo flute line in the music played over the store loudspeakers. It was a good thing they played hip-hop at the gym. No flutes there.

The hostess of the place seated them at a small table in the dark back corner. It was as far away from the music as possible, per his request.

"How'd you know where I was?" he asked Nan.

"It was written on your calendar. Not so hard to figure out."

"You didn't have to sneak in like that."

"You've refused my every invitation."

"I've been busy," he countered.

"You've refused because you didn't want to talk to me. Desperate measures for a desperate situation." She ordered a salad. Jim had a burger.

He sighed. "I'm sorry I've been so standoffish."

"Completely self-absorbed, I'd say."

"I've had a lot on my mind."

"The dress didn't work?"

He practically winced. She was a good enough friend not to say, "I told you so. Next time listen to me."

"I don't think it was the dress or the trip or anything I did," he said. "I just don't think she wants to get involved with anyone."

"Even someone as perfect as you?" Nan said wryly.

"My timing's off. I'm out of practice. I haven't gone out with a girl in too long. Why didn't I fall in love with you? That would have made things easier."

"It would have made things a lot more complicated," she said, realistically enough.

"You like me. I like you. Why wouldn't it work out?"

"Because we're not in love with each other. We're good colleagues and friends. We trust each other's taste and ideas. We work seamlessly together. We're good ballast for each other. And that's about as far as it'll ever go."

"Next time I'll listen to you. I'll do exactly what you say."

"I appreciate the confidence."

"But what am I supposed to do now? Work doesn't distract me. The gym tires me out. No matter how many reps I do, I can't get her out of my mind. And all the plays and movies I go to bore me to tears."

"I think you need to wait it out," Nan said wisely.

"I've waited for more than fifteen months, and finally something changed in my life. Everything looked so right . . ."

AT HOME Jim flipped on the TV for company but couldn't find a single channel to stop at. The comedies weren't funny. The talk shows were inane. The dramas undramatic. The reality shows showed nothing of reality. What he wanted was a love story. One with a few twists and turns to keep him interested but with the assurance of a happy ending. He'd always assumed that his life would have a happy ending. Where was that now?

He took a carton of coffee-Heath-Bar-crunch ice cream out of the freezer and grabbed a spoon. Carrying it, he ate out of the carton as he searched the apartment bookshelves. Lois would never have tolerated eating on the run like this. Even when they lived in a dump on the Lower East Side, she'd insisted that standards be maintained. Standards. What good would they do now?

He'd teased her endlessly about those romances with their purple prose and pastel covers. But that's just what he wanted.

Standing on a chair, he reached for a book on the top shelf. *Love at Last*, it said. Nothing he'd ever bought or read. This cover had a field of daisies and an embracing couple, the woman in enough pink muslin to cover a car and the man in a black top hat. What was so romantic about that? He took one last spoonful of ice cream, put the rest in the freezer, went back to the bedroom, lay down, and read.

The story caught him immediately with its careful historical details and descriptions. And the vocabulary. A reticule, a curricle, a cravat, an eyeglass, a footman. It took him a few moments to realize that the phrase "making love" did not mean what it did in today's language. In fact, it was more to the point. Making love was speaking your romantic mind. It took words to make love. If only he could blame Lois for the green dress and the ill-fated flight to Boise.

"I thought it would be easy to be in love again, Lois," he said aloud. "I wanted to do things right this time. I didn't compare her to you. This would be different. A new start. A fresh start at love. Can't you understand, dear? Love was rescuing me from the pit your death left me in."

It was a pit of regrets, missed chances, false starts, failed opportunities. The grief that haunted him was filled with conversations he wished he'd had. Words he wished he'd spoken.

He rolled over to her side of the bed. "Tell me what my mistakes were with you. Let me find the book that explains it. Let me hear from some friend. If it's not something you wrote down in purple, give it to me somehow. I don't care how. I couldn't live with you, and now I can't live without you. You're going to have to do something about that."

He closed his eyes and muttered before he dozed off, *"Jesus Christ, have mercy upon me. Make haste to help me. Rescue me and save me. Let thy will be done in my life."* A habit, good or bad, he wasn't even sure anymore.

Twenty-Nine

"Jim?"

"Hello," he said into the phone. He did his best to make his voice sound alert and awake but knew he was failing miserably. He'd been all prepared to proclaim, "Wrong number." Then he heard the familiar voice. The voice he couldn't get out of his head.

"I'm sorry to call so late."

He looked at the clock. *1:15. Not that late.* He might have still been pacing the floor with another carton of coffee-Heath-Bar-crunch. "It's not so late."

"I woke you," Elizabeth said.

"No."

"I have a huge favor to ask. An old friend just arrived from Germany . . ." There was a pause on the line. "He needs a place to stay, and none of his friends seem to be around."

"Have him come over."

"It'd only be for one night. I'm sure he'll find something after that."

"That's fine."

"I hate to impose."

"I've got plenty of room. I don't mind." If he did a favor for her, she might be indebted to him. "Come right over. I'm never around during the day. He can hang out here for as long as he likes. I've got an extra bedroom with a TV in it. It'll be perfect."

"Thanks. We'll be over in a minute."

We, he thought.

Jim raced through the apartment cleaning things, dumping dishes into the dishwasher, gathering up newspapers in a pile, throwing dirty clothes in the clothes hamper that Lois had insisted on buying when they were newlyweds. He would have vacuumed if he'd had time. Sheets? Did he have clean sheets and towels? He opened the linen closet and rummaged around. Lois used to keep the sheets in neat piles.

Yes, there was one clean pair of sheets that would fit the sofa bed and a green towel, right where his sisters-in-law had left them. Neatness seemed to run in their family. He dashed down the hall and took his trash down to the basement. He had just returned to his apartment when the late-night doorman called: "You have visitors. Elizabeth and Alberto."

Elizabeth and Alberto. Like a couple.

"Send them right up."

In the bathroom he splashed some water on his face and ran a comb through his hair. The buzzer on his front door rang. He opened the door to a scruffy, dark-eyed man with a Peruvian knapsack in one hand and an instrument case in the other. Handsome in a Bohemian way.

"I'm so sorry," Elizabeth said, looking harassed.

"I would have been fine on her floor," the stranger said.

"This is Alberto. He plays the French horn in the Dusseldorf Opera House and is taking a week's vacation in New York."

"And hoping to hear the finest flutist in America," Alberto added.

"Come on in."

"You've got a big place," Alberto said.

"We bought it when my wife was on a soap," Jim explained.

"She was an actress," Elizabeth said.

"Can you stay for a minute?" Jim asked Elizabeth.

"I've got to rush home. I've got a lesson first thing in the morning and a rehearsal. A busy day."

Alberto hung his head in apology. "My arrival was unexpected."

"I'm glad you were awake." Elizabeth's words to Jim were soft.

"Lots of books." Clearly Alberto was someone to whom "Make yourself at home" need never be said. He'd already taken off his shoes and was running his fingers along the spines of the books.

"My wife liked to read," Jim said.

"I like reading too." Alberto took down a three-volume history of the Civil War. "Did you read this?"

"Only the first part. I didn't get past Gettysburg."

"The last volume is the best," he said, laying down his intellectual standards like a duelist's glove.

And in that instant of male competition, James B. Lockhart realized who Alberto must have been to Elizabeth. An ex-boyfriend and musician, proud of his knowledge and talent. Always looking to show it off. "I'll have to try it sometime."

Alberto turned to Elizabeth. "Can I see you for lunch tomorrow?"

"I've got a student at noon," she said impatiently.

"How 'bout after that?"

"I have a rehearsal at three."

"We can have dinner."

"I'm playing in a show."

"After that."

"Too late."

"The day after tomorrow. Saturday. Breakfast."

"OK," she said, relinquishing.

Jim eyed the two with growing curiosity . . . and irritation. It seemed that Alberto's persistence broke her down.

"We'll talk more about Germany," Alberto said, kissing her on the cheek.

"Good night," she said quickly. "I really appreciate this," she told Jim. "More than you can know."

So he was right. He had read the unspoken desperation behind her call and in her eyes—an erstwhile boyfriend who wanted to be back in her life.

It seemed like an episode from some bad TV show. The two guys trying to make up the foldout couch together. Both of them being very polite, talking about the best way to tuck the corners in when the only thing they had in common was a woman.

"She's really great," said Alberto.

"An excellent flutist."

"I've been thinking of her ever since I went to Germany."

Jim said simply, "We haven't known each other for very long." He didn't want to go into detail.

"She needs a man who really appreciates her."

"I flew out to Boise to hear her concert. She had the audience in the palm of her hand."

"Do you have another pillow? I've got a real crick in my neck."

"SCOTT, WHAT do you do if the girl you're interested in asks you to house her ex-boyfriend?" Jim asked the next morning.

Scott was waiting between reps and staring in the mirror, searching for his abs beneath his shirt. Someday they'd show up, and he'd announce it to the whole world.

"You say no."

"What if it's the first chance you've had to talk to her in a week, and you want to prove that you can be a friend?"

Scott gave him the eye. "Is that what you want to be, a friend?"

"It'd be a start."

"You'll lose all your cachet. No glamour to it. You're proving that she can walk all over you."

"She's not walking all over me. I'm helping her. She doesn't like this guy anymore. She couldn't put him up, and I'm doing it for her."

"Nice guys finish last."

"That must explain your appeal," Jim said wryly.

"I'm a nice guy where it counts," Scott said. He lifted up the corner of his T-shirt and saw only stomach.

Jim could just hear Scott's internal dialogue. *If only I had less flab. The abs are there. They just can't be seen.*

"I'm nice to my friends," Scott continued.

"That's what I want her to be for me."

"Is this the one you flew across the country for?"

"Yes."

"If she didn't flip over that, then she's not worth a subway token. Or a Metro card. Forget her. She's just using you."

"I'm glad to be used." If it meant housing the ex, he'd do it.

"It's your life," Scott said, going back to his weights.

Jim returned to his set of overheads and the mental discipline that went with it. *Jesus Christ, have mercy upon me. Make haste to help me. Rescue me and save me. Let thy will be done in my life.*

The last time he had prayed, he received a phone call out of the blue from Elizabeth. Who knew what might happen next?

"YOU LOOK better today," Nan said that morning when he arrived at the office.

"I haven't had any sleep."

"It suits you well."

"She called me last night after I got home."

"Did she want to apologize?"

"She wanted me to do her a favor."

"Well?" Nan's right toe tapped slightly as she waited for a response.

"Give her ex-boyfriend a place to stay. He's visiting here from Germany."

Nan's jaw dropped. "You said yes?"

"He's not such a bad sort. Not really my type. Short and dark and full of pronouncements about everything. Politics, music, art, my bookshelves."

"You can tell a lot about a girl from the company she keeps."

"I can tell that he was the wrong guy for her."

"Being with the wrong person says even more," Nan said tartly.

"Think of what I can find out about her. I'm going to go home tonight and cook him dinner—if he's still there."

"If he hasn't stolen all your earthly goods."

"He's not that bad. After dinner, I'll find out all about her. What she likes. What she's interested in. What I did wrong."

"You're a glutton for punishment."

"Nan, don't you see how much better I feel? There's hope. That's all I need—hope. One sliver of it."

ELIZABETH HAD hardly slept. She had come back to her apartment, put on her nightgown, turned off the light, and tossed and turned. She could still smell Alberto in the room. That peculiar odor of cigarettes, hair gel, old corduroys, and a horn. She couldn't understand why a horn smelled, but it did. Leathery and polished and musty, like an orchestra pit.

The orchestra pit is what had drawn Elizabeth to Alberto in the first place. He loved music abjectly, passionately. He would have died for music. Practically did. Unlike Elizabeth, he'd had to put himself through conservatory. The son of a contractor and his librarian wife, he grew up in Middle Village, Queens. ("Middle class from Middle Village," he'd say.) His father wanted him to become a lawyer. His mother wanted him to do anything that would make his father happy. Problem was, Alberto had fallen in love with music at a young age, and he refused to give it up.

It used to make Elizabeth feel guilty. Here she'd had music lessons handed to her on a silver platter. Tuition at conservatory all paid for. Alberto had to do it on his own. He worked in construction for a year and went back to school until the money ran out. Then he'd find another money job: crewing on a barge in the Great Lakes, drilling for oil in Alaska, cleaning bathrooms in Las Vegas (and playing in a band). On the ship, in the tundra, on the Strip, he still practiced his horn.

He was so sure about music and his abilities. His powers of concentration were extraordinary. He would skip a meal if it meant he could get more practice time on a concerto. He took no phone calls for hours if he was analyzing a piece. Not only would he study the notes on the page, but he'd read ten biographies of the composer. He could tell you where a piece was written, whom it was dedicated to, and what had preceded it.

Every note Alberto played made musical sense. Phrases progressed to their logical conclusion, tempos moved at a rate that startled—lightning fast or sustained at such an agonizing pace that you were amazed he pulled them off. Alberto could smoke two packs a day and still have the lungs to carry a phrase longer than any other horn player.

He was known as a brilliant player. Brass ensembles sought him; teachers praised him; colleagues listened in reverence.

But there always seemed to be a moment in a musical relationship when things went bad. He would challenge a beloved professor one too many times. He would come late to a brass quintet rehearsal too many times. He would argue with a conductor.

For years Elizabeth saw her role in life as his protector. She could calm him, get him to reason, convince him to stay quiet for once. She could explain his passion for music, his knowledge, and what he'd learned from his research on a composer. She could also admit she was stunned by the beauty of his playing. When she was hired for a studio job or work in a chamber group, she quietly petitioned for Alberto's inclusion. No one could argue with his abilities. And if she were also in the group, he would behave.

But Alberto acquired enemies almost as fast as he earned fans. Once during a concert Alberto pulled the rest of the brass away from the conductor's tempo in a near disastrous move. Elizabeth could do nothing from her position in the flute section. It was only the first violinist who managed to bring the rest of the orchestra to the brass's pace while giving the woefully incompetent conductor the illusion that he had reinterpreted the piece.

"What were you doing?" Elizabeth asked afterward.

"He's an idiot," Alberto said in a rage.

Another time he had a disagreement with the first trumpet about a note. One note in a transcription that the trumpeter had done himself. Alberto said the note was wrong; the trumpeter said it was right. Alberto brought in an orchestral score to prove it. The trumpeter could not be persuaded. At the last minute Alberto canceled out of the gig, leaving the group hanging.

"You're not going to make any friends that way," Elizabeth had said.

"Who needs friends like that?" was Alberto's reply.

Their relationship might not have gone on so long if Alberto didn't occasionally leave town to take a job with a regional orchestra. Elizabeth often thought he'd have been better suited for some solo instrument like the piano, where he could have decided on tempos and phrasing without being at the mercy of colleagues and conductors. But then again, he'd probably pick fights with his manager or terrorize some provincial hostess.

While he was out of town, he'd call her from Wichita or Milwaukee or Carson City and play her his horn over the phone. He could actually make the thing talk, and it made her laugh to hear him answer questions with different musical phrases. With Elizabeth he was at his most charming. He praised her playing. He brought her flowers. He gave her suggestions on repertoire. He introduced her to other musicians as "a brilliant flutist." He talked endlessly with her about composers, making her feel that she was as smart as he was.

She had thought their weaknesses complemented their strengths. She was diplomatic where he was direct. She was reasonable where he was ardent. She was deliberate where he was impulsive. Together as a couple they could be brilliant. The whole greater than the sum of the parts.

But after six years she began to wonder if he would ever learn from her. He was self-contained, his own best audience as well as performer. His opinions always counted for more. His career would make a greater mark on the world than hers.

It finally occurred to her that sheer talent was not the most important thing in a career. In praising him she had neglected to acknowledge her own gifts of patience, caring, kindness, dignity, courtesy. They counted too.

What she needed was a break. But how? People looked to them as a couple, depended on them that way. The invitations came jointly: "I'd like you and Alberto to come on our New Jersey tour." "Could you and Alberto play this gig for me next weekend?" "I'm organizing some master classes this summer—it would be great to have you and Alberto there." At her lowest moments she wondered if she were being asked just to be Alberto's baby-sitter.

Then one day, out of the blue, he asked her to marry him. Maybe he was heeding the warning of her own impatience. Sensitive and oblivious at once, he dropped by her apartment with flowers, a ring, and two tickets to Las Vegas. "Come on, Lizzie," he said, "let's just do it. Everybody thinks of us as a couple. Let's become one for real."

"I don't think I want to get married that way," she'd said.

"Are you telling me you don't want to get married at all?"

That was exactly what she was saying. What she'd been saying to herself all along. Loving him as a musician didn't begin to translate into loving the man. She had grown since they had first started dating. She could go on a concert tour without his coaching. She could play an audition without playing the piece for him first.

Saying no was painful. She had reassured him that she had enormous respect for him. She was still in awe of his musicianship. She hoped they could still be colleagues. Six years couldn't be erased like that.

Two weeks later he booked a flight for Germany. One day he just showed up to say good-bye. "See ya" were his last words to her. "See ya" was their end.

She told herself she didn't care . . . but that was far from the truth. They'd known each other too long. She hated that she'd hurt him, but there was too much to tell him. More than she could ever say.

THIRTY

THE MORNING after Alberto arrived, Elizabeth called Dorothy. "Why didn't you tell me he was coming back?"

"Lizzie, what time is it? It feels like seven o'clock in the morning."

"It is."

"I don't wake up this early," Dorothy said. Her voice was groggy. "I don't do anything this early."

"How do you think I feel, coming home to find Alberto at my door?"

"So he did come."

"He told me he called you."

"I never figured he'd do it. Never thought he was brave enough. His ego is so fragile I couldn't imagine him swallowing enough pride to speak to you again."

"That's what's so awful. He just acts as though he'd never left or he never asked me to marry him and I never said no." Elizabeth became more and more impatient. "He's acting as though he's back from one of his tours or a short gig with the Omaha Symphony. He says he wants me to come back to Germany with him. He'll launch me on my career over there."

"What did you tell him?"

"What could I say? I was too stunned to answer."

"Where's he staying?"

"That's what's awkward."

"What do you mean?"

"He's staying with Jim." Elizabeth could picture Dorothy rolling her eyes.

"You've asked *Jim* to put him up?"

"What else was I to do? It was past midnight. No one else was around. I wasn't going to ask you to put him up. I'm not having him on my floor. I was desperate."

"No wonder you called."

"What am I going to do?"

"He's not your responsibility."

"He is now."

"Did you ever tell Jim about him?" Dorothy didn't sound pleased.

"No."

"Well, he's going to find out . . . and think about the source. All those stories from Alberto. It's almost as though you're trying to even the score. You know all about Jim's wife, and now you want him to know about the man in your past. Exhibit B has just arrived and is probably now snoring on Jim's sofa bed or spilling coffee grounds on Jim's kitchen floor."

"I feel terrible."

"If you cared so much about Jim, you could have been nicer to him back in Boise or Ogden or wherever you were." Dorothy wasn't letting her off the hook.

"It's not the same."

"Lizzie, how many months since you last saw Alberto?"

"Almost nine now."

"You should be over him and on to the next guy, and if you're not, then he has given you the perfect opportunity to bring some closure to the relationship."

"I hate that word."

"Fine. Pick your own. But that's what you need. Closure."

Elizabeth hung up and looked to her stack of Harriet Muellers. They were to blame for the mess she'd gotten in. If she hadn't gone to that church rummage sale, she wouldn't have picked up the books. Then she wouldn't have known so much about Jim Lockhart and his perfect marriage. He'd just have been a guy and that would be it. She wouldn't have been so intimidated by his generosity.

Or was it something else that had gone wrong? Like the past that haunted her? People didn't even mention Alberto to her anymore. They didn't ask about him. It was as though the two of them had never been together. She had few pictures of the two of them and those were deep in scrapbooks that she hoped she wouldn't have to look through until she was half-dead. Probably wouldn't even remember his name by then.

Closure. She already had closure.

So now that he was back, why did she still feel she had to fix him? Why did she still feel responsible for him? If this was love, it was not the kind of love she wanted. She would not be some man's Mother Superior. She needed something bigger in her life than that. She wished for a love so bold and commanding that it would wipe out any memory of Alberto.

IMPORTANT ANNOUNCEMENTS were made at Babcock, Crier, and Nelson at 3:00 on Friday afternoons. That's when you were called on the phone and asked if you could "come upstairs for a few minutes." The whole office watched as you walked down the hall, past the cubicles of assistants and junior execs looking for you to fail so they could fill your office someday. Everybody noticed, but no one looked up. No one dared give you any eye contact.

You came to the elevator and had to wait. The wait was interminable. While you were there, a client would walk by or a salesman would be sitting in the lobby wondering why you hadn't returned his phone call. The receptionist would act as though nothing was wrong. Didn't everybody go up to the twenty-second floor on Friday afternoons to stretch their legs or check up on the boss's ficus plant?

Usually this trip up to the twenty-second floor was preceded by rumors that only added to the tension and gossip. Who would be called? Who would be canned? If a whole department was about to be laid off, the rumors had plenty of time to fly, filling the vacuum left by lack of work.

Jim didn't have the luxury of being prepared by rumor. When he received the call on Friday afternoon, he was surprised. During his long silent walk down the corridor of cubicles, he asked himself if there'd been any rumors. Any water-cooler gossip or e-mails flashing across computer screens? He was still thinking about his houseguest and wondering if he'd left enough cereal for breakfast.

And now he'd have to prepare some speech justifying his employment at Babcock, Crier, and Nelson. Wasn't that what people did on their ride up to the twenty-second floor? Preparing a speech there'd be no time to deliver. The ax came too swiftly. No mercy for final speeches. Emotional outbursts were discouraged by the soft carpets on the twenty-second floor and the wood paneling.

Jim thought of Lois. When he started at Babcock, Crier, and Nelson, he used to fantasize about what he'd say to management on the twenty-second floor. "Think of what it'll be like when I tell them I quit," he'd told Lois. "I just want to see their faces."

Now he wouldn't be given a chance. They were going to let him go, just like that. All for ditching out of the office for a quick trip to Boise. What else could it be? After all he'd done for Babcock, Crier, and Nelson. The long hours. His undying devotion. The success he'd had in picking top talent. Finished.

The clock in the reception area on the twenty-second floor said 3:00 when he stepped out of the elevator. The receptionist smiled and said warmly, "Joan is waiting for you." He walked down the long corridor lined with abstract prints and watercolors. The people who sat at their desks looked up at him and raised their hands in greeting. No shame whatsoever. Couldn't they allow a man the dignity of a lonely walk to doom?

Joan rose from her glass-topped desk—impeccably clean—extended a hand and kissed him lightly on the cheek. It could have been the company Christmas party. "Thanks for coming, Jim. I know how busy you are."

"It's good to be busy," he said. "I like it that way."

"You're one of our hardest workers. You've done an outstanding job of identifying talent. It's work like yours that distinguishes Babcock, Crier, and Nelson from the other firms." She acted as though she were giving a pep talk.

"I enjoy my work."

"Have a seat." She gestured to a black leather sofa and glass-topped table in one corner of the office. It had all the personality of hotel furniture.

"Thanks."

"You're probably wondering why I called you up here."

He stared at her face and tried to imagine what role she'd fit in the commercials produced by Babcock, Crier, and Nelson. Too old for housewife, too young for old lady. Her hair was a perfectly dyed blond, her skin stretched tightly across the forehead, giving her brown-penciled eyebrows the effect of a constant question. She had a nice smile and white caps on her teeth. Only her hands betrayed any signs of age. They were wrinkled like ostrich leather.

"Three o'clock is when big announcements are usually made around here," he replied. Where was the human-resources representative who would escort him back to his desk?

"I won't beat around the bush." Of course she'd say that. "We have some big changes to make around here, and we want you to be a part of them."

The nerve of the woman.

"Yes?" Jim said politely. *Lois, I've been here so long that I can't even fake rebellion. Remember how I imagined that I'd stand up and shout that the company could just go jump in a lake? The words won't even come now. I've become one of them. I even like them. I like my job. I want to keep it.*

"We want you to be the head of the whole creative department," she announced, smiling magnanimously.

"What?" His mouth hung open.

"Before you decide, you should know how we came to this decision. We asked our creative people whom they would most like to work with. We talked to the producers, directors, writers. Your name was mentioned in almost every conversation."

"This is unexpected." *To say the least.*

"You have excellent management skills. You're good at putting out fires, and you have a diplomatic way of building consensus with different groups. We don't think we could make a better choice."

"Do I have time to think about it?"

"Of course," she said. Her fingernails clicked against the table. Should he tell her about the smudge of lipstick on her perfectly white teeth? "Give it the weekend."

"Thanks." He stood up.

She rose too. "Just one more thing. Don't tell anyone about this yet. We'll make a formal announcement after you decide."

"Don't you think people are talking already? I mean, they've seen me come up here."

"Tell them we just had a short discussion about the department."

Jim paused at the door. "You want me to head it, right?" he asked, just to be sure.

Joan beamed her most beatific smile. "You're our man."

JIM COULD barely process the news. He repeated it to himself as though he were writing it up for a PowerPoint presentation:

1. I'm going to become the boss.

2. In charge of the whole department.

3. I'm being promoted over half a dozen heads on this floor.

He couldn't help being in awe of the prospect. It was nothing he had sought out or planned. He hadn't laid out a strategy to rise to this level like some Roman general. He hadn't calculated whom he should impress, or how much work he should do. He hadn't even dreamed of what it would be like to have that corner office. The whole thing had come to him unimagined, unearned. An act of grace. Come down from heaven.

Did this have anything to do with the prayer? Was this why Lois had insisted on giving those holy words to him? Did she know, somehow, that they were more than just words? That they could change his life?

The concept was heady, dizzying.

"What was that all about?" Nan asked him in his office.

"I'm not sure." He wasn't lying.

"What's Joan want?"

"She told me I was doing a good job."

"Glad she noticed you're here."

Nan should have been given the promotion. She was far more deserving. Perhaps he could convince Joan that Nan was a better choice for the leadership of the creative department.

The only explanation that he could accept was that he was being set up somehow. He would be the fall guy for some other company plotter and strategist. A figurehead that could easily be knocked down. Nothing else was going right in his life. Why should this be happening at the office?

He returned to his e-mail and started to work on a database of talent. Colleagues kept dropping by just to let him know what they were doing and how hard they'd worked. Maybe the rumor had already spread.

After enduring as much of this as he could take, Jim decided to leave. He put on his overcoat and his scarf, and walked out of the office far earlier than usual. The commuters pressed toward their trains and buses, converging in platoons of tan raincoats and dark topcoats on Penn Station, Grand Central, and Port Authority. People rose from subway tunnels like brigades and tumbled out of office lobbies, all of them calculating how many minutes they had to make it to the platform. But even the streets of New York looked different—miles away, somehow, to Jim.

He strolled through the lobby of one hotel, remembering sitting with Lois late one night listening to a friend play and sing at the piano bar. He crossed Fifth Avenue at St. Patrick's and recalled walking through the church once—such a tourist thing to do—and watching Lois light a candle. She had put a few bills in a box and slipped a prayer card in her pocket. What had led her to do that? They weren't a churchgoing type of couple. Just Christmas and Easter and weddings. Times when it was nice to be reminded that God was in charge. That was all.

He paused at Rockefeller Center to see the skaters glide across the small square of ice. Like skating with Lois the first time back in school.

"You wouldn't catch me dead skating down there," Lois had said of Rockefeller Center. "Not enough space."

He kept walking west toward the theater district. The theaters had been the center of their world. Friends were in shows, or they knew friends of friends in shows. Knowing the lighting designer or costumer or the woman who had made the lead actress's handbag gave them a right of ownership. Someday their names would be up in lights. They were meant to be stars.

All that had been taken away from Lois by her illness and death. Her dreams had been interrupted before they were done. And for Jim the budding actor? The dream had been postponed. At first he could nurture it vicariously when he sat in a darkened theater and watched some performer who would be perfect for an ad at Babcock, Crier, and Nelson, but his life had followed a different route. He had had other successes, not the ones he had dreamed of.

Without thinking about it, he headed now for the old French restaurant run by the old Breton women. Even though the place was no longer there, he could stroll down memory lane. Standing on that block west of Broadway, he wished he could still smell the remnants of the meal they had eaten. His imagination would have to do the work.

Right after the crème brûlée and before the espresso, they had flipped the coin. She won. He lost.

It hadn't really turned out that way. He had won. She had lost.

His hands in his pocket, his face to the wind, he spoke to Lois now. "It's all right. It really turned out all right. All this time I wanted to blame you, but life went too fast around us both. I thought I was pausing to let you move ahead. Guess what? I moved ahead too. You know what? I'm OK with where I am. They want to make me a big muckety-muck. What a laugh! A job I was only going to do for a year or two until you got your big break. It turned into a career."

He tried the prayer again, the thing that had been his lifeline for the last sixteen months. *Jesus Christ, have mercy upon me. Make haste to help me. Rescue me and save me. Let thy will be done in my life.*

Maybe there had been Someone behind all the scenes helping him. Reading between the lines of his life.

After all, he hadn't sunk into despair but somehow had survived. Up until now he had thought the point was to fight your way through. To work hard to make your future happen. But perhaps that's not what needed to be done. Perhaps what he really needed was to give up, give in, let go. To say good-bye to his own plans—what he thought he should be doing.

And I thought I'd be rescued by love, he thought. *By Elizabeth.* But now that didn't seem likely. Instead, a fantastic job—something he'd never dreamed of or considered—was being thrown his way. Just what he'd wanted, without even knowing it. But certainly not *when* he wanted it. *Timing is everything*, he thought. So why did his timing seem to be way off?

THIRTY-ONE

JIM HEARD Alberto even before the elevator in his apartment building stopped at his floor. The sounds of the French horn floated down the hall and tumbled into the elevator shaft. He had the strange sensation that he was rising to meet the music, like smoke rising to meet the ceiling. At first he thought it was a recording, but the resonance was too strong and the timbre too real to have come from any speakers.

He hurried down the hall, imagining the complaints that would come from Mrs. Kleinman in 7H or Mr. Dichter in 7F. "A person couldn't even think straight with all that racket next door," Mrs. Kleinman would say. "I lost my hearing from shellfire," Mr. Dichter would explain, "and I can still hear that noise."

But the music was good, the sound pure and true. It was like a call through the woods for a chase with the hounds. It would be good for a horse ride through the royal forests of France. No wonder Elizabeth fell for this guy. He made music fit for a king.

Jim turned the key in his lock and pushed open the door. He could only open it a crack. The door to his own home was chained.

"Alberto," he called through the crack in the door. "Alberto!"

The music stopped midphrase. Footsteps padded across the floor. "Who is it?"

"Me, Jim." He could see a half-dressed Alberto through the crack in the door. "Let me in."

"You've got to close the door first," Alberto said.

"I know. It's my home."

The chain came up. Alberto opened the door. He was wearing a sleeveless undershirt like Marlon Brando in *A Streetcar Named Desire* and orange boxer shorts that were baggy enough to double as a kilt. "Your neighbors keep interrupting my practicing," Alberto said. "That lady even opened the door after I closed it. That's why I locked it."

"She's a real busybody."

"Busybody? She loved my playing. Said she wanted to bring her daughter over to hear it. I told her it wasn't a performance. I charge for performances."

Jim hung up his overcoat and looked into the living room. Books had been taken down from the shelves. Music was spread out on the floor. A half-eaten chicken carcass in a styrofoam carton sat on the coffee table along with three empty cans of Pepsi. The armchair had been moved across the room to the window, the sofa was pushed against the wall, and the round antique table was sitting in the middle of the room.

"What on earth—?" he began.

"I did some redecorating," said Alberto. "When I play, I walk around. And there were some things I wanted to change."

"Thanks a lot."

"You can put them right back. Want a Pepsi? I got a whole six-pack. The rest are in the fridge."

"I'll get something of my own." Jim picked up a handful of books and started to reshelve them, but the right spots weren't vacant. How exasperating. The man was intolerable. How could Elizabeth stand him?

"I changed the organization of your books a little. It was too confusing the way you had it. Alphabetical works OK with fiction, but it's a bad way to go with history."

"That wasn't necessary. I knew where everything was."

"No problem. You can put them back."

The phrase "no problem" was one that particularly irritated Jim. *And anyway*, he wanted to tell Alberto, *it is a problem. I find it a problem.*

Jim went into the kitchen to discover three dirty saucepans, six plates, and a couple of mugs soaking in the sink. He couldn't imagine how Alberto had used three saucepans, and he didn't feel like investigating what was in the murky water. He opened the refrigerator door and found the three remaining Pepsis.

Popping the top off one can, Jim returned with the soda in hand to the living room. Alberto was putting the horn in its case.

"Haven't played in a couple of days," Alberto said. "Wanted to see if I still had the chops. We musicians are a little like dogs. We can't settle in our territory until we've played in it."

"Evidently you can't settle down until you rearrange the books and the furniture too," Jim said sarcastically.

"Minor improvements."

"The music sounds good. You're very accomplished."

"It's my job. I'm one of the best."

Spoken as if it were doctrine. Inarguable.

"What were you playing?"

"It's French. Saint-Saëns. My romantic showpiece. I use it as an encore when I want to leave the crowd yearning for more. I never do it for a really discriminating audience though. Too obvious. It's not sophisticated enough for fine musicians."

How had Alberto managed to turn a compliment into an insult?

"What brings you here?" Jim asked.

"I wanted to see Elizabeth."

So that's what this visit was going to be about. Two grown men fighting over a girl.

"She's a wonderful woman."

"We went out for six years. There's no one else I could have stood being with for that long."

No one else could have stood you for that long. "I've only known her for a little over a month," Jim admitted.

"Have you heard her play?" Alberto whistled. "She's an incredible musician. The best."

"Why do you want to see her?"

"I think Elizabeth should check out Germany. They'd love her over there."

"She seems to be doing well here. Makes a decent living."

"Making money isn't what it's all about," Alberto said. "Artistic expression is part of it too. At least she wouldn't have to spend her time playing for Broadway shows."

"It doesn't seem like she considers it a hardship." Jim couldn't help bristling at Alberto's snobby tone . . . or defending Elizabeth.

"Tell me, Jim." Alberto ran his hand through his thick, dark hair. "What interests you in Elizabeth?"

"I've been impressed by her playing."

"Is that all?"

"She's an attractive woman."

Alberto's deep eyes focused intently on Jim's. "There must be more to it than that."

Jim could feel heat rising to his face. He hated confrontation, but he was being pushed. No, *baited* was more like it. And by his houseguest.

"Alberto, I don't know you very well, but by an odd set of circumstances you are my guest. I would like to be as hospitable as possible. But I should make my own situation very clear. I am in love with Elizabeth. She's beautiful. I love her hair, her eyes, her smile, her skin. I love the way she stands when she's playing the flute. I love her voice when she talks on the phone and the way she looks out over the top of her eyes when she's talking to you."

"I know that look." Alberto nodded, almost encouraging Jim.

"I love her independence. I admire the way she's built a career for herself, never choosing the easy way out. Always going for the challenge. She doesn't just do Broadway shows. She puts together concert tours and travels through the West and the Midwest. I love her integrity and her artistry."

"Her integrity would be well served in Europe."

"I'm not finished yet."

Alberto waved his hand impatiently. "Go on."

"I love her walk. I love her apartment. I love that she's such a big reader and can't even fit all the books she'd like to read in her apartment. I think she's generous. She's a good teacher. She's clearly a good friend. She's classy, smart, kind, and she's even nice to old boyfriends for reasons that don't seem clear to me."

Alberto smiled. His teeth were incredibly white for a smoker's. "I'm irresistible."

"I hope she finds you resistible because I believe I'm much better for her, and I will do all I can to convince her of it. I may not be a world-class musician, and I can't talk up a storm about symphonies and concertos and wind quintets, but I appreciate all that she does, and I intend to support it in whatever way I can."

Jim paced as he delivered this monologue, and Alberto sat on the couch.

"You know what you remind me of?" Alberto said when Jim had finished.

"What?"

"One of those books on your bookshelf. One of those romantic novels that Elizabeth is always reading."

"Which one?" Jim asked, half-irritated but desperate to know anything useful about Elizabeth.

"Something by Harriet Mueller."

"You ever read any of those?"

Alberto waved away the idea with disdain. "Of course not."

"DOROTHY."

"Alberto. Where are you calling from?" Dorothy was stretched out on the floor of her apartment, trying to get a kink out of her back while she talked on the phone.

"A very nice place between Columbus and Central Park West. Nice guy who lives here. Circumstances lead me to dislike him, but I can still tell he's a nice guy."

"Alberto, don't you make a mess of things."

"I've been laying it on rather thick. He doesn't discourage easily."

She sat up. "What have you been doing?"

"Making a general nuisance of myself. I did a little redecorating too. I just want him to know where things stand."

"Stay out of it. Elizabeth's mind is made up."

"She hasn't made any commitment to him."

"No, she hasn't. But she's not heading off to Germany either. At least not yet." Dorothy rolled to one side, working out the kink beneath her shoulder blade.

"I'm only encouraging her for professional reasons. She needs to try something different musically."

"She needs to put you behind her. You two were never good for each other."

"I've changed."

"It doesn't sound like it. You've been perfectly rude to your host, which is obnoxious."

"OK, OK. I've got to hang up now. Mr. Nice Guy is coming out of his bedroom."

She sat up. "You mean, he's been there all this time while you've been talking to me?"

"Changing his clothes."

❧

JIM WOKE up on Saturday morning at the first glimpse of light. He hated to linger in bed. Never liked to lounge. The sun was up, and he had to get up and do something.

He put on his sweats and running shoes and dashed outside. As always, it surprised him to see so many people running around the reservoir early on a Saturday morning. What was going on in their lives that kept them from sleeping? Were they hosting the ex-boyfriends of their would-be girlfriends?

He bought a bagel at the end of his run and ate it as he walked back to the apartment. He was so intent on not making any noise that he took off his shoes in the hall and didn't turn on any music while he showered. No doubt Alberto could sleep through the bombing of Pearl Harbor, but Jim didn't want to test it. He combed his hair, slipped on his clothes, and got out the door again before his guest arose.

The air was warmer than it had been all week, and the sky had turned a brilliant blue. The sky had been clear like this when Lois had died . . . the days even warmer. It had been October, a few days of Indian summer.

Jim used to tell himself that it was God's consolation. God's promise that life would go on. Brilliant blue skies and bright sun when his soul felt so very cold and distant. A shred of comfort in the worst days of his life.

He walked uptown to the hospital. He could have taken a bus or a subway, but he knew the walk would feel good. Being outside in the bracing air. Getting away from Alberto. Listening for Lois. Thinking of her.

"We'll battle this thing," had been Lois's war cry from the very beginning when she'd found out about her cancer. "We can beat it."

A lot of good that triumphant spirit did her, he thought. From chemo to radiation to brief moments of remission—to more treatments because the cancer had spread, eating away at her body. From the breast to the lymph nodes to the brain. Or maybe it had always been in the brain and just didn't show up for a while on the machines.

There were tests and more tests, then long periods of recuperation at home. Jim had somehow kept up his work. His medical insurance had covered half of the expenses, anyway. Her insurance covered the rest. He was grateful for the job. It helped with the bills, but also gave him a break from the sickness and the symptoms that dogged her.

When he was away, her friends visited. They called and brought flowers, food, and copies of her books. Jim had figured that Lois was glad he wasn't around. She could read all those old books she loved.

Now he realized she must have been writing in them then too.

They hadn't talked much in the evenings. She was usually tired, and all he could think of saying was what had gone on at the office. How interesting was that? But on those days when she could barely make it from her bed to the bathroom, she was writing to him. Using all her energy to tell him how much she loved him.

No one had warned him how long death took or how brutal it was. In the theater it always came swiftly. The heroine would cough a few handkerchiefs of blood, and the next moment she'd swoon in her lover's arms, gone after a final monologue.

Nowadays people weren't allowed final monologues. They were in hospitals wrapped up in tubes with machines monitoring every last breath. They had machines to show when the breathing stopped. There were lights to flash and ventilators to turn off.

When Lois went into the hospital the last time, both of them had known it was the end. One last radical surgery. One last attempt at the tumor. They wouldn't be able to get it all, the doctors said. The tentacles had spread too far, too deep. But Lois wanted to try. As long as she could have more life, she wanted it. As long as there was hope.

"Are you scared?" he'd asked her before the operation.

"No," she'd said. And he'd known by her expression that she meant it. In the last month, something had happened to her. It was as if her entire outlook had been transformed, little by little. Fear had disappeared, while the longing for hope and a future remained.

Her face was bloated from the medication she'd been taking. She looked like a newborn baby with her bald head. She didn't even have eyebrows or eyelashes. "A cue ball," she called herself. His cue-ball wife.

How could she not be scared? he wondered. *He* was scared. Scared of losing her. Scared of all the days to come when he wouldn't wake up with Lois by his side.

And all he could say was, "I'm sorry." Sorry that this was the way things were going. Sorry that she was dying. Sorry that they didn't have more time.

"Don't be," she'd said. She had her hospital gown on. She never wore it unless she had to. She'd beg him to bring her pajamas from home. She'd keep her bathrobe with her in every hospital room. A real bathrobe that she'd bought from Bloomingdale's with her first check from the soap opera. Hospital gowns were an indignity, she claimed. An insult. Stripping all humanity from a patient.

"You don't have to do this," he said one last time.

"Yes, I do. I have to continue grasping on to hope. Believing that I'm doing the right thing by trying."

Grasping on to hope. In the light of the statistics for this kind of cancer, any hope was a risk. And yet, isn't that what Lois had done in her career as an actress? Taken a gamble at nearly every role she'd played? Lately, even he'd been starting to think that their marriage had been a gamble on hope. Like any marriage. Like love itself.

Was there anything that was permanent? nonchanging? risk-free?

Lois caught his glance and held it, as if she sensed his inner turmoil. "I'll be waiting for you," she said, her words coming out slowly.

More and more lately, she had been talking about that. Trying to explain what she believed . . . and what life after death would be like.

Jim had tried to understand but always felt as if he were standing behind a curtain backstage while the real drama was going on. So he said simply, "I know you will." He'd clasped her hand. "And Lois, I won't forget the prayer."

She smiled, her lips parched and chapped. "I know you won't. That's why I gave it to you. Promise you'll use it. Those words will take you further than I ever could."

He squeezed her hand gently. "I'll do everything you tell me to."

He bent down to kiss her, then she was taken away on the stretcher into the operating room. Jim had liked the surgeon, one of those clean-scrubbed Eagle Scout types. The man had gone over the odds with both of them, stressing the dangers of the operation. "A procedure," he had called it.

Procedure. Such a euphemism for ripping out part of the brain.

That's why Jim needed to go back to the hospital today. He wanted to face the worst of his memories, and the worst was in a hospital corridor. He entered the lobby, and someone asked him what floor he wanted to go to.

"Seven, please. Oncology," he said.

No one even looked for identification. You wouldn't go up to oncology if you didn't have to.

There was the usual assortment of people in the elevator. Orderlies, doctors, relatives with balloons and flowers. *Every one of them has a story*, he used to think. They all had some tragedy they were trying to make the best of. They all knew the hopeful expressions: "We'll beat this thing." "You'll be back on your feet in no time." "You'll be fine in a few days. Don't worry."

OK, some people did get better, but for how long? The cancer was stopped for a few years, after months of miserable treatments, but then the patients were right back in the ward, waiting for surgery, radiation, chemo.

Misery.

He got out on the seventh floor and walked down the halls. Nobody cried up here. He'd never heard any outbursts of tears or sobbing. Everything was businesslike. It was worse than Babcock, Crier, and

Nelson. Files, computer printouts, clipboards, forms to sign. Sickness and death was a business.

"She's our favorite," the nurses used to tell him. Everybody liked Lois. So good-natured. Such a quick wit. So pretty. "We all love being with her." Of course, Lois was always good for an audience. She gave her best. She didn't like to disappoint. A real people-pleaser. No diva acts in the death chamber. She was a company player. A trouper.

Jim looked for one of those nurses now. One of the women who'd loved Lois so much. He could never quite figure out who was on what shift. They just appeared, looking at him sympathetically. They gazed at Lois with the awe of star-struck fans.

"But she died," he wanted to tell one of them now. "A lot of good all your hard work did for her." It couldn't keep her alive.

No matter how hard doctors and nurses worked, they couldn't save her. God—the boss, the director, the producer . . . the one Lois had come to believe was in charge of her life—would still have the last word, Lois said. He would decide when to drop the final curtain. He would determine who got the last bow.

And by doing so, God had dropped the curtain on Jim's future and his hope. On any trust that he might have had in a good God. As Lois slipped away into eternity and whatever awaited her there, Jim was left standing in the dark . . . holding only the words to a prayer that had meant everything to her in her last days.

Jesus Christ, have mercy upon me . . .

Jim walked down the long corridor with the floor-to-ceiling window at one end. Just seeing it stirred up his anger—made him want to push a wheelchair through it and watch it fall to the ground. Anything to shake up the calm of the corridor and floor. To confirm by the crash of metal the brutal reality of death.

He came to her room and stood outside. *707.* "It's one of our nicest," a nurse had told him. "You have a real nice view of the river from here, and it gets plenty of afternoon light."

A lot of good a nice view did for someone who can't see, hear, or speak. That's what Lois was at the end, after that last surgery. A body in a bed. An unrecognizable body at that. He would stare across the room at her for hours, looking for something that would remind him of who she was when they were first in love. He realized how much was gone from a person when you could no longer stare into her eyes. All Lois's eyes gave back was emptiness. They were staring inward, lost in some otherworldly destination.

The doctors didn't have to tell him the surgery didn't work. Now they could only wait. No one could say for how long. No one would even say what they were waiting for. One last glimpse of consciousness? One final word?

"This will make her feel better," a night nurse had said, pointing to the morphine dripping into her veins.

"Can she wear her own pajamas now?" he'd asked. Lois wouldn't want to be seen in the ugly hospital gown.

"Of course," he was told.

The hospital was glad to handle any request now. Jim recognized the position from work. When everything's gone wrong with a client, you give in to the smallest request because you want to salvage the relationship somehow. But no request granted will make a shred of difference in the outcome.

Her family flew out to see her one last time. Her father, who had never really liked Jim and seemed to blame him now for his daughter's death. Her mother, who encouraged everybody to pray for Lois.

Pray? Jim had thought. As though prayer could do anything at that point.

Her two sisters came. Melinda stayed in a nearby hotel. Emily stayed in the apartment with Jim, when he managed to go home.

They came, and then they left. Lois didn't die when she was supposed to. It wasn't a matter of days. She lingered, near death, for weeks. Jim went back to work and slept at the hospital at night. The flowers had dried up and had to be ditched in the trash. Lois, who never lingered too long for a curtain call, lingered too long at the hospital.

Jim listened outside room 707 now to see if anyone was inside. He looked for a name beside the door. No one. He entered. The bed was empty; the curtains around it pulled back.

Once again he saw her eyes. The eyes that registered nothing, even when he rubbed lotion on her hands or feet, trying to make some connection with her.

The nurses had urged him to talk to her in those final days, and he had tried. But half the things he wanted to say seemed so meaningless: what Nan had said at work, what the client wanted, what shows he wished he could see if he weren't in the hospital. What did those matter? The deep things, the hard things to say, didn't come out. He couldn't find words for them. And she had no words for him either.

There were times he wanted to weep. To throw himself into her arms and plead, "Lois, tell me what I should do without you!"

He was at the office when the nurse called.

"She's going," he was told. "Come quick."

He'd hurried as fast as he could to the hospital. The taxi he'd hopped into got stuck behind two buses and a stalled truck at Fifty-seventh and Fifth. He got out and ran until he found another taxi on the other side of the traffic jam.

She was breathing heavily when he came into the room. Her breaths came so slowly that he expected each one to be her last. He sat next to the bed and held her hand. He kissed her forehead. He whispered into her ear, "It's OK. I'm going to be OK. I'll manage OK."

With his cell phone he called her parents and her sisters.

"We'll be right out," they all said.

He turned off the phone after that. He didn't want to be interrupted by their explanations of flights and hotels and just when they'd arrive. He wanted to be alone with Lois.

He put his ear down to her lips to feel the air come if it came. There were the softest of exhales and then huge intakes of breath that were such a struggle it was a wonder she didn't give up.

He stood up for a moment to look out the window. To look at the blue of the sky. To calm his soul for what he knew was soon to come.

When he looked back at Lois, he knew it was over.

No more breath.

THIRTY-TWO

ELIZABETH CALLED Dorothy from a pay phone between her matinee and evening performances.

No one used pay phones anymore, Dorothy told her. Everyone had cell phones. Everyone but Elizabeth Ash.

But Elizabeth didn't want to be at a phone's beck and call wherever she went. People could leave messages at her home, and she could call from pay phones. Life didn't need to go so fast.

Except for now. She stood in the chill on Eighth Avenue, with cars whizzing by. A note on the pay phone said it could take no incoming calls. As though she were some drug dealer setting up shop on the corner of West Forty-fifth. Every three minutes she had to put in another quarter, and her quarters were running out.

"Alberto's concerned about my future here," she said. "He wants me to audition at some places in Germany. He thinks I could have a great career over there."

"Do you want to go to Germany?"

"The one thing I could always trust Alberto on was my music. He's always had good advice about it."

"Yeah. And he's always telling you that you shouldn't play for Broadway."

"Maybe I shouldn't. Maybe I need to find other markets."

"Why?"

"Things are changing here. More places are using computers for music. It's easy to imitate a flute sound."

"And that's why you're supposed to go to Germany?"

"We're not getting together. It's just a career move. I want to go over there and check things out. I'm free next week. The conservatory has its midwinter break, so I don't have to give any lessons. I'm not playing in a show. The freelance work is slow this time of year. I could go and come back in a week."

"I'm listening for some enthusiasm in your voice."

"Please deposit twenty-five cents . . . ," the voice on the phone said.

"Just a second." Elizabeth deposited another quarter.

"Aren't you running away from something?" Dorothy asked.

"There's nothing urgent going on."

"I mean, something personal."

"If you mean Jim, I think it'd be good to put some distance between us. He's a good guy. He was really nice about putting Alberto up for two days. He did me a favor."

"Isn't Alberto still there?"

"No. He's gone to Melvin and Dave's. We had breakfast together, and he told me then."

"What about the books? Have you told Jim about them?"

"The Harriet Muellers?"

"Yes."

"I brought them to breakfast and asked Alberto to take them back to Jim's when he packed up his stuff. He said Jim had books all over the place . . . so he'd never know if a few were added. Alberto had even tried to rearrange them."

"So you didn't write a note or anything explaining why you had them?" Dorothy sounded shocked.

Elizabeth paused. "I couldn't. I just couldn't."

She didn't have the heart to tell Dorothy what else she had given Alberto to leave at Jim's.

"Someday you're going to have to tell him about the books."

"I know." Elizabeth sighed.

"Do you plan on still seeing him?"

"Sure," Elizabeth said doubtfully. "We can be friends."

"I'd like to express complete confidence in you, Lizzie," Dorothy said in her most exasperated tone, "but I have to confess that I don't know what you're doing. Why are you being so skittish?"

"Skittish?"

"So on-again, off-again. What's gotten into you?"

"I guess I was thinking about Jim and his wife. Remember how she wrote about the two of them meeting and coming to New York and establishing themselves? Well, I was thinking about the incredible bond they had. They were the world to each other. They were ready to conquer the world. There's a bond you have with someone you've been with at that part of your life. No one else can take the place of that."

"You're going backward. You need to move on."

"That's why I thought it would be a good idea to check out Germany."

"If you feel so certain, why are you calling me from a pay phone?" Dorothy shot back.

"Please deposit twenty-five cents," the voice on the phone interrupted.

"I've got to go," Elizabeth said.

"Don't do anything drastic without telling me."

JIM LIKED going into work on Saturdays. No interruptions. No ringing phone. He would plow through a pile of papers at his desk and bring some order to it. Mondays felt better when everything on his desk was in order. He went to the office after visiting the hospital. He took out the newspaper to study the theater listings. With a red pen he circled the show times of a few plays he could see. A matinee and an eight o'clock curtain. Anything to stay away from his apartment.

Maybe it was Alberto's musicianship that appealed to Elizabeth. No doubt the man was very charming. No question that he was an excellent horn player. And he had a rough Bohemian look that women probably found attractive.

But Elizabeth seemed smarter than that. And so much classier. What had made her stick around Alberto for six years? What was his appeal? All that Bohemian talk and musicianship, all that exotic passion and charm?

Was that what was missing in Jim in Elizabeth's eyes? Did she see him as a stuffy casting director who played well by company rules? In fact, so well that he'd been promoted without even trying?

Was it possible to have a life that just seemed to happen by accident? Was there anything that determined the shape or direction of a life? What—or who—was behind all this? Is that what he was looking for at the hospital?

His only escape seemed to be work. Watching some actors perform in a downtown theater would be a relief. He could pretend he was looking for someone chic to do an insurance commercial.

JIM DIDN'T get home until after 11:00 on Saturday night.

No sound of a horn drifted down the hall.

There were no brusque greetings from neighbors with critiques of his guest's playing.

Jim let himself into the apartment, fully expecting to be greeted by Alberto's mess. But the coffee table and sofa had been returned to their usual positions. The extra towel was folded next to the sink. The sheets had been stripped from the sofa bed and were folded on top of it. The kitchen sink was immaculate. The dishes in the dishwasher were clean. The carpet looked vacuumed; the trash had been emptied.

In the middle of the living-room floor was a note:

> *I found another place to play my horn.*
>
> *Thanks.*
> *Alberto*

Elizabeth must have done this, he thought. He could imagine her coming by to pick up Alberto, being appalled at the mess he'd left and getting out the vacuum cleaner, folding the sheets, washing the dishes. She'd probably dictated the note.

It pained Jim to imagine Elizabeth in his home without him being there. Would she have noticed the round mahogany table? Would she like the pillows that went with the pattern on the sofa? Would she have looked closer at the books?

Jim didn't usually care about his physical surroundings. Lois used to say he'd be comfortable in a monk's cell. Lois had handled the decorating and redecorating. Since her death he hadn't once considered changing the curtains or reupholstering the armchair.

Until now.

He took off his overcoat and his shoes. He sat down in the armchair across from the TV. That's when he spotted the FedEx box, at the top of the cabinet. He knew exactly what was in it. After all, he'd traveled with it from Boise to Ogden in a rented car. He'd hoped she'd keep it. Now it was here. What was he supposed to do with a green silk dress that had been worn a couple of times? It was meant for one person.

One and only one.

DOROTHY COULDN'T bear watching her good friend fall in the wrong direction. If there were some way she could physically restrain Elizabeth, she would have. Not that Dorothy disliked Alberto. They'd had some good times together. He was fun and droll and could be very witty.

One evening they'd gone together to hear Elizabeth play at some music festival on Long Island. Elizabeth's wind quintet was superb as always, but the sponsor of the event was a woman in a fluffy, light green dress ornamented with ostrich feathers. She'd waltz on and waltz off announcing the different performers. At one point Alberto had leaned over and whispered to Dorothy, "Think that's what she wears to sleep?" Dorothy thought she'd never stop laughing.

He was a brilliant musician. Dorothy still had his CD with two horn concertos—a limited release—and if she ever felt like listening to classical music, she'd listen to Alberto. He could make a French horn sound like a violin. That lyrical. Never a bleep or a burp in his playing.

But he was wrong for Elizabeth. He overshadowed her. She made too many concessions to his talent, his career. Theirs was not a good partnership. Too often Elizabeth took the backseat when he was around. The relationship was all wrong.

Now was the time to act. Dorothy still had the two Harriet Muellers from the Thrift Shop. Perhaps if she gave them back to Jim and explained about the other copies that Elizabeth had, Jim would get back in touch with Elizabeth. See what they had in common. Build a friendship. Become more than Alberto ever could be.

But there was one big problem with that plan. She would have to betray a friend.

Maybe Lizzie would understand, especially if things turned out all right. But what about Jim? What if the whole thing backfired? Dorothy could end up alienating a powerful casting director.

No, she couldn't just call him up and drop the books by and explain everything. Dorothy didn't dare jeopardize the career that she had so carefully crafted and built. If only she could get someone else to do the favor. Someone who had less invested in the whole event but still cared.

Someone like Mrs. Halladay, the Thrift Shop lady.

The Thrift Shop was not open on Sunday, Dorothy knew, but the church had to be. And surely someone as dedicated as Mrs. Halladay would be there. The woman seemed to make it her goal in life to connect people to donated goods. Finding just the right things for the right people. Dorothy couldn't imagine Mrs. Halladay saying no to such a request as hers.

So on Sunday, Dorothy woke up early. She put on the least amount of makeup possible and her most conservative dress. Picking the two Harriet Muellers off her shelf, she dropped them in her large canvas tote bag.

From the back of the church, it was hard to find Mrs. Halladay. Half a dozen other women in the pews seemed to have the same hairstyle—gray hair molded into a helmet. Dorothy spent most of the service staring at the backs of heads and the napes of necks where a string of pearls was clasped. She stood up when hymns were sung, bowed her head at the prayers, and dropped a ten-dollar bill into the offering plate. At the end of the service she watched the worshipers walk down the aisle to the doorway, where they shook hands with the pastor and said nice things about his sermon.

Mrs. Halladay was not among them.

It was only when the church was half-empty and the organist had finished a flamboyant piece of Bach that Dorothy spotted Mrs. Halladay. She was near the altar carrying a vase of forsythia. Dorothy could barely see the face behind the splash of yellow, but the dress, the walk, and the hair were unmistakable.

Dorothy walked up to the altar steps. "Mrs. Halladay. I met you at the Thrift Shop."

Mrs. Halladay peered around the flowers. "Yes. I need to take this into the kitchen. Just follow me."

Dorothy followed. "You had so many great things there. I came in with my friend Lizzie. I don't know if you remember, but we were looking for these books by this author—"

"Harriet Mueller."

"You remember."

Mrs. Halladay nodded briskly. "I try to remember what all my clients like."

"The two books I bought. I shouldn't have taken them. They don't belong to me. There's this guy—"

"Yes, remember I met him."

They were in the church kitchen now. Mrs. Halladay was emptying out the vase and wrapping the forsythia in butcher paper.

"I was thinking that it would be nice if you could call him up and give them to him. They have some really personal messages in them. They belong to him. If you don't know how to reach him, I could give you his number."

Mrs. Halladay paused as she folded the paper around the flowers. "I know how to get in touch with him, but I won't return the books to him."

"Why not?"

"Miss Hughes, isn't it?"

"Call me Dorothy," she said, startled that the woman had such an astonishing memory for names and details.

"Dorothy, I try to make sure that everything at the Thrift Shop goes to the right person. It's a sort of stewardship at our church. People give things to our rummage sales and the Thrift Shop, and we see that they find new owners. Even the things we don't sell, we make sure they find a home. I don't like to throw anything away. I'd rather have it sent to Africa at a loss than just get thrown away. That's our ministry."

"I see." But Dorothy really didn't see the point at all.

"So when it came to those two books, I had to make a decision. Who were they meant for? Not who owned them previously. I had a very strong feeling that day. They were meant for you."

"For me?"

"To give to your friend."

Dorothy picked the two Harriet Muellers out of her bag. "She didn't want them."

"Then save them for her. Till when she's ready for them."

Dorothy was crestfallen. "I'm afraid that will never happen."

"Miss Hughes, I've been thinking a lot about your young friend and that young man. I think the best thing is for the two of them to talk frankly to each other," Mrs. Halladay said firmly. "In fact, I'm convinced of it. I brought this up in my prayers this morning. Those books were meant to draw those two together, for some purpose . . . whether they know it or not."

"How can we make that happen?"

"We can encourage, dear," Mrs. Halladay said with a regal smile, "but we cannot force. If God wants their love to bloom, it will happen according to his plan and in his time . . . not ours."

Thirty-Three

"Elizabeth."

"Oh, hi," she said into the phone.

She had told Jim that her other friends called her Lizzie or Liz. He was the only one who always called her Elizabeth.

"I wanted to talk to you." He had hoped this was a reasonable time to call. After brunch, on a Sunday afternoon. "I wanted to thank you for your note."

"You really came through in a pinch. I'm so grateful. Alberto's friends came back, and he was able to stay with them."

"But your thank-you note for the dress. That was very kind of you."

She hesitated. "I wanted you to know that I liked the dress. I was really touched. It was a very nice thing to do."

So he'd lost his timing. Somewhere between Lois and work and life. He couldn't read people anymore. He couldn't tell what they thought or what they'd think.

"I know I didn't really know you well enough to send you a dress," he apologized. "The idea just came to me. It had been so long since I'd had a wild urge like that, I figured I'd better follow it."

"I understand," she said. "Will you be able to return the dress?"

"There's a place I can take it." He was thinking of the Christ Church Thrift Shop. "They take anything."

"I hope Alberto wasn't obnoxious."

Jim couldn't help feeling irritated. He wanted to tell her, *Stop apologizing for him. He's a grown man, for goodness' sake.* But he held back. "He's very talented. He was practicing his horn when I came home from work the other day. I could hear the sound all the way down the elevator. It was beautiful."

"Did that cause any trouble?"

"The neighbors liked it. No one complained."

"I'm glad you heard him play. You need to do that to understand Alberto. Not until you've heard his music can you really know him."

Like you. "You must have helped him clean up the place."

There was silence on the other end of the phone line, then, "He cleaned it up?"

Jim's hopes plummeted. "Things were pretty much back to normal when I came home last night."

"His apartment was always very neat."

"This one was when he left it." He had so wanted to believe that Elizabeth had visited his place and fixed it up. But it had been all Alberto. Disappointment made him brave. "Are you and he getting back together again?"

Again, there was hesitation. "I don't know," she murmured.

She could have said that it was none of his business.

"I'm not going to try to talk you out of it."

"Thank you."

"I wish that we could start out all over again."

"I like you a lot," she said. "That's what I was trying to say in the note. It's not that I don't like you. I wouldn't have asked you to do that favor with Alberto if I didn't like you."

"Glad to hear it." But his heart felt numb. Cold.

"Could we leave it at that?" There was a pleading in her tone that he hadn't heard before.

"I wish we could get to know each other better," Jim said. "I realize I don't know half about you, and you don't know much about me."

"I know."

If I hadn't pushed it, he thought. *If I hadn't rushed things . . .*

"Is there anything so far that's given you the wrong impression?"

"Nothing about you."

Then about whom?

"Well?"

"The timing's just not right," she said.

"OK. Well, I wanted to thank you for the note. It was very thoughtful of you."

"It was the least I could do."

JIM LOOKED for a mat to stretch out on. He'd gotten to the gym so early that the yoga class was still going on. They must have started at five, humming to themselves and sitting on their mats. He'd visited the class once to see what it was all about. The stretching was good, and the breathing felt great, but he kept waiting for the workout to begin. He hadn't built up a sweat.

"You're too results-oriented," Lois would have said. "Yoga is about process."

So he had adopted another process. As good as yoga for him. Stretching, pumping some iron, running on the treadmill.

There was a small room for boxing at the gym that had a few mats in it. Usually there was some guy pummeling the punching bag in there and someone else skipping rope. Today it was empty. He took out a mat and lay down on it, staring at the dull, flat, ugly glow of the fluorescent lamps overhead.

Hands spread apart, knees to the left, head to the right. Stretch. Reverse it. Knees to the right, head to the left. Hold it for twenty seconds. He'd read somewhere that a stretch had to be held for at least twenty seconds to do any good. He closed his eyes and counted to himself.

Crunches next. Up, down, up, down. Counting to himself. *Thirty to the left knee, thirty to the right.* People looked pretty funny when they did crunches. He felt pretty ludicrous doing them too. Like an oil derrick going up and down. But that was the thing. Sometimes you had to get over being self-conscious to do anything important in life. You had to get over feeling silly for going to the gym or really caring about your job or telling a woman that you loved her beyond reason.

"Jimbo, what're you doing in here?"

"Hey, Scott. I wanted to do some stretching and crunches before I hit the weightroom."

"Have a good weekend?"

"It was OK. I did a little work in the office."

"Girls flip for you," Scott said. "Why don't you go out?"

"Guess I had work on my mind." *Work, the best excuse.*

Scott shook his head. "See you in the weightroom."

Jim looked forward to the promotion at Babcock, Crier, and Nelson. He liked challenges. He wasn't sure how good he'd be, but he needed to try. There were a lot of things you never knew you could do until you tried them.

"A real learning curve," people would say at work. Stretching and growing. Like coming to the gym.

He turned over and began a set of push-ups. Once he could barely do ten. Now he could do a set of fifty like any marine.

Down, up, down, up, down, up.

It was amazing what you could accomplish with some self-discipline and hard work. You could really grow when you set your mind to it.

Lois was right. He was results-oriented.

But then there were other things that never came to him, no matter how hard he tried. Like drawing. Improvising on the piano. Perfect pitch. Lasting love.

And something or someone worth living for.

That was the crux of the issue, wasn't it?

Everything since Lois's death had become rote, meaningless. There was no spark, no life.

Jim stopped at thirty-nine push-ups. He could have gone for fifty, no problem. He probably could have gone for sixty or seventy. He was in great shape. Physically at least.

But now he realized how much his soul was in need of a workout. He knelt and stretched his hands out over his head, almost lowering his head to the mat. He had the room to himself. If anyone walked by, they'd just think he was doing some necessary back stretching.

The words came automatically. That was the wonder of the prayer: *Jesus Christ, have mercy upon me. Make haste to help me . . .*

The words had been a gift from Lois. Their last dinner out together. She could hardly hold anything down, but she had wanted to go to the little French restaurant. Both he and she knew it would be their last time . . .

They took a cab that late afternoon, an unusual extravagance. Jim made the cabby stop right at the front door. When Lois stood at the curb for a moment, he was afraid she was going to get sick. He was ready to turn around and head straight back home.

But she just stood there, one foot in the gutter, her head down. Finally she looked up. "I'm OK."

Without even being told, the waitresses were clued in. They'd seen the progression from the vital, energetic woman Lois had been to this pale, thin waif. She didn't even wear a wig that day. Just a Mets cap over her bald head.

"*Bonsoir, monsieur. Bonsoir, madame*," the plump Breton woman exclaimed, holding open the door.

It was still early. No theatergoers yet or tourists. Just a few old-timers from the neighborhood. They looked on sympathetically.

Jim hated their sympathy. It was as though she had one foot in the grave.

"We'd like to have dinner," Jim said. He acted like 5:30 on a Thursday night was the most fashionable time to dine.

"I have just the table for you." The plump Breton led them to the back corner, where a table awaited them with a red and white gingham cloth and a yellow chrysanthemum in a cut crystal vase.

Jim pulled out Lois's chair and seated her. The waitress brought a handwritten card with the day's specialties. Boeuf bourguignon, steak hachée, pot-au-feu, soupe á l'oignon. None of the specialties had changed in all the time they had frequented the restaurant, yet the gravy-spattered card was still served up as though every word on it were new.

"What do you want?" Jim asked Lois.

"Everything."

"Are you sure your stomach will take it?"

"I want to have everything we usually do."

They ordered as though there were no tomorrow. A first course, a second, and a third. Lois had the *escargots* slathered in butter, thick with garlic. Jim, the onion soup with croutons and Gruyère cheese melted on top. It hardly mattered that Lois didn't have more than a bite of escargots or the veal or the pâté or the salad. Her face was flushed, but her voice was strong, maintaining the illusion of good health. She was, Jim thought, like a veteran actress giving the performance of her career and then going home to die. Gertrude Lawrence in *The King and I.* Gone before anyone ever knew she was sick.

"This was a good place," she said.

"It still is."

"For us it was."

"They've always been nice to us."

"Promise me you'll still come here," she said softly.

"Sure."

But even as he promised, he knew it wasn't likely he could keep that promise. The place was already on its last legs. One of the waitresses had told him that their lease had expired. The women would return to Brittany, and the restaurant would become some new chic place with no atmosphere or memories.

"You've helped me."

"I haven't done much."

Her blue eyes focused intently on him. "You've always been there."

He thought of the many times when he hadn't been there. "Thanks."

"There's one thing I want to give you to keep."

"What's that?" Some memento from childhood? Something she kept in her top bureau drawer?

"I hope it will help you as much as it's helped me."

The waitress came to their table. The restaurant was filling up, but there'd been no pressure on them to leave. They could have stayed there all night if they wished.

"How about dessert?" she asked. "We have a delicious *tarte au poire.*"

Lois smiled. "That sounds good."

263

"Two slices," Jim said. "With whipped cream."

They'd barely eat one slice between them, but now was not a moment to hold back.

"Remember when I went into St. Patrick's?" Lois said. "Before chemo? I picked up a prayer card there. I began to repeat the words to myself every day. Especially at those times when I thought I couldn't get out of bed to face one more day. The words brought me comfort. Calmed me inside, so I could go on."

She took a sip of water, as if her throat were parched. "The longer I said those words, something began to happen in my heart. I realized they weren't just words of comfort, going into a void. They were a prayer, and they were going somewhere. *To* Someone. Someone who has given me hope. Purpose. Meaning. Someone I can trust to take me through this."

He held her hand across the gingham tablecloth. The pear tart arrived, and they both took a bite.

Then Lois moved her fork around in the whipped cream. "I want you to know the prayer too."

"OK." His mouth was half-full of pear tart and whipped cream, but he would have promised her anything. Anything to please her.

"Promise me you'll say the words."

"I promise." He chewed.

"The prayer is very simple. It's easy to remember the words once you get used to the rhythm. You don't have to go to St. Patrick's—or any other church—to say it. You can pray the words anytime."

"I could say it at work."

"Or the gym."

Back then Jim couldn't imagine uttering a prayer in the sweat-soaked, macho gym with its hip-hop and rock playing on the loudspeakers. Still, "Yes," he promised. "At the gym."

"Repeat it after me."

He swallowed the slice of pear tart and leaned forward. She closed her eyes and lowered her voice, although no one else seemed to listen or care. "It goes like this: *Jesus Christ, have mercy upon me. Make haste to help me. Rescue me and save me. Let thy will be done in my life.*"

Maybe because he'd been an actor, accustomed to memorizing long speeches, he didn't have to repeat it more than once for the words to stick. She said it twice and he had it. Like the Pledge of Allegiance or the preamble to the Constitution, it was one of those things. Once it was in your head, you could never lose it.

"Let me hear you say it," she said. And he repeated it in the French restaurant before the remains of *tarte au poire* and the yellow chrysanthemum.

He had no idea how much he'd use it in the months to come. He didn't know yet that it could block the sounds of the loud rock music or hip-hop at the gym. It focused his heart. When he first heard it, he didn't think he needed any rescuing or saving. It was Lois who needed the rescuing, so he could understand why she had grasped onto that prayer . . . onto those particular words. And why she'd held them like a lifeline until the moment she took her last breath.

But now as he lay on a gym mat, beneath a swaying punching bag, Jim realized how much help he'd derived from that prayer and how much more he still needed it.

Jesus Christ, have mercy upon me . . .

How he needed to feel God's mercy. A healing touch. His heart had been broken when Lois died, and he'd stopped trusting in any "higher power" in the universe. If there was a higher power even around, why had Lois—who so deserved to live—died?

Make haste to help me . . .

So he'd given up. Closed down the walls of his heart even as he'd said the prayer. He wouldn't break his promise to Lois, but he hadn't really seen where the words would help. Where anything or anyone could help. So he'd said the prayer like a mantra to focus his energies away from the pain of losing the only woman he'd ever loved.

Rescue me and save me. Let thy will be done in my life.

He had done everything he could to make his life work, but still he needed rescuing. Some will higher than his own needed to do the work.

THIRTY-FOUR

ELIZABETH BEGAN making the calls that would give her a week off. The conservatory was on vacation, but she had other lessons to cancel. She made the calls in the late morning, in hopes of not finding anyone at home. She could just leave a message on answering machines. "Hi, this is Elizabeth Ash. Something's come up that will take me out of town for several days, so I'm going to have to cancel our lesson this week. We're still on for next week though. I'll see you then."

Out-of-town gigs were to be expected if you had a professional flutist for a teacher. Elizabeth tried to convince herself that they made her look even more desirable. Truth to tell, many of her students would be only too delighted at finding her gone, and so soon after her concert tour. It would give them a reprieve from practicing. Take a bit of the pressure off.

She let the quintet know she was going to be gone. She caught the clarinetist at home. "I'm going to check out the career possibilities in Germany," she explained.

"Will you see Alberto?" he asked.

"Probably," she replied.

She inspected the refrigerator for any food that would expire in her absence. One container of cherry yogurt and a quart of milk. She would manage to finish them off before she left. Then she gathered her dirty clothes to take to the laundromat. She was not going to come home to an apartment of dirty clothes.

Just when she'd put them all in a large canvas bag, her buzzer rang. She panicked. Had she forgotten some appointment? She turned on the intercom.

"Let me in," Dorothy said. "We need to talk."

"I don't want to talk."

"I'm coming up."

"Stay where you are. I'm on my way out. I've got to do laundry."

Elizabeth locked the door and carried the laundry down the steps. She found Dorothy standing on the stoop. She was holding two Harriet Mueller books.

"You never asked about these," Dorothy said.

Elizabeth frowned. "Now is not the time."

"I'll come with you to the laundromat."

"I don't need any help."

"Come on, Lizzie. We need to talk."

"OK, then, you'll have to fold and sort."

The laundromat was in an uncongenial basement room beneath a Korean deli. Elizabeth always assumed that the people who diced the melons and pineapples upstairs also took the quarters out of the washers and dryers. On Monday morning at nine-thirty, when most people were at work, it should have been quiet. But all the dryers were tumbling, and only two washing machines were empty. Wash Monday.

"Colors in that one, whites in this one," Elizabeth said.

"I think you've got him wrong."

Elizabeth didn't need to ask who the *him* was. "I don't want to talk about him."

"I know you don't, but I do. That's why I brought these books."

"They don't belong to you, and they don't belong to me. You should give them to him."

"Not without reading parts of them to you."

"In here?"

"Nobody's paying any attention to us."

Most of the people doing their laundry had headphones on. They were lost in their own worlds.

"That's spying."

"It didn't stop you at first."

Elizabeth exhaled in exasperation. "That was before I knew who he was."

"I'm starting to agree with Mrs. Halladay. She thinks you picked up those books for a good reason. That they were meant for you."

"I should have put them back down, then and there."

"Why? Because they changed the way you thought about Jim?"

"Because they were none of my business." Elizabeth poured in the detergent and deposited her quarters.

"They *were* your business, because they opened your heart. And you were at a point in your life when nothing short of a miracle could have done that."

"As long as I didn't know who I was reading about, I could picture the man and the woman and their perfect relationship. It was my own little fantasy."

They sat on the hard plastic bench next to a fellow whose headphones were playing music so loud that Elizabeth could hear it over the rumble of the washers and dryers.

"Lizzie, there's nothing wrong with little fantasies."

"There is if they become real."

"All the better."

"Not if you're supposed to step into the picture."

"What was wrong with the picture?"

"Being told I'm the 'One and Only' when I knew there was another who had the same role."

"But she's dead. Doesn't he deserve a second chance?"

"With the same language? He needs someone else."

"He wants you."

"I can't measure up. They had a wonderful relationship. She was perfect for him."

"Things weren't perfect. Listen. Listen to what she wrote." Dorothy turned to one of the Harriet Muellers and read aloud:

"I can't put my finger on just where things went wrong.
Maybe it was after we made that agreement at the restaurant.

Who could know that I would be so successful? Suddenly everything I touched was gold. Fool's gold.

"You see?" Dorothy said. "There were all sorts of jealousies and tensions."

Elizabeth shrugged. "She was a success."

"She was really upset when he didn't come to an opening night of hers."

"I'm sure he was busy."

"See. You're defending him already," Dorothy pointed out.

"I wanted to see things from his side."

"But this proves that they didn't always talk about their problems. They didn't work things out."

"They should have."

"Of course they should have. We all should, but sometimes we don't. We're not perfect. None of us."

Elizabeth watched the clothes tumbling on top of each other in the washing machine, the soapsuds clouding the window. "I'm not up to it. I don't think I'm right for any guy. Maybe musicians just should stay single."

"Then why are you trotting off to Germany to be with Alberto?"

Elizabeth stiffened. "I'm not going there to be with him. I'm going for professional reasons. Alberto and I have a professional relationship. I respect him professionally."

"And you can't respect Jim? He's the best in his profession. I've seen a lot of casting directors, and he's as good as they come. Diligent, courteous, hardworking."

"It's a different profession."

"You're afraid, Lizzie. Your heart flipped for this guy, and then you refused to follow."

"You yourself said there were jealousies and tensions in his relationship with his wife."

"There are tensions like that between any creative people. It comes with the territory. Just because it went wrong with Alberto doesn't mean it'll go wrong with someone else. Lizzie, I've always admired your courage. The way you've pursued your career. Balancing the money jobs with the things that really fill you up artistically. You need to show the same courage in a relationship."

Elizabeth shook her head. "I don't have it in me."

"Then you're going to have to find it, because if you go off with Alberto and don't patch up things with Jim, you are making the biggest mistake of your life."

Elizabeth looked searchingly at her friend. "I'm not like you, Dorothy. I don't have your energy or confidence. I wouldn't have gone to that silly rummage sale, or the Thrift Shop, if you hadn't goaded me."

"That's why I'm goading you now." Dorothy smiled. "I can't let you mess this up."

"I just need to get away." Elizabeth stared at the machine with the clothes tumbling on top of each other.

"Lizzie, you need to take a risk. You know the way you step out on a stage without a scrap of music and play a fabulous concerto entirely from memory?"

"That takes practice."

"In time, risking becomes easier. But you have to take that first step."

"It's too hard." She turned back to Dorothy.

"I want you to call up Alberto and say no. Then I want you to call up Jim and tell him what you know about him. Explain why you have been so hesitant. Give him the books back. These too. And start all over again." Dorothy placed the Harriet Muellers in Elizabeth's hands.

"Why?"

"Because it's what you want to do. But you're afraid to."

"I don't have the nerve," Elizabeth murmured.

"Read these. And then do it."

"NAN, HAVE a seat."

"I'm always sitting down in your office," she said. "Why are you getting so formal all of a sudden?"

"Because I'm about to tell you something that I shouldn't tell you."

"Office gossip?"

"Not exactly."

Nan pulled up one of the bentwood chairs across from his desk. About the only reason he figured he merited such a big office with room enough for a desk and two chairs was that he was always interviewing people.

"Maybe you should close the door first."

A closed door at Babcock, Crier, and Nelson was a sure sign of an important meeting going on. Even when Jim was interviewing potential actors and actresses for a commercial, he kept the door open. He liked to see how they dealt with interruptions.

"Sure."

"Nan, you've always been my closest friend in the office. The one person I tell everything to."

"You tell me what you want to tell me. I don't ask."

"I know. You don't pry. Well, what I'm about to tell you is something that I shouldn't tell anyone—at least not yet. And I'm not sure it'll be good news to you. I'm still trying to figure out if it's good news to me. But I can't go forward without talking to you."

"You're talking in circles."

"I'm sorry. I'm talking about my conversation on Friday with Joan. She wants me to take over the department." He searched Nan's face for any sign of disappointment. "She wants me to be the head of it."

"That's great!" Nan said. Her dark eyes were impenetrable.

"You really think so?"

"You'll be wonderful at it."

"It's not at all what I expected. I wasn't really gunning for the job. I didn't even think they were considering me."

"I did."

He was startled. "What do you mean?"

"Joan asked me about you and your abilities a couple of weeks ago. She gave me this big long interview. It didn't take me long to figure out what she was driving at. They want someone who's really creative and also organized to run the department."

"When did this happen?" He sat back in his chair.

"It must have been when you were away. When you went off to Utah or Nevada to see that woman." She grinned.

"Stop grinning. Don't tease me. It was Idaho."

"That's right. The ticket to Boise."

"Why didn't you tell me?"

"I didn't want to build your hopes up."

"You knew that I was going to become your boss?" He cocked his head to study her.

"Not in so many words."

"I promised to give her my answer by the end of today."

"And what is your answer?"

"That I'd like to do it. But I'll only do it if you become my number two. I want you to be promoted to assist me. Everything that I don't know about this business you know, and everything that I can't do very well, you can do."

"What about the flutist?"

"What do you mean, what about her?"

"Does she figure into this decision?"

Jim frowned. "I wish she did. I don't know if she figures into any part of my life right now. But Lois figures into this decision. I have her to thank. I got into this work because of her. It was just going to be for a short time, but it's turned into something I really like doing."

"And do well," Nan volunteered.

"I'm going to take the job. As long as you'll back me up."

She nodded. "You can count on me. As always."

MONDAY WAS not Veronica Halladay's regular day to be at the Thrift Shop. She usually had her hair done on Monday and shopped for the week's groceries. But her stylist was on vacation—he'd gone to the island of St. Bart's for a long weekend—and Mr. Halladay was out of town on business. Mrs. Halladay thought of those bags that were still in the back room at the Thrift Shop. Books, clothes, board games, pots, pans—some of them left over from the rummage sale. They gnawed at the back of her mind like an unsent thank-you note. She wouldn't be at peace until she went through them.

She let herself into the basement shop at half-past eight and started working.

Some people loved gardening, others needlepoint. Some found satisfaction in music, others in painting flowers on china. Some adored cooking, others writing. For Veronica Halladay, happiness was going through boxes in the back of the Thrift Shop. Time no longer mattered. She became lost in the dusting, shining, appraising, cataloguing, and pricing.

Who knew what she might find . . . an autographed letter in a humidor? A first edition of Dickens or Trollope? A ruffle of antique lace sewn on an old bridesmaid dress? It took someone like Mrs. Halladay to know what could be salvaged, what could be marketed, and what was even too good for the Thrift Shop. Signed first editions, for instance, were sold on consignment at a fine antique bookseller on Madison Avenue, and the proceeds were donated to the church.

"What do you see in that old stuff?" people would say. "Stories," she would have said. An old tennis racket, an art nouveau vase with a chip in it, sheet music from the 1930s. They all told stories if you listened close enough.

She thought about the things in her own house. Her husband's silver money clip. It always reminded her of their first date at the Rainbow Room. She could still see him taking out a ten to tip the coat-check woman. Or there was the small Chinese parasol she kept in the back of the hall closet. Mr. Halladay had bought it for her on a vacation at the Jersey shore. And she still had the program from *La Boheme*, when he had fallen asleep in the second act but wiped a tear from his eye in the fourth.

It wasn't the things themselves that were important. It was what they said about people. The memories they evoked.

Mrs. Halladay believed that the people who came to the Thrift Shop would find new memories in the old things.

Like the sad-looking woman in the well-worn gray suit. A two-dollar silk scarf could bring some color into her days.

Or the punctilious fellow who always bought old prints of Europe. By now his walls must be covered with pictures of Montmartre, the Leaning Tower of Pisa, Cologne Cathedral, and Piazza San Marco.

She thought again of Elizabeth Ash and the Harriet Muellers. Had those used paperback books brought something good into Elizabeth's life? Mrs. Halladay couldn't be sure. She couldn't be certain that Elizabeth Ash would look back fondly on a volume of Harriet Mueller the way Mrs. Halladay treasured an old opera program or a faded Chinese parasol.

Now she came to a box of books. Wearing a pair of old gardening gloves, she dusted them off and shelved them. *The Life of Doctor Johnson* by Boswell. The collected poems of Emily Dickinson. *Lose 30 Pounds in 30 Days.*

And at the bottom a paperback romance by Harriet Mueller. *Whither Thou Goest.* With a familiar purple script.

Weighing her options, Mrs. Halladay carried the book to the front desk. She stared at the two cards—one with the name James B. Lockhart Jr. on it. The other with the telephone number for Elizabeth Ash.

And then she slowly dialed Elizabeth's number.

THIRTY-FIVE

"IT'S NOT really my book," Elizabeth said when she walked into the Thrift Shop. Mrs. Halladay had insisted she come in. She said it couldn't really be explained by phone. Could they talk in person, just the two of them? "It doesn't really belong to me."

"Tell me about it," Mrs. Halladay said. She sat on a stool behind the counter at the Thrift Shop and set a stool on the other side, encouraging confession.

"You've seen some of these books, haven't you?"

"Of course. And your friend Dorothy explained your fascination with them."

Elizabeth sank down on the stool. At once she realized she wanted to be here. She needed to talk to a neutral party, and Mrs. Halladay had such trustworthy gray eyes that Elizabeth felt she could say anything without feeling foolish. It would be a relief to explain everything.

"I was fascinated with them at first," she said. "I came across the first three volumes at the rummage sale. When I bought them, I didn't know there was any writing in them. I just thought they'd be good stories to read. I've always liked Harriet Mueller's books, and I hadn't read these three, or if I had, it was years ago. You've never read Harriet Mueller, have you?"

"I'm afraid not."

"The plots are set in the Regency period. They're really well researched. I learned a lot of English history in them. All about Beau Brummel and Bath, George IV and Mrs. FitzHerbert. When I came to nineteenth-century history in high school, I discovered that I was very solid on a couple of English decades, thanks to Harriet Mueller."

"I like books like that."

"They give you a whole world." It was a relief to be understood, even on something as basic as Harriet Mueller. "You come to know the characters and their habits. You care about them. Sometimes the covers are a little cheesy, but there is nothing cheesy about the stories. You can trust Harriet Mueller on the emotional details of a plot. When a man and woman fall in love, they are really meant for each other—even if it takes them the whole book to figure it out."

There was a glimmer of humor in Mrs. Halladay's gray eyes. "Ah . . . so it takes the two a while to figure that out, does it?" She cleared her throat. "Sounds like real life . . . in some cases."

"Real life, yes," Elizabeth said thoughtfully. "There's something very honest about them. People have honest feelings. They don't get over-wrought and dewy-eyed. The heroines are strong, like I wish I could be. I guess I would describe the books as comforting. You always know they will have a happy ending."

"I like a story with a happy ending."

"As long as it's an honest ending. I don't like happy endings that aren't earned. The hero and heroine might have some difficulties, but you need to see them working things out. You need to know they're going to make it. That they're going to be all right together."

"We all deserve happy endings. And I believe a man and a woman can be meant for each other. That their love is meant to be. That it doesn't just happen in romance novels like the Harriet Muellers."

"Do you really think so?" Elizabeth looked at her earnestly. Suddenly this older woman, this complete stranger, seemed as trustworthy as Harriet Mueller.

"I didn't for some time," Mrs. Halladay said.

"Why not?"

"The first time I fell in love, I fell for the wrong man."

It was hard to believe that Mrs. Halladay, so crisp, so polished, so seemingly sure of herself, had ever made a mistake.

"You don't look like things ever went wrong for you," Elizabeth said . . . before she thought better of it.

Mrs. Halladay didn't give the all-encompassing benevolent smile that Elizabeth expected. She looked bemused. "Before I moved to New York, before I met Mr. Halladay, I looked for security and happiness in all the wrong places. But then I didn't know any better. I grew up on the wrong side of the tracks in a small Southern town, and all my mother told me was that I would have to make it in this world by my face."

"What do you mean?"

"Those are the kind of things she would tell me. Her whole philosophy of life was, 'Don't say anything. Don't do anything. Just be pretty. Then you'll find a man.'" Mrs. Halladay smiled apologetically. "It was a different era."

Elizabeth smiled encouragingly.

"Well, the man she found for me was on the right side of the tracks," Mrs. Halladay continued. "His father owned the bank and the racetrack and the only nice restaurant. And even though the son was feckless, he could be very charming. Very persuasive. He persuaded me that he would take care of me and make me happy. I believed him." Her jaw became a stern line. "And it nearly killed me."

Elizabeth winced. "Was he abusive?"

"Not physically. But psychologically, yes. He drank lots and worked very little. He managed to convince me that I was worthless. That without his family's money no one would be interested in me. He took me shopping. Told me what to buy and what to wear. It got so I couldn't make a decision on my own. If he wasn't around, I just stayed in my bathrobe, afraid to leave the house without his approval."

"But you did leave?"

"One day there was an audition at the local community theater for a production of *Plaza Suite*. I was given the small part of the bride. He laughed when I told him. Said that I would embarrass myself. Actually, it was the perfect part because I spent most of the play locked in the bathroom." Mrs. Halladay shrugged. "That I could do. And when I came out, wearing this beautiful wedding dress, everyone clapped. I discovered that when I was on stage I wasn't shy at all. I could be somebody."

"Did you come to New York to be an actress?"

"No, not then. I wasn't ready. I still wanted to make the marriage work. I thought if I did everything he said—and one play a year—he would still be happy with me. It took me a long time to realize he could never be happy with me because he wasn't happy with himself. He couldn't make me right because he couldn't make himself right. No matter what dress I wore or how I did my hair, I wasn't going to please him."

"I would have given up trying." Elizabeth thought again of Alberto. She had gotten away once from his influence. Would she be putting herself back in his hands if she took this trip to Germany?

"It wasn't that easy. I really wanted to please him. I thought that he was right. Fortunately, I found a few friends who helped me see that pleasing myself was important. And, even more, that I had to risk being the person God had created me to be. On the good days, I could believe it . . . and I tried to be that person. The rest of the time I just prayed that God would make him happy with me."

"How'd you get out of it?"

"One night he drove back from the country club by himself and smashed into a telephone pole. Killed himself. He was drunk and shouldn't have been behind the wheel of a car at all." Mrs. Halladay looked down. "My first thought was entirely selfish."

"What was that?"

"I thought of all the times I had been with him in a car when he was drunk like that. I could have been killed too."

"It must have been a relief to have him gone."

Mrs. Halladay's head snapped up. Her eyes grew intense. "No. It was terrifying. I felt incredibly guilty. I thought it was my fault. As though I could have stopped him. As though I could have done something. Most terrifying of all, now I would have to do something with my life. I would have to make something of it. The decisions were frightening. All I wanted to do was stay inside in my bathrobe."

"Sometimes I feel like that," Elizabeth agreed.

"One day I was hiding out and the doorbell rang. I thought it was just the gardener, or I wouldn't have opened the door. Instead it was a man I'd known from the theater company. He told me he was moving, and he wanted to say good-bye. He offered his sympathies and hoped that I would still do some acting. He also said that he wished he could see me some more. In the end, he moved to New York and I followed."

"Did you come here to be an actress?"

"That was the excuse. I really came here to make something of my life. It wasn't going to happen down there."

"Did you see the man again?"

The spark of amusement was back in Mrs. Halladay's eyes. "Eventually I married him. But by then I knew what I wanted to do."

"You mean, be his wife."

"That was part of it. The other part of it was this. The Thrift Shop. I loved things. I was especially good with things. I could have had a brilliant career running a gift store, I suppose. But my first husband had left me with a lot of money, and Mr. Halladay made good money, so there was no reason for me to work. I could give my time to a place like this."

"So when did you fall in love with Mr. Halladay?"

Mrs. Halladay's eyes turned misty. "It took a long time. I couldn't fall in love with him until I was ready to stand on my own two feet. Until I knew who I was. Who I was created to be. He waited, the dear man."

"I feel so confused," Elizabeth said. "I thought I was in love with one man, but now I know he was wrong for me. It's just that he looked so right. And everybody else thought he was so right. Or at least they acted like that. They thought we were the perfect couple."

"It's *your* life. *You* have to decide what to do with it. No one else on this earth can do that for you."

Elizabeth felt a tremor go through her. "It's terrifying. What if I make the wrong decision?"

"God can help you. He helped me. And he was very patient, because it took a long time. But he can't help you unless you listen to your heart. That's often how God speaks to us."

"How do you know?" How could anyone know? That's what was so frustrating. Elizabeth was afraid she'd start crying. Had she ever felt so vulnerable?

"Because that's how he spoke to me. Over and over again . . . until

I finally decided to listen. And it was only when I listened and acted on his words that I could move ahead. I lost my fear of risking because I saw something bigger than myself to believe in. Finally I was able to act—to take that leap of faith. To believe in him. And my life changed. *I* changed." She patted Elizabeth's hand. "To move past your fears, you have to act. Take that leap of faith."

"I suppose that's why I'm here. And why you called me about the book."

"Oh, yes." Now Mrs. Halladay became very businesslike. "This one." She held up the cover of *Whither Thou Goest*.

The title alone was enough to jar Elizabeth. She didn't dare look inside for what had been written. Not yet. "How much do I owe you?"

"Nothing." Mrs. Halladay laughed. "For all the trouble the other books caused you, I don't think you owe us a cent."

"You don't have to do that."

"What I'd really like to give you is peace of mind."

Just then the sleigh bells jangled on the door behind Elizabeth. She turned.

The silhouette in the doorway was familiar. Tall, broad-shouldered, dipping slightly as though he might bump his head on the threshold. Elizabeth stood there, holding *Whither Thou Goest*. She wanted to run but stayed rooted to her spot, surprised by how glad she was to see him.

"Jim!" Quickly she slipped *Whither Thou Goest* into her purse.

He looked just as surprised . . . but in a good way. "I didn't expect to find you here."

"I come here sometimes. They have real bargains." *And a lot more besides,* she was thinking.

"They do."

"Are you off work?" Elizabeth asked.

"It's lunchtime."

"Oh."

"I wanted to make a donation to the Thrift Shop."

When Elizabeth saw the familiar FedEx box under his arm, she felt a pang of guilt.

"How nice of you," Mrs. Halladay said, taking out a slip of paper to write up a receipt.

"It's a dress," he explained. "Green silk. I guess you'd call it a ball gown."

"We can always use nice dresses. We have a group of ladies at the church who make prom dresses for girls who can't afford them. Perhaps we could use it for that."

There was silence in the shop.

Elizabeth felt Mrs. Halladay's gray eyes on her and then on Jim.

"You know," she said firmly, "we're not officially open yet. It's not one o'clock." She stood up. She seemed on the verge of kicking them out.

Jim turned to Elizabeth. "Do you want to have lunch?"

She hesitated. She thought of all the things she had to do, especially if she was going to Germany. On the other hand, if she wasn't, she had already canceled her life for a week. There was nothing to do.

"Sure," she said.

And out of the corner of her eye she caught Mrs. Halladay studying the two of them . . . as though this was just the sort of ending she had orchestrated.

THIRTY-SIX

"WHEN I first read them, I didn't know they were yours. I didn't know who they were for."

Elizabeth and Jim were sitting at a small table in a bagel shop. She had lox on hers, and he had cream cheese and chives.

"I don't understand," he said. "What books are you talking about?"

"Books with writing in them."

He raised an eyebrow. "Like most books."

"I don't mean the stories in the books. There was another story in them. Someone had written to you in the books, except I didn't know that then. I didn't know they were meant for you."

He drew in a breath and sat back. "Romances by Harriet Mueller?"

"Yes. You know the ones." She found herself blushing. It was the one time she hated having a fair complexion because the blushing showed. She could fight it from rising to her face, but it would still burn across her chest and come up her neck. She could feel it happening now.

"My wife read Harriet Mueller. She loved those books. She wrote in them too. Underlined stuff in them. Whenever she wanted a break from the world, she'd curl up on the couch and read a Harriet Mueller."

"I know all about that, Jim."

"You read them like that too?" He looked at her, hope shining in his eyes.

As though this was one more convincing reason for them to be a couple.

"That's why I bought them at the rummage sale. The three that belonged to your wife. Dorothy dragged me there."

"Where?"

"The church rummage sale. In addition to the Thrift Shop, they have a big rummage sale every year. I'm not a big shopper, but I do like old books. Especially out-of-print paperbacks. I don't have much room in my apartment for many, but I keep buying them anyway."

She realized she was blathering . . . stumbling all over herself to justify her actions when there was nothing really that needed justifying. At least not about buying the books.

"Tell me about the writing in them."

"I found it almost immediately. The purple script. A few sentences at the chapter headings. When I thumbed through the whole book, they told another story."

Jim looked away. "She wrote that way because she couldn't think of any other way to reach me. She was so sick at the end and so weak, the books were all she could reach. So she wrote just a few sentences here and there."

"Yes."

"It was Lois writing to me." His eyes met hers.

"I didn't know that at first. I hadn't even met you then. I was just reading a story. It was as interesting to me as any Harriet Mueller. How you met each other in college. The things you did together. The plays. Skating."

"Was that in there too?" He seemed amazed.

"She was reminiscing. She wanted to remind you of the past. She talked about the two of you moving to New York and doing theater together. I should have put two and two together when we went out for dinner that first time and you told me about coming to New York. Or when we went skating. I should have realized you'd done all this before with someone else."

"It's an old story."

Elizabeth looked down at her hands. She'd been wringing them unconsciously. "I wanted to return the books to the right person. Dorothy and I came to the Thrift Shop intending to do just that. But Mrs. Halladay said she didn't know who had donated them. There was no record."

He nodded and took a bite of his bagel. "I came to the church to look for them too. The books were donated by my sisters-in-law. The two of them helped clean up the apartment. They went through Lois's things at a time when I couldn't have done it."

"So you knew about them?"

"I knew that Lois loved reading romances. But it took me a long time to discover the messages she'd written to me in them. I just happened to come across one of them one night in my apartment."

"Mrs. Halladay gave us two more books."

"How many do you have?"

Elizabeth could feel the renewed rush of color and warmth across her face. How could she explain that she'd asked Alberto to put the first three she'd found on the shelves in Jim's apartment, without him knowing? "I've read five. *Secret Vows, A Lark for Love, What Price Glory, The Captain's Dream,* and *Stalwart of the Ionic Club.*"

"You've got quite a collection."

He was smiling. She couldn't tell if he was joking. She wondered if he had found the first three in his apartment. Had he figured out by now where they had come from?

She tried to explain. "I wanted to give them back. I was trying to find out who owned them. I figured whoever had given them away didn't realize there was writing in them."

"You're right. Not until I found one in my apartment."

"When?"

"One night when I was feeling really down I remembered how Lois would read romances to cheer herself up. A stack of her books was still on the nightstand, and I picked one up. It happened to be a Harriet Mueller. That's when I found the purple script. Discovered she'd been writing to me. And she made clear that she'd written in several volumes."

Elizabeth asked the question that had been on her mind for a while: "Why didn't she just put it down in a letter?"

Jim turned to the cashier. Someone bought a dozen cinnamon-raisin bagels and the cash drawer clanged open. Outside a kid walked by, jamming to whatever was on his headphones.

"Lois was playful like that," he said. "She liked games, treasure hunts. Hidden things, puzzles. I'm also convinced she didn't want me to find the messages right away. She knew I wouldn't be ready yet."

"You loved her."

"She was my wife."

"I don't know how you can ever get over a loss like that."

"You can," he said very calmly. "When you fall in love again."

"But how can you ever fall in love again?"

"I didn't think it would be possible. But it is." His eyes searched hers, as if trying to read through them and into her soul.

Elizabeth picked up her purse from where it was hanging on the back of her chair and took out the book from it. "Today Mrs. Halladay gave me one more she just found this morning at the bottom of a bag. *Whither Thou Goest.* I haven't even looked inside. It's yours."

Jim took the book and opened the pages. His expression softened. "Lois would have liked you."

"I'm sure I would have liked her."

"She would have found it amusing that you discovered the books before I did, and that then I found you."

Elizabeth kept thinking of what Mrs. Halladay had said. That some things are meant to be. That they're heavenly ordained. Was this one of those things?

"I wanted to tell you as soon as I put it together," she said.

"When was that?"

"Mrs. Halladay figured it out. After you came into the Thrift Shop looking for the books, she called me. She had promised to phone if she came across any other Harriet Muellers."

"Ahh . . . she's a clever one." Jim chuckled.

"She knew that I had the other copies, and if you were ever going to get them, I would have to give them to you. She didn't know that we . . . had met already."

"Trying to be a matchmaker, was she?" His smile grew wider.

"She was trying to get the books back to the right person, that was all," Elizabeth said quickly.

"So the first time I met you, you already knew who I was."

"No, not right away. Not until later, when Mrs. Halladay and Dorothy put it all together. Who the books belonged to. Who you were."

"It's like it was meant to be," Jim said. "The two of us coming together. Like a story that has to be told."

Elizabeth could feel her impatience rising. Hearing Mrs. Halladay's words come out of his mouth didn't help. "But don't you see, Jim? That's why it won't work. You've had a perfect love. I've read about it . . . and all the love between the lines too. You and Lois were devoted to each other. You gave up your own acting career so she could have her career. You sacrificed for her."

Jim held up his hand, stopping Elizabeth. "Wait. Where did you get that idea?"

"You told me about it and I read about it. You were her One and Only. That's how she described you. How could anyone replace that? How could *I* even hope to replace that?"

He appeared puzzled. "I'm not asking you to replace that. I thought we were starting something new."

"I didn't feel like that. When you came to hear me play in Boise, when you sent me that dress . . ."

He still had the dress. It was there at their feet in the FedEx box.

She swallowed hard and plunged ahead. "When you sent me the note that went with the dress, I thought you were following a familiar script. You were saying the same old lines. Calling me your 'One and Only.'"

Jim couldn't hide his hurt. "They weren't meant that way."

Elizabeth's foot bumped the FedEx box, and it brought back that moment in the motel room. "It was so hard for me, Jim. I'd heard them first when I read the messages. I'd heard them in my head. You and Lois had something very special. I couldn't imagine coming after that. I could never measure up to what you had before. It wouldn't be fair to you . . . or to me."

"Don't you understand? Can't you see why she wrote everything she did? It was because things *weren't* perfect. Just the opposite. The pressures her career put on both of us were enormous. The jealousy, the tension. She had to go away on tour, and at the same time I was getting more involved in my job. We drifted apart. We weren't the perfect couple at all."

"Was there another woman?" She had to ask.

He shook his head. "It's almost worse. We got really busy with what we were doing. Wrapped up in ourselves and our egos. Before she got sick, I wouldn't have been surprised if she had asked me for a divorce. There was an opening night of hers that I missed. Something came up at work, and I completely forgot all about it until it was too late. She was so hurt, and I was so aloof I couldn't apologize. We didn't even talk about it—just buried it. I suppose I resented her successes. It took something awful like cancer to get us back together."

"It didn't seem like that from what she wrote."

"Elizabeth"—he said her name—"that's exactly why she wrote it. She was rediscovering our love, and she wanted me to rediscover it too. At the end."

"After she'd gone?"

"After I'd gotten over my worst grief. I'd look at the books and remember the good times. I'd recover. It'd be healing. The remorse would go."

"Are you still remorseful?"

"I'm sorry. Sorry for thousands and thousands of things. But remorseful? No. We loved each other. We did it badly at times, but we had a few last months to be with each other. To reconnect. The messages were for that."

"It doesn't sound like much of a romance."

"It was bigger than that. It was life. The kind that isn't always in front of you. The kind where you have to look closely to get at the true meaning."

"I guess I didn't understand. I didn't read it that way." Elizabeth wanted to get up and leave. There was too much to think about and reconsider. *Whither Thou Goest* sat on the table between them, its unread message waiting to be heard.

"What about the other books?" Jim asked.

"I left three of them in your bookshelves. The other two that Dorothy gave me later I have at my place."

Jim looked startled. "My bookshelves? In my apartment?"

"I had Alberto put them there."

"Don't go to Germany. Please, don't." His brown eyes pleaded with her, urging her to stay. "I know you have to do some things for your job and your career. Everybody does. But I don't want to lose you. We have our own story to write."

He was not like Alberto at all. He was gentler, more gracious. Straightforward and kind. She had hardly given him a chance.

"But I've already canceled everything for this week. I'm almost all packed."

"Good. That'll give us more time to spend together. I'll take the rest of the week off from work."

"How can you?"

"I wouldn't be worth your time if I didn't do that."

They both stood up at the table. As their eyes locked, he leaned toward her and kissed her, the table still between them. They backed away.

"OK," she said.

"Tonight we're going to the opera."

"How can you get tickets?"

"I can get tickets to anything. Here, take the dress. It was meant for you."

"You take the book."

THE FIRST thing Elizabeth did was call Alberto. Even though she told him she wasn't going with him to Europe, he said he wouldn't give up hope entirely. If she couldn't come now, she'd come later. He had great confidence in his powers of persuasion.

His one nasty parting shot was to ask Elizabeth if she still intended to play Broadway shows. She replied that, of course, she'd do them from time to time if she was lucky enough to get asked. She would not be pulled down to his low level of musical snobbery. There were all kinds of music, and she was glad to be involved in all of it, thank you very much.

JIM'S RETURN to the office at three-thirty in the afternoon was greeted with many raised eyebrows.

"Nan was looking for you," the receptionist said.

"Lisa was looking for you," said the bookkeeper.

"You've had a couple of phone calls," Lisa said.

Far be it from her to ask where he had been for three-and-a-half hours and why he wasn't remotely apologetic about his absence.

"You have several appointments waiting," she said.

"Tell them I'm sorry. I'll see them in a minute." A few interviews. He could get them over with quickly. "And could you find Nan for me?"

"She's in your office."

"Thanks, Lisa."

Nan was sitting at his desk, going over some papers of her own, waiting for him. She looked like she might even drum the desk with her fingers. "I won't ask where you've been."

"I'm glad."

"I've been sitting here for the past hour hoping to catch you before anyone else does."

"Half the office looks like it wants to catch me."

"Joan wanted to talk to you. She actually came down and asked me where you were. I had no answer."

"I had an important meeting."

"You need to tell her what your answer is."

"I know what my answer is. You do too."

"It'd look pretty funny if I was the one to give her the message."

"I want the job. I actually think I'd be good at it. I'd enjoy it."

"Good." Nan gave a crisp smile. "Are you sure you're ready?"

"Of course not. But I'll depend on my friends to guide me." *And the words of a prayer to point me in the right direction every morning.*

289

"I'm with you all the way."

"Nan, do you ever pray?"

She blinked. "Why do you ask?"

"Just one of those things. Most people do, you know."

She looked evasive. "I try to be different from most people."

"But do you ever have those times when you need the kind of help that can only come from outside you?"

"I suppose I do." It was clear she wasn't going to say more.

"Right now that's the only thing that's starting to make sense about my life. That Someone greater than me is in charge . . . and will help with what I'm about to do."

"The new job?"

"No. The request I have for Joan. I'm going to say yes and then take the next week off."

"You're crazy. There's so much work to be done. You've got to take charge."

"I've got to take charge of something else too."

"The flutist?"

"My life."

"The workaholic takes a week off?" She looked dubious.

"She needs to know that no matter what I do, she's my top priority. I don't want to blow it. Nan, can you do a big favor for me? I've got some appointments waiting. Can you talk to them?"

"Maybe."

"And the appointments I've scheduled for the rest of the week?"

"You'll owe me big-time."

"I do already." Without even taking off his overcoat or putting down his shoulder bag, Jim turned on his heel.

"Where are you going?"

"To the twenty-second floor. To see Joan. Wish me luck."

THIRTY-SEVEN

THE OPERA *Lucia di Lammermoor* had a very sad ending, but Elizabeth couldn't be sad. She felt almost giddy feasting on the beautiful music, gorging on it. In the final act, in a riveting scene, the soprano sang a duet with a flute. Just flute and voice. Elizabeth imagined the technical challenge of it. Playing in the orchestra pit, yet staying together with the coloratura soprano on stage.

But even as she admired the musicianship, she was transported by the music. Giving herself up to it, she didn't wonder about who was sitting next to her and why she had chosen to be with him. She had decided, for once in her life, to take a risk. To step out of her place of comfort. She didn't doubt for a moment that she'd made the right choice.

The rest of the week she had nothing to do. No lessons, no rehearsals, no jobs. She slept in late and waited for Jim's call.

"What do you want to do today?"

"I don't know," she answered.

"I have an idea." He always did. An itinerary and plan. Together they did all those New York things that she had promised herself to do for years. It was as though she were seeing the city for the first time. They went to the Frick, admiring its Whistlers, its Fragonard room, its Old Masters. They took the subway up to the Cloisters Museum, where they sat together for half an hour studying the unicorn tapestries . . . sitting in the half light and seeing how the tightly woven threads created a story.

"The unicorn needs to be caught by a virgin, according to the mythology," Jim said. "The hunters chase him, but it's the woman who catches him."

"What's he doing with the water?" She looked at a panel where the unicorn was dipping his horn in a stream.

"He's purifying it."

"What's happening in that one?" she asked.

The unicorn pranced behind a fence.

"The unicorn is caught. In its own garden."

"The flowers are beautiful." All those tiny threads making beautiful daisies and hyacinths, roses and climbing vines. All that beauty.

On an unusually warm March day, they took the Staten Island ferry across the harbor and back. Going nowhere. Just enjoying each other's company. They sat outside on the upper deck and watched the New York skyline grow smaller as they crossed the harbor. Then they watched it grow bigger as they returned. From the vantage point of the ferry, the sky was bigger than any buildings and the bay was immense.

Elizabeth had the calming sense that the world was bigger than they were. That there was indeed a plan for it. That it would go on, and any crisis they faced would be small by comparison.

"Do you like New York?" he asked.

"It can be ugly and pushy and full of rude people. It can be dirty and dark. But sometimes it becomes beautiful."

It was interesting how going to Germany had receded as a possibility, like the Statue of Liberty growing smaller and smaller behind them. "How's it seem to you now?"

"I can't imagine living anywhere else on earth." Her hand brushed against his, and automatically their fingers entwined. There was no self-consciousness about it.

"The city looks so peaceful from this distance."

"It's hard to believe there are people working in those buildings."

"People calling clients and negotiating fees. Buying things and selling things."

"Or coming up with creative ideas. Like you."

"I've needed this week off."

"I'm glad you took it."

"It's harder for you. Canceling your lessons. You're a freelancer. If you don't work, you don't get paid."

"I can't work if I don't take a week off every now and then. I've learned that. I become an automaton."

He nodded. "Sometimes I need to be hit over the head to be reminded to take a vacation."

"Did Lois have to hit you over the head?"

It was the first time in the week that either of them had mentioned Lois. It was as though they wanted to wait until their own love was strong enough, sure of itself, to linger over the past.

"I wish she had. It would have been easier for both of us if I'd slowed down every once in a while."

"Stop and smell the roses."

"I didn't do that until she was very sick and I had to be with her. By then it was almost too late."

"Almost?"

"I was taking her to her chemo appointments or visiting her at the hospital. 'In sickness and in health' the wedding vows say. The 'in health' part is really important."

"What was she like?" Elizabeth asked.

"Smart, funny, romantic. Strong-willed, stubborn sometimes. Loyal. Warm. A wonderful actress. Not stagey like a lot of actresses. Very real."

It surprised Elizabeth that she could hear these words and feel no jealousy. "I'm sorry I never met her."

"On stage she was a lot like you. The way you make listeners focus on the music. No matter how many times I saw her in plays, I could always lose Lois. She would become another character."

"Would you have felt any differently about her if you hadn't found the Harriet Muellers?"

"I would still be thinking about her, but the books gave me the words for my thoughts. They connected me to something she gave me before she died."

A sea gull hovered over their heads, waiting for a crust of bread or an old French fry.

"What was that?"

Jim pointed to the sea gull. "Do you ever wonder how they can stay right with you on a boat without ever flapping their wings?"

"No." Elizabeth laughed. "I can honestly say I've never wondered about that."

"It was a prayer," he said, answering her question.

"What was?"

"What she gave me before she died. The words to a prayer. Something she found on a card one day when we visited St. Patrick's. She didn't even have the card anymore. She had committed the words to memory. And she wanted me to memorize them. She told me to say them. Remember them when she was gone."

"What were the words?" Elizabeth's fingers had slipped from Jim's hand.

"You don't really like prayers and things like that, do you?"

"It's not that I don't like them," she said. "I just don't know what to do with them."

"You don't have to do much. Just accept them."

"That's easier for people like you and Dorothy. People who don't have doubts."

"I've had plenty of doubts since Lois's death," he admitted. "Doubts about me . . . whether there is any real meaning or purpose remaining in my life. Doubts about whether I'll ever find love again. Or whether I want to find it again. But the prayer Lois gave me helped me refocus. Calmed me. Gave me comfort. Pointed the way to the real Source of power."

"What is this prayer?"

Jim closed his eyes. *"Jesus Christ, have mercy upon me. Make haste to help me. Rescue me and save me. Let thy will be done in my life."*

Elizabeth listened. "Say it again." Like a singer picking up the words from a neighbor, she mouthed the words. "Again," she said. She repeated it inside her head. She would try it on her own.

Jim opened his eyes. "I haven't said it aloud like that since Lois died."

"Does it spoil it?"

"Not at all. It seems even stronger."

The ferry was getting close to Manhattan. Passengers were picking up their bags and briefcases, moving to the exit. The trip was almost over.

"The thing about it," Jim said, "is that when I say those words, I can ask for things I don't even know I want. I can believe in God again. Somehow praying those words softened my heart, a little at a time. Prepared it to ask for what seemed so impossible that it would never happen."

"Like what?"

"Like you. I didn't know I needed you and wanted you before we ever met. My heart said it when my head couldn't."

The sea gulls hovered for a moment over their heads, then abandoned the upper deck, en masse, and swooped down to the water as though they'd been choreographed.

"I'm ready," she said.

"Ready for what?"

"Dorothy was talking about how much I needed to step out and take a risk. In life . . . and especially with you. For me it is like stepping out on stage without any music and playing from memory."

"That's what falling in love is like."

"Somehow it's easier to do the one when you've done the other," she said. "Taking a risk like that."

"And then you'll be caught like the unicorn."

Elizabeth leaned her head on his shoulder as they both relaxed against the bench. "I thought it was the maiden who caught the unicorn."

"Love caught them both."

<hr>

"JIMBO, WHERE have you been?"

"Around."

"You haven't been here for days." Scott scratched his head as if he were stumped.

"I was on vacation."

"Where'd you go?"

"The Cloisters, the Met, Carnegie Hall, the Staten Island ferry."

"But those places are all here in New York. Unless you went to some mockup of New York, like that casino in Las Vegas."

"That's what I said. I was around."

"Some vacation. You need a real change of scenery."

"I've had it. I didn't go into the office at all. I just did some sight-seeing at home."

Jim leaned back on the bench next to Scott. They did bench presses in unison, with more grunts and groaning from Scott than Jim. Five days away from the gym, an unconscionably long time, and Jim felt better than ever. He could do longer sets and heavier weights than he had in months. It must have been the break or the rest . . . or love.

Jesus Christ, have mercy upon me. Make haste to help me. Rescue me and save me. Let thy will be done in my life.

Why was he even saying the prayer now? He didn't need anything. He didn't want anything. All he wanted to do was praise. Breathe thanks to God with every exhale.

There was a clank of weights from Scott. "It must be that girl."

"Pretty good guess."

"When a girl keeps you from a workout, you've got it pretty bad."

"Or pretty good. Depends on how you look at it."

"Are you going in to work today?"

"Not yet. I'm taking one more day."

"Won't they get rid of you for this? Taking all this vacation time."

"They've given me a promotion."

Scott whistled. "They must be out of their minds."

"I thought you said I was the one who was out of my mind."

"Are you getting a big raise?"

"I guess so. I haven't gone through the numbers yet."

"When it comes to investing all that extra loot, don't forget your friend Scott. We've got mutual funds that would be perfect for a guy like you . . ."

"THERE YOU are," Dorothy said on the phone. "Where have you been hiding yourself?"

"I've been around."

"I haven't been able to raise you on the phone."

"I've been busy."

"I guess I should be lucky you answered this time."

Elizabeth yawned. "I was going to bed."

"Not without an explanation."

"About what?"

"So far my spies have spotted you at the Metropolitan Opera, at Carnegie Hall for a piano concert, and at the Frick. Someone said they even ran into you at the Cloisters Museum, but you looked so dewy-eyed she was sure it wasn't you. Not the purposeful, businesslike flutist we know."

Elizabeth could hear the teasing in her friend's voice.

"I've been taking a little vacation at home."

"By yourself?"

"Dorothy, you know the answer to that."

"Just one question: are you OK?"

"I don't think I've ever felt better in my life."

"What have you been doing?"

"All those things you promise to do someday when you live in New York and never get around to. I'd already canceled all my lessons and rehearsals so I had the whole week free. We even took the Staten Island ferry."

"My spies weren't diligent enough to tell me about that."

"I think I finally figured out what you meant about taking a risk. All those things you said about stepping out on stage with no music and how I had to trust that I would play the right notes."

"I'm glad to be quoted saying wise things."

"You were right. I needed to give Jim a second chance. Even though at first it seemed like the hardest thing on earth. I didn't want to be hurt again. But then I just decided that I had to do it. And once I told him about the books, saying yes to spending the week with him seemed so easy. Guess I really was stuck in a rut."

"How did Alberto take it?"

"He understood. He had to understand. Alberto can be the densest person on earth until you finally get through to him. And then he gets it. He went back to Germany."

"He approves of Jim?"

"I wouldn't go so far as that. But he understands that I need to stay where I am."

"Did you give Jim the rest of the Harriet Muellers?"

"I told him everything. I don't know why I hesitated in the first place. I had it all wrong. I misread their whole relationship and idealized it. They loved each other—that seems clear—but things weren't always perfect."

"Things *aren't* always perfect."

"They learned from each other though. She gave him a lot."

"No more than you'll be able to give him. Or he gives you. I think you're completely right for each other. I knew that from the first time we all went out together—and if you want further proof, just ask Mrs. Halladay!"

"Speaking of Mrs. Halladay," Elizabeth said, "we had an interesting conversation. The weird thing is that once you start thinking about *how* you're meant for someone, then you have to consider Who meant you for each other."

Dorothy laughed. "I can just hear Mrs. Halladay now. 'Now you're getting it!' she'd say, nodding that silver helmet-head of hers. 'That's what the Thrift Shop is all about. Second chances for things . . . and people.'"

THE EARLY dose of spring weather lasted clear into the weekend, so Jim and Elizabeth decided to visit the Central Park Zoo. They watched the sea lions diving for fish and barking like dogs. They enjoyed the damp warmth of the rain-forest exhibit, like a summer's day at the beach. Then they stared at the polar bears tumbling off their cold rocks and splashing into the water. Polar opposites.

"One of the polar bears had to go to a shrink," Jim said.

"You're kidding me."

"I read about it in the newspaper. He was getting all morose, so they brought in an animal psychologist."

"What was the diagnosis?"

"He was lonely. That's all," he said, grabbing her hand.

Holding hands, they walked to the Plaza Hotel. Crossing Fifty-ninth Street, Jim spotted a colleague. He pulled Elizabeth behind a newsstand.

"What was that about?"

"I just saw someone from work, and I didn't want to have to explain what I was doing in town and why I wasn't in the office all week. Let him think I was in the Bahamas. I don't want to share you with anyone yet."

Elizabeth laughed. "I haven't seen anyone I know for days. Dorothy says her spies have noticed us. But I've been oblivious."

"I went to the gym once and saw my usual workout buddies."

"I talked to Dorothy, but I haven't needed anyone else."

"I'll take that as a good sign." He grinned.

"It is a very good sign."

Girls in crisp starched dresses and boys in blue blazers sat with their grandmothers under the palms at the Plaza. Older couples who looked like they were celebrating their fiftieth wedding anniversaries reminisced beneath the stained-glass skylight. Tourists with Bloomingdale's bags at their feet sat at the white-clothed tables, peering around the room for a sight of Eloise. One man raised his hand to flag down a white-gloved waiter. The waiters themselves had perfect manners, just snobbish enough to make everyone feel they were exceptions in a rough and rude world.

"I've never eaten here," Elizabeth said.

"Neither have I. I've only walked through and stared at everyone else, wondering why they were spending so much money for a cup of tea."

"Do you still feel that way?"

"Not sitting across the table from you."

They ordered a plate of pastries and two cups of tea. The waiter bowed obsequiously as he picked up their menus and backed away.

"You haven't told me about the last Harriet Mueller," Elizabeth said.

"*Whither Thou Goest?*"

"What's in it?"

"You."

Elizabeth could feel the color drain from her cheeks. "What do you mean?"

"Remember how I said that I thought she'd like you? Well, she anticipated me meeting you."

"We never knew each other. I never met her. Never saw her."

"She knew, though, that I'd fall in love again someday. It's what she wanted to happen. For me. That's why she wrote in the Harriet Muellers. It was something she knew I wouldn't even listen to right after she died. I wouldn't have been ready. But someday, she knew, it was what I'd need."

He put his hand in the pocket of his overcoat that was on the back of his chair and took out a volume. He began to read:

"Someday, I know you will meet someone special. I hope that she is just the right person for you. She could be a lawyer or a banker or a stockbroker. I would prefer that she were in the arts somehow. A musician or dancer. But no matter what she does, I pray that she is very good to you. Have fun together. Enjoy each moment you're with each other. Take time off. Go out to dinner. If there's any money left in my estate after all these medical bills, do it on me!

"But remember, she doesn't have to replace me. What we had was one thing. Very special to both of us. What you have with her will be something equally special because it's new. I hope I can look down on you. I will smile, I will laugh, I will entreat God above to bring this happiness to you because life wasn't meant to be lived alone. I love you, dear. And love means wanting you to be fulfilled long after I have left this earth and gone to the next life.

"From time to time, I expect you might think of me, but don't do it with any guilt. I'll be the one looking down at your wedding, crying buckets of tears. Tears of happiness. Because, more than anything else, I want you to be happy."

Tears brimmed in Elizabeth's eyes, but she was determined not to cry. "She was generous."

Jim reached down again and felt in the other pocket of his overcoat. He took out a small velvet-lined box. His fingers fumbled as he opened it. Inside was a ring with one medium-sized diamond. Not a big showy one. One that was just right. Just meant for Elizabeth.

"I want to give you this as a promise."

"Of what?"

"I want to promise you that I'll always be supportive. I'll always listen. I won't get too busy. I won't be too impulsive. I won't boss you around. I'll hear as much as you want to be heard. Life wasn't meant to be lived alone."

"No," she said.

"I want to have more weeks like this. I want to have a life of this. I can't imagine living without you, Elizabeth. It has nothing to do with Lois. This is us. This is what we are and what we'll become. I'm very happy. Happier than I've ever been before. Because of you."

"I might not always make you happy. What if I make you angry? What if I disagree with you?"

"I think we'll manage. We've managed this far, haven't we?" He kept the ring in the box and reached his hand across the table, grabbing hers. Elizabeth looked down. The image came to her again of stepping out on stage and taking a big breath, lifting her flute up to her lips and then playing. Playing without any music in front of her, only with the music inside her head. If ever there was a time to risk, this was it. If ever there was a time to trust, this was it. To trust not only this man, whom she'd come to love, but the One who was orchestrating the music of her life.

"Yes," she said.

"Will you marry me?"

"Yes."

EPILOGUE

VERONICA HALLADAY didn't generally pay much attention to the commercials on TV. She didn't watch much TV anyway, other than the news with Mr. Halladay and an occasional series on public television. She was partial to those BBC dramatizations of classic English literature—Dickens, Trollope, George Eliot. Anything that had good historical details. Long dresses with bustles, women with parasols, dining rooms with full china settings, a character penning a letter with quill and ink. She liked the plots of the shows, of course, but even more so, she liked studying the accoutrement of daily life. It was what her work had been dedicated to. Giving new life to secondhand things.

Someone had given the Thrift Shop a television. One that seemed to be in good condition—other than a few scratches on the side and a smudge on the screen. A squirt of detergent would be able to clean that up. The real question was, How would it play?

She plugged the TV in and turned it on.

The color looked fine and, even without cable, the reception was all right. She switched the channels and got a good clear picture on one of the soap operas. The thing would pull in a good price for the Thrift Shop. Why had the donor passed it along? Probably wanted something bigger or newer or more luxurious. Think of the client who'd pick this one up. How delighted he or she would be!

Mrs. Halladay was coming back with a rag to clean it when a commercial came on. She paused to watch. It was very clever, and Mrs. Halladay above all appreciated creativity and wit from anything on TV, particularly when it came so close to home. The ad showed a thrift shop, not unlike Christ Church's Thrift Shop, with a long shelf of books. On one side of the shelf a young woman was thumbing through a copy of a romantic novel, her eyes lost in the plot. On the other side of the shelf a handsome young man was reading a similar book, absorbed by the romance.

She could tell what would happen, of course, even in thirty seconds. The two would move down the row of books until they were facing each other. Then they would look up, going from the romance in the book to the real thing. It would be an advertisement for heart-shaped chocolates or breath mints or hair gel. You could never know for sure in some of these commercials. It wasn't like a used-car commercial or a testimony for weight loss. They liked to keep you hanging.

Mrs. Halladay hung on, watching. The couple kept staring at the books. Never looking up. Never making eye contact. Never connecting. Then the screen went blank, and the announcer made his plug. Something to do with life insurance. "In a world where the odds are against happily ever after, be secure."

She was about to fire back a reply that the odds weren't always against happily ever after. That some couples found each other and did very well together. Look at her relationship with Mr. Halladay, after all. Or that young couple who had gotten to know each other through those books at the Thrift Shop. Surely they were doing fine now. She hadn't had one more night of lost sleep about them since she'd called Elizabeth about the *Whither Thou Goest* book. A perfect title . . . for a wonderful outcome. The good Lord had even cast her in a modest role for that love story.

Just then the commercial switched back to the couple.

Their eyes lifted from the books. They looked at each other and smiled. The music swelled, the screen filled with sunlight. The books dropped to the floor as they walked out of the store together.

Happily Ever After.

"Yes," Mrs. Halladay said out loud. "That's more like it." Whoever made the commercial was very perceptive. If you waited long enough, if you were patient, if you had faith in the One who controls all things, things worked out. Not always *how* you expected them to, not always *when* you expected, but they worked out.

People met and married and had children. They bought houses or sold them, ridding themselves of the things they had acquired. Treasures they no longer needed. Things that found their way to the Thrift Shop.

She turned off the TV. It would find an excellent new owner. He would walk out with a bargain. The money would come to the church.

It was a win-win situation. Just as Mrs. Halladay expected.

She made it so.

A Note from the Author

READING BETWEEN the lines of this novel, you might wonder how much of the author is in the story. Quite frankly, much of it feels deeply personal.

No, I don't work in advertising like Jim, the male protagonist. And, thank God, I have not lost a wife to cancer. My wife, an accomplished writer, is very much alive.

But the Jesus prayer is part of my daily life. As I've written in my spiritual memoir *Finding God on the A Train*, I use the prayer when I pray on the subway train every morning on my commute to work. And yes, I've been known to pray those words in between sets at the gym (although I can't bench-press nearly as much as Jim!).

I love books and all kinds of reading. My wife, Carol, was the one to introduce me to the world of historical romances, especially the incomparable novels of Georgette Heyer, which Carol has read countless times. Carol and I now have two teenage boys.

When I first came to New York, it was to pursue singing and acting. These days most of my singing is done in our church choir and in a local Gilbert and Sullivan troupe. My main work is with *Guideposts* magazine, where I am the executive editor.

I couldn't be happier with the way my life has taken shape. No need to read further between these lines!

Rick Hamlin

•